ADVANCE PRAISE FOR *STARVATION LAKE*

"*Starvation Lake* is one of those books that won't shake its grip. Bryan Gruley is off to a phenomenal start!"

—MICHAEL CONNELLY

"Like a slap shot from the blue line: powerful, deadly accurate, and a hell of a surprise. A truly impressive debut."

—STEVE HAMILTON

"Tough storytelling and compelling writing."

—MICHAEL HARVEY

"A tremendous read, a twisting ride peopled with vivid characters and a wonderfully evoked sense of place."

—MARCUS SAKEY

"Authentic and thought provoking."

—C. J. BOX

"Introduces a welcome, human voice to crime fiction readers."

—GEORGE PELECANOS

Advance praise for
Starvation Lake

———

"A great debut from a major talent."

—Harlan Coben

"*Starvation Lake* is a wonderful surprise! It is one of those books that won't shake its grip. Bryan Gruley is off to a phenomenal start!"

—Michael Connelly

"Bryan Gruley's *Starvation Lake* introduces a welcome, human voice to crime fiction readers."

—George Pelecanos

"A terrific debut by a talented author to watch . . . *Starvation Lake* is a smorgasbord of colorful local characters, a great sense of place, hockey, PBR, small-town newspapers . . . but most of all the clinical dissection of a little town with big secrets. Authentic and thought-provoking."

—C. J. Box

"*Starvation Lake* is a tremendous read, a twisting ride peopled with vivid characters and a wonderfully evoked sense of place. You heard it here first—Bryan Gruley is here to stay."

—Marcus Sakey, author of *The Blade Itself* and *Good People*

"Bryan Gruley digs into the frozen ground of northern Michigan and unearths a gem. Tough storytelling and compelling writing; *Starvation Lake* is a wonderful debut."

—Michael Harvey, author of *The Chicago Way* and *The Fifth Floor*

"*Starvation Lake* is like a slap shot from the blue line: powerful, deadly accurate, and a hell of a surprise. A truly impressive debut from Bryan Gruley."

—Steve Hamilton, author of *A Stolen Season* and
A Cold Day in Paradise

"Like Gus Carpenter, his small-town newspaper hero, Gruley has an eye for the telling detail and a nose for a great story. The hours you spend in Starvation Lake will fly by with this exciting debut. A terrific book."

—Kevin Guilfoile, author of *Cast of Shadows*

"A terrific debut. Gruley is a gifted stylist who wraps a first-rate mystery into a gritty and discerning portrait of small-town America with insights worthy of a Sinclair Lewis novel."

—Ken Wells, author of *Meely LaBauve* and *Crawfish Mountain*

"You can see the journalist's eye for detail in every passage. A deeply atmospheric book that hooked me from the start. I can only hope there is more from Bryan Gruley and protagonist Gus Carpenter for many years to come."

—Ace Atkins, author of *Wicked City* and *Devil's Garden*

for pjn

Starvation Lake

The cast-iron railing wobbled in his hand as he climbed the porch steps. He nearly fell over. After three tries, he decided the doorbell didn't work. The screen door wouldn't give, so he stripped off a glove and rapped on the aluminum frame. Paint the color of pea soup was peeling off the face of the inside door.

A cold drop of rain leaked through the awning over his head and splatted on the back of his neck. He put a hand to his neck and looked up as another drop splashed on his cheek. "Shit," he said, taking a step back and pulling his camouflage jacket tight around the package tucked within.

He looked down the street. Not a person in sight. Two Fords, a Chrysler, and his Chevy pickup truck waited at the curb. A single porch light flickered wanly in the dusk. Two doors down, charring from a fire blackened one side of the house, and wind ruffled the drapes where a windowpane had once been. He looked down. Brown stains pocked the concrete porch, down the three steps, and along the walk to the street. The stains seemed to grow bigger as they neared the curb. He hoped they weren't blood.

He rapped again. Dammit, he thought, I knew I should have just sent it the usual way. Four hours down to this shithole city and now I gotta wait around? How the hell does the guy work in this dump? There's a darkroom in there? He looked at his watch. If he could get this done in the next hour he would still have time to visit one of the Windsor clubs before heading home.

He heard something moving inside, then footsteps on the other side of the door. He swallowed hard and took another step back. Just a delivery, he thought. Just leave the thing and go.

The door eased open a crack. He smelled cabbage and cigarettes. A woman's pale round face appeared above the hand holding the door. She seemed to be wearing nothing but a flannel shirt that drooped to her knees.

"What?" she said.

"Riddle. Got something for Charley."

He slipped the manila envelope out from under his coat.

"Riddle? You a joker?"

She had an accent he didn't recognize. Jesus Christ, he thought, is she going to understand a word I say?

"It's my name. Is Charley here?"

The envelope was wrapped in tape and rubber bands. She looked at it with contempt.

"No Charley. We don't want no delivery."

"This is the address he gave me." He glanced at the address plate nailed to the brick. "Cecil Avenue, right?"

A man's voice called out from inside. "Magda!"

She yelled at him in her language. He barked something else, sounding closer now, and she stormed away, leaving the inside door ajar.

The man swung the door open wide. He stood barefoot in a pair of paint-stained sweatpants and a gray T-shirt that said Property of Detroit Lions. A single brow overhung his dark, sunken eyes. He held the door with one hand and kept the other behind his back.

"What you want?"

"I was supposed to bring this for Charley."

"Charley?" The man almost smiled, then decided against it. "Jarek."

"Jarek?" Riddle chuckled nervously. "Jarek, Charley. Got it. Can I leave this for him?"

The man shifted his weight from his left foot to his right, keeping his one hand hidden. Riddle tried not to look at it.

"You are from up north?" the man said.

"Yes, sir. About four hours."

The man stared at Riddle for a moment. "Why do you wear army jacket?" he said. "Are you in military?"

Riddle glanced self-consciously at his camouflage jacket. "Oh, no sir. This is for hunting. Deer, rabbits, you know."

"Aha. You are a killer then. Did you bring gun?"

"My gun? Oh, no sir. That's locked up at home, yes sir."

The man tilted his head slightly. "Would you like to come in?"

"Thank you, but no, I really have to be going. Got a long haul back. Got other deliveries to make, you know. Sorry."

"Other deliveries?" The man leaned forward. "What other deliveries?"

Riddle glanced down the street again. Still not a soul. The last light of afternoon was nearly gone. "Nothing," he said. "I just have to get back."

"Jarek is not here."

"No?"

"No. Not here anymore."

"I see. Well." Riddle tried on what he imagined to be a business-like smile. "Do you know where I can find him?" He wished he hadn't asked the question the second it left his lips.

"Jarek will not be back. You can leave it with me."

The man pushed open the screen door with his hidden hand. The hand held an unlit cigarette. Riddle gave the man the envelope.

"OK, then," Riddle said. "You'll send it back to the usual place?"

The man slammed the door without another word.

february 1998

Y ou can never look into their eyes. Not once. Not for a second. Not if you're a goaltender, like me. Because the guy shooting the puck wants you to look there. Then he'll glance one way and shoot the other, or he'll draw your eyes up just as he snaps the puck between your legs. Or he'll lock on you just long enough to remind you that he knows exactly what he's about to do and you don't, that you're just wishing and hoping that you'll guess right. That you're not at all in control.

Then you're dead.

It was nearly midnight. I was tending the hockey goal at the south end of the John D. Blackburn Memorial Ice Arena. And I was yelling for help. Soupy backpedaled across the rink to give me some. It looked like he'd make it just in time to cut off the other team's winger when his skate blade caught a gash in the ice and he went flying. His helmet, an old three-piece Cooper held together by skate laces and friction tape, bounced off of his head and went skittering into the boards.

"Fuck me!" he shouted.

Boynton sidestepped Soupy and the helmet and veered to the center of the ice, heading my way, alone. He was tall and lean, dressed all in black, and he kept his head up as he crossed the blue line, looking for my eyes. I focused on the puck as he slid it back and forth, from the back of his stick to the front. My team was up, 2–1. Less than a minute remained in the game. My left hand, steamy inside my catching glove, whacked once against my belly, involuntarily, and shot out to my side, open and ready. My right arm pressed the bottom edge of my goalie stick against the sandpaper ice. I dropped my squat an inch, dug the inner toe of my right skate into the ice, and glided back six inches, a foot. I tucked my head into my neck. The thin slick of sweat beneath my mask stung my cheeks. I blinked, hard.

I didn't want to be there. In a drafty hockey rink reeking of refrigerant. Late. In a two-stoplight town clinging to the south-eastern tip of a frozen lake in northern lower Michigan. I'd left the place years before, a failure, intending never to return. Now I was back, against my weak will, after failing miserably someplace else. By day, I was the associate editor of the *Pine County Pilot*, circulation 4,733, published every day but Sunday. By night I tended goal in the Midnight Hour Men's League, surrounded by men I'd known as boys. In between I waited for something to change my life, to get me out of Starvation Lake again. That's what goalies do. They wait.

When Boynton had closed to fifteen feet, I felt him drop his right shoulder as if to shoot. Just then, the puck bounced on something—a shaving of ice, a sliver of wood—and tottered on an edge. I glimpsed the chipped scarlet paint of a logo on the underside. I dropped to one knee and flung my stick forward, catching just enough of the wobbling puck to flop it back over Boynton's stick blade. It trickled behind him, and Soupy, bareheaded, swooped in and golfed it clear.

Boynton kept coming, though. I was trying to get to my feet when his stick cracked me under the left ear, below the edge of the mask. A shock of pain tore through my jawbone and rippled down my neck. Boynton's knee speared my chest and I toppled over backward, my head bouncing on the ice as he fell on me. The smells of snuff and hops and sweat and tape filled my nostrils. I could hear a whistle shrieking, again and again. I opened my eyes. Boynton's face was two inches away, a grin beneath dark eyes. "Lucky fuck," he spat before I blacked out.

My wait was over.

The needle punctured the skin along my jawbone and I dug my fingernails into the soft wood of Leo's workbench as he stitched me. I had tried to numb the left side of my face with a fistful of snow, but the pinpricks stung anyway. The cut took six stitches to close.

"Thanks, Leo," I said. The air in the big steel shed behind Blackburn Arena was sweet with gasoline. I sipped a beer in a circle of light spread by a bulb hanging from the high ceiling. Leo moved out of the light to toss his stitching needle into a wastebasket. It *ping*ed on one of his empty 7-Up bottles.

"Try to be more careful," Leo said, emerging into the light again. "You boys aren't boys anymore."

For something like thirty years, Leo Redpath had maintained the rink's compressors and ice scrapers and Zamboni machine. He performed the odd carpentry and plumbing chores that kept the dressing rooms, snack bar, and restrooms in working order. Mostly he kept to himself, content to tinker in his shed and tend to the Zamboni he affectionately called Ethel. And although Leo was no doctor, his workbench sometimes doubled as an operating table for players who didn't want to bother with the local clinic. Leo had been doing it so long that he barely left scars anymore.

"See the game tonight?" I said.

"I never watch," Leo said.

I smiled at his lie. The stitches tugged at my chin. I could make out his wide, hunched-over shape shuffling around in the shadows surrounding Ethel. "You don't see hockey like that too often in Starvation Lake."

"I'm sure no truer words were ever spoken," he said.

"It's that deceptive speed, eh, Trap?" The voice came from the other end of the shed. Soupy walked in with a beer in one hand and two more dangling from a plastic six-pack holder. "We're even slower than we look."

It was one of his favorite lines, and he laughed at it, by himself.

Leo stepped out from behind Ethel. "Well, if it isn't Sonja Henie," he said. "Was that a triple salchow that landed you on your derriere?"

"Derriere?" Soupy said. "Derri-fucking-aire? Haven't we told you like eight million times to speak English around here? I think the word you're looking for is 'ass,' my friend. And who the hell is Sonja Henie?"

"Leo didn't watch," I said. Talking hurt.

"True," Leo said. "But I did catch a glimpse while carrying a box of Junior Mints to the snack bar."

I jumped down from the workbench. My teeth rattled when I landed. "Well, then, maybe you noticed whether Soupy punched Boynton's ticket on his way past?"

"Blow me, Trap," Soupy said. He stood a head taller than me, long and lanky in a blue denim overcoat with the words "Starvation Lake Marina" encircling an anchor embroidered over the left breast. Thick blond curls furled out from under his red woolen cap. "Gave you a chance to shine. You ought to thank me."

"I would have but I was unconscious."

I finished my beer, tossed the can at the wastebasket, missed, and motioned for one of Soupy's beers. Leo picked up the empty.

"Ultimate Teddy Boynton assault and battery," Soupy said. "You poke-check him, he runs you over." While I was out cold, as Soupy explained, Boynton threatened to punch a referee, who threw him out of the game. "The bastard probably didn't mean to knock you out. Or who knows, maybe he did." Soupy took a long pull on his beer. "He probably didn't like your editorial."

I had no idea Soupy read editorials. "Probably not." I looked around the shed. Leo had disappeared behind Ethel again. "We have a meeting tomorrow."

"With Teddy boy?" Soupy asked.

"And his lawyer."

"His *asshole* lawyer, Trap."

"Of course."

Soupy touched his beer to the side of his head. "Try to keep your head up this time, huh?"

"Quiet, please." Leo was trying to listen to the police scanner. It sat on a stack of milk crates, keeping him company on slow nights. We heard some crackling and some beeps, then the voice of the dispatcher, Darlene Esper. She was talking with a deputy on his way to Walleye Lake. A snowmobile had washed up onshore.

"Christ," I said. It was probably nothing. But every local over the age of fifty had a police scanner next to the bed, on the garage workbench, or on the shelf over the washing machine, and they'd all be talking about that snowmobile on Walleye Lake at Audrey's Diner the next morning. I grabbed Leo's rotary phone and dialed the sheriff's department. One of the perks of being associate editor of the *Pilot* was knowing that number by heart. Darlene answered.

"Deputy Esper," I said. "Gus Carpenter." I hoped for a chuckle. Darlene and I had grown up next door to each other. Our mothers had finally given up trying to marry us. So had Darlene.

"Gussy," she said. "You hear about the sled?"

"Yeah."

"You better get out there. Sheriff's out there."

"Dingus? Why, is there an all-you-can-eat buffet?"

"Just go, Gus."

I lingered on the phone—her voice always got me that way—but she'd already hung up. I zipped up my parka, fished out my truck keys. "Leo, thanks for the embroidery," I said. He didn't answer.

"Can't keep away from her, can you?" Soupy said.

"Good skate, Soup," was all I said.

As I stepped into the night, I heard him call out: "Mrs. Darlene Esper—sweetest ta-tas in Starvation Lake."

My pickup nosed down the icy two-track road that wound between the pines to Walleye Lake. I'd often wondered why it was called that. No one had ever caught a walleye in its mucky, weed-clogged water. A carp maybe, or a sucker trout. Never a walleye.

I grew up a few miles away, on Starvation Lake. My dad died of colon cancer when I was seven, so it was just Mom and me in our yellow clapboard house on the southern shore of the lake. We had a rickety dock, a dive raft, and a fishing boat with a ten-horsepower outboard motor, everything a kid needed to love summers on a clear blue lake. Over the long winters, I played goalie, the little guy barely taller than the net, for the town's youth hockey team, the River Rats. I was the goalie for the greatest of the Rat squads, the one that for the first time beat the mighty teams from Detroit, when no one thought it could be done. And I was the goalie who allowed the overtime goal that cost us our one and only chance to win the town a state championship.

It was a shot I should have stopped, a fluke really, a stupid lapse, that cost us the state title in our very own rink, right there in town in front of just about everybody who lived within fifty miles. I couldn't really blame them for not forgiving me, for looking at me out of the sides of their eyes and shaking their heads, for calling me "sieve" and "funnel" and "pylon" behind my back, sometimes even to my face, if they'd had enough to drink. I'd replayed my mistake in my mind a million times. I had trouble forgiving me, too.

It shouldn't have mattered, of course. We were just boys playing a game. But when the River Rat teams that followed us failed to come close to winning a state title again, the townspeople concluded that my flub had cursed them forever. My coach, Jack Blackburn, seemed to agree. He was the guy who'd taught me to play goal when I was just a little kid missing his dad, who'd befriended my mom and come to dinner on Sundays and regaled Mom and me with stories of his hockey triumphs in his homeland, Canada. But after we lost that state final, Coach never had much to say to me. It was like he'd just sliced away the part of his brain or his heart that had me in it. We would see each other at the rink or on the street and he'd say, "Gus," and I'd say, "Hey, Coach," and he'd just keep going and I'd turn and watch him walking away. He stopped coming to dinner, too.

All I wanted to do after that was get out of there. I went to college downstate, took some journalism classes, started working summers as a reporter at the *Pilot*. I caught the news bug and, after graduating, joined the *Detroit Times*. I worked there for better than ten years, mostly covering the auto industry, and never thought I'd return to Starvation Lake, except to visit Mom. I'd loved Detroit, loved waking to the chirping of hungry gulls and walking alone to work along the Detroit River while the sun burned a golden streak across the water. I loved my job and, just before I left, I'd been working on the best story of my life, a story I thought might win me a Pulitzer prize. Instead it cost me my job, my reputation, and my life away from Starvation. Before I knew it, I was back in Starvation, working at the *Pilot* again, an unmarried thirty-four-year-old without a prospect in sight.

Tire tracks crisscrossed the flattened snow at the Walleye Lake boat ramp. Snowdrifts usually made the beach inaccessible to anything but snowmobiles, but only a foot or so of snow had fallen so far that winter. I left my truck and edged along the bank toward the flashlight beams bouncing in the gloom. Dark bluffs ringed the semifrozen lake, which lay still and gray beneath the low sky. Cracks and dimples showed in the rough ice along the shore. Here and there slabs of ice floated just beneath the surface of the silver water. My boots skidded in mud and I grasped at dry cattails for balance.

"Whoa, there!" A flashlight beam swung up into my eyes. "Freeze where you are, please." It was Pine County sheriff Dingus Aho.

I tried to shield my eyes against the glare. "It's me, Gus Carpenter." I felt for the notebook in my back pocket but decided to leave it there for the moment.

"Nothing for you here, Gus," Dingus said. "I'll call you in the morning."

About twenty yards behind Dingus, a deputy played a flashlight along the shoreline. I caught a glimpse of an object lying on the beach, about knee high, triangular, pale yellow, striped with dripping weeds.

"That a snowmobile?" I said.

The sheriff stepped in front of me. "Just checking a situation," he said. The flashlight glare obscured his face, but I could see the brass badge stuck to the furry flap on the front of his cap. "Police business, Gus," he said. "I'm afraid I'm going to have to ask you to leave."

"Leave?" I almost laughed. "You think I wanted to come out here? It's a public access, for God's sake."

"You been drinking?"

Christ, I thought. I had my notebook out now and was patting myself for a pen. "I had a beer after hockey," I said.

The deputy had walked up. Now two flashlights shined in my eyes. Apparently I didn't have a pen. I wasn't about to ask Dingus for one.

"Look," I said, "I don't mean to hassle you, but I've got a paper to put out tomorrow, and I have to talk to you first thing."

He shrugged. "Good evening, Gus. Drive carefully, eh? You wouldn't want to get pulled over with your breath like that."

I steered my truck up the two-track. At the crest of the bluff, I turned left onto Route 816. I drove a few hundred yards, flicked off my headlights, and pulled onto the shoulder. I had to wait while my eyes adjusted to the blackness. Then I crossed the road and scrambled down the bank and into the woods until I could peer down to the lake's edge. My toes curled against the snow that had settled into my right boot.

Dingus and the deputy crouched over the yellowish object in the intersection of their flashlight beams. Dingus kept scratching at the side of the thing, then looking where he'd scratched. He did this three or four times, then stood up, walked a few steps down the shore, and sank to one knee. It was hard to see him in the shadows, but it looked to me like he bowed his head as if to pray, or to cry.

Thirty minutes later, I poured myself a Mason jar of water and sipped it in the dark at the kitchen window of my second-story flat. Across Main Street at Enright's Pub, I could see Soupy's head in its red wool cap bobbing around in the amber light of last call. He still wore his coat, and he hugged his mug close to his chest as he laughed.

My dinky apartment, where I'd lived for the six or seven months since I'd been back, sat directly above the *Pilot* newsroom. I rented it from my boss, the *Pilot's* executive editor. At $125 a month, it fit my shrunken budget and kept me from moving back in with Mom, though I loved visiting her around dinnertime once or twice a week.

Enright's went dark as Soupy and the other diehards spilled out the front door. I'd left my lights off so Soupy wouldn't come stomping up my stairway for a nightcap. He walked half a block in one direction, toward the lake and his marina, then stopped and reversed course, walking back along Main to where his truck was parked. As he passed the tavern, he reached into his coat and pulled out the half-filled mug he had sneaked out.

I walked into what passed for my living room and sat on the arm of the recliner. I set my water on the plywood tabletop that rested on four cardboard boxes. Three were marked on the sides with the word Trucks. They were filled with notebooks, photographs, and folders I had collected while working at the *Detroit Times*. I hadn't gotten around to throwing it away.

I thought about what I'd seen on the beach at Walleye Lake. Yellow was the standard color of the old Ski-Doo snowmobiles that had been popular many years before. The thought sent a little chill down my spine. My coach, Jack Blackburn, had died on a yellow Ski-Doo. He'd been riding with Leo Redpath late on a Saturday night when his snowmobile broke through the frozen lake and he went under. Neither his body nor his snowmobile was ever found. But Coach Blackburn had gone down on Starvation Lake, not Walleye. So that couldn't have been his snowmobile that Dingus had gone to see. Then why did I feel nausea slithering around in my gut like a worm? What was Dingus even doing out there, and why had he seemed so jittery? What if it was Coach's snowmobile?

I was too tired to walk down to the *Pilot* and leave a note on Joanie's desk, so I picked up the phone and dialed her extension, figuring I'd leave a voice mail. I heard half a ring, then a click, then a rustling sound.

"McCarthy," she said.

"Joanie?"

There was a pause. "Yes, Gus, it's Joanie. I'm sleeping."

"At the office?"

"I forwarded my calls. What do you want?"

"Dingus. You need to call him first thing."

"What?"

"Sheriff Aho. Ask him about the snowmobile that washed up on Walleye Lake. Or at least I think it was a snowmobile. He wouldn't say. Might be nothing, but he was acting pretty weird."

"You spoke with him?"

"I went out there."

Another pause. "Well," she said, "I have a bunch of stuff on my plate."

"Uh-huh. But I need you to check with Dingus first thing."

"OK, boss," she said, enunciating it so as to remind me that she wasn't in love with my being her boss. She was young and smart and bent on getting out of Starvation Lake as fast as possible. Like I'd once been. I remembered that feeling of impatience for what would come next, and how soon, and whether it would come at all, whether you'd get stuck at some small-town rag writing about drain commission meetings while everyone else went to big cities and big stories.

I finished the water and put the jar in the sink. Outside, Soupy's truck was gone. Next to Enright's, the backlit sign in the window of Boynton Realty glowed dully. Soupy and Teddy Boynton and I had all played together for Jack Blackburn. I shivered in the darkness. Was Coach back now? I wondered. Had Dingus seen his ghost on the shore of Walleye Lake?

three

A narrow inner stairway descended conveniently from my apartment to the *Pilot* newsroom, but I rarely used it. I preferred to take the outside stairs to the parking lot out back and walk a block to Estelle Street, turn up to Main, and double back to the *Pilot*'s front door. It got me some fresh morning air and helped me sustain the illusion that I had a life separate from work.

Walking up Estelle, I heard the staccato drip of melting ice in the rain gutters of Pine County State Bank. I turned onto Main, and the heart of the town opened before me. Two-story brick-and-clapboard buildings flanked the two-lane street, which ran flat between angled parking spaces to the lake. Down my side of Main stood the *Pilot* and the shuttered Avalon Cinema. Beyond lay Kepsel's Ace Hardware, the law office of Parmelee Gilbert, a Dairy Queen, and, at the edge of the beach, Jordan Bait and Tackle, where Main veered west and disappeared. Across from the bait shop, Soupy's marina squatted where the Hungry River spilled into Starvation. Coming back toward me along Main was Teddy Boynton's office, Enright's, Sally's Dry Cleaning and Floral, Audrey's Diner, and Fortune Drug.

The lake was named for a drought that had nearly dried it up in the 1930s until the Civilian Conservation Corps built a dam to divert the nearby Hungry River. From the sidewalk outside the *Pilot*, I could see clearly down to the lake, silent and white, a seven-mile-long crescent encircled by hills, palatial summer cottages, and smaller year-round homes snugged beneath the pines, oaks, and birches. Starvation's population could more than triple with the vacationers who drove hundreds of miles from Detroit and Chicago to boat, swim, fish, ski, hunt, snowmobile, and party. Tourist dollars had built Starvation's new schools and paved its roads and helped put its children through college. But the town had seen better days. In the past decade, roughly since Coach Blackburn died, more and more tourists had defected to the bigger resort towns on Lake Michigan and to Sandy Cove, a town seventeen miles east that had spent boatloads of money advertising its own clear blue lake in travel magazines and on billboards along I-75. Teddy Boynton had a big idea for fixing Starvation, which was why he was coming to see me this morning.

The front door to the *Pilot* jangled shut behind me. Like just about every door on Main Street, the *Pilot*'s was equipped with little toy bells.

"Morning, Till," I said.

"Good morning," Tillie Spaulding said. "Did you bring me tea and croissants?"

"Gosh," I said. "Forgot again." This was our morning ritual. Tillie asked and I apologized. I supposed that someday I might actually bring in tea and croissants, though first I'd have to find croissants in Starvation Lake.

Matilda Spaulding had been Miss Michigan as a lissome blond teenager, the pride of Starvation Lake in 1963. Two hours after a Main Street parade in her honor, she left to make movies in Hollywood. She made a TV commercial for foot powder, met a producer, got married, got pregnant, got an abortion, got divorced, and came home. There was no parade upon her return. Since 1971 she'd been society columnist, occasional news reporter, and unofficial receptionist for the *Pilot*. She had dated virtually every eligible bachelor within thirty miles of town, and a few who weren't bachelors anymore, while developing a fondness for whiskey, rocks, with a maraschino cherry. She leaned on an elbow at the front counter, a cigarette crooked in her long fingers. She pointed it at my chin.

"What happened to you?"

I instinctively touched the stitches on my jaw. They stung. "Boynton ran me over last night," I said.

"Ted Boynton?" Her voice hadn't yet lost its morning croak.

"Just about beheaded me," I said. I grabbed a *Pilot* off the counter.

"Oh, pshaw, Gus. You boys have known each other forever."

"Maybe that's the problem." Checking the front page, I noticed we had used the wrong photograph for the local youngster who had speared a six-pound bass on Blue Lake. "Anyway, he's coming in this morning."

She stubbed out her half-smoked cigarette. "Should I get doughnuts?"

"No. This is a business meeting, and I think Teddy convened it last night." I started back to the newsroom.

"Hold on. You owe me a quarter."

NLP Newspapers Inc., the company that three years before had purchased the *Pilot* from its original owners, Nelson P. and Gertrude X. Selby, had started making employees pay for their paper.

"Put it on my tab," I said.

"Gus."

I walked back and slapped two dimes and a nickel on the counter.

At ten o'clock, Tillie ushered Teddy Boynton and another man toting a briefcase back to the *Pilot* newsroom.

Buzzing fluorescent lamps lit the windowless room. It was just big enough for a watercooler, a knee-high refrigerator, a combination copier and fax, and four gray steel desks. The air tasted of stale coffee and copier ink. I cleared one swivel chair of grease-spattered chili-dog wrappers, another of a pile of newspapers. Teddy approached me with his big hand outstretched, flashing the smile I knew well from high school. These days it adorned refrigerator magnets advertising his real estate company. His eyes flicked over my bandaged jaw. "Hell of a game last night," he said.

"Really? I don't remember much. Must've hit my head on the crossbar."

"It'll sneak up on you. Meet Arthur Fleming."

Fleming, a short, pear-shaped man in thick glasses, was an attorney from Sandy Cove. He had represented the town the summer before when a movie-theater chain was deciding whether to close the theater there or the Avalon in Starvation Lake. Sandy Cove prevailed after offering twenty thousand dollars to rebuild its theater's balcony. I shook his hand. "You're not representing Sandy Cove?"

His eyes wandered disapprovingly around the room. "Not on this matter."

Boynton grinned again. "He's all mine," he said.

Boynton unrolled a blueprint and spread it across my desk. "You may think you've seen this before, but you haven't," he said. As big and broad as he looked in his hockey gear, he always seemed bigger in a jacket and tie. "We've tweaked a few things and, just between us, I'm not sure our zoned-out zoning board has absorbed it all." I felt him peek to see if I was smiling. "Like here," he said, pointing. "We've moved the Jet Ski docks farther down the beach so we don't have kids shooting out in front of boats . . ."

Teddy wanted to build the Pines at Starvation Lake, a marina with a luxury hotel, a restaurant, and a fifty-foot-tall waterslide. He had the land. He had most of the money lined up. He just needed a change to the local zoning ordinance. But the zoning board, five old men who seemed flummoxed by all the legal, financial, and environmental issues involved, was balking. Plenty of townspeople felt the marina was just what Starvation needed to steal business back from Sandy Cove. Others thought Boynton owned enough.

I had written the editorial that led to the stitches on my jaw. I didn't care how much of the town Teddy owned, and I thought the new marina was probably a good idea, but I argued that there were still questions about how the development might affect the lake. Unless Boynton offered more money to keep the water clean, I argued, the zoning board should think hard before approving the project. Besides, we already had Starvation Lake Marina, which Soupy had inherited when his father died the summer before.

Although it was fifty-three years old and in need of repair, the town had to find ways to help it.

"You saw our editorial?" I said.

"I did," Boynton said, his face hinting at a scowl. The zoning board was scheduled to meet again the following Monday and, with the editorial fresh in their minds, the members were likely to demand more money.

I propped a boot against my desk. "Well," I said, "I doubt we're going to change our view."

"We'd welcome that, of course," Boynton said, "but that's actually not why we're here. Arthur?"

Fleming jumped up and his glasses slid down his nose. He pushed them up with the heel of his left hand, set his briefcase on my desk, and pulled out a thick document sheathed in clear plastic. "We have some research we think might be enlightening, Mr. Carpenter, to the citizens of Starvation Lake," he said. "We'd like to show this to you on an off-the-record basis."

I hadn't heard that phrase since Detroit. Fleming must have fantasized that he was a big-city lawyer rather than a glorified notary public with a mercenary streak. "Sorry," I said. "No off the record."

"Gus," Boynton said. "All he means is, if you use this stuff, we'd prefer you didn't say where you got it."

"Mr. Carpenter," Fleming said.

"Call me Gus."

"Gus, then. We've simply compiled publicly available information that paints a broader picture of the implications of the zoning board's responsibilities—and, in fact, the *Pilot*'s responsibilities—to the community."

I looked up at the clock over Joanie's desk. There had been a time, not so long ago, when I'd believed that things were either true or they weren't, no matter where they came from. "Tell you what," I said. "I'll *look* at it off the record. But if we think it's worth a story, we'll have to say who put us onto it."

Fleming looked at Boynton, who shrugged. The document thudded on my desk. Beneath the plastic, the cover page was blank but for an identifying label, "Campbell/7364opp," typed in tiny black letters. On the next page was a table of contents divided into four categories: (I) Recent Litigation, (II) Formal Complaints, (III) Affidavits, and (IV) Tax Liens and Related Matters. Beneath each were a variety of references to Starvation Lake Marina, Alden C. Campbell, and Angus F. Campbell. Alden Campbell was Soupy. Angus was his father, who had been the marina's proprietor until Soupy found him lying face-up on a dock on the morning of July fourth, dead of a heart attack. I flipped through the document. There were excerpts of lawsuits, sworn statements by people who had business with the marina, copies of overdue tax bills, complaints filed with the Better Business Bureau. I'd known Soupy was having trouble running his father's business, but not this much.

"Looks like Soup's got his work cut out," I said.

"The real question," Fleming said, "is whether the young Mr. Campbell is cut out for the work. His record seems to demonstrate—"

"He's only been doing it for, what, not even a year."

"Come on, Gus," Boynton said. "He grew up in the damn place."

Fleming quieted his client with a raised palm. "It's true Mr. Campbell has been managing the property for slightly in excess of seven months. But it's also true that in that short span he has managed to exacerbate the relatively dire financial straits the business was experiencing at the time of his father's death. It's debatable as to whether his father would've been able to right this sinking ship. Perhaps. But he is not with us. Under his son, this ship has done nothing but take on more water."

Enough with the nautical metaphors, I thought. "It's not the *Pilot*'s job to make judgments about who is or isn't a good businessman."

"Arguable," Fleming said. "I would argue it is certainly your job to alert the public if a business's lack of viability has the potential to impact the public interest. In the case of the Starvation Lake Marina, we fear that its next public filing will be for bankruptcy. That could have catastrophic consequences for this community—the loss of its sole marina, the very heart of its economy."

"What do you care?" I said. "Then the zoning board would have to let you guys go ahead."

"Too late," Boynton said. "By the time all the shoes dropped, I'd lose an entire season. The lenders won't go for it. I've put a lot of time and money into this. If Starvation Lake doesn't want it, somebody else might."

That explained the presence of the Sandy Cove lawyer. "Clever," I said.

"It's no sin to play hard."

"No," I said, scratching my stitches.

Fleming cleared his throat. "Incidentally, you should know that we're contemplating showing this same material to Channel Eight."

He was goading me. Although the *Pilot*'s owners, NLP Newspapers, didn't especially like controversial stories and the legal inconveniences they could sometimes bring, they hated it when Channel Eight had a story before any of its newspapers. If we got beat to an important story about the marina, I was certain to catch hell from corporate, and Fleming probably knew it.

"Jeez, Ted," I said, "why didn't you just tell me all this when you had your stick down my throat last night?"

Boynton hitched his chair up closer. The metal wheels squeaked on the linoleum. "Look, Gus," he said. "Your buddy Soupy—our buddy Soupy—is a fuckup. Great guy, great hockey player. But a fuckup. You know it and I know it. Should the whole town suffer for that?"

"Who's a screwup?"

We all turned to see Joanie standing there in her orange parka, clutching a notebook in her left hand. Over her shoulder hung a backpack that was half the size of her. Her hair, a wild, flaming bush that matched the color of her coat, billowed around her head and spilled over her shoulders. As always, she seemed out of breath.

"Where's the fire?" I said.

"Just got back from the sheriff's. Who's a screwup?" She couldn't bring herself to say "fuckup." She didn't like profanity, didn't use it, didn't like when anybody else used it. She gave me a little speech once about how senseless it was to use "fucking" as an adjective. "It's not a pencil," she'd said, "it's a *fucking* pencil. It's not a lamp, it's a *fucking* lamp. Barbarians and fools talk like that." I'd grinned and said, "*Fucking* barbarians, you mean?"

Boynton stood and offered his hand. "Ted Boynton," he said. "And it's not me who's the fuckup."

Joanie frowned. "So who then?"

Boynton laughed. "I'm sure your boss will fill you in."

Joanie's eyes fell on the document. Then she looked at me. "What happened to your chin?" she said.

"Fell out of bed," I said.

"I got some stuff on the snowmobile," she said.

"OK," I said. "Just give us five more minutes."

"Going across the street," she said, meaning Audrey's Diner. "Looks like the thing was registered to someone, John Blackberg or Blackston or something."

Teddy Boynton sat up and turned toward Joanie.

"What was that?" I said.

"I thought you needed five."

"What was the name?"

She pulled out a notebook and flipped through it. "Blackburn," she said, shooting me an irritated glance before she turned to leave.

Teddy turned back to me. "Holy shit," he said.

four

My computer screen displayed a list of five news stories, two features, and a few briefs that had to be edited and sent to the presses in about six hours. I had to hustle. Our staff wasn't much of a staff since NLP stopped letting us replace the young reporters who inevitably came to the *Pilot* for just a year or two before leaving for a bigger paper. Essentially, there was Joanie, Tillie, and me to write stories, and a photographer. My boss, executive editor Henry Bridgman, had been spending a lot of his time huddling with the suits at the corporate offices in Traverse City. We had a few blue-haired ladies who freelanced now and then. It was next to impossible to put out a six-day-a-week paper with such a tiny staff. I filled a lot of the paper with wire-service copy and barely rewritten press releases.

Joanie had written most of the stories on my screen, including the one at the top, slugged BIGFOOT. I punched the story up:

> By M. Joan McCarthy
> *Pilot* **Staff Correspondent**
> A glass case on Clayton Perlmutter's kitchen table contains what some might consider to be a bizarre treasure. Perlmutter's prize is a three-inch-thick mound of hardened brown feces, which the retired house painter claims came from a Sasquatch, the mythical "Bigfoot" creature rumored to roam the woods of northern Michigan.
>
> But some people think Perlmutter is the one who's full of it.

I couldn't help but smile, both at the lead paragraph itself and at the unlikelihood that it would run in the *Pilot*. We did our best not to put fecal matter in the paper, at least intentionally.

"What's so funny back there?"

"Nothing, Tillie," I said.

The *Pilot* and other papers in our area ran stories every few years on Clayton Perlmutter and his Sasquatch Institute. Invariably, the stories ushered readers through Perlmutter's dank garage, where he kept his collection of blurry photos, scratchy audiotapes, footprint casts, and maps of Sasquatch sightings. And they quoted Perlmutter about his one-man campaign for a state law that would prohibit the killing of the Sasquatch.

I had expected Joanie to file something equally harmless. Reading her story, I saw I'd been mistaken. She quoted zoologists from Harvard and the Smithsonian discrediting the notion that the Sasquatch had ever existed. She cited a retired local photographer who said he'd helped Perlmutter doctor snapshots of a brown bear. The real news showed up halfway through: For years, Perlmutter had been getting state money to support his organization. In his grant applications, he had said he was maintaining a museum.

> Documents obtained by the *Pilot* under the state Freedom of Information Act show Perlmutter has garnered at least $32,235 in eighteen state grants since 1985. In periodic reports to the state, Perlmutter has said only that the state money had been used for "sundry uncompleted research projects." When asked, Perlmutter said he had "no obligation under the First Amendment" to address these matters.

I loved the story, even felt a pang of jealousy at Joanie's ability to nail it. But I doubted it would fly with the corporate guys. It wasn't just their usual skittishness that was giving me pause. My job was on the line. The bosses at NLP had balked at hiring me after my abrupt departure from the *Detroit Times*. Only Henry Bridgman's personal guarantee had persuaded them—that and a year of probation. One bad slip and I could be gone from the *Pilot*—and maybe the whole newspaper business—for good. I didn't like it, but I decided I had to let the NLP lawyers vet Joanie's story. That created another problem. Expecting something tamer, I'd planned to splash the Bigfoot story across Saturday's front page. Now I needed something else.

Up front, Tillie was leaning against the counter with the *Detroit Times* spread before her. A bluish cigarette haze hung around her bleached-blond head.

"Hey, Till," I said. "What's in the news?"

"Aren't newspaper editors supposed to keep up with the news?" she said.

"I suppose."

"Indeed. Well, it's all Monica all the time."

"Who's Monica?"

"She's a little hussy who worked in the White House," Tillie said. "She had a little thing with the president. He stuck a cigar in her you-know-what."

I cringed, less at what Tillie said than at having to hear it from her. "Her last name's Lewinsky?" I grabbed a phone book. "I need a favor, Till."

She crushed her cigarette out. "Please, Gus, not a Selby."

The *Pilot*'s former owner, Nelson P. Selby, had some peculiar ideas about "localizing" national news. One of his favorite gimmicks was to have reporters interview local people who happened to have the same surnames as people in Washington or New York or Hollywood who were making news. So, when General Schwarzkopf was leading the U.S. military in the Gulf War, some poor *Pilot* reporter sought out the three Schwarzkopfs—one may have been a Schwartzkopf—in Pine County to ask what they thought. None were related to the general. A retired plumber wondered if the general had a homely dog, like General George Patton. A widowed schoolteacher thought Schwarz-kopf a handsome man who shouldn't wear sunglasses when being photographed. I'd sneered at this sort of story when I was in journalism school and later as a reporter in Detroit. Now I riffled through a phone book and told Tillie, "There are three Lewinskys in the county, all spelled S-K-I. And there's two LOW-inskys. If you're desperate, there's a Lewinskas."

"Oh, we're plenty desperate," Tillie said. "What happened to Bigfoot?"

"Problems," I said. "Don't forget to get a photo. It'll have to run big."

Tillie was looking in the phone book. "Here's old Artemis Lewinski," she said. "He could definitely run big."

I winced again. "Copy by four, OK? Where's Joanie?"

"She went for coffee."

"Oh, no," I said. She'd been gone too long. I hurried out without a coat.

Every head in Audrey's turned as I walked in. Then every head turned back to the round table in the corner. Four men, three wives, and a sister-in-law sat there with Joanie, who was nodding and scribbling in her notebook, her backpack parked on the floor between her feet.

I was too late.

I stationed myself behind Joanie's left shoulder. She didn't look up. Their plates hadn't been cleared; I smelled grease and cinnamon. Elvis Bontrager was talking. He glanced at me from beneath the brim of his Lawson's Lumber Land cap. The back of the cap was made of plastic mesh, and I could see the rows of thin hairs like wires jutting from his pink scalp. A fleck of Canadian bacon clung to his left cheek as his jowls worked.

"The thing was, I mean, the real thing with Coach was, it didn't matter who we were playing, they could be bigger or faster or, you know, fancier than us, and he don't care, he'd figure out how to beat them."

"A strategist then?" Joanie said.

"Always a good game plan."

Everyone nodded. Elvis looked at me. Here it comes, I thought.

"But Coach Blackburn, unfortunately, had to have the players actually play the game, right, Gus?" he said. "What happened to your face?"

He meant my stitches. "Puck," I said.

"Well, at least you stopped one, eh?" Elvis chuckled and turned to Joanie. "You know, miss, Gus is pretty famous around here. He was witness to the end of an era in Starvation Lake hockey. Hell, he was the one who ended it. Tell her, Gus. You know what happened. God knows none of us do."

Joanie lowered her notebook. "What happened?"

Elvis shrugged. "Nothing. Gus here just lost us a hockey game. A state *championship* hockey game. Our one and only."

Joanie looked as though she didn't quite understand. "That's it?"

"Miss," Elvis said, leaning forward, "he lost that game and we ain't come close to a state championship since."

"Oh," Joanie said. She looked at me. "So you jinxed them?"

Elvis had another laugh. He didn't like me because I gave up that goal, and because, yes, to a superstitious person, and there were plenty in Starvation Lake, including me, I had jinxed them. But he also didn't like me because I had broken the heart of his niece when I went off to Detroit to work at a newspaper instead of marrying her, as Elvis and everyone else had expected. Her name then had been Darlene Bontrager, but later she married a minor-league hockey player named Esper who suffered a mysteriously chronic back ailment and now spent his days playing video golf at Dingman's Bar. Darlene Esper was the sheriff's deputy who had called me about the snowmobile in Walleye Lake.

I'd gone off to Detroit so that someday I might be able to come back to Starvation and walk up to Elvis and tell him, "Why don't you go to hell, so what if I lost a stupid hockey game years ago? Look at me now, a big-city reporter, a Pulitzer Prize winner." But there I was, just another local loser who worked at the little paper across the street with the shaker shingles over the door and the sign in the window that read, "Peerless *Pilot* Personals Will Put You on the Path to Pleasure and Profit." Screaming would have felt great. Instead I managed a tight smile and said to Joanie, "What's all the interest in the coach?"

"The snowmobile," she said. "Looks like it could've been his."

"Weren't you out to Walleye last night, Gus?" Elvis said.

"Yes, but I—"

"We heard they found a pair of Jack's old skates inside, all rusted out."

Joanie scribbled furiously in her notebook. This was just what I had feared. If I didn't get her out of there fast, by nightfall we'd be hearing about sightings of Jack Blackburn, and maybe the other Elvis, too.

"Sounds like you all know a lot more than I do," I said. I put a hand on Joanie's shoulder. "We need to get the paper out."

She shrugged my hand off and stood. "Come on back, Miss Joanie," Elvis said. "I'll buy you a cup."

The door had barely shut behind us when she turned to me, florid with anger. "Why did you do that? I was getting good color."

"Color for what?"

"For the snowmobile story you told me to do."

"Blackburn died on Starvation Lake," I said, "not Walleye."

"Whatever. The cops think it might be his."

"*Might* be?" I noticed Elvis craning his neck to see us through the window.

"They got the registration—part of the registration number—and it matches. I mean, part of it matches what's—"

"Part of it? Did Dingus confirm it?"

"No. D'Alessio."

Pine County sheriff's deputy Frank D'Alessio was young and dumb and a notorious skirt chaser. "I'll bet it's not on the record, though, huh?"

"So?"

"So you've got part of a number and the word of a deputy who won't go on the record. You don't really have a goddamn thing, do you?"

"Watch your language, please."

"This is a small town, Joanie. Asking questions about stuff you don't know to be true is no different than gossiping to everybody here."

"Well, maybe this town's too small."

"Maybe. Just don't bring me this stuff until you have it nailed."

"OK, boss," she said. She veered to cross Main without me but had to wait for a car to pass. She spun to face me again. Her hair had fallen across her eyes. I knew D'Alessio. He'd be all over that.

"What about the Bigfoot story?" she said.

"What about it?"

"Do you need anything more?"

"Not right now."

"Meaning?"

I glanced away. Soupy's truck was parked in front of Enright's. "It'll run next week. Got to have it lawyered first."

"Lawyered? Bullcrap! They'll cut out all the stuff about the grants and all the crap Perlmutter's been peddling all these years. And you can run the usual little piece of crud instead of a story that might turn a few heads."

"You don't know that."

"But you know, don't you, Gus?"

I watched, speechless, as she turned and darted into the street, holding up her hand to slow an oncoming pickup.

five

No way was I going back to Audrey's for lunch. I walked around behind the *Pilot* and climbed the wooden stairs to my apartment.

I took bologna and ketchup from the fridge, a frying pan from the dish drainer. I turned on the stove and tore the bologna into ragged strips in the pan. The meat sizzled into crisp curls. I dumped ketchup all over it, turned the heat down, and laid two slices of white bread on a paper plate.

Out the window, I stared at Soupy's truck, still parked in front of Enright's. I hit the play button on my answering machine. My mother reminded me about coming for Sunday dinner. Somebody hung up. Then a reedy voice filled my breadbox of a kitchen.

"Gus," it said. "I wish you'd return my calls. Tuesday's the drop dead."

"Then I'll call you Tuesday," I told the machine.

The voice was the Detroit lawyer I had had to hire in my final days at the *Detroit Times*. I turned the stove off and scooped the crispy bologna onto the bread.

"Jesus," I said.

My best reporter—my only real reporter—was angry with me. Teddy Boynton was trying to blackmail me. My old coach had resurfaced. And now it looked like I would finally have to deal with the mess I had made in Detroit. I sat down in the recliner to eat. But I wasn't hungry anymore.

The sandwich spent the afternoon in the newsroom fridge, while I edited stories and wrote headlines for Saturday's *Pilot*. The school board was seeking a special tax to pay for a swimming pool. A cellular phone company cut the ribbon on a store in the mini-mall. A frustrated mother called the sheriff's department for help putting her eleven-year-old son to bed. And the River Rats were headed downstate for the first round of the state hockey playoffs. I spent most of an hour translating Tillie Spaulding's Monica feature into readable newspaper patter. She couldn't write, but she surely could find the strange.

She dug up eighty-three-year-old Gloria Lowinski, a nurse who thought President Clinton and his wife should try tantric sex, and a CPA named Barton Lewienski, who insisted Republicans had paid the intern to seduce Clinton. There was a French poodle named Monica and a cashier at a burger joint called the White House who said, "Monica who?"

I held my nose and sent the thing to the printing plant.

Joanie didn't turn in her story about the snowmobile until 5:12, eighteen minutes before deadline. It began:

> Pine County sheriff's deputies think a snowmobile that washed up
> on Walleye Lake may have belonged to John D. "Jack" Blackburn, the
> legendary youth hockey coach who died in a snowmobile accident
> ten years ago.

Reading the rest, I saw no more evidence to support that assertion than Joanie had let on outside Audrey's. Nor did she attempt to explain how the snowmobile, if it was Coach Blackburn's, had surfaced on Walleye Lake after sinking in Starvation. She was sitting at her desk, marking up a notebook with a red pen. She hadn't said a word to me all afternoon.

"Joanie," I said. "You haven't nailed this snowmobile thing."

"Fix it then."

"Too late," I said, annoyed. "Corporate'll raise hell if we keep the plant overtime. I'm spiking it." Just as I turned back to my computer,

I heard a metallic *thwup* against the wall facing me. Two feet over my head, a wet brown stain seeped down the wall. A Diet Coke can hissed on the floor beneath.

"Jesus," I said, wheeling around to face her.

She was standing now. "Jerk," she said. "I could've worked on Bigfoot, but I spent the day chasing your stupid snowmobile, and now you kill that story, too? You're so full of crap."

She had a point. And I could handle her calling me a jerk, but in my short career as an editor I'd never had a reporter throw something at me. I had no idea what to do. But I wasn't about to fire her when the suits weren't about to let me replace her. So I just said, "Calm down, Joanie."

"Don't tell me to calm down. Don't tell me anything."

Tillie appeared in the doorway in her fur coat with the little mink claws dangling from the shoulders. "What's going on back here?"

I looked at Joanie. "You're a loser," she said.

Tillie walked over, picked up the can, and dropped it in a wastebasket. "Can you children please clean this up? Good night."

Joanie and I sat in silence. I wanted to get up and tell her how unprofessional and immature she was. Her story was all guesswork. Maybe she'd guessed right. Or maybe not. But she was right—we couldn't just ignore the damn snowmobile. The clock said 5:26. Son of a bitch, I thought.

My eight-paragraph revision said merely that police were investigating the appearance of part of a snowmobile on the Walleye Lake shore. I left a single reference to Coach Blackburn, in the last paragraph:

Police have yet to determine ownership of the snowmobile. They noted similarities to one owned by John D. "Jack" Blackburn, the legendary youth hockey coach who drowned in a snowmobile accident on March 13, 1988. However, that accident occurred on Starvation Lake. Neither his body nor the snowmobile were found.

I printed it out and walked it over to Joanie. Her eyes flitted across the page. She tossed it on her desk. "Whatever," she said.

"Whatever?"

"Put it in the paper. That's your job, isn't it?"

"Joanie. Is the story accurate?"

"So far as it goes, yes."

I went back to my desk. As the story disappeared from my screen, I felt Joanie standing behind me. I turned to see she was wearing her parka. "I'm going to make it even more accurate for Monday's paper," she said.

"OK," I said. I nodded at the wall. "You going to clean this up, too?"

"Nope," she said. I waited until she was gone to get the mop.

When I walked into the smoky tunnel of Enright's pub, Soupy was standing at his corner of the bar, in his denim coat and red cap, yelling at the bartender to turn up the jukebox. On the TV over the bar, a local weatherman was placing a turtle on a circular chart cut into pie pieces labeled snow, sleet, sun, clouds. Each night, the turtle would crawl dumbly to one of the pieces, and that would be his forecast. He got it right about as often as the weatherman.

"Hold your horses," said the bartender, Dave Lubienski. He rummaged behind the cash register for the TV remote. Loob was a quiet guy who spent mornings working as an assessor at Town Hall and afternoons building elaborate clocks and birdhouses that he sold to downstate tourists who overpaid. He also tended bar and played for Teddy Boynton's team in the Midnight Hour Men's League. "Mute button don't work," he said. He clicked the volume to zero, turned toward Soupy, and saw me. "Evening, Gus."

"Loob," I said.

Soupy turned and spread his arms wide, feigning surprise. "Well, if it isn't Mr. Trapezoid himself." He'd been calling me Trap since we were nine, playing a tabletop hockey game I'd gotten for Christmas.

Soupy had dubbed his goaltender "Tommy Trapezoid," after the shape of the little metal figure. Because I was a goalie, he started calling me Trapezoid, too, Trap for short.

Loob set a Blue Ribbon on the bar. The first icy swallow burned my throat. "Another day, another miracle," I said.

"The trusty *Pilot*," Soupy said. "Michigan's finest mullet wrapper." Our motto, printed each day for fifty-seven years beneath the masthead, was actually "Michigan's Finest Bluegill Wrapper." Soupy liked to switch the fish around, though. "Long day, Trap?"

"Long day." I gave him the two-minute version, skipping Boynton's visit.

"That Joanie's a piece of work, eh?" he said. "Not much of a looker, though, is she?"

"I tend not to assess my employees by the shapes of their asses."

"Of course, but Loob here, he might have issues, right, Loob?"

Loob replied on cue. "You can drink them pretty, but you can't drink them skinny."

"Yes, sir," Soupy said, downing his beer with a flourish.

There were no tables in Enright's, just eight stools, the long, whiskey-colored bar, and an elbow rail along the length of the opposite wall. Above the rail hung a collage of photographs of boys in the blue-and-gold uniforms of the Hungry River Rats. There had once been some of me, but smart alecks kept defacing them, and the bar's owner mercifully took them down. Our old coach smiled at the center of the display, just his face in black and white, the deep-set eyes, the knife-blade cheekbones, the silver hair combed straight back. "Jack Blackburn, 1934–1988," read the inscription.

At the other end of the bar hung a photograph of Soupy Campbell, then sixteen, leaping into the air with his hockey stick raised high and his mouth agape in a joyous whoop. It was the night we had beaten Paddock Pools of Detroit in the state quarterfinals. Late in the game, with the score tied at 2, Soupy had stolen the puck from a Paddock winger and weaved his way through the rest of the team until a single defender stood between him and the goalie. The goalie didn't see Soupy's shot until it was whizzing past his left ear into the net.

Soupy left Starvation after our last year with the Rats to play on a scholarship for Northern Michigan University. I was at Michigan, but we made a point of seeing each other whenever Northern traveled to Ann Arbor for games. He dazzled them his first year, and in his sophomore season got drafted in the third round by the National Hockey League's St. Louis Blues. He left Northern abruptly before his senior year and tried the minor pro leagues. He played in western Canada, Salt Lake City, Fort Wayne, finally Hershey, Pennsylvania. Every now and then he'd show a flash of the old brilliance, but mostly he played just well enough to hang on. There were rumors of drug and alcohol use on the hockey grapevine. He tore up a knee, dislocated a shoulder, got arrested in Erie, Pennsylvania, for riding through downtown atop a car naked and drunk in the middle of the night. He married a woman in Flint, had a daughter, got divorced. I asked him about it all a few times, and he grinned and said, "Ancient history, Trap. If I dwell on my screwups, I might remember how much fun they were and start repeating them." He returned to Starvation around the time of Coach Blackburn's accident and worked with his father at the marina. Now, with his father seven months dead, he owned it.

"Tell me, Soup," I said. "Isn't it kind of inconvenient to park your truck here all day when the marina's three blocks away?"

"Hey, Mom," he said. "I came in for one."

"Uh-huh."

"One right after another." He laughed and jabbed at my shoulder with his bottle. "Got a bug up your butt, Trap?"

The day's aggravation had me just irritated enough to want to extend it. "I hear you've got some legal trouble," I said.

"Trouble?" Soupy said. "Nah. Just some lawsuits." Loob set fresh beers down. Soupy leaned closer to me. "Lawsuits are one of those real-world things, Trap. You're in business, people sue your ass."

"Your old man have as many lawsuits?"

"Oh, yeah."

"Does the zoning board know?"

"Know what?

"About all this?"

"All this?" Soupy tore off his cap and tossed it on the bar. "What *this?*"

"The marina, Soup."

"The marina's fine."

I wasn't as worried about the town as I was about Soupy. He was no expert at selling or repairing boats, or at running a business, but he knew enough to keep himself in shoes and beer in Starvation Lake.

"And if Boynton builds his marina?"

"Fuck Boynton," Soupy said. He turned to Loob. "I'll be collecting a hundred bucks from his sorry ass tomorrow. Who's your money on, Loob?"

Loob smiled laconically. "Not Gus."

They meant the annual Starvation Lake Shoot-Out, to be held the next day before our league playoffs began. Shooters paid twenty dollars for five one-on-one chances to score on a volunteer goaltender. The proceeds bought practice jerseys for the youth teams. Coach Blackburn had started the Shoot-Out when we were kids. This year, I was the goalie, thanks to Soupy, who'd volunteered me. The shooter who scored the most goals won a wool hat embroidered as "The Stanley Cap." But it was really about bragging rights and side bets. Soupy had won four of the last five Shoot-Outs. Boynton had won the other.

"You can afford a hundred bucks?" I said.

"If I know I'm going to win. Fuck Boynton and his fancy-ass marina."

"Good luck."

"Yeah, and fuck you, too, Trap. The zoning board is going to shoot Teddy boy down like a porcupine from a tree."

Soupy figured he had an edge. Two board members had been friends of his father. Another once worked at the marina.

"Maybe," I said. "But what if they do? What if Boynton walks away then and you tank, isn't the town screwed?"

"Is that what fuckface Teddy told you?" he said. I started to answer, but he waved me off. "I know, you can't talk about what goes on inside the holy hallowed walls of the mullet wrapper. But I know Boynton and his fat-ass lawyer have been peddling those lawsuits. I'm not so dumb, Trap. You want my permission to put that shit in the paper? Is that it?"

"I don't need your permission, Soupy."

"Look," he said. "The town will not be screwed." He set his beer down. "Snow's been iffy this year, so we haven't rented out as many snowmobiles as I'd like. But I already got people coming for boats. I've been a little distracted with this Boynton stuff, but we'll take care of that and everything'll fall into place. Shit, Trap, you hate your job, why don't you come over and we'll run the place together? Hell, we used to just about run it."

"I don't hate my job, Soupy."

"You remember the cat, Trap?"

When we were fifteen, both working at the marina, we pooled our earnings to buy a used sixteen-foot catamaran. We took it out on breezy summer evenings after work. Soupy sat and handled the tiller. I buckled on a harness and stood on the pontoon behind him. When a stiff wind caught the sail, my pontoon would lift out of the water and I'd stand up, the bottoms of my feet crooked hard against the pontoon's edge. I'd lean way back against the harness to keep the boat from flipping, my body nearly horizontal over the water rushing by, Soupy working the tiller, his hair flying, both of us laughing and yelling at the setting sun.

"That was the ultimate, Trap. Better than hockey even."

I loved him like a brother, but he didn't make it easy.

"Will you be at the zoning board Monday?" I said.

"Fucking-ay," he said. He smiled and spread his arms wide. "Hey, man, look—the marina's got to last at least through summer. I already ordered the softball shirts."

six

I left Enright's a little after eleven and walked along the river to the
lake to clear my head of the smoke and alcohol. The wind whistled
low through a birch stand at the far end of South Beach. Across
the lake, dim lights of homes on the bluff made hazy silhouettes of
the fishing shanties dotting the lake. I looked toward the darkness
past Pelly's Point, where Coach Blackburn had gone down.

He had come to Starvation in 1970 from Canada, where he'd
played hockey into his twenties and then had been a coach, first of
little kids, then older ones, finally sixteen- to nineteen-year-olds, Canada's best amateurs. He left Canada, he told us, because he couldn't
stand the cold anymore; he longed for warm summers. He said his
brother-in-law, who was from Kalamazoo downstate, had told him
Starvation was one of the prettiest lakes anywhere.

He started a heating-and-cooling business and bought a cabin
in the woods a few miles west of town. That first winter, he built a
rink outside in the clearing next to his cabin. The town had plenty of
backyard rinks, but none like Coach's. He encircled his with slatted
construction fence for dasher boards and made goal nets from two-
by-fours and chicken wire. He lined up red and blue milk crates for
team benches and erected a huge blackboard for keeping score. He
made it known that all of Starvation Lake's young skaters were welcome to come to "Make-Believe Gardens" to play hockey.

On Saturday mornings in January and February, when it was so
cold that our skate blades squeaked on the ice, there'd be ten, fifteen,
twenty of us out there in helmets and hockey gloves, our Detroit
Red Wing and Chicago Blackhawk and Toronto Maple Leaf jerseys
pulled on tight over thermal underwear and flannels and wool sweat-

ers. We'd stop at noon to wolf the sandwiches and cookies our mothers had packed. Coach would hand out push brooms and we'd line up across one end of the rink and sweep until the ice glistened in the sun. Then we'd play until dark, and sometimes after, if enough of the dads who'd come to collect us were willing to wait a while and shine their car headlights out over the ice. Sometimes five or six squeezed into a station wagon with Coach to drink beer and watch the last game of the day.

Usually Coach was on the ice. He called penalties and broke up fights and tended to bloodied noses and bruised ankles. Every hour or so, he'd whistle play to a halt and gather us around. "Listen up, eh?" he'd say, and we'd mug at one another about his Canadian accent. He'd show us the best way to scoop a rolling puck off the boards, how to throw a hip to knock someone off his skates, why it was better to shoot low because the puck might glance off a leg or a stick and fool the goalie. While he coached, his fuzzy mutt, Pocket, sat on a milk crate watching, his head swiveling back and forth as the puck moved up and down the rink. Whenever somebody went near Blackburn, little Pocket would bark his nails-on-blackboard bark. He did a lot of barking.

Originally, I had wanted to play forward, like the Detroit Red Wings' great right wing, Gordie Howe. But my dad's favorite Red Wing had been a goaltender named Roger Crozier. Like me, Crozier was small and feisty and Dad liked how sometimes he would flop to block a shot and then right himself by grabbing the crossbar over his head. After Dad died, I decided I would be a goalie, like Crozier. No one at Make-Believe Gardens objected; everyone out there wanted to score goals, not stop them. At first, I wasn't much good at minding the net. Mostly I just flung my body in front of the puck, hoping it would hit me. Maybe my lack of ability looked like fearlessness, though, because Coach Blackburn noticed. One day after we'd played from morning till dark, I sat in a snowbank, exhausted, staring at the ice caked in my skate laces and rubbing my neck where a puck had left a welt the size of a half dollar. Coach crunched up next to me and said, "You're all right, Gus. If I ever get to coach a team around here, you're going to be my goalie."

That spring, after Make-Believe Gardens had melted away, Coach showed up at my house one morning with a pair of goalie's leg pads, a goaltender's stick, and another of his homemade nets. All that summer, he came over two or three times a week and shot tennis balls at me. He showed me how to kick my legs at a shot, how to cut down angles, how to gauge whether a breakaway skater would shoot or deke. And he told me again and again to avoid the temptation to be a goaltender like Crozier, who nearly always flopped to the ice to stop a shot, kicking his legs to each side in a butterfly fashion. Coach didn't like floppers. He said goalies who flopped tended to give up goals over their shoulders. And young players liked to shoot high because it looked cooler than shooting low.

"Floppers look fancy, eh?" Coach would say. "Up and down, up and down, the girls like that hotdog stuff, eh? But you might get a crick in your neck from watching those pucks go flying past your ear. Your job isn't to look good, it's to stop the puck, and if you want to stop the puck, you got to be a stand-up goalie. Especially you, Gus, because you're short, eh? You're barely standing up even when you're standing up." He'd smile then and muss my hair. "The floppers lose control, Gus. You don't see anybody else out there flopping around, do you? So stand up. Hold your ground. You can't control what's going on in front of you, but you can control what happens in your little corner of the world."

My mom started inviting him to stay for dinner. He fell in love with her Swiss steak and mashed potatoes. I wished he'd fall in love with Mom.

Two years later, he was asked to coach the River Rats, Starvation's travel squad, with five teams at different age levels. The Rats had consistently won their fair share against northern Michigan competition, but they'd never been able to skate with the powerhouses from Detroit—the Pipefitters, Evangelista Drywall, Capraro's Pizza, Panorama Engineering. Year after year, a Rats team emerged victorious from the state regionals thinking they were the ones who would finally eliminate one of the Detroit squads, and each time, they got crushed. It wasn't only that the Detroiters were bigger and faster, which they were. They just seemed to know something about hockey that we didn't. When they stepped onto the ice before the game, none of them even looked at us warming up at the other end.

Blackburn took over the Rats team for nine- and ten-year-olds. The way it worked, if he did well, he'd keep coaching that same group of boys as we rose through the older leagues. We had our first practice at the town's semi-indoor rink. There was a roof and two sides, but the other two sides were open to the elements. The wind cutting through barely ruffled the slicked-back hair on Blackburn's hatless head. He gathered us around him at center ice, standing still and straight as a goalpost while we fidgeted and tottered on our blades, our baggy jerseys drooping to our knees, our helmets like fishbowls on our heads. He knew most of us, of course, but he acted as if he'd never seen us before. "The Hungry River Rats, eh?" he said. "You don't look so hungry to me. But we'll get you there. We'll do what we've got to do to reach the ultimate goal." He paused. "There are goals"—he pointed at one of the nets—"and there are goals. I'm talking about the *ultimate* goal. Does anyone understand?"

We knew ultimate. Soupy had started us using the word as a substitute for "cool." Bobby Orr was the ultimate. Whoppers with cheese were the ultimate. Still, we stood there dumbly. Coach skated a little circle around us, sizing us up. He stopped where he'd begun and propped his stick up straight on the edge of its blade, the butt end scraping his chin. His eyes fell on mine.

"Gus?"

"Yeah."

"No, Gus. 'Yes, Coach.'"

It startled me. He'd come to Sunday dinner plenty of times without ever correcting the way I addressed him. "Uh, yes, Coach," I said.

"Come on, Gus. You know 'ultimate.' Didn't you just say the other day that your mother's mashed potatoes were the 'ultimate'?"

The others tittered. I felt uncomfortable. "To play hockey?" I said.

"Of course we're here to play hockey, Gus, or you wouldn't be out here in these goofy outfits."

I ventured again, "To play good hockey?"

"Well, we'll certainly have to play good to reach the ultimate goal, but first we have to know what it is. Can anybody help me?"

Again, silence. Then: "To win?"

It was Soupy.

"Alden Campbell," Coach said. "You're quite a smooth skater, son. Like a swan. Anybody ever tell you that?"

"Nope—I mean, no, Coach."

"From now on, you're the swan—Swanny. That all right with you?"

"I don't know, Coach."

"What's the ultimate goal, Swanny?"

"To win, Coach."

"To win what? A game? Two games?"

"All the games, Coach."

Blackburn shook his head. "No. Not all the games." He stopped and looked around again, catching each of us by the eyes. I felt as if he was about to tell us a secret. "The ultimate goal, boys, is to win one game. One game." He held up a finger. "That one game, boys, is the Michigan state championship final. Of course we're going to have to win a few others on the way. And we're going to have to lose some, too. But that's all right. Did you hear me? That's all right. Because losing's good for winning, boys. Hear me? Losing is good for winning. We're going to lose some, and then we're going to win. And we're going to win that one game. The state championship." He waited for it to sink in. "Understand?"

"Yes, Coach," we answered in unison.

He grabbed the whistle dangling at his neck and blew a short blast. "OK," he said. "Let's skate."

A year later, our parents called a meeting. They weren't happy with Coach Blackburn. He wasn't the friendly, easygoing guy they'd laughed and drank with at Make-Believe Gardens. He'd had the gall to ban the parents from watching practices. He told them he didn't want their kids looking to their mommies and daddies for help when Coach was making us skate endless circles and sprints and stops-and-starts without ever once putting a stick to a puck. He'd go around before those no-puck practices and put short stacks of pucks at each face-off dot. We weren't allowed to touch them. "Dying for those biscuits, eh?" he would say. "Makes you hungry." Word got back to the parents that a few of us had lost our breakfasts out there.

Worse for our moms and dads, we weren't winning. We had finished that first season under Coach 23–27 and didn't make the state playoffs. The parents blamed Coach, of course. For skating us without pucks. For making us play a defensive scheme he called the "Rat Trap" that slowed the game and kept us from scoring many goals. For inviting top-notch teams from Ohio, Illinois, Wisconsin, and, scariest of all, Detroit, to come up and play us on weekends. In the past, the Rats had avoided the Detroit teams until the state playoffs, but Coach said that only by playing those great teams repeatedly could we learn and then exploit their weaknesses. Of course, every time they beat us by six or seven goals, he reassured us that losing was good for winning.

But what really had the parents in a lather was that Coach had begun to recruit players from outside Starvation. On a low rise behind his cabin he'd built three small plankboard houses where those out-of-town players could board from September to May. He called the buildings and the players "billets." Billets were common in Canada, brand-new to northern Michigan. The day before the parents called their meeting, Blackburn had cut a local player, Jeff Champagne, in favor of a billet from Racine, Wisconsin, named Teddy Boynton.

The parents assembled around the picnic tables in the snack bar at our town rink. My mother sat at a table in the back. The smells of mustard and popcorn wafted on the air. Don Champagne, Jeff's father, spoke first. "This is our town and our rink that we built with our own hard-earned dollars, and we don't need a bunch of out-of-town folks who didn't put a dime into our rink," he said. "The River Rats ought to be players from Starvation Lake, and Starvation Lake only."

Soupy and I and the rest of the River Rats waited outside, as Coach had instructed, but we peeked and eavesdropped through the cracks in the door, as Coach no doubt had expected. He sat alone at a table facing the parents and listened, wordless, as one parent after another stood to complain about the billets, the no-puck practices, the Rat Trap. Just about everyone had something to say, except my own mother, which wasn't at all like her.

When every argument had been repeated two or three times, Coach smiled and placed his hands flat on the table. "Folks," he said. "First, I'd like to apologize for a little lapse in communication. It's a new season. You're all welcome to come watch practices. If the boys forgot to mention that, that's my fault." Outside, we snickered; Coach hadn't said a word to us about lifting the practice ban. "Second, no-puck practices will be more the exception than the rule this year. Your sons are all fine athletes, but, let's face it, they weren't in the best physical shape. Maybe too much of the pop and potato chips, eh?" He winked. "Hockey takes a lot of stamina, and the only way to build that stamina—the only way I know—is skating. This year, though, the kids'll be seeing more pucks. After all, you're right, the puck's a pretty big part of the game." A few parents chuckled.

He stood. "As for the various other ways we've approached the game, I'm afraid I'm not going to be able to apologize." His smile melted slowly away. "I'm going to be a little bit blunt with you now, folks. Please don't take it personally. I really love this town and the lake and how you've all welcomed me here. And I love your boys, every one of them, even the one—*especially* the one I had to cut from the roster." He was moving slowly around the room now, looking at each parent, one by one. "I don't come from here. Don't have kids of my own. So I don't have all that—that *emotion* you have tied up in watching your kids. I think I can be a little impartial, if you know what I mean. I've won a few championships in my time, and I think I know what it takes."

"Come on, Jack, we all want to win," Champagne piped up. "But why do we need players from Timbuktu to do it?"

Coach steepled his hands beneath his chin. "Good question. Here's the answer." He paused. "Because the players we have aren't good enough." He waited in the silence that followed, which was more awkward for the parents than for him. Then he repeated it: "Because the players we have aren't good enough. I'm sorry, folks. We have a few guys who are fast enough, or skilled enough. We have one boy who can skate with anyone in Michigan." I elbowed Soupy in the ribs. "We have another who's going to be the best stand-up goalie this town has ever seen." Soupy shoved me back, and Stevie Reneau smacked me on the back of the head. "And we have a few other good players in Starvation Lake. But we don't have enough. Not if we want to reach the ultimate goal."

He let the phrase linger on the air, as he had with us. He'd never used it on the parents before. As if on cue, Champagne finally said, "And what would the ultimate goal be?"

"Well," Coach said, "why don't I have your sons tell you?" He looked in our direction. "Boys?"

After practice earlier that afternoon, Coach had placed a cardboard box in the middle of our dressing room floor. We'd watched as he sliced it open with a pocketknife, reached in, and pulled out something wrapped in clear plastic that he held up for us to see. "What do you think, boys?" Inside the plastic was a shiny blue jacket with gold stripes on the collar and cuffs, and gold piping along the sleeves.

A River Rats logo was stitched over the right breast and a player's name—"Stevie" this one read—over the left. We all jumped up, oohing and ahhing. "The *ultimate* ultimate," Soupy said. We'd never had team jackets before. Coach had told us to stow them in our hockey bags until the parents' meeting.

Now the seventeen of us filed into the snack bar in our new jackets, as Coach had told us beforehand. It was the parents' turn to ooh and ahh. We formed a tight semicircle around Coach, Soupy and I on either side of him, again as he had instructed. He laid his hands gently on our shoulders. Surveying the room, I saw my mother smiling from her table. She'd probably known about the jackets ahead of time.

"Gus," he said. "Can you tell the folks here, what is the ultimate goal?"

All the parents' eyes were on me. I stuffed my hands in my jacket pockets and blurted, "To win one game, Coach."

"Just one, Gus?"

"Yes, Coach."

Champagne snorted. "One game?"

"Why don't you let him finish, Don?" It was the voice of Francis Dufresne, who was leaning on a vending machine in the back of the room. Dufresne didn't have children, but he never missed one of our games. The bar he owned, Enright's, ran a shuttle bus to the rink on game nights.

"Gus," Coach said. "What is that one game?"

I gave the answer. A few parents seemed to sit up straighter. Coach turned to Soupy. "Alden. Is the ultimate goal to win *all* the games?"

"No, Coach."

"Why not all the games, Alden?"

"Because losing is good for winning, Coach."

"Say again?"

"Losing is good for winning, Coach."

"This is ridiculous," Champagne shouted.

"Boys," Coach said, looking around at us, "how many games are we aiming to win?"

"One, Coach," we answered in unison.

"And that game is?"

"The state championship, Coach."

"Hear, hear," Dufresne said. He'd moved away from the vending machine to hover over the sitting parents, a short man in a black leather jacket who seemed to take up more space than he actually did. "The best damn town in the state of Michigan ought to be able to prove it's the best at the best damn sport there is." He raised a fist to the level of his shoulder. "We've been doing this for, what, twenty years? We've got someone here who's telling us what it takes. It's time to stop whining and do it."

Lenny Ziolkowski, the father of Paul "Zilchy" Ziolkowski, stood. Mr. Ziolkowski played poker on Friday nights with Coach, Leo Redpath, Soupy's dad, and a few other dads at Blackburn's cabin. "Jack's got a tough job," he said. "We ought to give him the room to do it, unless someone here thinks they can do a better job." He glared momentarily at Champagne. "We're not out there on the ice with him, but our boys are, and the boys sure seem to like him."

I looked up at Coach then. I saw a spark in his eye I'd never seen before, a spark like the one I saw in the eyes of shooters bearing down on my net. It wasn't there long, and it scared me at first, but the fear didn't last, because I knew Coach was on my side.

"Folks," he said. "Tell you what. I cut a boy from the team yesterday. Maybe I got a little ahead of myself. I'd like to restore him to the roster, effective immediately. I can't guarantee he'll play a whole lot, but he'll have every chance to earn it." He looked directly at Don Champagne now. "If you'll get me the right size, I'll order Jeff a jacket first thing tomorrow."

Champagne just nodded. Then I saw my mother waving her hand. "Yes, Mrs. Carpenter?" Coach said.

My mother talked fast, and I worried she'd say something nobody would understand. But it was clear enough. "I would just like to say, I don't know about anybody else, but I think the boys look just adorable in their jackets."

"Adorable?" Dufresne cried out. "Bea, we don't want adorable hockey players."

"Oh, all right, Francis, wonderful then or—oh, I don't know!" She started to clap, and then Dufresne started clapping, and pretty soon the whole room, even Champagne, was applauding. By the time the meeting ended, Coach had persuaded the parents to chip in for a new skate-sharpening machine, and Dufresne had offered to organize a committee that would investigate installing new benches in the dressing rooms.

That Sunday, Coach came to dinner at our house. Mom made fried pork chops and baked potatoes with gravy. We didn't talk about the Rats at first, but Mom finally asked how he thought the meeting had gone. Coach shrugged as he reached for a bowl of peas and carrots. "You know, Bea?" he said. "It's like I always say. They don't care how. All they care is how many."

It was late in our fourth full season that we finally proved ourselves. By then we were whipping all the teams up north and had beaten some good squads from as far downstate as Ann Arbor. But the Detroiters still had our number.

Griffin Hawks, a team from the suburbs west of Detroit, came up for a pair of weekend games. Friday night we blew a 2–0 lead to lose 4–2. There were tears in the dressing room afterward. We'd never come so close to beating a Detroit team. Coach normally would've told us hockey wasn't for crybabies and ordered us to listen up, eh, here's how we gave up those last two goals. But on this night he just stood by the door, hands folded behind his back. When we'd all gotten our clothes on and our bags packed, he raised his arms for silence.

"Men?" he said. He never called us that. "Are you ready?" We lifted our wet heads to meet his gaze. "Ready for what, Coach?" one of us asked, and Blackburn shushed him. "Are you ready?" he said again. "You better be ready. Because tomorrow will be the biggest night of your life."

I got an inkling of what he meant just before the next day's game. The guys were warming up our backup goalie, and I was in a corner shoveling pucks out to the shooters when I noticed one of the Griffin coaches standing on their bench, gnawing on an unlit cigar in his black-and-orange Griffin jacket. He was watching Soupy. Soupy was skating tight figure eights, backward, with a puck on his stick, flipping it back and forth like it was glued to the blade, his head up, gathering speed as he circled. The coach leaned to his right and called another coach over. He said something to the other coach and gestured toward Soupy. They both nodded.

We weren't invisible anymore.

As we played that night, word was getting around town that the Rats were about to beat a team from Detroit. Later I heard that Francis Dufresne had made a bunch of phone calls. Whenever play stopped, I glanced into the stands. It seemed as if more people were there every time.

By the start of the final period, the bleachers were filled. I hadn't seen that since the Red Wing old-timers had come to town for an exhibition game. As we were lining up for a face-off just to my left, I heard banging on the glass behind me. I turned to see people lined up all along the glass, two and three deep, neighbors and friends and people I'd seen on the street and at church, some I'd never seen before. The game was tied at 2, and those people were pounding on the glass, shouting my name and my teammates' names, yelling for us to hang in there, we could do it, we could win. As I turned back to the game, I slammed the heel of my stick into my catching glove and drew down into my crouch and I could feel my heart pounding, swelling as it never had before, and I knew that we could not possibly lose. And I knew that I'd known this even before the game had begun. Just as Coach had known.

With less than a minute to go in the game, we were still tied when a Griffin wing deked past a Rat at the blue line and swooped in alone on me. First he faked a shot, trying to get me to drop, but I held my ground as he fired a low, hard bullet to my left. The puck looked huge to me. I kicked my left leg out at precisely the right instant and deflected it across the ice. Soupy gathered it up in stride and bolted down the left side of the ice, the crowd shrieking, the clock counting down to twenty-nine seconds, twenty-eight, twenty-seven . . . Soupy charged into the Hawks' zone and launched a rising shot that caught their goalie off balance. The puck caromed off his shoulder to Jeff Champagne, who had sneaked to a corner of the net, alone. He took a backhand swipe and knocked it in.

I've never heard anything louder than that rink at that moment.

Although we were eliminated in the state playoffs by Detroit's O'Leary's Heating, we knew we could play with anybody. Two seasons later, we made the state quarterfinals and fell to Byrd Electric, another Detroit squad, 5–3. When our bus pulled onto Main Street after the three-hour ride from Flint, everyone at Enright's spilled outside to cheer us. We smiled and waved, but the older Rats—Soupy, Teddy, Stevie Reneau, Brad Wilford, me—knew we had just two years left to win that one big game before we'd be going off to college or jobs or whatever else the real world held. Coach seemed unfazed, though. Before we departed the bus that night, he told us yet again, "Losing is good for winning."

We made it a step closer the next year, upsetting Paddock Pools in the quarters when Soupy scored on the end-to-end rush memorialized on the wall at Enright's. We thought we'd finally get our shot. But in the semifinals we were routed, 7–1, by the Pipefitters, a street gang of a team from the steel-making furnace of downriver Detroit. It seemed like they were all big and hairy except for number 17, a scrawny winger named Billy Hooper who skated like his feet had touched molten metal. He scored four, and to this day I can't remember seeing three of them until they were behind me. Even Soupy had trouble staying with

Billy Hooper. We stayed downstate to watch the Pipefitters demolish O'Leary's in the final, 9–2. Hooper scored three, assisted on two others, and was named MVP of the tournament. Late that night, our bus pulled into the high school parking lot where our parents sat waiting with the exhaust snaking around their cars and trucks. Coach stood at the front of the bus and called for quiet. Then he said, "Men—are you ready?" We knew what that meant. We filed silently off the bus.

Though we had yet to reach the ultimate goal, there was no doubt in our minds that we would in our last year together. In the meantime, our success against Detroit's best hockey teams meant Starvation Lake wasn't invisible anymore either. It was no longer just another town up north with a good breakfast joint and a smoky tavern. The town council bought a billboard on I-75 proclaiming Starvation as "Hockeytown North. Home of the River Rats." Local kids begged us for autographs. Girls came from Sandy Cove and Kalkaska and Mancelona to hang out at our practices. Francis demanded our old sticks and skates to hang in Enright's. Coach had River Rats caps and T-shirts and stickers made. The town turned blue and gold.

There was green, too. All those people from Detroit and Chicago and Cleveland and Milwaukee who came to Starvation for hockey saw how beautiful the place was and returned to buy lakefront lots and build cottages. Their money lured a McDonald's and a Pizza Hut, a fudge shop, and two new souvenir stores on Main Street that hung Rats T-shirts in their windows. New business swamped the marina, and Soupy's dad added a refueling station and a big section of dry dock. The town built a little zoo along the lakeshore where tourist kids could ride a miniature train past white-tail deer, red foxes, bobcats, and snapping turtles. New housing developments sprouted around the lake.

The money behind a lot of the building came from Francis Dufresne, who recruited Jack Blackburn as his pitchman. When the time came to persuade the town council to approve construction of this new motel or that new subdivision, Coach would don a sports jacket and his self-assured smile to present the plans to the council while Dufresne watched from the back of the audience, nodding with satisfaction as the council voted his way again and again. The two of them built Starvation Lake into a bona fide resort.

Everything changed after Coach's accident. Whether from grief or inertia or bad luck, the town seemed to lose the momentum it had had. One summer, a faulty fuse box started a fire that shut down the marina just as the boating season was getting started. The next year, a putrid outbreak of algae left a gooey green slick floating on the lake surface. Sandy Cove and other towns started siphoning off the business. Dufresne and his new partner, Teddy Boynton, kept building, but they kept moving farther from Starvation, becoming silent partners in projects in other towns, even Sandy Cove. Eventually the hockey suffered, too.

The whole town had lost something. It wasn't easy to pinpoint, but it was more than just a hockey coach. Jack Blackburn had showed Starvation Lake how to win. Somehow, without him, people forgot.

"Gus?"

The woman's voice pierced the wind on South Beach. I turned to see Sheriff's Deputy Darlene Esper, née Bontrager, trudging through the snow toward me. I'd known her forever and could tell immediately that she didn't want to be on that beach, talking to me. She'd come out of a sense of duty to someone who grew up with her, whom she'd once loved, who had broken her heart.

"Soupy said you might be down here," she said.

"Yeah?"

"Yeah. I thought you'd want to know."

"About?"

"The snowmobile. We're pretty sure it was Blackburn's," she said.

"How can you be sure?"

"All we have is the front part, you know, the whatchamacallit, the cowl. But the registration numbers match up."

"So? That could be a clerical screwup or something."

Darlene took one obliging step closer. Her eyes were huge onyx marbles. "There's also a sticker, like, a decal, next to one of the headlights. It's all faded, but you can tell."

The River Rats logo. A snarling, toothy rodent in skates and helmet, carrying a hockey stick like a pitchfork. Coach had had decals made every year. I remember seeing them on the insides of his kitchen cupboards.

"OK," I said.

Instinctively, Darlene reached for my elbow, then loosed it just as quickly and stepped back again. I stared at the shadowy boot prints she'd left in the snow at my feet. "Well," I said, "it's not like Coach died all over again."

"It's pretty weird, Gus."

"What do you guys think happened?"

"I don't know. Maybe the tunnels?"

The tunnels. Many a boat had sunk in Starvation Lake never to be found. The cops would drag the lake and send scuba crews down, but boats that sank in plain sight seemed to have been swallowed up by the lake bottom. Around town the favored theory was that the lake was part of a serpentine network of underwater tunnels linking dozens of inland lakes to Lake Michigan. Sunken boats were sucked into the tunnels and out to the big lake. Like Bigfoot, the legend persisted, even though no one had ever actually located one of the tunnels.

"Come on," I said.

"I've never seen Dingus like this. Calling meetings, in the office before eight, on the phone all the time with the state police. He's reopening the whole investigation."

My chest tightened. "Of the accident?"

"Yes. The accident." She looked away. "But what do you care? You weren't around ten years ago, were you?"

"No, I wasn't. What else do they know?"

She shook her head. "Dingus and the guy deputies were whispering about something tonight. They didn't share it with me."

I thought of Joanie. She wasn't going to be happy with me. She'd had the story exactly right.

"I'm sorry," I said.

"No. You just want the story."

"Will you give me a break, please, Darlene?"

"Did I have to come out here and tell you this?"

"No. Thanks. I'm sorry."

"You're always sorry."

She turned to leave. Up the street I heard Soupy howling something over the rumble of revving pickup trucks, the sounds of Enright's emptying. I knew I shouldn't, but I did anyway. "Darl," I called out. "Give me a ride home?"

She didn't even turn around.

seven

I was out of bed at 5:45 the next morning. I wanted to see Leo Red-path before the *Pilot* hit the streets and the codgers at Audrey's started talking.

I found him in the back of the Zamboni shed at the rink, hunched over his workbench in a pale wash of light. A faded River Rats cap hung on a nail above his head. "Good morning, Mr. Carpenter," he said without looking up. "The Shoot-Out doesn't begin for several hours, you know."

"I've got to tell you something, Leo."

Although he'd never played and wasn't really a student of hockey, Leo was the closest thing the River Rats had had to an assistant coach. He drove our bus on out-of-town trips. He filmed our practices. He kept tape handy and the water bottles filled. During games he worked the bench door for players hopping on and off the ice. Even as we grew into adults, he still took care of us, supplying pucks, sewing up gashes, keeping a few beers in the fridge. He turned to me while wiping his hands on a rag. I could tell he already knew.

"The police were here last night," he said.

"Oh."

Leo had been with Coach on Starvation Lake that night. Off the ice as well as on, they were nearly inseparable. They drank and hunted and fished and snowmobiled together. On that night, they'd been out riding and had a few drinks around a campfire in the woods west of the lake. Leo never said much about that night. The police interviewed him and he was quoted briefly in the *Pilot*. At Coach's funeral, he declined to give a eulogy. I asked him about it one night in the Zamboni shed and he acted as if he hadn't heard me. When I asked again, Soupy told me to leave him alone. "He feels guilty enough," Soupy whispered. Leo kept working at the rink, but except when he was steering Ethel around the ice, you rarely saw him. He slept on a cot in the shed some nights and otherwise retired to his mobile home off Route 816.

He quit drinking after Coach's death. On the pegboard above his bench he took to pasting aphorisms he'd clipped from books about addiction recovery: *Today, I will embrace each minute of my day with joy and wonder . . . Today, I will leave shame behind and move forward into peace . . . Today, I will face the truths about myself and lose my fear of acknowledging their presence in my life . . .* Leo never spoke about the sayings, and we understood not to ask.

Since Coach's death, Leo seemed a man in constant pain, constantly trying to talk himself out of feeling it. I wished there was something I could do to make him feel better.

"Did the police tell you anything?" I said.

"Not much. They said something about those tunnels."

"They told you that?"

"Not in so many—well, I don't suppose I'm supposed to talk about it. Are you interviewing me?"

"No. What did you tell them?"

He shrugged. "What could I tell them? Nothing's changed, Gus. Jack was a foolish man sometimes. There was nothing anyone could do."

I didn't think he really believed that. "You went to my mom's house that night, right? After the accident?"

"It's all in the record. You can look it up. But I'm kind of busy right now, Gus. I'll see you later?"

On my way out I caught a glimpse of Leo's reflection in a sheet of Plexiglas leaning near the door. He had turned to watch me leave. He wore the expression of someone who was straining to remember something.

eight

At 6:35, I was the only person in Audrey's Diner. I took a seat at the counter. "Morning, Gussy," Audrey said. "You know what you want?"

"Morning, ma'am. Egg pie, please."

Audrey DeYonghe was a surprisingly unplump woman in her sixties who had run the diner alone since her third husband took off with a buxom blackjack dealer he'd met at an Indian casino in Gaylord. He had shown up one morning a year later to beg Audrey's forgiveness, but by then she had taken up with a gift shop proprietor from Petoskey—also a woman in her sixties—and told her husband, while her breakfast patrons stilled forks to listen, that divorce papers were waiting on a chopping table in the back.

Ordinarily, a love interest like Audrey's would've caused a stir in Starvation Lake. But her diner was the only good breakfast place nearby. And a good breakfast place is as essential to a northern Michigan town as a reliable propane supplier. No one made a fuss. Besides, Audrey was nice. And she baked a wicked gooey cinnamon bun.

The diner was blessedly quiet. I gazed down the counter at the photograph of old Red Wing Gordie Howe hanging on the wall. Audrey was no hockey fan, but Gordie Howe happened to be her girlfriend Molly's uncle, and he'd signed the photo. Beneath it lay a copy of that morning's *Pilot*. I ignored it. I wanted to eat in peace and get out.

"One egg-pie special," Audrey said as she set my breakfast on the counter. Cheddar cheese and scrambled eggs bubbled up through a golden cocoon of Italian bread. I stabbed at the crust with my fork and steam billowed from the sausage, bacon, potatoes, green peppers, mushrooms, and onions baked inside. I had to let it cool before I dug in. Sometimes when I ate something I really liked, I ate in small bites, to make it last. That wasn't necessary with an egg pie. The hard part was getting a single forkful with every ingredient in it. Since I was a kid, I had averaged about two all-ingredient mouthfuls per pie.

"So what do you think?" Audrey said.

"About what?"

"About anything."

I smiled. She always did this with me. "I think I like your new hairdo."

"Oh, yes, and the hairnet makes it all the more stylish, don't you think?" she said. "But thank you, dear. What else is on your mind?"

"What's been the talk in here lately?"

"Oh my gosh, if I hear about that snowmobile again. It's all I heard in here yesterday, and then the hockey, and then of course, well, you were in here for a little." She folded her arms across her chartreuse smock. "Sometimes I don't like some of those people much."

She meant they'd talked about me, and that goal I let in. "Yeah," I said. "I don't know. Maybe it is the tunnels."

Audrey loosed a scornful whoop as she turned for the kitchen. "Sure, dear. And there are flying frogs in the lake, too!"

As I savored my first bite—eggs, cheese, potatoes, and sausage, minus the rest—I heard a clattering on the sidewalk outside. The door jangled open and I turned to see three children in identical black-and-gold snowmobile suits clump into the diner, each carrying a black helmet. Behind them lumbered a man the size of a meat freezer bursting at his own black snowmobile suit, stitched with a name—"Jimbo"—over his left breast.

I turned quickly back to my plate, hoping he hadn't noticed me. I listened while he herded the children to one of the big tables in the back. Then I felt a hand on my shoulder and saw another stuck out over my egg pie.

"Gus?" came a foghorn voice. "Jim Kerasopoulos."

Kerasopoulos was the general counsel of NLP Newspapers, owner of the *Pilot*. "Jim, how are you?" I said. "Got the whole brood here?"

"Three of 'em, anyway," he said. "Linda's got the other two at some cheerleading thing. The snowmobile trails are cooked out by Traverse. They're still nice and white over here."

"Yep." I remembered the *Pilot* lying on the counter and wished I had brought it nearer to my plate.

"I was going to stop by your—hey, kids. Kids! Excuse me." His children were banging their helmets on the table. "Do you want your French toast?" he said. "Let's put the helmets down." He turned to Audrey and ordered three French toasts, an egg pie, and four orange juices. Then he sat down on the stool next to mine. "I wanted to talk to you anyway about that story you have about the gentleman who hunts the uh, the—"

"Bigfoot?"

He slapped his palm on the counter. "That's it. Perlman."

"Perlmutter."

"Exactly. Quite the character. And a very interesting story." He put on the thoughtful look that lawyers affect when they want you to know that they can see things to which you are hopelessly blind. "Maybe a tad *too* interesting, if you catch my drift. Your reporter, what's her name?"

"Joanie. McCarthy."

"Exactly. She has done some very, shall we say, aggressive report-ing here. The documents she uncovered are very interesting, perhaps even persuasive." He interrupted himself. "Gosh, all that money Perl-man's been pulling out of the state kitty, I wonder how much more it costs me in boat-use fees." He chuckled at his little joke. "But, but," he said, his thick brows furrowing into one at the bridge of his nose, "what's crucial to remember here, Gus, is that Mr. Perlman is a *private* individual. You know what that means."

"Perlmutter. And yes, I know." It meant that, according to libel law, it would be easier for him to sue us and win than a public figure, like the sheriff.

"Does he have an attorney?" Kerasopoulos said.

"Yes. But neither of them are saying much."

Kerasopoulos's kids were banging their helmets again. "Have we made every attempt to give Mr. Perlberg a chance to respond?"

"We have. Joanie went out there once and talked to him. But since he figured out what she had, he hasn't returned her calls."

"Exactly," Kerasopoulos said, rapping a finger on the counter for emphasis. "This is a gentleman who seems perfectly at ease with the tedium of paperwork. And he's an aggressive individual who obviously has a good deal to lose. Put those together and you have a lawsuit."

"He's a thief who's been defrauding the public for years," I said, and immediately regretted it.

"Whoa there, partner. That's for others to decide. We simply submit facts in as fair and balanced a way as we can. Are we clear?"

I looked at my congealing egg pie. "We're clear."

"I used to be a reporter myself, Gus."

You used to be skinny, too, I thought.

"We may have a problem here," he said.

"Jim, this is a legitimate story."

He stood. "If you were sure of that, Gus, you would've just run it. But you sent it to us for our opinion, and I'm giving it to you."

I wanted to tell him to take his double-wide ass back to his corner office with the drawings of duck blinds and lighthouses and golf holes on the walls and stop sticking his nose into things. I wanted to tell him he was a small-timer and he would always be a small-timer, making the money that paid his boat-use fees off little towns whose newspapers he neutered daily. Except that he was right, at least partly. I could've just put the story in the paper and taken my lumps from corporate, maybe even lost my second newspaper job in a year. But I'd been covering my ass, playing to the bosses, securing my own small-time future. And now, by blurting out the truth about Perlmutter, I had put the story in even greater danger of never seeing print. I felt like smacking myself.

"Look, Jim," I said, "let me see if we can get Perlmutter to respond."

"You do that," Kerasopoulos said. "You know what I always say: We can never be second with something that matters to our readers. Right? OK. Listen, I've got to get back to my kids before they wreck the place. You made the right call on this, Gus. We appreciate the caution."

I pushed the egg pie away and looked out the window. Standing in the street with a *Pilot* folded under his arm was Elvis Bontrager. He was talking with someone I couldn't see. I stood to leave. Audrey turned from the griddle. "Gussy, you barely ate."

"Sorry, Mrs. DeYonghe. I'm not feeling so hot. The pie was great, really."

"Feel better. And give your mother my love."

I eased out the door, trying to keep the bells from jangling. I saw Elvis was talking with Teddy Boynton. I hurried down Main Street, head down, rock salt crunching under my boots. "There he is," I heard Boynton say as I swerved down the alley next to Enright's. It dawned on me that in two days I'd had two meals ruined by lawyers.

At the Hungry River I slowed and turned toward the lake. Across the frozen river lay the snow-covered beach where Boynton wanted to build his marina and hotel. A sign on the property showed an artist's rendering of a creamy white four-story hotel on a golden beach, a pavilion of shops crowded with people at picnic tables beneath powder-blue umbrellas, and a sparkling bay dotted with sailboats, cruisers, and powerboats. Only the zoning board—and Soupy's opposition—stood in the way. With the board's approval, Boynton's lenders would release the first $5 million he needed to start construction.

Over my shoulder hovered Starvation Lake Marina, a four-story hulk of corrugated steel painted the dull green of a brontosaurus. I walked up to the door of the business office and cupped a hand over my eyes to peek inside. A tower of pizza boxes had toppled in a corner, and a garbage can overflowed with empty beer bottles and cans. A wall calendar was stuck on the previous July, when Soupy's father had died. I walked around the side of the building and felt beneath the water meter for the magnetized box that held the spare key.

Inside, the office reeked of stale hops and pepperoni and the lingering sweetness of marijuana. I snatched a dusty page off one of the chest-high stacks of paper on Soupy's desk. It was a summons ordering Soupy to court at 9:30 a.m. on Friday, January twenty-fourth.

"Way to go, Soup," I murmured.

I recalled that he and I had gone ice fishing that morning; he hadn't said anything about a court date as he polished off a six-pack before 10:00 a.m. Two unmarked file folders rested alone next to the stacks of papers. I flipped one open. Inside was a two-page letter, dated four days earlier, from Arthur Fleming, Boynton's lawyer. It proposed a "joint venture" in which Boynton Realty would take a 25-percent interest in Soupy's marina and, in return, Soupy would get 1 percent of the Pines at Starvation Lake and an immediate cash payment of thirty thousand dollars. The venture would continue to operate Soupy's marina "so long as it is deemed fiscally prudent," and the cash would help Soupy "resolve outstanding litigation." In return, Soupy would drop his opposition to Boynton's marina at Monday's zoning board meeting. It wasn't a bad deal. The cash would come in handy, and the stake in Boynton's marina might be worth a lot someday. But it wouldn't take long for Boynton to decide it was no longer "fiscally prudent" to keep Soupy's marina alive.

I picked up the other folder, but before I could open it, I heard a metallic groan in the dry-dock area, where boats reclined in tall steel racks like sleeping birds. I sidled over to the window to the dry dock and saw the huge steel door at the other end rumbling upward. Light spilled in beneath it, revealing a pair of boots and legs in silhouette. Tatch, Soupy's right-hand man, was starting work. I ducked down and scurried for the back door. Taking a quick step outside, I swung the door closed behind me and immediately flopped up in the air and onto my rump. "What the hell?" I said.

I sat up, wincing, and saw at my feet a pile of slimy carp and sucker trout, barely alive, puckering their mouths. I scrambled to my feet, disgusted. "Fucking fish?" I said, kicking at a carp. "How the hell did you get here?" Fish blood and guts were slopped across the snow; some of the fish had been slit open. I looked around but saw no one. "Not funny," I said, as if someone could hear. "Not funny at all." I hustled down the river walk, brushing snow and fish scales off my butt and wondering if anyone had seen me in the marina. The dying fish I left for Soupy.

At my apartment I hung my coat, stinking of fish, on the stair rail outside. I hauled out my hockey bag and zipped it open on the living room floor. The smell wasn't much better than my coat. My gear felt clammy as I laid it out to dry. Leg pads, arm pads, chest protector, pants. Catching glove, blocking glove, protective cup. Skates, mask, a stiffened towel, a canvas pouch holding tape, laces, Bengay. I wished I had unpacked it after the game Thursday night. Now it would feel heavy when I played that night, and I'd be a hair less agile or, worse, I'd *think* I was. Thinking was everything. If you didn't think you were going to stop every single shot, you wouldn't. If you lost that focus for a sliver of an instant, the puck would be behind you. Even on one of your off nights, after you'd given up four or five goals, you had to keep *thinking* you could stop them all, or just like that there'd be seven or eight behind you, and Coach would pull you and you'd have to skate off the ice while everyone on your bench and the other team's bench and in the stands watched with scorn or pity or both.

I sat down in the recliner with my favorite piece of gear, the blocking glove I wore on my right hand, the one that held my goalie stick. I unwrapped the shiny black electrical tape wound around the thumb. With its wide rectangular shield, the glove looked like a big waffle.

I had considered it my lucky waffle—or, as Soupy nicknamed it, Eggo—since the day the dogs got to it.

I was thirteen then. I'd been watching television one afternoon— the Three Stooges, I think—when I heard growling from Mom's laundry room, where my hockey stuff was airing out. I hurried in to find our two mutts, Fats and Blinky, in a snarling tug-of-war with the waffle. "Damn dogs!" I yelled. But it was my fault. I'd forgotten to close the laundry room door. I ripped the glove away and swung it halfheartedly at the dogs. As they scampered away, their toenails clicking on the linoleum, I noticed a tatter of leather jutting from Blinky's mouth. My heart sank. I turned the waffle over. The thumb was gone.

We had a regional playoff game that night. I couldn't play with a bare thumb sticking out of my glove. I cornered Blinky and traded her a dog biscuit for the thumb. Mom was out shopping, so I took the waffle and the chewed-off thumb next door. Darlene was doing geography homework at her kitchen table. "You're such an idiot, Gus," she said, but I could tell she was glad I'd brought my problem to her. We showed the glove to her mother, who worked part-time at a shoe repair and had once mended a tear in one of my leg pads. After inspecting the glove, she cast a disapproving look at me.

"This cost your mother a fortune, Gus."

"Yes ma'am, Mrs. B."

"And you need it by six?" She shook her head and handed the glove and thumb back to me. "I'm sorry. It's euchre night, Darlene's father will be home any minute, and I have dinner to get."

I looked helplessly at Darlene. She grabbed her mother's hand and pulled her into the hallway off the kitchen. I heard them whispering. When they returned, Darlene was smiling. "You children," her mother said, snatching the glove back. "It might not be fixable, you know."

I thanked Darlene at the door. "I just hope Daddy doesn't mind pancakes for dinner," she said. "It's all I know how to make."

I wore the glove that night. Just to be safe, I wrapped black electrical tape around the fresh leather stitching on the thumb. For some reason I liked the way it looked. Our opponents were a bunch of fast kids from Grand Rapids. But I had the shiny black tape. I stopped all but one of their forty-eight shots and we won, 3–1.

In the twenty-one years since, I'd replaced every piece of my goalie gear, except for Eggo. Before every game—I never missed once—I applied fresh tape to the stitching, always the shiny black stuff, wrapping it exactly as I had that night when I was thirteen. All the tape really held was my confidence.

It made no sense, of course, but superstitions are as much a part of hockey as elbows to the nose. We had to put our pads on a certain way, tape our sticks a certain way, line up the water bottles on the bench a certain way. Stevie Reneau had to take a cold shower right before games. Wilf had to puke, and kept a bottle of ipecac in his bag to induce if his butterflies weren't going to do it. Zilchy refused to sit next to a goalie in the dressing room, nor would he speak a word until the opening face-off.

Soupy had more superstitions than a witch doctor. He had to sit directly to my left. I had to be sitting there when he sat down; he couldn't sit first. No one could touch his equipment while he was dressing; if someone accidentally did, Soupy had to strip down and start all over again. Just before we went out to the ice, he had to reach around my head and smack me on the right shoulder and give me a last word of encouragement. "Tonight, you're a brick wall," he would tell me, or, "Tonight, you're a giant sponge, sucking in everything and spitting it back out." In his last couple of years with the Rats, he started wearing skates four sizes too small for his feet; he insisted he couldn't skate his fastest unless his toes were jammed in so hard that they hurt. That was especially weird, I thought, but that was Soupy. Some nights he would sit for half an hour after the game massaging feeling back into his arches and toes. Even now, in his thirties, he kept wearing skates he could barely get on.

Coach Blackburn tolerated our rituals because they made us believe in ourselves, while insisting that he himself had never fallen for such silliness. We knew otherwise. Coach had his own little secret superstition. He always—always—stepped onto the ice with his left skate first. If he had to take a little hop and skip to stagger his stride before he stepped out, he did it so that his left blade hit the ice before his right. Soupy called him on it once before a practice, thinking it funny; Coach responded by announcing that this would be a no-puck practice. We never mentioned his superstition again.

Now I leaned back in the recliner with the retaped Eggo in my lap and closed my eyes, preparing for the Shoot-Out that would begin in an hour. I tried to picture the rink, how the overhead lamps would drape shadows along the sideboards, how the skaters would veer and feint as they bore down on me, how the puck would spin and flutter and rise and dip coming off of their sticks, how I would try to slow it down in my mind, try to make it look bigger.

The phone woke me.

"The snowmobile was Blackburn's," Joanie said. "Without a doubt."

"I heard."

"Yeah. Yesterday. From me."

"You didn't have the cops saying it, Joanie."

"No, no signed confession. No fingerprints on the gun."

"What are the cops saying now?"

"Haven't been down there yet. But there was this fat guy at the diner—his name's in my notes—and he had this whole theory about the coaches from Detroit supposedly hiring someone to kill Blackburn and dump him in Walleye."

The locals always had had trouble accepting that Coach himself might've done something stupid. "That'd be news to Leo," I said.

"The guy who was with Blackburn that night? I went to see him too. What a weirdo."

I let that go. "The cops talked to him."

"How do you know?"

"Bumped into him at the rink."

"Uh-huh." She was getting her back up again. "Look, this is *my* story: Big-shot coach dies and then the town that worships him finds out it might not have happened the way they thought. Bet you AP picks it up."

She was right, but I didn't want her to be. Part of me wanted to know what had happened. Part wanted to leave it all alone.

"Actually, Joanie, it's the *Pilot*'s story. And I've still got to live here."

"You played for Blackburn, didn't you?"

"A long time ago."

She paused. Then she said, "Do you know anything about where he was before he came here?"

"A little."

As a boy I'd sat for hours poring over yearbooks and game programs he'd given me from his years playing junior and minor league hockey in Canada, and his later years coaching teenagers there. At Sunday dinners, he regaled Mom and me with tales of coaching juniors in western Canada.

"OK," Joanie said, "so the *Pilot* clips say he came here in seventy after four seasons coaching the St. Albert Saints in, um, Alberta. There's a couple of quotes from Blackburn talking about his four years there. 'Four fantastic years,' he keeps saying. But all I can find is he coached the Saints for three years. Doesn't look like he was even there in sixty-six. I called a newspaper up there and got a woman who put me onto this geezer who's like the unofficial team historian. He told me Blackburn came in sixty-seven and left in seventy."

"So?"

"Actually, 'skedaddled' is what the guy said. And the team was really good that year, like, they won some big championship. But

Blackburn leaves? What's up with that? I asked the guy, and he said it was ancient history and got off the phone."

"Maybe the guy's memory isn't so good."

"Maybe. But I gotta go. Later."

It made no sense. Why would Coach lie about something so mundane as how many years he spent coaching a hockey team? He must've counted wrong, I thought, or my recollections were faulty. I closed my eyes and pictured him sitting across the dinner table while Mom cleared the dishes. I could clearly see him speak that phrase: "four fantastic years." His past was easy enough to check. One of the boxes beneath the makeshift table at my feet contained the yearbooks and programs Coach had given me. I made a mental note to look through them later. Now I had to get to the Shoot-Out.

The puck zipped past my left shoulder and grazed the left goalpost before smacking the mesh at the back of the net.

"Can't see it, can't stop it," Teddy Boynton said as he sped past me. He spun on his skates and taunted me as he backed away: "But you're expert at missing pucks, aren't you, Carpie?" I'd heard that one a few times before.

The Starvation Lake Shoot-Out was nearly over. I'd faced more than a hundred wrist shots, snap shots, slap shots, backhanders, and dekes in a series of one-on-one showdowns. I'd stopped most of them. Thirty shooters had been eliminated. Now it came down, as it did most years, to Soupy Campbell versus Teddy Boynton. Each had three final shots. I'd stopped both of their first efforts. Teddy had just scored on his second, a slapper that caught me leaning to my right. I plucked my water bottle off the top of the net, flipped my mask up, and skated away from the net for a breather.

All afternoon, I'd been struggling not to think about Coach's unsettling reappearance in my life. It was damned hard to do while standing in Blackburn Arena. When he'd arrived in Starvation Lake, the rink was just a sheet of ice protected by two thin steel walls and a roof that sagged under the weight of snowstorms. With the help of Francis Dufresne, Coach had gotten the town to replace the roof and close in the ends of the rink. He finagled new dressing rooms, showers, a scoreboard, bleachers. Each time he went before the town council, he brought along three or four River Rats. We stood at his side in our satin jackets as he made his pitches, our smiles polite, our hair combed neatly, our hands folded behind our backs, just as he had instructed.

"Today, Trap!" It was Soupy shouting from center ice, where he stood flipping a puck back and forth on his stick.

"Relax," I said, as much to myself as to Soupy. I leaned my head back and doused my face with water. Above me in the steel rafters I glimpsed the faded blue-and-gold banners marking the Rats' progress in the state playoffs, 1977 to 1981: regional finalist, regional finalist, state quarterfinalist, semifinalist, runner-up. I leveled my gaze and looked past Soupy to a banner that had hung at that end of the rink for as long as I could remember. It read: "To win the game is great, to play the game is greater, to love the game is the greatest." I skated slowly back to my net, set the bottle down, and pulled my mask down over my face. Slapping the blade of my goalie stick once against each goalpost, I lowered myself into my semicrouch and yelled, "Bring it on."

Soupy was what hockey players admiringly call a "dangler," with hands that cradled the puck as if it were no heavier than a tennis ball. He could dangle it between his skates, behind his back, one-handed, backhanded, skating backward, on one knee. All the while the puck stuck to his stick like a nickname. He had a thousand moves that he'd practiced for hours in his basement or late at night on a patch of ice behind his garage. He liked to practice in the darkness, the darker the better, so he was forced to rely not on his eyes, but on simply feeling the puck on his stick blade with his amazingly sure hands. That way he'd never have to look down, he could always be scanning the ice for an opening or an open man, and he'd always be ready when an opposing defenseman was lining him up for a hit.

He'd worked on one particular move for most of a season. He'd gotten the idea when we were playing in a tournament in Detroit. One night in our hotel room, we picked up a Canadian TV station broadcasting indoor lacrosse. The players ran around on a shiny concrete floor resembling a hockey rink, flinging a ball from thin sticks fitted with webbed leather baskets. "Man," Soupy said, "if you could cradle the puck like that, how cool would that be?"

After practices, while the rest of us undressed, he'd take a bucket of pucks and position himself behind a net. With a puck at his feet, he'd try in one motion to scoop it up, raise it shoulder high, step out to the side of the net, and then sling the puck, lacrosse style, into the upper corner of the goal. He quickly mastered the scooping part but had trouble keeping the puck on his stick as he sidestepped out from behind the goal. Some nights the rest of us would come out of the showers and stand on the bench teasing him. But he kept at it. Coach watched, too, but he didn't say anything, at least not at first.

One afternoon I came out of the dressing room late and was nearly out the door to the parking lot when I heard the *whang* of something hitting a goalpost. I knew Soupy was the only one on the ice, so I dropped my gear and walked back to see. He was standing behind a net with his back to me. There were four or five pucks at his feet, and a couple in the face-off circle to the right of the goal. Six or seven others lay in the net. I watched silently as he snatched up a puck, took two quick steps to his left, and whipped his stick around until it clanged on the goalpost and the puck flew into the high corner of the net. "Holy shit," I said. Soupy turned and grinned.

Coach spoke to Soupy about it for the first time before our next practice. Stickhandling drills were fine, Coach said, but he didn't want to see any lacrosse shots during games. He called it "a fancy-ass fag move."

Coach never used profanity around us, and he forbade us from using it. "Fag" and "faggot" were in a different category. Coach used them all the time to define for us what hockey was and wasn't. Elbowing an opponent in the chin was hockey; kicking his skates out was a fag move. Scorers who could take a hit were hockey players; scorers who shied from the rough stuff were fags.

Soupy never tried the lacrosse shot again in practice. But one night he swore me to secrecy and told me he'd kept practicing it behind his garage.

"For what?" I said.

He shrugged. "Coach is a dickhead."

"No, he's not. Are you saving it up for something?"

He smiled to himself. "I don't know. Maybe."

"Maybe my ass."

"Maybe I'm just a fag."

Now Soupy shoved the puck out in front of him and took three long strides toward me. I eased out from the net to cut off the angle. He gathered up the puck and, as he swerved left, I followed.

On most goalies, Soupy liked to fake a shot that would make them drop to the ice, then he'd either snap the puck over one of their shoulders or cut hard, flip the puck to his backhand, and skate around them in a burst to the open side of the net. But as a stand-up goalie, I wasn't as likely to drop. Soupy usually tried to beat me with a low shot to one of the corners, or he'd drive hard right at me and try to juke me to one side and slip the puck past me on the other.

He raised his stick high behind his left ear. I braced myself for the explosion of wood and rubber while staying on my toes in case this was just the first part of whatever Soupy had planned, the part meant to fool me. But he wasn't trying to trick me. His stick whipped down and I heard the blade drive through the puck and saw it jump off the stick right at me. Not to my left or my right or even at my feet, where I might have left an opening, but right at me, chest high, the easiest of shots to stop. It hit me just above the sternum and I smothered it there with my catching glove.

Something was wrong. Soupy never hit goalies square in the chest.

I watched him as he snagged another puck and headed to center ice to take his final shot before Boynton took his. Teddy was laughing and yelling, "One more and it's oh for three and a hundred smackers for me, baby. Looks like you'll be emptying out your pop machine."

They had once been friends, in our early years with the Rats. On the ice, they made a splendid pair. Soupy was the swift defenseman who set up plays with tape-to-tape passes and scored dramatic goals on end-to-end rushes. Teddy was the rough-and-tumble forward who mucked for pucks in the corners and scored his own scrappy goals on rebounds and deflections and scrums in front of the net. Teddy loved turning Soupy's perfect passes into goals; Soupy loved how Teddy peeled opponents off the puck. They were pals off the ice, too, chasing the Sandy Cove girls and swiping beer from unlocked garages.

Our last year together, a rivalry developed. To a degree, it was no surprise. Soupy was being recruited by four or five big hockey colleges. Teddy, who lacked the speed and hands to play at that level, was living in Coach's billets and wondering what came next. But there was more to it than just hockey, something I couldn't put a finger on. They spoke less and less. They sat at opposite ends of the team bus. I asked Soupy about it once and he brushed me off: "Teddy's just a jealous fuck."

I wondered back then if Coach had something to do with it. Soupy—or Swanny, as Coach called him—had always been the favored son. But our last season together, Coach took to calling Teddy "Tiger." It bothered Soupy, though he tried not to show it. By the time Soupy returned to Starvation Lake years later, his hockey career in shambles, Teddy owned more property than anyone but Francis Dufresne and was one of the wealthiest businessmen in northern Michigan. Soupy and Teddy avoided each other, but their men's league teams—Campbell's Chowder Heads and the Boynton Realty Land Sharks—played just about every season for the league title, just as Teddy and Soupy faced each other most years in the finals of the Shoot-Out.

Soupy had to score now and then hope I'd stop Boynton on his final shot. He circled at center ice, once, twice, three times before he started toward me. "Oh-fer, oh-fer, oh-fer," Boynton chanted as Soupy skirted the blue line and flipped the puck to his forehand, then back, then back again, trying to mesmerize me. I knew his eyes were searching for mine but I stayed riveted on the puck. And then, in an instant, it was in the net. Maybe my eyes saw what happened. My brain sure didn't. One second the puck was in front of me, big as a pancake, and I started to reach out with my stick to poke it away. The next second, it was gone. Soupy drew it back to himself like a blackjack dealer and spun around on his blades, a full 360-degree spin-o-rama. I lost the puck in his whirling skates. Then I felt its dull weight glance off my left instep and heard it thud against the back of the goal. It was the perfect dangle. Everyone watching whooped and whistled while I whacked the puck out of the net and Soupy glided away.

"Holy shit, Carpie," Boynton shouted. "Put your dick back in your pants." They all laughed, except Soupy, who slid slowly along the boards across from Boynton, glaring. I turned around and grabbed my water bottle. I wasn't really thirsty, but there was nowhere else to hide.

"Carpie!" Boynton shouted. He stood with the puck at his feet, ready for his last shot. "Looks like Coach is back from the dead. You think he heard *you* were back from the dead and wanted to see if you still sucked?" I heard some of the others chuckle. "Brings back memories, huh?"

I barely had put the water bottle back when he leaped out and drove hard right at me. Usually that meant a shooter was going to try to deke rather than shoot, but Teddy, whose puckhandling wasn't nearly as nimble as Soupy's, almost always shot. He loved to aim between the legs so I pressed my leg pads together and kept the bottom of my stick hard against the ice as I moved backward with his strides. Just inside the blue line, he veered slightly to his left, my right. Yeah, here comes a shot, I thought. The puck was on his forehand. I scrunched my head down and stiffened. Teddy veered farther to my right. I slid around in that direction, squaring myself to the puck. He wound up for a slapshot. As his stick blade reached back, he said, "Hooper."

Hooper.

I couldn't help myself. It threw me so badly that I took my eye off the puck and glanced up at him. He wasn't looking, though. He was aborting his shot and snatching the puck away and cutting hard to his right. When I looked down again, the puck was gone. Off balance, I kicked out my left leg, sprawling, and flailed at him with my catching glove. But he was by me. Over my shoulder I watched his backhander snap the mesh in the upper left corner of the net. He stopped next to the goalpost and stood over me, gloating. "Thanks, Carpie," he said. "Good old Hooper."

"Fuck off, Teddy," I said.

Billy Hooper was the star winger for the Detroit Pipefitters who had scored the winning goal on me in the 1981 state final.

"What the fuck was that, Trap?" It was Soupy, who'd skated up behind me. I stumbled to my feet and saw he was angry.

"You can go to hell too," I said

"Jesus, Trap, Helen fucking Keller could've stopped that."

"Then next time get Helen fucking Keller to play goal."

"Whose side are you on?"

"Whose side are *you* on?" I dropped my catching glove and grabbed him by the jersey. I told him what Boynton had done. At first he looked at me blankly. Then he turned and stared across the ice at Boynton, who was laughing it up again with the other guys. "Goddamn it," Soupy said. He turned back to me. "Goddamn it, Trap."

"Soupy, what the hell is going on?"

Ignoring me, he scooped up a puck with his stick, flipped it into the air, and caught it in his left glove. Then he stopped and, assuming a baseball hitter's stance, tossed the puck up over his head. As it came down, he took a hard, fluid swing at it and connected with a solid *thwack*. The puck flew haphazardly at Teddy Boynton. He saw it at the last second and ducked. It missed his head by a couple of inches. "What the fuck was that?" he yelled, digging toward Soupy. "I'll be wearing the Stanley Cap this year, fuckhead." The other players grabbed him, laughing, while Soupy skated off the ice.

. . .

Pine County sheriff Dingus Aho's office smelled of gunmetal and powdered sugar. I waited in an angle-iron chair in front of his desk, my hair still damp from the quick shower I'd taken at the rink. I scanned the shelf behind his desk. There were cans of pepper spray, handcuffs, some *Field & Stream* magazines, a framed photograph of a woman whose face I recognized but whose name eluded me.

I wanted to ask Dingus myself about the snowmobile. I tried to tell myself it wasn't because I didn't trust Joanie, but it was. Despite my years away, despite my desire not to be there, I still felt that I knew these people and I could get them to tell me at least a semblance of the truth. Part of me wanted to hear that it was all a mistake, that the snowmobile wasn't Coach's after all. Mostly I wanted to hear a good reason why the sled wound up in Walleye.

I heard Dingus in the hallway just outside his door. "Call me when you hear something," he said. He stepped into the office. "Where's the redhead?" he said as he squeezed into the chair behind his little steel desk. Graying tufts of hair covered his bowling-pin forearms. He wore his cocoa uniform with a mustard tie secured by a brass clasp in the mitten shape of Michigan. "Thought she'd just about moved in here now."

"Thanks for helping her out, Dingus."

"Am I to be dealing with you now?"

"He was my coach."

"Ah," he said. He grabbed a piece of paper off a stack on his desk, peered at it, then replaced it, facedown. "How'd the Shoot-Out go?"

"Fine."

"I heard there might've been an incident."

"Boys will be boys."

"For sure. So how can I help you?"

Dingus had come to Starvation Lake from a tiny Upper Peninsula town populated by Finns named Heikkala and Pikkarainen, and his voice still carried the gentle lilt of their accent. He'd been sheriff for six years. People liked him. He was friendly and mostly docile.

He stayed within his modest budget and didn't try to pump up his revenue by setting traffic-ticket quotas for his deputies as so many other sheriffs did. He also rarely left his office except for lunch at Audrey's or, lately, to go on the TV news. Perhaps because he faced re-election, Dingus had become a regular on Channel Eight, which most days was desperate for local news and happy to put him on camera, whether it was to announce a new safety-belt campaign or to show off new jackets and caps for crossing guards. Yet Dingus on TV was usually as wooden as the lectern he hauled out for press conferences. Only his singsong accent and the dancing of his handlebar mustache saved him from being a total bore.

I had a notebook out but hadn't opened it yet. "The snowmobile at Walleye," I said. "Did it really belong to Coach?"

Dingus smiled. His head gave a barely discernible shake.

"No?" I said.

"Can't help you."

"Come on."

"No comment. You know what you know."

Nobody loved the cat-and-mouse more than small-town cops. It made the tedium of their jobs more bearable. Still, Dingus's "no comment" was confirmation enough for me. "So how the heck does the sled wind up in Walleye?" I said. "And please don't tell me the tunnels."

He sat back and placed his hands flat on his head. "Strange things happen, Gus," he said. "Remember Felix?"

Everyone in town knew the story. Felix, a golden retriever, dove into an ice-fishing hole on Starvation just as his master, Fritz Horn-beck, was hauling up a perch. Felix was going after the fish, but he missed and disappeared beneath the ice. Hornbeck, who was into his second bottle of blueberry schnapps, assumed the dog had drowned. But an hour later, Felix emerged from another ice-fishing hole in a shanty half a mile away, shaking off lake water in front of Elvis Bon-trager. It was the talk of Starvation for weeks.

"That's your comment?" I said. " 'Strange things happen'?"

"No. No comment at all."

"Come on, Dingus." Joanie was going to raise hell with me for interfering with her story. It'd be worse if I had nothing to show for it.

Deputy Frank D'Alessio walked into the office and, without noticing me, handed Dingus a steaming mug and a thin file folder. "Forensics, chief," the deputy said. Dingus shot him a look, and D'Alessio turned and saw me.

"Ah, jeez," he said. "Gus."

"Frankie," I said. "Forensics?"

He glanced nervously at Dingus, then started for the door. "You're playing tonight, right?" He meant our playoff game. "See you out there."

I smiled at Dingus. "Forensics on a snowmobile?"

Dingus shrugged. "Routine stuff," he said. "And that's off the record." He stood up from his chair, closed his office door, and sat down again. The name of the woman in the photograph came to me: Barbara Lampley. Dingus actually displayed a picture of his ex-wife. What man did that?

"Off the record, Dingus? Give me a break. Has the *Pilot* ever burned you?"

He folded his meaty hands on his desk. "Not yet," he said. "I'd really like to help you, Gus, but fact is, I have an ongoing investigation here."

"Ongoing or reopened?"

"No comment."

That gave me an idea.

"Can I get a copy of the original police report from 1988?" I said.

"Tell you what," he said. He pushed back from the desk, pulled a drawer out, plucked a sheet of paper from inside, and handed it to me. "Fill her out and we'll get back to you."

The sheet was a form for requesting records under a state public-disclosure law. "Dingus, I can't wait for this," I said.

"Well, I'm afraid somebody else has asked for the same report, and I asked them for the same thing."

"Joanie?"

"No, not the redhead."

"Who then?"

He shook his head. "That's all."

I couldn't imagine who else would be interested in that report.

"Are you going to drag Walleye?"

"Sure," Dingus said. "With an icebreaker."

This wasn't like Dingus. He usually gave it up once he saw you were serious. Did he have more at stake here than I knew? I recalled watching him from the woods on the night the cowl washed up, how he knelt in the shadows on the beach. I didn't remember him being a close friend of Coach, but then I wasn't around Starvation for years.

"Hey," I said. "Isn't that Barbara Lampley? Your ex?"

"What of it?"

"You're a better man than me, Sheriff."

"OK," he said, pushing away from his desk. "We're done here."

"No, tell you what, Dingus, I'll take your advice."

Remembering Barbara reminded me that Dingus had been a deputy once—maybe during the original investigation. I slapped the information sheet down on his desk and scribbled my name, the *Pilot* address, and my request for the 1988 file on Coach's accident. I handed it to Dingus. He stared at it for a long moment, then looked up at me, holding my gaze as if he were sizing me up. We really didn't know each other very well. I guessed that was going to change. "All right," he said. "We'll process it within the required ten days."

ten

Glassy cobwebs arched over the stairway down from the *Pilot* newsroom. I flicked a switch and gray light filled the basement, a dank concrete vault the size of a one-car garage. Along three walls stood wooden racks holding black binders of *Pilot*s dating to the 1970s, dates etched in gold lettering on their sides. The one I wanted was marked "March 1–March 15, 1988."

I hefted the binder from the rack and set it on a slab of Masonite laid across two file cabinets beneath the stairway. Pink Post-its jutted from the edges of the binder—Joanie's doing. I flipped to the newspaper marked by the first Post-it, Monday, March 14, 1988. Coach's death covered the front page. The headline bannered across the top read, "Blackburn Dies in Snowmobile Mishap." Beneath it a photograph showed cops standing around a patch on the frozen lake, the headlights of their snowmobiles and ambulances illuminating the early morning gloom.

There was a story recounting the reactions of local people, a story about other recent snowmobiling accidents, and a story about Blackburn's coaching career headlined, "Proud Coach Put Starvation Hockey on the Map." That story wrapped around the same smiling mug shot of Coach that hung on the wall at Enright's. Another picture showed Make-Believe Gardens, Blackburn's billets fuzzy in the background.

The main story began, "Legendary hockey coach John D. 'Jack' Blackburn disappeared on Starvation Lake early yesterday in what appears to have been a drowning in a snowmobile-related incident." Police offered scant details, the story said. There were unhelpful quotes from a few lakeshore residents and a brief, unrevealing interview with the sole eyewitness, Leo Redpath. I pulled out another binder and skimmed the next several papers. Photos showed that police encircled the accident scene with yellow tape at a fifty-yard radius. Townspeople in long coats and wool hats gathered along the perimeter to watch cops in scuba gear drop into the jagged hole in the ice. Some left flowers. The bouquets froze and wind scattered the petals so that flecks of scarlet and gold and violet speckled the hard gray lake. The cops kept the tape in place for three days. By then the sheriff's department was talking a bit more freely and the *Pilot* had pieced together a version of what had happened.

As they often did on Sunday nights in winter, Coach and Leo had gone riding on the trails that wound through the woods north of the lake. They stopped at their usual places, the Hide-A-Way, Dingman's, the Just One More Saloon. A bit before midnight, they parked their snowmobiles in a clearing a mile from Starvation's western shore, built a bonfire, and shared a bottle.

Coach wanted to do some "skimming." I'd done it a few times with Soupy and other friends, mostly in high school, always when we were drunk. We'd take our snowmobiles and find patches of open water on Starvation or Walleye or one of the other area lakes, and we'd hammer the throttles until we were moving fast enough to skim across the water to solid ice. It was kind of like jumping barrels on a motorcycle, only dumber, because it was usually dark and, as I said, we were drunk. Pine County outlawed skimming after two kids drowned on Little Twin Lake one night in 1982.

Everyone knew Coach loved to skim as much as he loved to dodge the cops who tried to catch him at it. "I'm going to die with my helmet on," he liked to say, and Leo would invariably respond, "You just might get your wish." Leo, who had never learned to swim, wanted nothing to do with skimming. Coach taunted him, but Leo would say, "I have no desire to spend my retirement years at the bottom of a lake." He didn't even like to watch. When Coach went looking for open water, Leo waited onshore, nipping at a bottle. On this March night, though, Leo relented. Why wasn't entirely clear, at least from the *Pilot*. The police quoted Leo as saying he'd simply had too much to drink, and, in fact, he never took another drink after that night. Later, when people asked him what had happened, he usually begged off by saying he was afraid that dredging it from his memory would send him back to the bottle.

Coach led Leo onto the lake beneath a moonless sky. Out past Pelly's Point, half a mile from shore, Coach and Leo stopped before a large pool of standing water shaped like a pear. Leo told police he lined his sled up facing the narrow end, and Coach steered himself into position to cross the wider stretch, spanning about twenty-five yards.

Half an hour later, just past 1:30 a.m., Leo banged at the door of my mother's house on the southwestern bank. She called the police.

Leo had chickened out.

He told the cops that, just before his snowmobile reached the water's edge, he had cut the throttle. Coach did not stop, of course. As always, Leo tried not to watch, but he turned to see after hearing Coach's snowmobile whine and splash and go silent. He saw Coach's helmeted head bobbing up and down in the water, heard his gurgling cries for help. "I didn't know what to do," the *Pilot* quoted Leo as saying. The rope they carried for such emergencies was stowed in Coach's snowmobile. The *Pilot* said Leo lay down on his stomach and edged close enough to the water to dampen the shoulders of his parka.

Divers found no body or snowmobile. Police said they thought the sled had sunk into the deep silt at the bottom of the lake and Coach's body had drifted away. They planned to dredge after the spring thaw. I pulled out another binder and looked for stories on the dredging. It never happened. The town council decided it would be futile and expensive, the *Pilot* said. Nor did the council desire to prolong the town's mourning. The sheriff then, Jerry Spardell, said he had no good answer for what happened to Coach except that perhaps he and his machine had been sucked into one of those underwater tunnels. Reading it, I shook my head in disbelief.

A cold sun shined on Jack Blackburn's funeral procession. Townspeople in River Rats caps, hats, and jackets lined Main Street as fifty snowmobiles draped in bedsheets dyed black crawled past, trailing plumes of exhaust and an empty hearse. A blown-up photograph atop the hearse showed Coach standing on a rink in his blue-and-gold sweatsuit, hockey stick in his hands, whistle dangling. I watched with Soupy from the storage room over Enright's. Now and then I cried. Soupy, who did not cry, laid a hand on the back of my neck and said nothing. Coach had taught me how to play goalie and how to love hockey and how to win. But that wasn't why I cried. I cried for the years in which Coach and I had barely talked since the day we lost that last game, since I'd left Starvation Lake. I cried because Coach had never taught me how to lose.

I closed the binder and stood there, my eyes fixed on the dates etched on its side, thinking. Why would Leo change his mind about skimming? He'd doubtless resisted plenty of other times when he'd had a lot to drink. Why hadn't anyone onshore heard Coach's cries for help? How could the city *not* dredge the lake, the expense be damned? And what about my mother, a witness once removed? She hadn't been quoted in the *Pilot*, not even declining to comment.

What troubled me most was that I hadn't pondered these questions before, or allowed myself to. Why was it that only ten years later I'd begun to feel that Leo's story seemed unlikely? Why only now was I wondering what my mother knew that she'd never told? At the time, perhaps, I was too distraught to think about it. And then I ran back to Detroit and tried to forget, while my mother and everyone else who knew how I felt was telling me to let it go, move on with my life. So I did. Now it was catching up with me, a nightmare that had been hiding all those years in the shadowy corners of my mind, unseen and unacknowledged.

As I slipped the binder back into its rack, I heard a creak in the floor above me. Shit, I thought.

Joanie was waiting at the top of the stairs. "Jerk," she said.

"Excuse me," I said. "Got a hockey game to get to."

She stepped in front of me. "What were you doing going to see Dingus? Checking up on me?"

"I wasn't checking—"

"You have no right."

"It's my job—"

"Bullcrap! Editors don't go around checking up on reporters behind their backs. Editors aren't supposed to be sniveling little chickens."

Some bosses might have fired her then and there. I told myself to calm down and walked past her into the newsroom and sat down on her desk. Of course I couldn't fire her, and not just because we were short-staffed. She had to help me figure out what had happened to Coach.

"Take it easy," I said. "You were right."

"Darn right I was right."

"No, I mean about the whole thing. It is a hell of a story."

"So what were you doing at the sheriff's department?"

"I don't know. I wasn't checking up on you, I swear. I think maybe I was checking up on me."

"What the heck does that mean, Gus?"

I got up and walked to my desk. My keyboard was buried in a pile of typed articles that had been dropped off by old-lady freelancers, who attended school board and parks commission meetings and babbled on in their stories about what the mayor was wearing and who led the recital of the Pledge of Allegiance. I spent my days rewriting that garbage into slightly better garbage that filled space between ads for pizza joints and lumber yards.

"Look at all this shit," I said. I turned to face her. "Look, I'm not trying to steal your story, OK? Christ, we work for the same paper.

Like it or not, I'm your boss, all right? And I . . . well, I wasn't *there* when all this happened, but I knew—actually I didn't know what I knew, then or now—oh hell, never mind. Bottom line, Dingus didn't give me squat. I filled out a request for the eighty-eight police report and he sent me home."

"I'll take your word for it," Joanie said. "But for the past two days it seemed like you were trying to keep me away from the story. Now you think it's a story. Well, hello! It's the biggest damn story ever to hit his town."

" 'Damn'? Watch your language, girl."

She actually blushed. "Sorry."

"Let's just work on it, OK? You know D'Alessio, right?"

"Yes," she said, blushing again.

"You might want to ask him about some forensics analysis they're apparently doing on the snowmobile. I did hear that while I was over there. Dingus wouldn't talk about it."

"It took guts to ask for that eighty-eight report," she said.

"Why?"

"Dingus wrote it. He was the deputy then."

We were quiet for a minute. Joanie leaned back against the copier and folded her arms. "You know what happened, don't you?" I didn't particularly want to hear. "There was no accident, Gus. Somebody killed Blackburn."

I gazed at a coffee stain on the tiled floor. In my mind I pictured the beach at Walleye Lake, felt the flashlights in my eyes.

"I'm glad you looked at the old papers," Joanie said. "Hard to figure, isn't it? I mean, do you really think that Leo dude was telling everything he knew? I don't. And underwater tunnels? Give me a break. The old folks at Audrey's might believe that junk, but you sure as heck don't."

No, I didn't, though I had tried to for a couple of days.

"Reminds me," she said. "I hear your coach was quite the ladies' man."

This was old news. "And?"

"Who knows? Could go to motive. Don't you think that's interesting?"

"Screwing's always interesting, but it's pretty tough to get into a family newspaper."

"So I should just ignore it?"

"No. You shouldn't ignore anything. You should look at everything and talk to everyone. Just don't assume everything you get is going to see print."

"Don't worry, I won't."

I looked up at the clock. It said 6:31. "I've got to fly," I said. "By the way, did you clear up the Canada thing?"

"The what?"

"The thing about Coach—about Blackburn not really being in that one place for four years?"

"Oh, right. Not yet. I called that woman at the newspaper again. It was weird, for a minute I thought she was going to cry. Anyway, she told me to call her at home tonight. Got to do my laundry first."

Upstairs, I shoved a stack of old *Hockey News* magazines off my makeshift coffee table and lifted the plywood off the cardboard boxes beneath. I opened the box that wasn't marked Trucks, the one marked Rats.

It was filled with old tournament programs, newspaper clippings, and photographs. I rummaged in the bottom and pulled out the dog-eared programs and yearbooks Coach had given me when I was a boy. I flipped through them once, then again more slowly, looking for a St. Albert Saints program for 1966–67, the season he supposedly wasn't there. Then I lined up all the programs across the carpet in chronological order, from Kitchener in 1954 to Moose Jaw to Kamloops to Kelowna to Victoria to St. Albert.

There was nothing from St. Albert in '66–'67.

I couldn't believe I hadn't noticed it before. I looked again. There was no program from that season. Was my memory fooling me? I sat on the floor remembering Coach leaning over his empty plate, telling us St. Albert was just too damn cold. The kids were great and they'd nearly won the title, he said, but he wanted those warm summers. "I had four fantastic years there," I could hear him saying. "But you know what? All good things come to an end."

eleven

The dressing rooms at Blackburn Arena were cramped rectangles with benches and clothing hooks nailed into cinderblock walls, showers that occasionally spewed hot water, and black rubber mats covered with spilled coffee and spat tobacco dip. The only difference was the numbers one through four on the doors. When we were the River Rats, and now that we were the Chowder Heads, we had to be in dressing room 3. That's where I found Soupy, Zilchy, Wilf, Stevie, and the rest of the boys before our 8:00 p.m. semifinal playoff game against the Mighty Minnows of Jordan Bait and Tackle. Soupy stood waiting for me to sit. I did and he plopped down on the bench to my left.

"Trapper," he said. "Pumped?"

"Sure," I grunted. I had way too much on my mind to be having pucks fired at my head. On my way in, I'd passed the Zamboni shed and spied Leo crouched beneath Ethel with a rag in one hand. It was briefly comforting to see him attending to his normal duties, as if nothing at all had happened the past two days.

"What's the score out there?" Soupy said.

As we dressed, the Boynton Realty Land Sharks were playing the Capraro's Pizza Pieholes in the other semifinal. The winner would play the winner of our game in the championship Monday night. The champs would get T-shirts and the runners-up would buy cocktails for everyone at Enright's.

"It was five to one Sharks when I came in," I said. "Saw Teddy just about behead Bobby Safranski with an elbow."

Teddy had always been tough, but over the years he'd grown mean—sneaky mean. Even the toughest players watched their backs around him, especially after play was whistled dead and the refs were busy lining up a face-off. That's when he might spear you with a stick blade or punch you in the back of the head.

The other guys jabbered as they tightened their skate laces and taped their shinguards. "He get a penalty?" Soupy said.

"Not Teddy. Refs never saw it." I leaned closer to Soupy. "What was up with you and him today anyway?"

"Me and who?" Soupy said.

"Don't. You and Boynton. At the Shoot-Out."

Soupy rummaged in his bag. "What do you think? I lost a hundred bucks. Wasn't a lot of fun. But everything's taken care of, don't worry."

"Meaning what?"

I was thinking of the settlement offer I'd read in the marina that morning. Had he changed his mind and taken it? I wanted to ask directly but didn't want him to know I'd sneaked in. Then again, maybe he already knew. Maybe he had left those squirming fish outside the marina door.

"By the way," I said, "were you fishing this morning?"

"Fishing? Shit, I was in bed till noon. What the hell's up with you tonight, Trap? It's time to play hockey now." He called to Stevie Reneau across the room. "Steve-O. Minnows got both Linkes tonight?"

Twin brothers Clem and Jake Linke were the Minnows' best players.

"If Jake got out of jail," Stevie said.

"Jail again? Now what?"

"He got kicked out of some Mancelona dive and got all pissed off and went up and down the street snapping windshield wipers off cars."

"Nice," Soupy said. "Could be both Linkes, Trap. Hope you brought your A game."

"Go to hell," I whispered back.

I opened my bag with an angry zip. Soupy elbowed me gently in the shoulder. I looked at him. His eyes said he didn't want me to be mad, but he also wasn't going to tell whatever he had to tell. Not yet, at least. "Come on, Trapper," he said. "Stop worrying. Ain't good mojo to talk business before games." He meant luck, but it was bad luck to acknowledge that luck was involved.

One day when Soupy and I were eleven, we were riding our snowmobiles when we stopped atop a hill at the border between Pine and Polley counties. From there we could look back and see the lazy crescent of the lake and the chimney smoke curling up from Soupy's house, where Mrs. Campbell was baking pies for a New Year's dinner our families planned to share the next day. Soupy wanted to sled down the Polley side of the hill into forbidden territory; our parents' rule then was that we were not to cross the Pine County line. But it was New Year's Eve, Soupy argued, so it was OK. He pointed to a clapboard bell tower jutting up through the trees below. "See that?" he said. "We can ring the bell." Before I could answer he was roaring down.

Ours were the only tracks scarring the snow around the one-room schoolhouse. It looked abandoned; boards covered all of the outer windows. Soupy creaked the front door open and we stepped inside. The vestibule smelled of moldy paper. Through the window of the locked inner door we could see the dusty desks pushed into a corner, textbooks stacked haphazardly on the wood floor. A rope hung down from a square hole in the ceiling.

"The gun," Soupy said. He ran back outside, returning with his Daisy BB rifle.

"Soupy," I said. "We're gonna get caught."

"Don't be a pussy."

"I'm not a pussy."

"Look," he said, holding up his gloved hands. "No fingerprints." He trained the gun on the door window and fired. The hissing BB left a pinhole at the center of a web of spidery cracks. Six more shots opened a hole the size of a fist. Gingerly, Soupy reached through the jagged opening. The door gave way.

The floor groaned as we stepped inside. "Smells like ass in here," Soupy said. I edged farther inside, holding my breath against the must. I reached up and clasped a mittened hand around the knot at the end of the rope. I yanked it once and jumped back. "Harder," Soupy said. I yanked again, and the rope gave way so easily that I fell backward. I looked up and saw rope and bell and shreds of rotted wood plummeting toward me. "Holy shit," Soupy yelled, and I rolled left just as the bell slammed into the floor. Soupy grabbed the back of my parka, yelling, "Let's get out of here!"

The cops found us the next afternoon, just before dinner at the Campbells'. Soupy and I were horsing around in the basement when Mrs. Campbell called down. She marched us in front of two state troopers standing on her boot rug in matching navy parkas and ear-flap caps. One wore thick glasses and smiled sheepishly, as if he was embarrassed to be there. Mr. Campbell stood next to them, arms folded, face pinched with aggravation. We'd interrupted his afternoon of drinking beer and watching football.

"Sure smells good," the trooper with the thick glasses said. "Got a turkey in the oven?"

"No," Mrs. Campbell said, giving us a look. "A goose."

Soupy and I stood shoulder to shoulder. "Boys," the trooper without glasses said, "we have a report of a breaking and entering out by—"

Soupy interrupted him. "It was me," he said. "I went in that school-house." He jerked a thumb toward me. "He was there but he kept telling me not to."

I looked at him in disbelief. "Excuse me, son," the trooper with the glasses said. "What we heard—"

Angus Campbell took a step toward us. "What the hell were you doing in Polley?" he said. "You know you ain't supposed to go that far, boy." His right hand twitched beneath his left elbow.

"I know, sir," Soupy said. "I'm awfully sorry."

"Sorry, my ass," Mr. Campbell said.

The trooper with glasses looked worriedly at Mr. Campbell. The other said, "You boys could've gotten hurt."

"How'd you get in?" Soupy's dad said.

"Broke a window, sir," Soupy said.

"Broke a window how, goddamn it?"

"BB gun, sir."

Mr. Campbell unfolded his arms and took another step toward his son. I felt Soupy flinch. "Sonofabitch," his father said. His eyes searched the room. "Where's the goddamn gun?" he said.

"Outside, sir," Soupy said.

"Sir," the bespectacled trooper said, but Soupy's father ignored him and stepped out the door. "Son-of-a-fucking-bitch," we heard him say as he slammed the door behind him. We heard him pick up the rifle and curse. Then we heard the gun barrel *whang* on the concrete porch, its stock cracking and splitting.

Mr. Campbell was sweating when he came back inside. He glared at Soupy as he brushed past us. Mrs. Campbell said, "Excuse me," and followed him.

Soupy and I were both grounded for a week. I didn't see him again until school the next Monday. His black eye hadn't quite healed.

The first thing I said was, "Why'd you do that?"

"What?"

"Rat yourself out."

He shrugged. "My old man would have whupped me anyway."

Late in the playoff against the Minnows, we led 2–0, and I was bored. The Minnows hadn't managed a shot on me since the middle of the game. My attention wandered to the bleachers, which were empty but for two women huddled beneath a green afghan up near the roof beams and three others chattering along the glass. They were all girl-friends of players. Wives were smart enough to stay home where it was warm and they couldn't hear their boneheaded husbands threatening to beat up referees.

I noticed Brenda Mack making her way down the bleachers and asked myself why she would waste a perfectly good Saturday night shivering in a hockey rink. I'd had a crush on her in grade school and never had tired of seeing her. She had married Wilf, but that lasted only four years. Now she was dating a Minnow. She'd just reached the glass to my left when I saw Teddy Boynton emerge from dressing room 2 behind her. His hair was wet, and he was carrying his hockey bag in his left hand. An image—a memory—flitted through my mind too fast for me to recognize. Teddy called out to Brenda and she turned and smiled and he dropped his bag to kiss her on the cheek. As they chatted, Brenda pointed out something on the ice, probably her new boyfriend, and I thought, Teddy'll have a two-hander-to-the-ankle for him next time they're on the ice together. Boynton picked up his bag again, and then it came to me.

Without thinking, I rushed out of my net toward Teddy, waving my stick over my head and yelling, "Hey, wait! Boynton!" He turned, befuddled, and dropped his bag. "Go fishing this morning, Ted?" I shouted. The picture now fixed in my mind was of Boynton standing on Main Street, talking with Elvis Bontrager. Instead of a hockey bag, he'd held a tackle box. Which explained the fish outside the marina: It was Teddy, letting me know he was watching.

Now, instead of answering my question, he looked past me and pointed, grinning. "Heads up, Carp," he said. I whipped around to see Clem Linke winding up for a shot from halfway down the rink. "Shit!" I screamed. I scrambled back toward my empty net but was still three strides away when Linke's shot sailed across the goal line. The Minnows whooped and banged the heels of their sticks on the boards as I skated a hapless circle in front of my net. I wanted to disappear under the bleachers. To punish myself, I looked back toward Boynton. I could tell from how he was gesturing that he was explaining to Brenda Mack how I'd left my net untended and let a goal in from a mile away. She put a hand to her mouth, giggling, while Teddy clapped and yelled, "Way to go, Carpie! Just like old times!"

twelve

A n hour later, I saw Boynton again, standing in the back of Enright's, sipping a Heineken and talking with Darlene Esper. She leaned against the jukebox, smoking. I'd learned since returning to Starvation Lake that she only smoked on Saturday nights when she came to the bar without her useless husband to drink White Russians in her tight jeans and black turtlenecks. I didn't go to Enright's every Saturday, but she avoided me when I did. I understood, but it still bothered me. It bothered me more to see her with Teddy.

I kept an eye on them through the smoke and the crowd from the other end of the bar where I stood with Soupy and most of the other Chowder Heads. It was impossible to hear what Boynton was saying over the din of chatter and the blare of "Whipping Post." He leaned to speak into Darlene's ear. She folded her arms across her chest. He leaned back, waiting. She shrugged. He said something else. Darlene shook her head no, once, then a second time. She glanced my way and caught my eye briefly, then turned back to Boynton, who was holding up his hands as if to say, OK, I give up.

"Leave it alone," Soupy said, elbowing me.

"What?"

"She's married. Let it go."

"So is Boynton."

"Fuck Boynton. What the hell were you thinking out there tonight?"

Despite my late-game lapse, we had hung on to win, 2–1. It meant we would play Boynton's Land Sharks for the league title Monday night.

"It was Brenda's fault," I said. "She's way too hot for her age."

"Roger that," Soupy said. "The butt that belongs in the Louvre." He shouted down the bar, "Hey there, barkeep! Four more Blue Ribbons, please."

Francis Dufresne turned and glared. He was helping Loob tend bar. Along with his near-constant scowl, he wore an ancient pair of Wallabees with no laces and a bleached-out River Rats sweatshirt. His short, blubbery body shifted around like a sack of rocks as he moved. Old acne scars clefted his pale cheeks, and his nose was like a red rubber ball a dog had used as a chew toy.

His appearance belied his good fortune in life. The story went that Francis had taken five thousand dollars he inherited in the late 1960s and, by investing wisely time and again in real estate, turned it into millions. Maybe the story was no truer than the tales of the underwater tunnels, but the locals believed it because they could see the results in the office buildings and restaurants and subdivisions he'd developed. First with the help of Jack Blackburn, and later Teddy Boynton, Francis had built most of Starvation Lake that had been built in the past twenty years and bought much of the rest of it. He was the first to notice the swelling wave of tourists that Coach and the River Rats were bringing to town, first to recognize how to capitalize on Coach's status by using him as a pitchman. Francis was smart and tenacious, but he hadn't the looks or the charisma to charm the locals into letting him and his partners own most of their town. For that he had Coach, and when Coach was gone, he had Teddy.

Francis and Teddy had done well together. Teddy was the outside guy, making the deals, selling them to the public officials, flashing the fridge-magnet smile. Francis, many years older, was the inside man, raising money, huddling with lawyers, making sure the paperwork was right. Between them, they owned just about everything in town. But Teddy, as he had prospered, had begun to chafe at hearing about Francis's role in his success. There were whispers that Teddy wanted Francis out of the new marina project.

I didn't know Francis well, but I liked it that he'd called all those

people to the rink on the night we beat Griffin. I liked it that he'd
hung on to Enright's, the thing he'd owned longest, and that he still
came in on Saturday nights to help sling beers. He'd been close to
Coach, and I thought he knew my dad a little as well. He set four
beers in front of us.

"Who won?" he said.

"The good guys," Soupy said.

"I wish I could say the same for the Rats," Francis said.

"Knocked out again?" I said. As the source of the Rats' long jinx, I
prayed every year that they would snap it.

"Indeed." Francis spoke with the hint of an Irish brogue, a hand-
me-down from his mother, whose maiden name was Enright. "Same
old, same old. Pipefitters again. Six to one. We were never in the
game."

"At least it didn't come down to one guy shitting the bed, huh?" It
was Little Timmy Wilford, Brad's younger brother, trying to be funny.
Little Wilf was barely six when we'd lost our last game.

"Eat shit, junior," Soupy said. "I don't recall your sorry-ass squad
ever getting out of the regional, let alone making a final."

"Let it go, Alden," Francis said.

"Lighten up," Little Wilf said, raising a palm in Soupy's face. "Just
messing with you."

"Jesus, junior, the hand!" Soupy said. He pinched his nose and
made a gagging sound.

Little Wilf turned the palm to his face and inhaled deeply.
"Ahhhhh," he said. "Hockey." Nothing smells worse than the inside of
an old sweat-drenched hockey glove, except a hand that just came out
of one. And nothing smells more like hockey.

"In my opinion," Francis interrupted, rapping a finger on the bar
for emphasis, "it didn't matter how well we played this weekend, we
weren't going to win. Not with that snowmobile washing up onshore.
You can't be playing hockey with ghosts flying around in your locker
room."

"Ghosts?" Soupy said. "Come on, Francis. You think those kids give a damn? What the hell's with everybody? All I've been hearing is this shit about Blackburn and his snowmobile. He croaked a million years ago. You ought to let it go."

Teddy was making his way toward us. He stopped to peer at the photograph of Blackburn, glanced back toward Darlene, then looked again at the photo. Francis turned to me.

"Saw your girl's article today, Augustus," he said. "I thought, Good for Augustus, he's not going to go crazy with this thing just so he can sell a lot of papers. But then, I'll be damned if your little reporter didn't come in here today, snooping around."

"Just doing her job," I said.

"She wanted pictures off the wall, for God's sake."

"She ain't so little," Soupy said.

"Did you talk to her, Francis?" I said.

Francis leaned close and put his hands flat on the bar. "Only to tell her that Jack Blackburn was one of the finest men ever to set foot in Starvation Lake. And that it's out of line to be digging him up like this. It ain't right, Augustus. Jack's dead and buried wherever the good Lord wished. Rest in peace."

"Amen," Soupy said.

"Well, sorry, Francis," I said. "The cops are investigating. You're always bitching about the county pissing away your tax dollars. Don't you think we ought to find out what the hell they're doing?"

"Hogwash, Augustus. Your job is to sell as many papers as you can. And for your information, I don't think Dingus and his bobbies should be poking around in it either. It's an election year, I know, but this isn't the way to go about getting attention. I think he ought to let the past stay in the past, just as I think young Mr. Wilford here ought to leave your past in the past, regardless."

"Regardless of what?" I said.

"Just as nobody needs to be asking whatever happened to you down in Detroit that got you back here, either."

"Right," I said. Not even Soupy knew how I'd screwed up in Detroit.

"Think about it." He clapped me on my hand. "I know you're a good man."

"Are we having an argument?" Teddy Boynton set his empty Heineken on the bar. "Give it up, Gus," he said. "Campbell's gonna have to pay his bar tab eventually. It must be up there with the federal deficit by now, huh?"

"Evening, Ted," I said. I looked past him and saw Darlene was gone.

"Theodore," Francis said, nodding.

"Francis," Teddy said. They didn't shake hands. Maybe the rumors of a rift were true. Boynton threw a ten on the bar. "That should cover me."

Francis shoved it back at him. "Your money's no good in here, Theodore."

"Give it to Loob then."

"No luck with Darlene, eh, Teddy boy?" Soupy said. "Why don't you try the high school? Maybe there's a sock hop."

"You got that hundred you owe me?"

"No, but I got an answer for you: Go to hell."

That stopped Teddy for a second. It wasn't just a smart-ass remark. Teddy looked at Francis, whose own look suggested that he, too, took Soupy's meaning.

"So that's it?" Teddy said.

"That's it," Soupy said.

"There's time to reconsider," Teddy said. "Don't be stupid, Soupy."

"Excuse me," Francis said. His eyes met Teddy's for an instant as he slid away. Now I understood. Soupy was telling Teddy to stuff his settlement offer. That would leave everything up to the zoning board. I wondered if Francis was in on Boynton's marina or not.

"Nothing to reconsider," Soupy said.

Teddy yanked his keys out of a coat pocket. "You know," he said, "you're a loser. And you make a conscious choice to be a loser every day. But you will come around. In the meantime, I'd appreciate you not winging pucks at my head."

"In the meantime, kiss my ass," Soupy said. "If I wanted to hit you, I would've."

"See you on the ice Monday night," Boynton said. "Want to double down on that hundred?"

"Fucking-ay," Soupy said.

"We'll talk tomorrow."

"No, we won't."

Boynton looked at me. "Thanks again for the memories, Carp."

As he headed for the door I excused myself to take a leak. Instead of going into the men's room, though, I ducked behind the crowd and slipped out the front door. I found Teddy unlocking his sport utility.

"How was the fishing this morning, Ted?" I said.

He was peering at a bar napkin he'd pulled from inside his coat. He put it back in his pocket. "You gonna do that story or not?" he said.

"Which?"

"The one about your loser friend we're gonna give to Channel Eight."

I'd forgotten all about it. "We're working on it."

"You'll hear from my lawyer."

"How was the fishing?"

"Fishing?" he said. He slammed the vehicle's door shut. His engine growled to life. He rolled his window down. "You know, Carpie," he said. "You're a sucker."

I figured if I went back inside, I'd be there till close, then Soupy would want to come up to my place for more drinks. Better to escape while I could. But my truck wasn't where I thought I'd parked. I hiked down Main to Estelle and around to the *Pilot* lot. There was the truck. Memory's going, I thought.

At my stairway I looked up and noticed a dull glow in my apartment window. Had I left a light on? Four steps up, I noticed my door was open a crack. I stopped and looked around. Break-ins almost never happened in Starvation Lake. Had I left the door open too? I crept to the top of the stairs and tried to peek inside. I couldn't see anything unusual but I smelled something. Cigar smoke. Cheap cigar smoke. I eased the door open with a boot, reached in, and flicked the wall switch. "Hello?"

Sheriff Dingus Aho sat in my recliner, biting a Tiparillo beneath his handlebar mustache. "Gus," he said, smiling. "You were parked illegally. I took the liberty of moving you before you got a ticket." He tossed my keys on the plywood table. "You know, you shouldn't just leave them in the ignition, son."

"And you shouldn't just let yourself into my house. Do you have a warrant?"

"A warrant? No. But I have this." He leaned forward and set down a thin blue file folder. "Please. Sit down."

I dropped into my sofa and picked up the folder. Before I could open it, Dingus reached over and lightly grasped my wrist. "Yesterday, you made a request for a report," he said. "You'll get a formal response from the county attorney in, oh, six weeks, maybe eight. So we need to agree that I was never here."

"All right."

"And you can't be putting any of this in your paper, at least not yet."

He let go of my wrist.

Inside the folder were four pages stapled together. The top three were a photocopy of a Pine County Sheriff accident investigation report dated March 13, 1988. Parts were smudged and barely legible. Scanning the spare description of Coach's accident, I learned little I didn't already know, although it noted that Leo Redpath "became visibly upset and approached a hysterical state." He kept repeating, "What's done is done. What's done is done . . ." The report was signed by Sheriff's Deputy Dingus Aho.

The fourth page was a photocopy of a receipt for $25,000 paid to the Starvation Lake Marina, "Angus Campbell, proprietor." It was dated April 12, 1988. Across the page someone had scribbled PAID FULL, CK 5261, FIRST DETR BANK. Nothing was listed under the purchases column. A signature near the bottom of the page was badly smudged. Beneath it I read something slightly more legible: "Ferryboat." The F on "Ferryboat" had a little tail on it like a fishhook.

I tried to look indifferent, but my mind was buzzing. What had upset Leo so? Was it simply losing a friend to foolish behavior, or was there something else? What did this receipt or Soupy's late father have to do with anything? Why would somebody in Starvation Lake want a ferryboat? I couldn't remember ever seeing one at the marina, though I suppose Soupy's dad could've gotten his hands on one if he had a buyer. What was Dingus after?

"Thanks, Dingus," I said. "But I have no idea what to make of this."

He blew out a plume of Tiparillo smoke. "There are some additional materials our attorney might give you," he said, "but I can tell you they're not terribly revealing."

"None of this is. You wrote this report. Help me out here."

Dingus stared at the pages in my hands. "I have an idea, Gus, but it's a little worn from age. I doubt you'd believe it. Nobody did way back when. And it cost me, let me tell you."

"Try me."

He stood. "I'm confident you'll figure it all out."

"Come on. Why'd you bother coming here if you're not going to tell me?"

He moved toward the door. "You know, Gus, I heard the rumors about how you had to leave Detroit. I hope you don't mind, but I made a few calls down there. You're a pretty enterprising guy."

"What's the hell's that supposed to mean?"

"Pretty gutsy guy, too. Anyway, I'm thinking you'll figure this out and shine a little light on this subject. Also, next time you park on Main, remember we changed the signs a few weeks ago. You had a front-page story on it."

"Dingus."

He closed the door softly behind him.

thirteen

I never set out to be a newspaperman. From the time I was twelve, I had worked summers with Soupy at the marina, long, hot days made longer by Soupy's dad chewing our butts. After two years at the University of Michigan, I decided to try something different. I'd taken a journalism class that year. It seemed easy enough. I liked sports, and one of our neighbors was Henry Bridgman, executive editor of the *Pilot*. Instead of scraping perch innards off boat decks, I figured I'd write about sports for Henry. Mom called him.

I showed up at the *Pilot* the next morning. Henry was sitting behind his steel desk, turned sideways at a typewriter. A copy of that day's paper lay on the desk. A headline on the front read, "School Board Mulls Millage Increase." Henry bit on a cigarette and stiffened his forefingers to bat out something hunt-and-peck style on the typewriter. "Christ," he blurted, cigarette jiggling in his mouth. "These bastards must be on drugs if they think they can get away with this." I had no idea what he was talking about. He stopped typing and stared at his words. "OK," he declared, and swiveled to face me. A grin creased his face, all bony cheeks and crinkly eyes. "I'll be goddamned," he said. "Did your mother give you my message?"

"Um." I glanced at my watch. "She said ten o'clock."

"Oh, holy Christ," he said, laughing in a hoarse guffaw, *haw haw haw.* "I get to do the dirty work then."

"Pardon?"

He *haw-hawed* again. "See, I don't really need a sports reporter."

"You don't?"

"Naw, hell." He screwed his cigarette around in his mouth, squinting against the smoke. "I can get some high school kid to do sports. I got real news to cover."

I wondered if "real news" had anything to do with a "millage," whatever that was. Why hadn't I just stayed at the marina? "OK," I said.

Henry let me cover the occasional high school track meet or baseball game. But mostly I covered the police, the school board, and, when Henry couldn't make the meetings, the town council. I forced myself to learn about police procedure, zoning variances, even millages. Henry had to rewrite some of my stories so they made sense. I didn't mind. I felt good about having comprehended enough to write anything down. There were night meetings to cover, but the hours were better than at the marina, my boss was not an asshole, and I was making a few more dollars. That's all I really thought about it. It was a summer job. Mom would ask how it was going and I'd say, "Fine." She wanted to hear that I'd found something to do with my life. I couldn't tell her that. In my mind, there was that summer and there was my future, and one had little to do with the other. Until I got my first big scoop.

His name was James Baumgarten, but his softball teammates called him Bubba. He had biceps like muskmelons and a fat tomato face, and he could hit a softball farther than anyone in Starvation Lake. Somehow Bubba wound up at Soupy's tailgater one night after his team had whipped our team, also called the Chowder Heads, sponsored by Soupy's marina.

Bubba and I got to talking over beer and bratwurst. His team, the Screwballs, was Starvation Lake's perennial softball champion, sponsored by a local manufacturing company, Perfect-O-Screw Inc. Every summer, it seemed, the Screwballs recruited a couple of outfielders built like Bubba. We never saw them around town except on Wednesday evenings, when they'd smack homer after homer over the 283-foot fence at Thinnes Park. Bubba was the latest Screwball ringer. I was a little surprised to hear he lived in Boyne City, more than an hour's drive away. I asked him why he would come so far just to play softball—there were leagues in Boyne City, after all—and he snickered like a little kid. It took a few beers, but Bubba finally confided that Perfect-O-Screw was paying him to play. "No shit," I said. I don't think he knew I was a newspaper reporter, and I didn't feel compelled to tell him. A few more beers and he was bragging that Perfect-O-Screw even reimbursed him for his mileage.

The company gave Bubba eighty-nine days of pay at the minimum wage and in return he hit long balls and agreed to have himself listed on Perfect-O-Screw's full-time payroll. He had never set foot in the factory except to pick up his uniform. "You can't be telling anyone this shit," he said. "I could lose my job."

"Your job? You mean left field?" I said. We both howled with laughter.

I probably would have forgotten about it, except that Perfect-O-Screw at that very moment was trying to persuade the town council to expand a tax break the company enjoyed on its land and factory. Two nights before Bubba and I had our little chat, Cecil Vidigan, who owned Perfect-O-Screw and pitched for the Screwballs, had appeared at a town council meeting in his black-and-gold Perfect-O-Screw softball jacket. He reminded the council that the company's original tax break had led to the hiring of six workers, a big deal in Starvation Lake. He said an expanded break would save it enough money to hire four more employees. "You see," he said, his whiskery scowl spreading into a smile, "it's a win-win for the company and for the community." Not to mention the Screwballs.

The day after hearing Bubba's secret, I visited the Pine County courthouse for a look at the company's property tax records. Inside the county clerk's office, eight rows of filing cabinets stood behind a panel of frosted-glass windows set atop a long oak counter. The place was empty except for Deputy Clerk Verna Clark.

She was a pencil-thin woman in her fifties, wearing an ash gray dress on which was pinned a name tag that said, "Deputy Clerk Clark." Henry had warned me about her. Years before, a county commissioner had raised a stink about Verna and her family because they lived a few miles outside Pine County. The commissioner, who wanted to replace Verna with his daughter-in-law, made an issue of Pine County employees actually living in Pine County. He dropped the matter after his daughter-in-law got a job with the county drain commission. But Verna, mindful of how the powers-that-be could snatch away her livelihood, had become a stickler for rules and procedure. A pain in the ass, in other words. Henry told me he once went to the courthouse for a county map, and Verna told him he'd first have to fill out a public-information request.

"Can I help you?" she asked me.

I told her what I needed. Without a word, she produced the one-page form for requesting public documents.

"Do I really have to go through all this?"

"It's county policy," Verna said.

"How long will it take?"

"Most people are able to complete it in two or three minutes."

"No," I said, growing annoyed. "How long to actually get the records?"

"The statute requires us to respond within ten business days."

"So I'll have it in ten days?"

"If the county attorney was to determine that the documents could be released, sir, we would then have a reasonable period of time to process and produce them."

"And how long could that take?"

"I'm afraid the statute doesn't specify."

"Could you at least guess?" Saying "at least" was a mistake. Her thin lips got thinner. She may have been a bona fide bitch, but it didn't help that I was young and stupid.

"Guessing isn't part of my job, but if I had to hazard an estimate,

I'd say that, assuming the county attorney approves, you could have the materials by Labor Day."

"That's three weeks from now."

She picked up the reading glasses dangling from a nylon cord around her neck and peered through them at a Chet's Sunoco and Party Store calendar taped on the counter.

"Two weeks and four days," she said.

I had to be back at college a week before that. "Look, Miss Clark, I'm—"

"Mrs. Clark," she corrected me.

"Mrs. Clark. I'm sorry, I just need a few names and numbers. It wouldn't take me more than an hour. Couldn't I just do this today?"

She tapped a finger on the form. "You'll need to fill this out."

I looked haplessly around the room, hoping to see someone who might be able to help me. There was only Verna. "This is not right," I said. "These are public records. The public has a right to see them."

Verna gave me a tight smile. "Then, sir," she said, "I suggest that you have the public fill out the required form."

After filling out the form, I stepped out into the hallway. The men's room at the end of the hall was closed for repairs. A plumber there told me I could use an employees' restroom around the corner.

I stood at the urinal fuming. I wondered if Verna Clark knew Cecil Vidigan or had friends or family working at Perfect-O-Screw. Goddamn Starvation Lake, I thought. Maybe there was a story, maybe not, but I couldn't let this small-town bullshit keep me from finding out. I had to see those records.

I washed my hands and stood at the sink, trying to figure out what to do. In the mirror I noticed a second door in the restroom. An idea popped into my head, so preposterous that I laughed. But I stood there thinking about it a little more and, after a while, it didn't seem so crazy.

That other door opened on a dimly lit corridor that led past a janitor's closet to yet another door, this one fitted with a frosted-glass window. I walked as quietly as I could to the frosted-glass door and put my hand on the knob. I turned it and gently tugged the door open. Through the half-inch crack I peered across a bank of filing cabinets to the counter where Verna Clark stood with her back to me, waiting on someone. I eased the door closed.

The inside of the janitor's closet smelled of soggy mops and Comet. I found a thermos, which I filled with cold water from the restroom sink, and a rolled-up bag of stale pretzels. I locked the door from the inside and sat down on a box of toilet paper. I'd written a story that summer about county budget cutbacks. One cut meant janitors didn't work Tuesdays and Thursdays. This was a Thursday.

I waited until after nine to slip into the clerk's office. The records took me a little while to find, but once I had the right drawer, I worked fast, jotting names and numbers on my legal pad in the light of a half moon slivering in through the blinds. I wanted to get out of the court-house as soon as I finished, but I feared someone might see me. So I refilled the thermos, cleaned off a big sponge to use as a pillow, and prepared to spend the night. I figured I'd sneak out as soon as the building opened in the morning.

The floor was hard and sticky, but sleep came. In a dream I slept on the edge of a cliff out West. I could hear water rushing by in a canyon below and invisible birds made of metal rattling around me in the darkness. Then I felt the cliff's edge slipping out from under me, felt myself rolling off. Jerking in my sleep, I bolted awake to the clatter of a tin bucket I'd kicked over. "Shit," I whispered. I lay still and lis-tened over my thumping heart. At first there was only the quiet hum of the old building at rest. Then I heard a knob turn—the door on the restroom—and then a footstep, then another, as a spray of light flashed beneath the door to my hiding place. Did the county budget include a line item for security guards? I couldn't remember. I sat up as quietly as I could and made sure I'd locked the door.

The light passed twice before finally stopping at the door. I heard a key being inserted into the lock. I looked desperately around the closet for some cranny into which I could disappear. Of course there was none. I squatted on one knee, thinking I could spring past whoever was about to find me. Then the door squeaked open and the flashlight beam blinded me and I froze.

"Gus?"

The voice was familiar. And the laugh that followed. "What the hell are you doing?" Darlene said.

She was wearing a dark blue cop's uniform with a patch stitched in gold and shaped like a badge over her left breast. "Vigilant Security," it read. Her hair was tucked up into a policelike hat sewn with an identical patch.

"Darlene," I said. "What are you doing here?"

"What am I doing here? I'm working. What are you doing here? Did your mom kick you out? Or do you like sleeping with cockroaches?"

"It's a long story. I came in this afternoon to look at some files. The bitch clerk wouldn't let me."

"So you broke into the county courthouse."

"No. I was already in."

"Do you think the sheriff would look at it that way?"

"Come on, Darl," I said. I was beginning to worry that she might actually take me in. "I never told your mom about Jitters."

We were nine years old. Darlene and I liked to careen down the dirt two-track of Jitters Trail on our bicycles and catapult over the bank into Jitters Creek. Of course our parents forbade this. One afternoon we were ski-biking, as we called it, when Darlene lost control and crashed into a small poplar along the path. Her bike kept rolling into the creek and started floating away. I chased it down the bank until it snagged in a fallen tree and I was able to dislodge it and bring it back. I found Darlene sitting on the bank, crying. She had a bloody cut on one cheek and had torn her new one-piece lavender bathing suit. Being a nine-year-old, naturally I considered teasing her, but thought better of it and instead solemnly informed her that the front wheel on her bike was badly bent and would need repair. Later we told her mother Darlene had slammed into a picnic table at the public access. Darlene hated to lie, so I did most of the talking while she stood next to me sobbing. Her mother bought it. Or at least we thought so.

"So what am I supposed to do, Gus?"

"Let's see. Forget you ever saw me here?"

"Hmm—I don't know."

I'd never seen her in her uniform. She'd wanted to be a cop since she was in high school, but I realized, kneeling there in the janitor's closet, that I'd never really taken it seriously until now. It seemed to suit her. Which made me feel glad, despite my predicament. There she was doing what she wanted to do with her life. I smiled.

"Are you really going to arrest me?"

Now she smiled, too. "I might." She leaned back against the door until it closed.

"What are you doing?"

"I don't know. A citizen's arrest?"

We didn't say anything for a while. We just looked at each other, me on my knee, Darlene in her uniform, the flashlight beam playing across my chest. My heart was pounding now from something other than fear. Darlene and I had gone on a few dates and gotten into a few clinches, but one of us had always stopped things before they went too far. I think we knew we really liked each other, and we knew I wasn't going to stay in Starvation Lake, and we knew that those two things could only come to pain. But there in the humming silence of the Pine County courthouse, with the town asleep around us and my stupid little secret hanging on the air, I guess it was easier for both of us to say the hell with it, this is our place, for now.

I sat back on the floor. She snatched her hat off and tossed it at me. I caught it against my chest and set it down next to the bucket I'd upended. Darlene locked the door and snapped off her flashlight.

. . .

I got my story. Bubba Baumgarten wasn't the only slugger on Perfect-O-Screw's payroll. I called some of the guys whose names I'd found in the courthouse records. As it turned out, there were six Perfect-O-Screw employees who hadn't done anything more for the company than catch fly balls and swing bats. Henry was so delighted that he never asked why I hadn't come in until noon.

"Christ," he said, "it's a double play. You nailed 'em screwing the city *and* the softball league."

More like a triple play, I thought.

Henry wanted to publish the story on the day the town council was scheduled to finalize Perfect-O-Screw's newest tax break. The day before the meeting, my phone rang just after 9:00 a.m. "Gus Carpenter," I said.

"What the fuck are you?" came the voice. I knew it from the softball field. I looked around for Henry. He'd gone for doughnuts.

"Mr. Vidigan?" I said.

"What the hell have I ever done to you? Did I strike you out or something? Will ruining me be a feather in your fucking cap? Will you be able to go to your bosses and say, 'Stop the fucking presses, I'm about to destroy Cecil Vidigan'?"

"Actually, Mr. Vidigan—"

"By the way, print a word of this and I'll come down and cave your goddamn skull in."

Then he hung up. My hands were trembling. What if I had the story all wrong? I wished Henry were there.

The phone rang again.

"Gus?"

"Yes, Mr. Vidigan. Sir, I had fully—"

"No, no, Gus, please." He took a deep breath. "I'm sorry. I shouldn't have said all that sh——, all those things. You're just doing your job. As you can imagine, Gus, this company, I've built it from the ground up. I've sweat blood, Gus. Cried tears, friend, real tears. And I think I've contributed a hell of a lot to this community."

"I understand," I said. "Do you think you could tell me—"

"Listen," he said. "Why don't you come out to the shop in the morning? I'll lay it all out, how this grimy little joint—I'm pretty damn proud of it—how it makes a big difference around here. What do you say?"

My hands still hadn't stopped shaking. "Well," I said, "I actually need to do this now."

"Now? Like today?"

"Yeah."

He cleared his throat, a little too loudly. "Look, Gus, today's just impossible. I got a huge shipment to get out of here."

"We can do it over the phone. What I'm working on is this tax abatement—"

"No. I can't do it now. Tomorrow."

Now that I'd heard his anger turn to feigned calm and finally to desperation, my initial fear of Vidigan began leaching away. I'd worried for a second or two that maybe he had a perfectly reasonable explanation for hiring softball ringers, that maybe my story wasn't a story after all, maybe I'd wasted my time breaking the law with Darlene at the courthouse. But now I was sure, without even hearing what he had to say, that I really did have a story.

"Mr. Vidigan," I said. "We plan to run this story in tomorrow's paper. If you want to comment, now is the time."

There was another long pause before he said, "OK. I get it. You want to fuck me at the town council."

"I just want to report—"

"Don't give me that happy horseshit. You just want a feather in your fucking cap."

"Mr. Vidigan, everything you say now is on the record."

"Oh, ho, ho, fuck you," he said. He sounded like he was choking. "Put this in your piece-of-shit paper: I will cave your goddamn—"

"If I don't hear from you or your lawyers, I'll assume you didn't want to comment. Thanks."

Now I hung up.

. . .

Henry went through the story with me line by line, asking what I knew, how I knew it, whether I'd double- and triple-checked all my facts. When we'd finished, he gave me one of his big, crinkly smiles and said, "Goddamn headline ought to be, 'College Kid Raises Hometown Hell.'" The actual headline, bannered across the top of the front page, read, "Town Strikes Out on Perfect-O-Screw Abatement."

That evening, the town council rejected the company's application for a new tax break, canceled the original abatement, and authorized the town attorney to sue Perfect-O-Screw for $83,174.98 in back property taxes. Cecil Vidigan didn't attend, but eighty-seven citizens did, quite a turnout for an August council meeting. I counted every one. For a few hours, people talked about something I'd done that had nothing to do with that state title game.

After the meeting, I went back to the *Pilot*. Deadlines had passed, the newsroom was empty, and I didn't have to file a story on the meeting until the next morning. But I didn't want to go home yet. On my desk I found a copy of that day's paper with a note scrawled across it in black Magic Marker. "Here's how you know you had a helluva scoop," Henry had written. "The mayor called to complain about not being quoted." I took it into Henry's office and grabbed a Bud out of the mini-fridge beneath his desk. I propped my feet up on the desk and reread my story about twenty times. I kept thinking, This is just what my professors taught: Comfort the afflicted, afflict the comfortable. I had exposed a cheat and saved the town money. That's what real journalists did.

But there was something else, too, that kept me sitting there reading my story again and again into the middle of the night. I was a short, skinny college kid who'd gone toe-to-toe with a captain of industry, or at least what passed for one in Starvation Lake, a man of means and stature and raw, purposeful anger. And I'd beaten him.

Two years later, after I'd graduated from college, the scissored-out clips of my Perfect-O-Screw stories would impress a *Detroit Times* editor enough that she'd hire me as a general assignment reporter for the business section. By then Perfect-O-Screw would be out of business, and Cecil Vidigan would be rumored to be running a golf driving range somewhere in the Upper Peninsula.

But on the night I changed his life, I sat with my feet up and a beer in my hand and decided that if something could make me feel this good for even one night, and it didn't hurt anyone who didn't deserve to be hurt, maybe it was something I could actually do, something I might actually be good at, something that might actually make somebody proud of me.

fourteen

The morning after Dingus surprised me in my apartment, I slept until eleven. Dinner at Mom's wasn't until twelve-thirty, so after showering and dressing I went down to the *Pilot* to square a few things away.

The newsroom was empty. I expected Joanie but left the ceiling lights off. I couldn't bear the buzzing of those fluorescent lamps when I was alone. Instead I snapped on my desk lamp and proceeded to clear the mess on my desk, filling most of two garbage cans with old printouts, newspapers, and disposable coffee cups. I opened Saturday's mail: lunch menus for the elementary school. A press release about promotions at a local insurance firm. A one-page announcement that the Starvation Lake Lions Club had named Emil J. "Bud" Popke as its Man of the Year. The Lions Club didn't send a photograph of Popke. I didn't know whether we had one, and Tillie didn't like me messing around in the photo file cabinets, so I jotted her a note to make a photo assignment.

As I worked, I pondered: What was Teddy Boynton really after at Enright's? What was on the napkin he pulled from his pocket? Why was Dingus being at once so solicitous and so evasive? Beneath it all I was dreading having to call my attorney downstate. My Detroit troubles were far from over.

I set the copies of the police report and the $25,000 receipt Dingus had given me next to my computer. I dialed Mom. Her answering machine came on, and I pressed the phone to my ear. My mother talked so fast that it often was hard to understand her recorded messages. But you had to listen because she constantly updated them for whatever was on her schedule: bingo, crochet, euchre, Meals on

Wheels. Sometimes she actually called her own phone to find out where she was supposed to be. This morning she rattled off something about church and supper and meeting someone named either Felicia or Theresa at what sounded like the community center. "Mom," I said after the beep, "I'm going to stop on the way over to start the Bonnie."

For Monday's *Pilot*, I'd gotten most of the stories and headlines ready on Friday and Saturday. All that remained were Joanie's two Blackburn stories, which she had yet to file. Which reminded me: Joanie had also been at Enright's. I guessed that she'd wanted to see the pictures of Blackburn and the Rats, and maybe chat up Francis a bit. But if she really was looking for people who knew Coach, why hadn't she hung around until the playoff games were over and all the skaters came in?

Just before noon, I grabbed my jacket and walked up front to check the answering machine. One of the five messages was from Arthur Fleming, Boynton's lawyer, left at 8:07 that morning. "Mr. Carpenter," he said, "please call me at your earliest convenience so we can review the status of the article we discussed." I went back to my desk for the document Fleming and Boynton had given me, but didn't see it lying where I was sure I'd left it. I rummaged through the stack of papers next to my computer, checked my in- and out-boxes, pulled open a couple of drawers, but couldn't find it. I looked under the desk and riffled through the stuff in the garbage cans. Still nothing. I decided I'd look later.

Half a mile from Mom's, I swung my pickup truck left off Beach onto Horvath Road. My dad had bought property in the hills overlooking the lake's southwestern end, not far from our house. Atop a short rise jutting from a copse of pines he built a one-car garage. There, he told my mother, he'd have the peace to pursue his hobby of rebuilding motors for go-carts, lawnmowers, and other gadgets. But most of his time he spent gazing out over the lake on a deck he built atop the garage. On summer evenings, he'd sit in a rocking chair with a beer and a cigar, timing sundown against what the weatherman had predicted.

He called it his tree house. It was a simple platform of two-by-eight planks ringed by two-by-four rails. In the rafters beneath it Dad built a closet with a door where he stowed cigars, a transistor radio, a miniature fridge, and some girlie magazines. He kept it locked, he said, because I was too young to be looking at those magazines. Sometimes he took me up on the deck, though, and we'd put the Tigers on the radio. I could still taste the potato-chip salt, the onion in the chip dip, the sweet orange pop washing it all down. Now and then Dad would joke with Mom that he was going to install a bumper-pool table and a wet bar and apply for a liquor license. Mom would say, "I'm sorry, I don't think you can get a license if no girls are allowed." Dad would wink and say, "Not worth the trouble then."

The garage eventually became home to the last car he bought before he died. Dad had worked construction, installing drywall, so he drove a pickup truck. But he always talked about owning a Cadillac, if only just for Sunday drives to Lake Michigan. He set aside a little money every week for years. For a while he had a second job on weekend nights. I didn't understand much about parents, but I knew Mom didn't like him working Saturday nights and neither did I because that's when we went to Dairy Queen and Mom never seemed to be in the mood without Dad around.

He was still short of affording a Caddy when his doctor told him about the cancer. When later tests confirmed his condition, he left the doctor's office and drove straight to a car dealership in Grayling. He bought a used 1969 Pontiac Bonneville, gold with a cream vinyl roof, power windows, power seats, air conditioning, and a trunk the size of a swimming pool. When he brought it home, Mom took a look at it and her face tightened up as if she were going to cry. "Oh, Rudy," was all she said. From my bedroom that night I overheard them in the kitchen, speaking in strained whispers. I couldn't make out everything, but it seemed my mother wanted to understand why after all that hoping and saving Dad hadn't gotten the Cadillac after all. My father kept saying something about an "investment." I didn't know what that was.

When I was old enough to drive, Mom wouldn't let me take the Bonnie because she said it reminded her too much of Dad. But she couldn't bring herself to get rid of it, either. We stored it in the garage beneath Dad's tree house. Every six months or so, I'd go up and start the engine and let it run for a while, and once a year, I changed the oil and the spark plugs and updated the license plates. Even when I was living in Detroit, I made a point to drive up and service the Bonnie. If I forgot or procrastinated, Mom got on me, though she never ventured up there herself. Sometimes on summer evenings I'd clamber up the ladder to the tree house and lean against the railing.

Dad had cut a two-track road straight up to the garage through an archway of pines. I parked my truck on Horvath and trudged up the snow-covered two-track to the garage. Icicles the size of baseball bats hung from the eaves. I unlocked the side door and stepped inside. It smelled faintly of oil. A blast of cold smacked me in the face as I lifted the big garage door open.

The Bonnie started right up when I turned the key. The radio reception wasn't good, but I could make out the voice of a news announcer from WJR, the Detroit station that carried Tiger and Red Wing games. I switched it off and pushed an eight-track tape into the player Dad had installed beneath the dashboard. Even though I never drove the Bonnie, as a teenager I'd liked to sit in it alone and listen to Dad's music. My father loved rock and roll. His favorite was Bob Seger. Dad and his younger cousin, Eddie, had seen Seger and his band live at a club in Ann Arbor in 1968, two days before Eddie went off to army boot camp. For weeks the Seger show was all Dad could talk about. Then came word that a rocket had torn Eddie's chopper from the sky over a jungle crawling with Vietcong. Dad got quiet after that. He took that second job. He found out about the cancer.

Through it all, he played Seger on the record player in the house, over and over, the same record, the same song.

I pushed a button on the eight-track and played it: *I just want a simple answer why it is I've got to die / I'm a simple-minded guy / two plus two is on my mind.*

The bass throbbed, the guitar wailed, Seger howled. I turned it up and closed my eyes, recalling a summer Sunday afternoon before Eddie was killed, before the cancer, before Dad got quiet. Dad was working on our dock. I was playing army with Soupy and some other kids. I came running around the house wearing a plastic helmet and carrying a toy rifle. Dad was waiting by the birch tree. Sweat stuck his T-shirt to the skin at his collarbone. "Hey, Gus," he said. "Want to play some ball?" I pulled up for just a second and said, "Not now." Hurrying past him, I glimpsed just enough of the look on his face to wish I'd said yes. But I kept running. Every time I thought about it, I wished I could go back and tell him yes. Whenever I visited the Bonnie, I made myself think about it.

The song ended. I opened my eyes. "Two plus two is on *my* mind," I said aloud, and I had a little laugh. Wind had dusted the hood of the Bonnie with snow. I turned off the car, brushed the snow off the hood with my sleeve, and closed up the garage.

As I pulled into Mom's driveway, I saw her working in the kitchen of the little yellow house she and Dad had built when Starvation was not a vacation destination and a dry-waller and his wife could afford a hundred feet of lakefront property. She was making gravy when I walked in. I put my arm around her and pecked her on the cheek. The aroma of her perfume mixed with that of the pot roast simmering in onions. "Smells good," I said.

She poked me in the ribs with her spoon handle. "Could you be sweet and get me a gravy boat? In the china cabinet, bottom shelf, back-left corner."

She was talking too fast. "A what?"

"A gravy boat, dear. Gravy boat."

In the living room I looked through the big glass sliding door at the still, white lake. I'd always thought the lake looked bigger and more dangerous in the winter. The china cabinet stood along a wall filled with photographs of Mom and Dad and me, and framed needlepoint designs Mom had made, including one of a goaltender in his ready crouch. I took the gravy boat into the kitchen. Mom hummed off-key as she worked. She was glad to have me home, despite the unpleasant circumstance of my return. She hadn't asked much about it. But then she'd never wanted me to go to Detroit in the first place.

"You had a busy week," she said as she ladled gravy from the steaming pan. "But, Gussy, how could you put that woman in your story? Here, let's sit." She set the gravy down on the kitchen table next to the platter heaped with beef and potatoes and carrots. She sat, as always, at the end near the kitchen and I sat to her right. Across from me a place was set, as always, for my father.

"What woman?" I said.

"Oh, you know, that whatshername, that nurse. Gloria. Gloria Lowinski."

That was the nurse in Tillie's Monica story. So somebody had actually read it. I speared a chunk of pot roast. "What about her?"

"Dear," my mother said, as if it were obvious, "Gloria Lowinski is the biggest blabbermouth in town. She talks about her patients at Dr. Johnson's office, for God's sakes. She doesn't need to be encouraged."

"Who's Dr. Johnson?"

Mom crooked an eyebrow at me as she spooned applesauce onto our plates. "A gynecologist, dear. Gloria is his nurse. I used to go there until, well, you don't want to know, but suffice to say that Gloria's lips were flapping and I finally had to switch to Dr. Schmidt in Kalkaska."

"Oh."

We ate quietly for a few minutes. I wanted to eat until I was too full and then go take a nap in the living room. I couldn't, of course.

I had a paper to get out. As I chewed I gazed across the table at my father's setting. After Dad died, Coach Blackburn had sat there for Sunday dinners, until he stopped coming.

"So," I said, "what do you think of the snowmobile thing?"

Either she didn't hear me or she ignored me. "Are you still playing your season, honey?"

"It's almost over."

"You sound like you're glad. It used to be I'd have to go out and drag you off the ice. Remember how your toes got frostbite? If you don't like to play anymore, why do you play?"

"I do like to play, Mom." Once I got myself to the rink and pulled my gear on and got on the ice, I usually did like to play, just like I once did. "I have a lot on my mind."

"If you say so."

"So what did you think about this snowmobile that washed up?"

"Not much, really."

That wasn't like my mother. "They say it's Coach's."

"Well, I don't see how that's possible when Jack died right out there on the lake. I stood at that window and watched all those people gawking at the hole in the ice. Unless you believe those silly stories about tunnels under the lake."

"Sometimes I wish I did."

"How's the roast? Good? I left it on too long."

"It's great. You know, I've had to deal with Dingus a bit. He's kind of weird."

"Oh, tell me about it. Dingus hasn't been right for years. He never leaves that office. Does he have a bunk in there or something?"

"Didn't notice. Has he always been this way?"

"You were still down in Detroit, son, but no, Dingus used to be out and about like anybody else when he was with Barbara. You'd see them at the Legion dances and at the Avalon, all over the place. Let's face it, honey, Dingus isn't the prettiest kitten in the litter, but he and Barbara made a very cute couple. He adored her."

"I guess so. He still keeps her picture in his office."

Mom shook her head. "Barbara. Now there's another one. What that girl was thinking, I will never know. Don't get me wrong, I love Barbara, I just—I never understood how she could just go off with somebody else."

"Somebody else who?"

Mom stiffened a little; she knew she'd said too much.

"It doesn't matter, dear."

"Come on. Who'd she go off with?"

"She didn't really—I mean she didn't actually marry somebody else."

"OK, but who?"

Mom started to get up. "I have cherry pie."

"Sit down, Mom."

She gave me one of those looks that said this was something I didn't need to know. And then of course I knew.

"Whoa," I said. "Coach?"

"Oh, my gosh, who cares? How did we get on this subject?"

"I knew Coach was the ladies' man, all right, but I didn't know about Barbara. Man, I missed all the fun when I was downstate. So Dingus divorced her?"

She sighed. "No, he didn't divorce her. He wanted her back. She wanted Jack. But Jack wasn't marrying anybody."

"And where's she now?"

"Last I heard, the IGA in Sandy Cove. Or maybe Kalkaska."

"Wow. Just like that." I scooped more potatoes onto my plate. "You dated Coach for a bit, Mom. What did you think?"

"No, I wouldn't call it *dating*. We went to a show once or twice, dinner a couple of times. No big deal, really. Now, your friend Tillie, she actually *dated* dated him."

I remembered seeing Tillie at a few of our games. She still had most of her beauty then. "Weren't they just drinking buddies?" I said.

"Well, maybe so. Tillie is everyone's drinking buddy, isn't she?" Mom stood. "Would you like ice cream on your pie?"

"Sure."

She went into the kitchen. I heard the microwave start, the freezer door open and shut, a fork clink. My mother was never this quiet. She came back and set the pie and a cup of coffee in front of me. "Thanks, Mom," I said. I nodded at the chair across the table. "Remember when Coach used to come to dinner?"

"Of course. The man was a garbage disposal."

"Do you remember how he always used to talk about coaching in Canada, how great the kids were up there?"

"Vaguely, dear. I never paid much attention to all that hockey stuff."

Yes, she did, I thought. She was always asking whether the parents in Canada were as obnoxious as the ones in Michigan. "You don't remember him saying anything about taking a year off from coaching, do you?"

"I remember him talking about all those championships he almost won." Four fantastic years, I thought. "Your mother's an old lady, Gussy. It's all a blur now."

I set my fork down. "Mom. I know we've never really talked about this."

"About what?"

"About the night Coach died."

I'd asked her only once before. It was the evening of Coach's funeral. We were sitting in the back of the American Legion hall. Drunken former River Rats and their dads were toasting Coach at a microphone. At first Mom pretended she hadn't heard my question. I asked again. She patted my knee. "Let's listen, dear." I persisted. "Didn't you hear me?" she said. I thought she was going to cry. I let it go.

Now she said, "That was so long ago. Who cares?"

"It's my job. His snowmobile washed up on the wrong lake."

"I'm sure it's all a misunderstanding and Dingus will clear it up."

"No, it's not a misunderstanding. Help me out here."

She sipped her coffee. "It was bingo night. Or maybe bowling night—sweet Lord, my memory's gone—I just remember I was sleeping like a baby, so I must've been out late. Leo must've been banging a while before I woke up."

"He was at the slider?"

"No." She waved toward the kitchen. "He came in the back door. I couldn't make him out at first, because there was something bright shining in my eyes—the headlights on his snowmobile—and I was half asleep. Scared the devil out of me."

If Leo really had come to the back door, then he would have come from the road behind the house. But why wouldn't he have come directly from the scene of the accident and crossed the lake and come up the hill to the sliding door facing the lake?

"And he came in the house?"

"Yes. I remember he had liquor on his breath because it turned my stomach. And he was loud, which wasn't like Leo. He said we had to call the police, call nine one one, Jack drowned in the lake. He kept saying—forgive my language, Lord—'Goddamn Jack, Goddamn Jack,' over and over, and he seemed so angry." She looked at me uncertainly. "It makes sense, doesn't it?"

"What?"

"That he was angry."

Why would she wonder about that now?

"Sure," I said.

She pointed at the living room. "He came in here. I tried to make him sit down, but he just stood at the window like this"—she wrapped her arms around herself—"staring out at the lake until the police came. Dingus was with them. They went out to the lake."

"Was he wet?"

"Who?"

"Leo. Was he wet? At least his shoulders and his head? Were there icicles in his hair?"

"Icicles? Why?"

"Because he just tried to pull Coach out of the lake."

"Well then, I guess he must have. I don't remember."

"Did you give him a towel?"

"Are you interviewing me, son?"

"Mom. You were here. I just want to know."

"What good is it going to do, Gussy?"

I finished the last of my pie. "God, that's good," I said. "Thanks."

"You're welcome, dear."

"You know, I went back and reread the *Pilot* stories from back then. I didn't see your name in there. How did you keep the reporters away?"

"I didn't, dear. Henry Bridgman called and called and I think he even stopped by one night. But the police asked me to keep quiet because they were investigating. I did what I was told."

"Dingus said to keep quiet?"

"Not Dingus. He was just a deputy. Sheriff Spardell."

"And what about the towel?"

She looked into her coffee cup. "Gus, that was so long ago. Why would I be worrying about—"

A flurry of loud knocks came at the kitchen door. Mom turned. "Who could that be?"

Through the kitchen window I saw Joanie's red Honda Civic parked on the road shoulder. "I'll get it," I said.

Joanie stood on the back porch in a hooded sweatshirt, her hands stuffed inside the belly pocket. I stepped outside. "Where's your coat?" I said. "It's freezing."

"I knew it."

"You knew what?"

"There's a bullet hole."

"What?"

"There's a bullet hole in the snowmobile. That's what the forensics were about. A bullet hole. Somebody shot Blackburn."

I glanced to make sure Mom wasn't standing behind me. "Keep it down," I said. "How do you know?"

She hesitated just long enough to make me resent her for not trusting me. "A department source," she said.

D'Alessio, I thought. Always working it. "OK. Good. Go back and start writing. I'll be there in fifteen minutes."

"This is huge."

"Yep. Good work."

I knew how she felt, knowing she had a juicy story. But I just felt empty and stupid, like I'd never known anything at all.

Inside, Mom was at the sink, scraping the roasting pan. "Sorry, Mom, duty calls," I said. "Dinner was fantastic."

She turned to hug me. She held the squeeze a little longer than usual. "I wish you could stay. I love you."

"I love you, too."

As I started my truck, I thought, She remembered Leo's liquor breath but not a towel because she didn't give him a towel, because she didn't need to.

I parked in front of the *Pilot* and crossed Main Street to Enright's. Inside, Loob was washing mugs behind the bar while music videos played silently on the TV overhead.

"Dude," Loob said. "Brewski?"

"Loob. No, listen—were you here all last night?"

"Came in around six-thirty." He jammed the mugs one by one onto a soapy brush sticking up out of the sink, then rinsed them in milky water.

"Did you see my reporter in here? Joanie?"

"You mean pretty-not-skinny?"

"Uh, yeah."

"Yeah, she was here for a bit. Two Diet Cokes. Left me a quarter."

"You talk to her?"

Loob held a glass up to a bar lamp, decided it was clean, and set it in the drainer. "I suppose."

"Francis said she was asking questions."

"She didn't ask me no questions." He dried his hands with a towel. "But she did give me a message."

"For who?"

"Teddy."

"Boynton?"

"No, Teddy Roosevelt. Man, goalies."

"What was the message?"

He grinned. "Heard you took a little holiday on the ice last night, Gus. Ain't you cured of that by now?"

"There is no cure. What was the message?"

"She wrote it on a napkin. But it's none of my business, Gus."

"Uh-huh."

As the main bartender at Enright's, Loob probably knew more secrets than anyone in town, except Audrey at the diner. The difference was, Audrey could keep them. Loob picked up the TV remote and changed the channel. The president appeared on the screen. He looked angry, wagging his finger. Loob shut it off. "Fugging joke," he said.

"Yep. Can you tell me what Joanie wrote?"

"Oh, I don't know, maybe an address and phone number."

"*Her* address and phone number?"

"How the hell would I know, Gus? Look, I got work to do."

"Francis here?"

Loob cocked his head and pointed past the photograph of jubilant Soupy on the back wall. "In his office."

As I started back, Loob called out, "Hey, Teddy banging her?"

"Not literally."

"Augustus! To what do I owe the honor?"

Francis Dufresne looked up from the cluttered desk where he sat counting money and punching a calculator. Thick stacks of ones, fives, tens, twenties, and fifties were piled neatly alongside a metal lockbox.

"Just checking to make sure you're in business."

"Ho," he said. "So long as Alden Campbell keeps drinking, I'll be in business. The apple doesn't fall far from the tree. Sit down."

His office was a converted closet that smelled of whiskey and disinfectant. I sat on some vodka cases stacked against the wall. Tacked behind his head was a dog-eared certificate that read, "Francis J. Dufresne, 1980 Northern Michigan Bartender of the Year." Next to it hung a bulletin board checkered with receipts and invoices and old River Rats schedules. At the top was a calendar from First Fisherman's Bank of Charlevoix, November 1986. A rendering on the calendar showed a woman in her Sunday best sitting with a grinning banker. Someone had penned crude quote bubbles over their heads. "I'll bet you'd like to screw me," the woman said, and the banker replied, "Sure would! No need to undress, though!"

Francis noticed me looking at it and smiled. "Some downstaters bought that old bank and then, guess what? No more free calendars."

I pointed at the nameplate. "What's the J for?"

"Not a thing, actually. Mother just fancied the sound of it. As if I was going to be somebody, ha!"

We talked about the weather and about the Rats losing again to the Pipefitters. Francis was kind enough not to bring up my distant past. Finally, he said, "What can I do you for?"

"Any chance you're going to be at the zoning board meeting tomorrow?"

He grunted. "How is your mom?"

"She's fine."

He set one stack of bills down, punched a few numbers into the calculator, and picked up another stack. "I've been thinking about her. And you, Augustus. This must be a difficult time for the both of you. I know you and Jack had a bit of a falling-out."

"He had his reasons."

"We all got our reasons—or our rationalizations. Sometimes Jack just took it too far. He did with you, in my humble opinion, and

I told him so. But he was a stubborn cuss. For Pete's sake, it's just a lousy hockey game. You were a damned fine goalie."

"Thanks." It sounded a little strange coming from the guy who made Coach his star pitchman, who used the town's love of hockey to open its collective wallet. But it felt good anyway.

"You know," he said, "it's too bad your dad's not around. Now there was a fine fellow, Rudy. I wish . . . well, you know. Can't do anything about the past. He was a friend, you know. You were just a little guy. We used to go fishing now and then."

My stomach rose and dipped. I had one sharp-as-a-knife memory of Dad's fishing. I was four or five years old, standing on my toes, peering across the big round picnic table behind my grandfather's house along the Hungry River. The table was covered with damp newspapers. Dad and Grandpa and Grandpa's brothers were cleaning the perch and bluegill they'd caught while I was still sleeping. There were a pile of fish filets, another pile of fish guts and scales, a bunch of longneck bottles of Buckhorn beer, and a transistor radio tuned to Ernie Harwell broadcasting the Tiger game.

"Really?" I said.

"Yeah. Bowled with him, too, up to Mancelona. He had one beautiful hook, he did. And whenever he got a strike, he'd spin around on one foot and take his beer and hold it out in front of him like a toast and say, 'How sweet it is,' just like old Jackie Gleason on TV. 'How sweet it is.'"

We both laughed.

"And then there was Jack," Francis said. "Hell of a coach, no denying that. But like I say, sometimes he just took it too far. All that stuff about how losing is good for winning." He stopped shuffling the bills and grinned. "I finally had to tell him, not in my business, Jack. Losing ain't ever good in business."

"So does that mean you're going to the zoning board?"

"Ho-ho, OK, you got some questions. Tell you the truth, I haven't really thought about it." Sure he hadn't. "I'm supposed to be up in Gaylord about the same time."

"So Teddy'll handle it?"

Francis resumed stacking the bills. "First let me ask you, are you going to be quoting me? You're a friend, so I'd like to be candid, but it's hard to be candid if you're going to be quoting me in the paper." He smiled. "Got too many dear friends to make into enemies, if you know what I mean."

I was reluctant, but I knew where I could find him. "All right."

"It's not like I have a flock of secrets to set loose," he said. "You've probably heard old Theodore and I aren't, well, we aren't working elbow to elbow as much anymore. I think the young fellow's sort of feeling his oats. He doesn't think he needs the old guy holding him back."

"Holding him back from what?"

"Ha! Lots of questions bottled up in that one, Augustus."

"Like?"

"Like"—he arched a bushy eyebrow—"does Mr. Boynton really want a new marina?"

"Why else would he be going to all this trouble?"

Francis chortled. "Well, I probably shouldn't be saying these things, Augustus. But I trust you. So let me just give you one little thought. It's something you probably wouldn't know unless you're in my business."

"Please."

"Well," he said. "Do I really want to say this?" He sat thinking for a minute. Then he said, "OK. We are off the record. And I mean no disrespect. Theodore is a capable young man. To his credit, he's built a few things. But mostly, he's not a builder. No, he's a bleeder. He bleeds things. Bleeds them dry."

"Like what?"

"Remember that little strip mall he bought out by Estes Corner?"

"I thought you both worked on that."

"I had a couple of dollars in it, but I was strictly silent. Theodore was the one who wanted to buy the thing. He said it had all sorts of potential, being at a crossroads, to scoop up traffic between Starvation and Sandy Cove. And at first he made like he was actually going to make some improvements and run the thing. But then he just bled it. Borrowed up to the keister, took the cash, put some in his pocket, and funneled the rest into his next victim, that duplex out on Morrissey. Then he bled that one, too."

"The strip mall's all boarded up."

"Yes, sir, 'tis. And you know where the cash for that originally came from? The old Avalon cinema. And where's that now? Boarded up. You see, son, Mr. Boynton is pretty good at the back-and-forth, at the negotiations. It's all a game to him, and he likes games, especially ones he can win. But he's not so keen on the actual running of things like stores and restaurants and movie theaters. Once he makes his deal, he wants to collect up his winnings and go home."

"But he doesn't have any winnings until he runs the things."

"You and I agree on that, Augustus. But that's not how Theodore sees it. That's why he and I aren't working so closely these days. He thinks I'm an old man with old-fashioned ideas, like owing everybody and their brother money is a bad idea, not a good one. Like keeping your money with the folks who made you what you are."

"What do you mean, Francis? You've been in on the projects in Sandy Cove and other places, haven't you?"

He leaned forward and wagged his finger in my face. "No, Augustus, see, this is where your paper hasn't gotten the facts quite right. Not that I can really blame you, because how were you to know? But I'll let you in on a little secret: Theodore and I have had some knock-down, drag-outs over these Sandy Cove projects, including that movie house we're supposed to be fixing up. I think our money should stay right here"—he pointed downward for emphasis—"and not be going hither and yon just because there's a few more dollars to be made, like we're a couple of damn carpetbaggers."

"Why don't you just walk away then?"

"Well, it isn't that simple when you've got all sorts of money tied up in the business, but I'm almost there. And that'll be a good day for Starvation Lake."

"What about the marina?"

Francis turned and began fitting the stacks of bills into the lock-box. "What about it? After the zoning board does Theodore's will—and they will, trust me, if not tomorrow then soon enough, because they're all so deathly afraid that Theodore and his lamebrained little lawyer might sue them—then I would be shocked, son, absolutely shocked, if a single piece of structural steel ever went up out there. Mark my words. Theodore has no desire to run a marina. That's a big, big operation. Alden is not much better than Angus was at running his show, but at least it's there."

"What's Teddy going to do if not build a marina?"

Francis snapped the lockbox shut. "Have you not listened to a word I said, son? He'll bleed it, bleed it for all it's worth. The minute he gets the zoning, his lender will release his first draw. Five million dollars, son. He's going to run that down the street to First Financial here and pay off some of what he owes on his other properties. The condos on the north shore, that strip mall. He's leveraged up to his neck. Why do you think he's borrowing the marina money from a bank down in Saginaw? Because nobody here'll touch him. Behind all the smiles and the handshakes, believe me, Mr. Boynton these days is a desperate man. One little thing goes wrong and all his debtors are going to come down on him like a shithouse of bricks."

"Aren't you in on the marina?"

"Well, yes and no. I have a sort of token investment presence, a few dollars, as a personal favor to Theodore, who's been with me on many a transaction, after all. I'll do everything I can to make sure he builds it. Maybe he'll surprise me."

As Francis talked, I thought of the deal Teddy had offered Soupy. If Francis was right, it would mean that Soupy would surrender his interest in the old marina in return for a potentially worthless stake in one that might never be built. Teddy would get a marina, all right, just not a new one. Soupy would be left high and dry. And if Teddy bled the old marina like Francis said he'd bled everything else, the town would be left high and dry too. I decided Francis probably didn't know about the settlement. "I worry about Soupy," I said.

"I'll bet you do," he said. "I worry, too. I knew his father. Alden's not a bad boy, just a little immature."

"That's for sure." Thinking of the marina reminded me of something. "I've got another kind of stupid question."

"No stupid questions, son, just stupid answers."

"Right. Did the town ever buy, or even consider buying, a ferry-boat of any sort? Like, maybe to take people across the river? Seems crazy, I know."

Francis chuckled. "Well, you're not so far off. There was some idle talk way back, must have been the late sixties, before Jack showed up and we got things moving around here. But why do we need a ferry for the river? A child can swim it."

True. Anyway, that marina receipt was from 1988. I stood to leave. "Thanks, Francis. You know, if you change your mind about being quoted—"

"Oh, no, don't even think about it. I want to help you. You know what you know now and you'll have to find ways to get it in your paper other than quoting your faithful barkeep. Maybe it'll give you something to do besides dig up Jack Blackburn's grave, God rest his soul."

"I'm going to be busy."

"Aren't we all? This working stuff is never going to be popular."

"You know," I said, "I wasn't around when Coach died. I just came in for the funeral. But maybe you know why they didn't drag the lake. Seemed like the thing to do, don't you think?"

Francis frowned. "Like I said, son, I really don't like digging all of this up. The remains, you know, they never smell so good, if you know what I mean. But on this, well, hell, it's been a long time, and I can't say as I remember. Something to do with the budget, I think. The town council made that decision. You could probably look it up. Have you checked the minutes of the council meetings?"

"Have not." I made a mental note to check in the morning. Because the county handled the town's records, too, I'd have to deal with County Clerk Verna Clark, who still presided over the files like a sentry at the castle gate. I allowed myself a moment's recollection of that night long ago in the closet, how Darlene's eyes glinted in the dark.

Francis grabbed his phone. "Excuse me one moment," he said.

I waited while he dialed. "And a good Sunday to you, my friend," he said into the phone. "Just quickly now—that matter we spoke about the other night? Right. I need it taken care of first thing tomorrow. Thank you."

He hung up. "Sorry," he said. "My memory's going so bad I have to do a thing as soon as it pops into my head or it's gone for a month."

"I appreciate your help. I know you'd rather we left this alone. You mind if I check in with you later?"

"I suppose not," he said. "I guess we can't leave the past buried, eh? I'll admit it, between you and me, I'd like to know just what the heck happened to Jack too. You're talking to Leo Redpath?"

"Trying to."

"Well, keep me undercover and I'll help you best I can."

I was glad to hear that.

fifteen

Back at the *Pilot*, black-and-white photographs of a couple in wedding attire covered Delbert Riddle's desk. The faint reek of a stogie and the tang of film-developing chemicals hung on the air.

"Stop the presses," I said. "Delbert was actually here?"

"I can confirm a sighting," Joanie said. "But the minute I started asking about pictures for my story, he was out the door."

In his twenty-nine years as the *Pilot*'s sole staff photographer, Delbert had taken a picture of just about everyone in Starvation Lake. The way he saw it, one good picture was plenty, no matter that over the years people got older, fatter, grayer, balder. "Readers understand," he'd say whenever he balked at taking a fresh picture of someone he hadn't photographed in a decade. "It's nostalgic for people to see how their neighbors looked a long time ago."

As for Delbert's own face, he rarely showed it at the *Pilot*, except to develop pictures, most of which, as far as I could tell, were for his sideline. I doubted those wedding pictures were for the *Pilot*, although I assumed—or hoped—he'd let us publish one. Henry kept him on, maybe because it was difficult to lure competent shooters to little towns with nasty winters. Delbert came through when we needed him. He also kept meticulous, alphabetized files of all the photos he'd taken in six steel file cabinets up front.

"What photos do we have for your stories?" I said.

"We could use a shot of Blackburn's funeral," Joanie said. "And one of Dingus."

"I should've thought to have a map made of where Blackburn went down. Too late now."

"He knew Blackburn, you know."

"Delbert? Yeah, he took pictures of him. Or at least one picture."

"He used to develop game films or something too. Said he made a few dollars off him."

Coach had had an 8-millimeter movie camera for recording games and the occasional practice. Leo operated it from the bleachers. I hadn't known that Delbert did the developing.

"Busy guy, Delbert," I said. "Though you'd never know it around here."

I sat down at my desk, and there, right where I thought I'd left it, lay the dossier on Soupy's legal troubles. I resisted the urge to ask Joanie if she'd borrowed it, figuring it was smarter to have her focus on her stories for now. I grabbed a pen and on my blotter jotted, "Council minutes mon a.m." Joanie sat across the room, still wearing her wool scarf. "Listen," I said. "I don't want to keep you from your writing, but how exactly do the cops know it's a bullet hole?"

She stopped typing and let her hands hover motionless over the keyboard, as though she were deciding whether even to acknowledge my question. Be patient, I told myself. She dropped her hands to her knees and turned to face me. Her eyes locked on mine, then went to the clock, then back. "I sent you the Blackburn sidebar," she said. "Now I really need to just write this. OK, boss?"

"Yes, you can write it, and we're going to run it, but first I need to know a few things, and I really don't need a lot of your 'OK, boss' crap right now, OK?"

What I'd heard at Mom's had unsettled me enough. Then came the news of the bullet hole, and Francis's accusations of Teddy. My head was filled with unanswered questions about $25,000 receipts and ferryboats and vague details in police reports. I was beginning to think everybody in Starvation Lake knew more than I did, and it was starting to piss me off.

"Take a chill pill," Joanie said. "I don't know much, but what I know, I know. There's a bullet hole, and that's news."

"Agreed. Got two sources?"

"Yes."

I assumed D'Alessio was one. "What does Dingus say?"

"Not talking."

The story would certainly raise a ruckus. Although the word "murder" wasn't about to appear in our stories, everyone would read it between the lines. Most people didn't want to hear that Jack Blackburn had been murdered. I wanted to be sure we were right. Or at least close.

"Let's just talk here, between us," I said. "Think about it. How the hell do you know there's a bullet hole in something that's been submerged in eighty feet of water for ten years? How can you be sure?"

She drew herself up in the chair and gave me a knowing smile. How sweet it was to have a dumb-shit editor ask you a question to which you had the perfect reply. "Well," she said, "they have a bullet."

"They do? What caliber?"

"Twenty-two."

Who in Starvation Lake owned a .22-caliber handgun or rifle? Just about everybody. It wasn't much good for killing deer, but it was handy for muskrats and chipmunks. "Where was it?" I said. "Did it lodge somewhere inside the snowmobile or—"

The phone on my desk rang. I slid back and grabbed it. "*Pilot*."

I heard static, then, "Trap." Soupy was on his truck phone. I could hear the pickup's rumble.

"Yeah?"

"I've got to talk to you, man."

"I'm on deadline. Drop down later."

"Not your office."

For some reason, Soupy would never come to the *Pilot*. Since returning to town, I'd asked him to meet me there a few times and each time he'd made an excuse.

"Enright's then?" I said. "Seven?"

Another burst of static made me pull the phone away from my

ear. "No," I heard him say. "Fuck." He'd been drinking. He sounded like he was talking with a mouthful of fishhooks. "Trap," he said. "I'll—" Static obliterated him. The phone went dead.

"What?" Joanie said.

I shook my head. "Where were we?"

"You asked where the bullet was. In the snowmobile, obviously. But I don't know exactly. My source was being a little cagey."

No, I thought, D'Alessio was too dumb to be cagey. "Hold on—were there any reports of gunshots being fired that night?"

"Not on Starvation Lake."

"Of course, and this happened—well, shit, we don't know where the hell it happened. Or even what happened. Are the cops saying—wait, are the cops actually saying it was murder?"

"The cops aren't saying anything, officially. But there's a press conference tomorrow. I overheard a dispatcher calling the TV guys."

"So that's your second source? Of course. TV brings the Dingus bear out of hibernation."

"Yes. So can I please write this now?"

For the next hour, the only sounds in the room were the clacking of our keyboards and the rattle of the printer. Joanie's profile of Blackburn contained all the salient facts: Make-Believe Gardens. The near-misses in the state tournament. The town's growing repute in amateur hockey circles. The letdown since his passing. The story noted that Blackburn, via his partnership with Dufresne, had become a fixture at local ribbon cuttings and dedications. The story also briefly recounted what the *Pilot* had reported about his accident, including what Leo told the police in 1988. Leo had politely rebuffed Joanie's effort to speak with him about it. The story said, "Redpath referred a reporter to his attorney, Peter Shipman, who declined to comment." I had to wonder why Leo would hire a lawyer, unless—I put the thought out of mind and turned to Joanie. "The sidebar looks good," I said. "But did you ever figure out what happened to that one-year gap in Blackburn's Canada period?"

"One second," she said, typing. "Um, no, sorry, didn't nail it yet."

The phone rang. I picked it up without thinking. "*Pilot.*"

"Keeeeee-rist," the voice on the line said. It was my boss, Henry Bridgman, calling from Traverse City. "What are you doing answering on deadline?"

I smiled. "I knew it was you and you must have something important to tell me, like what kind of polish you use on Kerasopoulos's Caddy."

"Haw! I meant to call yesterday but all I had was goddamn budget meetings. On Saturday, for Christ's sake. Even missed the Wings game. I swear I spend half my days here picking goddamn doughnut sprinkles out of my teeth. Anyway, I won't keep you, just wanted to slip you a little intelligence. Got good news and bad news."

"Bad first, please."

"You won't believe this. They're canning our motto."

"No way. 'Michigan's Finest Bluegill Wrapper'?"

"Yeah. Apparently they did some focus groups, who told them it's an anachronism, and not all that professional. Tell the truth, I can't believe it lasted this long."

"We'll catch hell."

"Not as much as we caught when I moved the crossword off A-2. Most folks probably won't even notice."

"What's the good news?"

"You didn't hear it from me, but your old pal's getting kicked upstairs."

Henry was finally going to make the move to corporate. That meant I had a shot at taking over as executive editor of the *Pilot.*

"Congratulations."

"Thanks. The missus won't be happy about moving over here, but these people sign the checks. As for you, I think I've got 'em sold. You know the town and the job and you know you made some mistakes before and it won't happen again. It won't be a done deal for a few days. But the job is yours to lose."

I'd figured my career was over when I left Detroit. I sent my résumé and clips to other dailies around the country. Most didn't call; maybe they'd heard I was damaged goods. For those who did inquire, I had a hard time explaining why I was leaving the *Times*. I found myself hiding out in my apartment, afraid to go outside where I might run into one of the other *Times* people. Eventually I ran out of money. With nowhere to work and nowhere to live, I figured I'd go back to Starvation Lake, spend a little time with Mom, maybe work with Soupy, regroup. After all, my problems really had begun there; I'd just carried them with me to Detroit. Besides, going home seemed fitting punishment for my mistakes in Detroit. Henry goaded me into coming back to the *Pilot*. "Just till you get your bearings again," he said. At least I could make a living, or half a living, doing something I didn't mind doing.

"Thanks, Henry."

"Not a problem. You'll get a little raise, and you'll go into the bonus pool. Now, one other thing: What's up with this story on the Bigfoot guy?"

I lowered my voice. "We've got a little more work to do."

"Well, you might want to go slow, eh? Let them put your name on the masthead before you start stirring the pot."

"Right."

"And by the way, I like my steak medium rare."

"You got it."

"What do you got going for tomorrow?"

"Hang on," I told him, hitting the hold button. Did I really want to tell him about the bullet hole? Would he tell me to hold off on that, too? Of course Henry had known Blackburn, had written some of the stories about his accident. But he didn't know yet what was really going on. It was too late to hold Joanie's stories. Better for Henry if he could tell his bosses he didn't know about them.

I got back on the phone. "Henry, I gotta run," I said.

"Be good."

. . .

After editing Joanie's bullet hole story, I ran down to Fortune Drug and picked up six Pabsts, a bag of nacho chips, and a container of cheese dip. I thought I'd treat Joanie. Over the years I'd learned that getting close to people I envied made me feel better, as if they could forgive my selfishness by sharing their success.

When I walked back into the *Pilot*, Joanie pointed at my phone, where the hold light was blinking. "Fleming?" I guessed.

"No," Joanie said. "Somebody Trenton? From Detroit?"

"Get rid of him, please."

"Does this have something to do with your, uh, situation down there?"

"Get rid of him and maybe I'll tell you."

Scott Trenton was the attorney I'd had to hire in my final days in Detroit. Joanie told him I was on deadline. There was a pause. Trenton was too scrupulous to say why he had called, but frustrated enough to use silence to express his displeasure. While she took down his number, I went up front and called Boynton's lawyer, Fleming. I hadn't done a thing with that dossier on Soupy. I didn't expect him to be there on a Sunday night, and he didn't answer. I left a message.

"So," Joanie said when I returned. She had popped a beer. "Who's Trenton and why does he keep calling you?"

I lifted her backpack off a chair next to her desk and set it on the floor.

"This thing weighs a ton," I said. "What do you keep in here?"

"Everything," she said. "You know, this Trenton dude left a bunch of messages on the machine yesterday."

"Not when I checked."

"Maybe they bounced to the Sound Off line."

Every Tuesday in the *Pilot*, readers were invited to respond to the weekly Sound Off question: Should deer hunting season be extended? What are your favorite spring flowers? Do you prefer powdered sugar or syrup on your pancakes? The answering machine recorded their phoned-in responses. Answers ran on Saturdays with photographs of the readers quoted.

"What's Till got for Sound Off this week?" I said.

"Something stupid about people shoveling off their roofs."

"It's always something stupid."

"No kidding. My favorite was the one that asked if people thought it was wrong—like a sin or something—to leave their Christmas lights up past Easter."

We both laughed.

"So what about Trenton?" Joanie said.

"No, no, wait," I said, trying to keep the subject changed. "Let's come up with something for Sound Off, something even funnier."

"Tillie'll be ticked."

"Tillie will get over it. Come on. Here, stoke those creative fires."

I opened two beers and handed Joanie one. She looked at her first beer, still nearly full. She shrugged. She set the fresh beer down, picked up the first, pulled her hair back from her face with one hand, and chugged the rest of the beer. Her hair tumbled back onto her shoulders as she loosed a guttural belch.

"Whoa," I said.

"I'm such a pig," she said, wiping the back of her hand across her mouth.

"I'm not sure you'll be able to do that at the *New York Times*."

She grabbed the next beer. "I've got it, I've got it," she said. "Listen. 'Sound Off: How do you keep your kids from belching at the dinner table?' "

"Not bad," I said. "But how about . . ." I looked around the room. " 'Sound Off: Should the county outlaw buzzing fluorescent lamps?' "

"Yes! And 'Sound Off: Why does every darn door around here have those little bells?' And 'Is there one eligible man around here who doesn't live in a trailer and start every morning with a tomato-juice-and-beer?' "

We laughed again and drank. "I don't know," I said. "I think maybe Tillie can out-stupid us any day."

Joanie propped her boot heels against the edge of her desk. "Do you really think I could make it at the *New York Times?*" she said.

She has the chops, I thought, and she's smart and usually solemn enough to fit in with those East Coast pinheads. But the evening's flash of silliness made me wonder if she might be better off in Cleveland or Chicago. I'd never send her to Detroit.

"Honestly," I said, "you really can't expect to be a reporter of that caliber unless you can and will use profanity with remorseless abandon. Try this: 'motherfucker.' Go ahead. Say it."

She stared at me blankly.

"OK. You might be able to handle New York," I said. "Though you might need a little more experience than the *Pilot*."

"No, duh. Did you ever have a chance to work there?"

"The *New York Times?* Yeah, right, and the *Pilot* outbid them for my services. No, Joanie, in case you hadn't noticed, my career has taken a slightly different direction. I'm thinking my next job will be covering volleyball for the *Needle*." The *Needle* was the paper at Pine County High School.

"Don't sell yourself short. I know about those truck stories you wrote."

"Yeah. That's why I'm up here in shitsville rewriting Kiwanis Club announcements."

"All right, all right. I got rid of Trenton. Now give it up."

She'd probably read about my departure from the *Detroit Times* in the *Columbia Journalism Review*, which had run a short item saying I'd resigned amid an unspecified controversy over my truck stories. "Carpenter declined to comment," the story said, "as did executives at the *Detroit Times* and Superior Motors, citing the possibility of litigation." Rumors had bounced around the *Times* newsroom, but no one knew the truth. According to my severance agreement, I wasn't supposed to talk about it. But who would know if I told Joanie?

"They want my source," I said.

"Your what?"

"They want the name of someone who helped me on those stories. They want me to give up an anonymous source."

"Who wants?"

"Superior Motors."

She let her feet fall to the floor and leaned forward. She looked at me hard, as if she'd never seen me before. "Gus, what in hell are you talking about?"

Hell? I thought. Joanie had said *hell*. I told her everything.

I had gone to Detroit when I was twenty-two years old, carrying with me the vain and preposterous goal of winning a Pulitzer Prize. And not because I thought it might help my career or fatten my wallet. What I wanted was to take whatever fancy certificate they gave you for winning a Pulitzer back to Starvation Lake and hang it on the jangling damn door at Audrey's, where Coach and Elvis Bontrager and everyone else could see it. Then they'd know who I was.

I almost pulled it off.

I spent most of 1996 writing about Superior Motors' XP-model pickup trucks. The trucks were big sellers that made big profits. But they had a problem. Their fuel tanks sat between the chassis and the outer shell of the truck like eggs in a vise. In crashes, the tanks ruptured and gasoline ignited, causing explosions and fires. Hundreds of people had been severely burned. Some had died. Superior had kept it quiet by buying the silence of victims and survivors with out-of-court cash settlements. Almost no one noticed until I started writing about it. Eventually, the TV newsmagazines started airing pieces, the national papers followed, the government started investigating. It was the kind of story you waited your whole career for. And it kept getting better.

One family, the Hanovers of Valparaiso, Indiana, refused to take Superior's hush money. Justin Hanover had been a seventeen-year-old basketball player with a decent jump shot who wore baggy jeans that hung to his butt crack and a fake diamond stud in his left ear.

He played chess and liked Nick Lowe records and had a girlfriend named Jennifer, one of four Jennifers he'd dated in high school. One night on his way home after dropping Jennifer off, he was broadsided by a drunk driver in a Honda Accord. Justin's 1991 XP pickup truck exploded beneath him. Eyewitnesses heard him screaming inside the flaming cab but couldn't get near enough to help him.

In the courtroom, the Hanover family's attorneys cited some of my stories as evidence that Superior executives and lawyers knew the trucks were dangerous but did nothing to fix them. My reporting showed that Superior had buried an internal study that portrayed the trucks as unsafe, that the company had attempted to hire a government investigator working on the case, that one highly placed executive was demoted after arguing that Superior should admit the trucks were unsafe. The jury found this behavior repugnant and awarded the Hanovers $3 million in compensatory damages—equal to Superior's latest settlement offer—and an additional $351 million in punitive damages, or $1 million for every known truck fatality due to fire. The jury's forewoman said jurors wanted to punish Superior for "a willful neglect bordering on the amoral."

A good deal of my reporting depended on a longtime source I had inside the company. As a mid- to high-level marketing executive, he had access to a great deal of valuable information, such as the next models Superior would be building, where it was closing or expanding plants, which bosses were hot or not. He'd call me with tips, feed me internal memos, confirm stuff I'd uncovered elsewhere. On occasion he leaked information that wasn't flattering to Superior. I asked him once why he did this, and he said, "If I don't dish some dirt, then the fluff has no credibility, does it?" Which was true. I didn't worry about his motives because I believed, foolishly, that motivations had little or no bearing on whether something was factual. It was either a fact or it wasn't, regardless of who happened to whisper it to you. And he had never fudged his facts or otherwise steered me wrong.

It would've been hard to pick him out of a roomful of Superior executives. Like most, he was white, trim, lightly tanned, with a charcoal suit, starched white shirt, dull red tie, every salt-and-pepper hair in place. He wore a smile as routinely as most guys wear a T-shirt. After we got to know each other a little, he told me to forget his real name and refer to him as "V." That way, he said, I was unlikely to unmask him even if I did slip and mention him around anyone from Superior.

One day in May of 1996, V left a message to meet him that evening at Fran & Jerry's, a pub on Detroit's northwest side. When I arrived, the front door was propped open to let the sun in. Stevie Wonder was singing through a tinny radio behind the bar. V waited in a varnished wood booth in the back. He had removed his tie. A thin stack of papers rested facedown in front of him. We ordered a Pabst and a Michelob.

"So what's up?" I said.

"You're busting our balls, my friend," V said. He meant the pickup truck stories. By then I had written just two or three.

"Pretty interesting stuff," I said.

"Sure," he said. "A kid in flames, a big, bad company, all the ingredients."

I didn't respond, but I was thinking, yes, all the ingredients. The waitress brought our beers. V asked for a glass. Then he removed reading glasses from his shirt pocket and placed them on his nose. He turned his papers faceup and scanned the first page, then the second.

"You might find this interesting, too." His eyes flicked up at me over the spectacles. "Off the record, for now?"

"Sure."

"And the fact that I'm giving it to you is totally off the record."

"Yeah, yeah."

At first, I couldn't tell what the pages were. The Superior letterhead marked them as clearly from inside the company, but they didn't look to be a memorandum. More like a script. Each page was filled with entries, some lengthy, some as short as a few words. One said: "Mark, it's Laurie, give me a shout back." Each was labeled with numerals that appeared to denote a date and time. The entries made frequent references to the XP trucks.

"This isn't Friedman, is it?" I asked V.

"That would be Mark Friedman, yes," V said. Friedman was Superior's general counsel.

"So Laurie would be, uh, Lauren Watson?"

"Wilson."

"Right." An assistant general counsel. "So this other guy's got to be, what's his name? Reichs." Howie Reichs was Superior's top safety executive.

I kept flipping through the pages. "I don't get it," I said. "It's like they're not in the same room. I can tell from these things"—I turned a page toward V and indicated the time-and-date notations—"that they're not even talking at the same time. Some of these are like an hour or so apart."

"Very good."

"It's not e-mail?"

"Close." The waitress set a tulip glass down. V picked it up and tilted it as he poured so that the beer barely had a head on it. "Not quite so modern."

"Voice mail?"

He nodded.

"Transcripts of voice mails?"

"Did you notice what they're talking about?"

"Yeah, your pickup trucks."

"You're selling yourself short, my friend."

I took a minute to reread the first few pages more slowly. "Oh," I said. "Holy shit."

The people on the pages were talking about me and my stories and some questions I had asked. "Look at this," I said. "They're plotting how to bullshit me. Friedman says, 'I think we can provide Mr. Carpenter an answer that will make him think we've actually given him one.'"

"Stop the presses," V said sarcastically.

"Goddamn voice mail. Where did you get this?"

"Not going there."

OK, I thought, you'll tell me eventually. "Can I keep these?"

V hesitated. I thought maybe I'd sounded a little too eager. The music faded. I heard traffic hissing past outside.

"You cannot quote from them," he said.

"What? Come on."

"No."

"Then what good are they?"

"You don't need to quote. You can read the lawyers' minds."

"But what good is it to read their minds about stuff that's"— I looked at one of the date notations—"two weeks old? That doesn't—"

"There's more."

"Like from when?"

"Like, for instance," he said, taking a dainty sip of his Michelob, "you called about that government study."

I had called that very morning about federal regulators preparing a new study of deaths in the trucks. "Jesus," I said.

A briefcase sat next to V. He snapped it open and drew out a manila envelope stuffed with paper. "Here," he said, handing me the envelope. "No quoting. Read, understand, use them to figure out what's going on. Better to fish where you know the fish are, am I right?"

I couldn't disagree. "Is this it?"

"Until tomorrow."

"Tomorrow?" I tried not to show my excitement. "How are you getting these?"

"You don't need to know. Use them productively. Or don't."

"Then why? Why are you doing this?"

V shrugged. "It's the right thing to do? You'd never buy that. Let's just say the truck people have it coming."

At Superior, there were car people, like V, and there were truck people. The car people had grown considerably less glamorous—and got less and less of the company's money—as pickups and sport-utilities had caught the public's fancy. But was it enough to turn V against his own company? Maybe. Or maybe I didn't care.

It worked like this: I'd open a line of questioning with Superior about some aspect of the trucks. Every Thursday after six, I'd walk to the bus station on Michigan Avenue, where I had rented a locker. I'd put a key in locker number 927, and remove three or four unmarked manila envelopes bulging with transcripts. I'd hustle them home and read what Superior lawyers and safety engineers and the occasional executive had said to one another about my questions. Then I knew exactly what to ask in my next round. I took care to word my queries generally enough so that the flacks wouldn't make connections I didn't want them to make. It wasn't quite like I was sitting on the nineteenth floor at Superior headquarters, but it was close.

The voice-mail transcripts helped me write some of my biggest stories, several of which found their way into the Hanover trial. When the verdict came down, *Detroit Times* editors started preparing to nominate my stories for a Pulitzer. None of the editors knew about the voice mails. Because I'd never quoted from them, I didn't feel the need to tell anyone about them. I told myself that this further assured that my source's anonymity would be protected. And why should it matter anyway, I thought, so long as the stories were right?

One Thursday in late November, I opened locker 927 and saw no envelopes. Damn, I thought. I'd assumed that V eventually would decide that the truck guys had had enough bad press and my gravy train would end. But way in the back of the locker I saw a single sheet of paper. I had to get up on my toes to pull it out. The paper looked to be a photocopy of a photocopy of a photocopy. The Superior letterhead was smeared black. A column of barely readable surnames, each matched with a six-digit number, ran down the page. I recognized the names of Superior lawyers and flacks. "No way," I said. The numbers had to be their voice-mail pass codes.

An old man sitting against the lockers turned to me as if I'd spoken to him. He was eating a Hostess Sno Ball wrapped in a wrinkled napkin. Pink flakes of coconut stuck to the front of his sweatshirt.

"What am I going to do with this?" I said.

"Up to you," he said.

Of course I had no idea why V had just given me the codes. I tried to reach him, without success. I thought maybe he'd gone on vacation. At the time I was working on a story that was supposed to wrap the entire year of truck news into one long, dramatic narrative. The bosses had ordered it up as the capper of our Pulitzer entry. I already had plenty of strong material for the story, but I wanted something really fresh and juicy.

I thought the voice-mail transcripts were probably stolen goods, although I didn't know for sure because V never broached the subject and I never asked. Reporters aren't supposed to accept materials they know to be stolen. Of course we take stuff all the time that we suspect has been procured through illegal or at least questionable means. It isn't quite like buying a car stereo from a fence, but when we suspect the stuff we're getting is hot, we justify taking it by telling ourselves that we aren't the thieves and the public is being served.

The rationalizations weren't so easy, though, when it came to the voice-mail pass codes. I hadn't stolen the codes, of course. And I didn't even know for certain that V had stolen them. But if I used them to listen to voice mails, and if listening to voice mails was theft, then, perhaps, I would be a thief. But would that be worse than knowingly allowing people to burn to death?

I didn't think about it too hard. I used the codes twice. After midnight. From a phone booth outside the bus station. A few didn't work; their owners had probably changed them. Others did work. The editors cleared space for my last great story to run on the front page on the last Sunday of the year.

Three days before, I attended an annual holiday get-together hosted by Superior. About twenty reporters, half a dozen flacks, and a few execs gathered at a restaurant in downtown Detroit for too many drinks, a dried-out dinner, and some phony laughs. Over the years I'd come to loathe the dinner, but I always worried that if I didn't go, my competitors might beat me to a story. I was waiting at the bar when I overheard two midlevel execs talking about a "purge." I hoped I'd misunderstood. At dinner I dropped a casual question. There had indeed been a round of early retirement buyouts the company hadn't publicized. Certain execs—V's name came up—had declined the buyout, but their bosses had leaned on them to resign.

I excused myself from the table and went to the men's room and locked myself in a stall. I hoped no one had seen my face go pale or the cold sweat bead up on my forehead. V had been gone from Superior for nearly eight months. He'd left weeks before he started giving me the transcripts. Now I knew, without having to ask anyone, that every single thing V had supplied me with was stolen, that he'd had an ax to grind and a reason—a bad one—to use me. So the motivations trumped the facts, after all. There was nothing I could do about the stories that had already been published. But as I sat there staring at the muddy shoeprints on the floor, I contemplated the bitter knowledge that there was time to spike my last great story—and along with it, my chance at a Pulitzer.

I was shivering at a pay phone when I finally reached V at home just after 1:00 a.m.

"You got fired and you don't tell me?" I said.

"You woke me up." V yawned. "I didn't get fired. I took a buyout."

"I needed to know."

"Why? You wouldn't have taken the transcripts then? You would've just told me to keep them?"

My temper was rising. "If I'd known you stole them and was trying to screw the company, goddamn right I would've told you to keep them." I said it, but I wasn't sure I believed it.

"So just forget it then," V said. "You didn't know they were stolen—and I'm not saying they were—but you didn't know, so you're fine. You can plead ignorance. Just take my last little gift and throw it away."

He was taunting me. "OK, Ernest," I said. Then I pronounced his full name.

V chuckled. "What are you going to do, get me fired? Remember, my friend, we were off the record. Blowing my cover would get you in more trouble than me."

He was right, of course. Many of the rules of journalism are dressed in shades of gray, but this one is black and white: If you promise a source anonymity, you never reveal his or her identity. You keep your mouth shut. You go to jail before you unmask an anonymous source. A reporter who ratted out a source might as well leave the profession for good.

I hung up the phone without saying another word.

Pellets of sleet pricked my cheeks as I walked home. I'm screwed, I thought. It wasn't V's fault, either. Sure, he hadn't told me the whole truth, but I had never sought it; hell, I'd avoided it. I'd worried less about his angle than I did about cops at the bus station suspecting me of drug dealing. And now, yes, technically I could plead ignorance about everything V had given me except that last little gift, the pass codes. On that count, I was dead. I'd used the codes to write my final masterpiece. The only way to absolve myself of that sin would be to go in that morning and confess to my editors.

Instead, I called in sick. I phoned in the final changes to my story. It ran that Sunday at the top of the front page and jumped inside to an entire page of copy dressed up with photographs and charts. The next week, I helped my bosses draft a letter nominating me for a Pulitzer Prize. All along, I kept telling myself that that last story— and every single story I had written about Superior's pickup trucks— was true, that none of what I had reported would ever have come out if I had not used the voice mails, that no one ever would have known how Superior had tried to cover up its deadly mistakes. The stories were right, I told myself, and that's all that matters.

. . .

Six months later, I was summoned to the office of Wendy Grimm, executive editor of the *Times*.

She sat behind a massive oak desk in a charcoal suit embellished by a bloodred silk scarf, her gray eyes fixed on a stapler she was fiddling with. A *Times* attorney named Ferris, whom I'd met once when he had reviewed and praised one of my Superior truck stories, sat glumly beside the desk. Grimm took her eyes off the stapler long enough to motion me into a chair. Her secretary closed the door behind me, shutting out the clatter of the newsroom.

"Gus," Grimm said. She set the stapler down. "We have an issue."

Wendy Grimm was a rising star in All-Media Corporation, the agglomeration of newspapers, TV and radio stations, and quick-copy companies that owned the *Times*. She'd come to the *Times*, her fifth newspaper in eleven years, only two years before and was expected to advance to the corporate offices in Dallas once she'd made her mark in Detroit. She'd had me in her office just a few months earlier to congratulate me on having my Superior truck stories selected as one of three finalists for a Pulitzer Prize in national reporting. That day she'd stood beaming at the framed certificates on the wall bearing witness to Pulitzers won by the *Times* in 1931 and 1954. "You're next, Gus," she'd said, knowing full well that my Pulitzer would be regarded by the corporate bosses as *her* Pulitzer.

After the *Washington Post* won the prize for a six-part series on the Congressional Budget Office, I'd actually felt relieved, because I had grown secretly terrified that winning the biggest prize might draw closer scrutiny of my reporting methods. Although I had continued to write an occasional story about Superior's trucks, I'd cut off contact with V, rid myself of the bus station locker, and successfully resisted calling the voice mails again. I thought I'd put the previous year's stories far enough behind me.

All of that changed when Wendy Grimm opened a desk drawer, took something out, and laid it on the desk in front of me. I immediately recognized the key to my old bus station locker, with "927" engraved on its bright orange fob. I felt Grimm and Ferris gauging my eyes and tried to stay calm through the sudden feeling that the bottom of my stomach was about to drop out.

"Tell us, Gus," Wendy Grimm said. "Just how did you go about accessing Superior's voice-mail system?"

"I didn't," I said. "Only a couple of times."

"Enough to get caught. Superior set up a trace."

Yes, I thought. But the stories were true.

We sat there for a moment in silence. Wendy Grimm broke it.

"So who was your source?"

"The stories were true," I said.

She picked up the stapler and slammed it down on her blotter. "Is that your rationalization for stealing property that wasn't yours?" she said. "Who was your source?"

I looked at Ferris, then back at Wendy Grimm. "My source was anonymous," I said.

"That isn't what I asked," she said. "Did you tell any of your editors about this person?"

"No one asked and, anyway, I didn't need to tell anyone because I didn't quote the voice mails."

Wendy Grimm pressed her lips together and leaned forward over her hands, which were now folded together so tightly that her knuckles were white. "Gus, Superior is threatening lawsuits and some rather unflattering publicity. If we knew who your source was, we might be more comfortable in trying to deter them. If it was someone at Superior, I want his or her name. You will give it to me. Now."

Normally a reporter would reveal an anonymous source's name to an editor, who would then be bound by the same oath of confidentiality. At most papers, including the *Times*, refusing to do so was an offense that could get you fired. But it was clear by then that I was a goner anyway, and that this wasn't about me or Superior or the trucks or even the *Times*. A fire was raging in Wendy Grimm's building and she had to extinguish it before it spread to All-Media Corporation.

"I'm no longer in touch with the source," I said. "He stays anonymous. That was my deal."

"*Your* deal, Gus? *Your* deal? Who do you think you work for? Do you realize how much shit you've brought down on me—on us, the *Times*, all of your colleagues?"

"Those trucks are burning people to death and Superior knows it. Every word I wrote was true."

She smiled the brittle smile of a climber who could feel the rungs of the ladder snapping off beneath her feet. "We're in a place now where that has become irrelevant. Totally irrelevant." She turned to Ferris. "Phil?"

Ferris unfolded his praying mantis arms and outlined the lawsuits Superior was threatening: libel, slander, invasion of privacy, theft. One way or the other, he said, my methods would become known. The paper, my colleagues, Wendy Grimm, All-Media, all would be disgraced. Further, a libel jury might well have to disregard any evidence I'd collected with the help of the voice mails, because they were stolen property.

"Libel my butt," I said. "Truth is a defense, as you told us over and over in your little newsroom seminars."

Ferris looked annoyed. "Truth is not a defense," he said, "until you've established what the truth is, until you've proven the truth."

Wendy Grimm's phone burbled electronically; she started to pick it up, then decided against it.

"Unfortunately," Ferris continued, "without the aid of your purloined voice mails, we can't prove very much, which means we'd be liable to lose a libel action."

"These people are killers."

"And we'd lose big," Wendy Grimm said. Her phone rang again; again she ignored it. "We're in discussions with Superior. The long and short of it is, we need you to resign, effective immediately." She placed in front of me a single sheet of paper. At the bottom I saw my full name, "Augustus J. Carpenter," typed where I was supposed to sign away my job. Until that morning, I had told myself that even if I did get caught with the voice mails, I'd only have to endure a beat change or maybe a suspension. They'd never fire me for writing stories that were true. Certainly not at Superior's behest, and not without a fight. But sitting there, with my name in capital letters staring up at me, I knew I was dead.

Ferris withdrew an expensive-looking pen from inside his jacket. "Sign, please," he said, "or we will be forced to terminate you."

"They're killing people."

Wendy Grimm's secretary ducked her head into the office. "It's Al on four," she said. "Better pick up." I could hear computer keys clacking in the newsroom outside. Grimm held up one finger to hold the call.

"I don't have time for this, Gus," she said. "Just sign the damn letter. Or don't sign, and you can get yourself into even more trouble." She pressed a button on her phone. "Security, please."

My brain stopped working then. I felt like I felt when we'd lost a hockey game in sudden-death overtime. When you lose like that, it happens so fast that at first you can't believe it. But then you see the refs leaving and the other team celebrating and you look up at the zeroed-out clock and the certainty of your failure tears through you like a tumbling bullet. Losing in regulation time doesn't hurt as much. The clock runs down. You prepare. In overtime, you just die.

I took the pen.

Soon, I was back in Starvation Lake. With my first *Pilot* paycheck I made part of a down payment on a used Ford pickup truck.

Two days before Christmas, my lawyer called. I had never met Scott Trenton, having hired him over the phone on the recommendation of another *Times* reporter who had used him for her divorce.

"The news isn't too frigging favorable," he said. I was in my kitchen, wrapping gifts for Mom. A robe, a fancy cribbage board, a gift certificate for dinner at a restaurant in Ellsworth. Freezing rain had coated my window with ice. For months I had heard nothing about my situation as the *Times* and Superior tried to negotiate a settlement that would avert a libel suit. Superior's lawyers would have loved to stick the paper for a front-page apology, but the company's executives weren't eager for anything that would draw more attention to their death-trap trucks.

Trenton explained that Superior was seeking the *Times's* cooperation in the Hanover litigation. The Hanovers were the Indiana family who had lost their son Justin in a flaming truck and later won the $354 million verdict against Superior, based in part on my stories. Superior had appealed. Now it wanted the *Times* to file an affidavit with the court stating that my stories were less than accurate, which might in turn nudge the court to throw the case out. The Hanovers would then have to decide whether to endure a second trial and another six to twelve months of reliving their son's death.

"It's not pretty," Trenton said. "So far, Superior and the paper haven't been able to agree on the language of the affidavit. But they'll get there. They'll probably file one minute before five o'clock on New Year's Eve."

There was more. In separate settlement negotiations between Superior and the Hanovers, the family had agreed to drop their lawsuit in return for Superior contributing $200 million to a fund that would subsidize alterations of the trucks for owners who wanted them. The Hanovers would also receive a $5 million cash payment, most of which would go to their lawyers.

"They won't get the windfall," Trenton said, "but some of the trucks might actually get safer."

"That's what they said they wanted all along."

"Between you and me and the barn door, Gus, plaintiffs always say that. Really most of them want a mountain of cash and maybe a CEO with his testicles in a bear trap."

"The Hanovers are good people."

He paused. "Yes, they are. Which is what makes this last little detail a bit of a problem. Superior has stipulated that a condition of their going through with the Hanover deal is you have to give them the name of your voice-mail source."

"They can't do that."

"They're doing it, friend."

"They must know who it is. They had the key to my damn locker."

"Whether they know or not, Gus, they want you to tell them, OK? If you don't, the Hanovers don't get their settlement."

"The hell with them."

"Then it's the hell with the Hanovers, too, because Superior says this is not negotiable. No name, the deal with the family's off, and they take their chances on the appeal, which won't be too good after the *Times* tells the court your stories are bullshit."

"But they weren't bullshit."

"Frigging tough to argue in the shoes you're wearing now."

My anger felt like it would suffocate me there in my kitchen, surrounded by wrapping paper and Scotch tape. I wanted to shove the phone through the icy windowpane into the pelting needles of rain.

"I can't fucking believe this."

"Believe," Trenton said. "And one more thing: If you don't give up the name, Superior will also go after you for felony theft."

"Why the hell do they care so much about the source?"

"I wish I knew. All their lawyers will say is they have their reasons."

"Right. They want to fuck with me. So, basically, I can screw the Hanovers or I can screw myself. Either way, Superior comes out OK, and tough shit for all the poor bastards who fry in their trucks."

"My advice?" Trenton said. "Give the guy up."

"How do you know it's—"

"Shut the hell up a second and listen to your attorney. You're pissed off and I don't blame you. But you don't owe this voice-mail guy or gal or whatever a thing. You two made a deal: He tells the truth, you protect his identity. But he didn't tell you he'd been canned. He lied. You couldn't know his motives were questionable. That's a breach of contract. You're no longer under any legal obligation to cover for him."

Technically, he may have been right, but I didn't think that V had lied to me. As a journalist, it was nice to imagine that, in extending the cloak of anonymity, you were protecting brave and noble people who were risking their livelihoods or maybe even their lives to tell you things you weren't supposed to know and were unlikely to learn otherwise. But a lot of the time—hell, most of the time—you weren't protecting the brave or the noble. Most of the time you were shielding lawyers and flacks and lobbyists and other dissemblers who knew exactly how to exploit your convenient little rule of anonymity so they could shape your story without leaving fingerprints. Yes, V hadn't told me the whole truth. But I never sought the whole truth. V told me what I wanted to hear, and I eagerly, willingly, hungrily swallowed it. He got what he wanted, I got what I wanted. And the truth was now, as Wendy Grimm had said, irrelevant.

"When do they need to know?" I asked Trenton.

"ASAP."

"Merry Christmas, Scott," I said, as I dropped the receiver in the cradle. Then I picked it up again and dialed V. I heard one ring followed by three high-pitched beeps, then a recording saying the number had been disconnected.

sixteen

S o have you told them yet?" Joanie said. We had finished the beers and most of the nacho chips while I was telling my story.

"Told them what?" I said.

"Told them to go to hell, what else?"

She wasn't letting me off the hook. "I haven't told them anything yet."

"Look, Gus. Maybe you shouldn't have stolen the voice mails. But what's done is done. You're still here, doing what you do. Don't mess that up. There's no wiggle room here. You can't give up a source. Period. Did the *Times* file that thing Superior wanted, saying your stories were bull?"

"Yep."

"Nobody noticed?"

"The court sealed it. But it'll be public when the ruling comes."

"Which is when?"

"Superior's lawyers are expecting it Friday. I have until Tuesday to decide. If I give up my source, they settle with the Hanovers and the appeal is moot. If I don't, and Superior wins the appeal, the Hanovers are screwed."

"The Hanovers are not your responsibility, Gus."

"Yes, they are."

"No. You cannot—wait, hold on." She yanked a pager out from under her sweater and peered into it. "Oh, gosh, I gotta go," she said. I watched as she stuffed notebooks and papers into her backpack and threw on her coat.

"Where are you going?" I said.

She ignored that. "Will you be in early tomorrow?"

"Probably. What's up?"

"Nothing."

"You'll do the Dingus press conference?"

"Yeah."

"The zoning board's at two."

She was almost out the door. "Oh, right. I wish I could do that, too, but looks like I'll be wrapped up with the cops."

I heard the bells jangle on the front door. I'd started collecting the empties when I heard the bells again. Joanie reappeared, breathless. "I got it," she said. " 'Sound Off: Do you believe there are underwater tunnels in the lake?' "

"Done," I said.

I left Tillie a note about the Sound Off question and went up the inside stairs to my apartment. As I reached the top I heard a voice outside. Through the curtains I saw Soupy sitting on the landing, his head in his hands, a bottle between his snow-slickened boots. His jacket was unbuttoned. He was shaking his head and muttering something. I stepped outside.

"Soup?"

He didn't look up. He just kept shaking his head. "What the fuck, Trap?" he was saying. "What the fuck you doing to me?"

"Soupy, what are you talking about?"

"You fucking know, Trap." He was drunker than he'd sounded when he called from his truck. Barely two fingers of whiskey remained in his bottle of Old Crow. I reached for it, but he pulled it away.

"The Crow, man," Soupy said. He took a swallow. "All I got. You want that, too?"

"Come on in, Soup."

"I'm fine, see?" he slurred. Then he tilted his head back and squawked like a crow: "Caw! Caw! Caw!"

"You're going to wake the whole town. Come in, please."

He tore off his hat and swiveled his head up toward me, his face a rubbery grin. "Quite a night," he said. "Two beers—make that three, three beers—and a shot with my dear old pal."

"Old pal who?"

"Teddy boy." He clamped an unsteady hand on the railing and wobbled to his feet. The whiskey sloshed around in the bottle. "My old chum."

Soupy took a slug and offered me the bottle. I reached again, but he yanked it back again, snickering. "I don't play that," he said. "So, so, so . . . Tell me, Trap. What the . . . what the hell were you doing in my office?"

So he really had been with Boynton, I thought. "Looking for you," I said, almost telling the truth. "It's a mess in there. Your dad wouldn't be happy."

"Now there's a goddamn news flash—my dad wouldn't be happy."

I thought then to ask him about the boat receipt Dingus had given me, but he was in no shape to answer. "Why don't you go home? Just walk. I'll bring your truck over tomorrow."

"Fuck the truck," he said, turning back to me. I was surprised to see tears in his eyes. Soupy was prone to drunken crying jags, but I knew there was something real beneath these tears because he was trying to hold them back.

"Jesus, Soup, what's the matter?"

He lifted the bottle to his lips, stopping just before he drank. "Teddy boy," he said. "He says you got a story about Coach."

"Yeah?"

"Leave it alone, Trap. Leave it alone. Ain't nothing good can come."

That's it? I thought. That's what has him so upset? The bullet hole story must have been getting around. But why would Soupy care? After our last defeat, he and Coach hadn't gotten along so well either.

"Dingus is holding a press conference. I can't help what the cops find out."

He let the bottle fall to his side. He looked dumbfounded. "Press conference? Fuck. Not that. Dingus knows shit."

"Well, what then?"

"Canada. You know."

"No, I don't. What are you talking about?"

"Don't mess with me." He pointed the bottle at me. "I can see your horseshit a mile away. Canada. Coach had a problem?"

Did he mean the gap in Coach's past? Had Boynton told him? How could Boynton have known? Unless Joanie told Boynton. She'd gone to him for an interview. Maybe he'd ended up interviewing her. Now Boynton was playing Soupy as he'd played her. But with what? Unless Boynton knew something about that missing year that Joanie and I didn't. There had to be something more.

"No," I said. "We don't have any story about Canada. Boynton's screwing with your head. Anyway, who cares what the hell Coach did in Canada thirty years ago?"

Soupy's lower lip trembled.

"Hey," I said, taking a step closer. "What is going on?"

"You're my best friend."

"What is it?"

"My only friend."

"Soupy. Goddamn it."

He was shaking his head, choking back sobs. "I don't know a fucking thing," he said. I put a hand on his shoulder, but he shook it off and started down the stairs. He knew something, all right, but he wasn't trusting me tonight.

"I wouldn't do anything to hurt you," I said.

Halfway down the steps, he stopped and turned and brandished the bottle. "See this piss-water? There's only one whiskey worse. You know which?"

I had no idea.

He yelled it. "Gentleman-fucking-Jack!" Then he reared back and flung the bottle over his truck into South Street, where it burst on a chunk of ice.

I had to blink back cigarette smoke when I walked into the *Pilot* on Monday morning. Tillie didn't look up from the paper she stood reading at the front counter. It was barely nine and her ashtray was already jammed with butts.

"Good morning," I said. "Did you see the TV truck out front of Audrey's?"

Tillie didn't answer. She leaned on an arm, obscuring her face. Something was bugging her. I grabbed a *Pilot* off the counter and slid a quarter next to Tillie's elbow.

"Kerasopoulos called," she said.

"Who?"

"At corporate. He didn't sound happy."

Joanie was at her desk, still in her wool cap and jacket, sifting through what looked like a stack of receipts. I spread the *Pilot* out on my desk. Joanie's main story, "Bullet Hole Found in Late Coach's Snowmobile," and the sidebar, "Blackburn Remembered as Strategist, Town Booster," filled the entire top half of the page. It was a nice display, with photos of the scene of Blackburn's accident, Blackburn hoisting a trophy, Blackburn cutting the ribbon at a pizza parlor. There was also that mug shot of Blackburn, the one that hung at Enright's, superimposed over the inscription "John D. 'Jack' Blackburn. Jan. 19, 1934–March 13, 1988." I wanted to savor it for a minute, feel like I'd accomplished something. But I had to call Kerasopoulos.

"Maybe I'll head over to the cop shop," Joanie said. "I was going to finally do my expenses, but that can wait."

That reminded me. I had been meaning to ask her about a phone bill. I fished through the pile on my desk. As I looked, I told her, "Listen, once Dingus's press conference gets going, just sit there and be quiet. Unless there's something you absolutely can't get from Dingus or one of the other cops on your own, don't ask any questions. You'll just be helping the TV people." I also didn't want Dingus thinking I'd told her anything about his visit to my apartment.

"Huh. Hadn't thought of that. Excuse me." She went into the bathroom.

I found the phone bill stuck to the back of the Bud Popke press release. It listed a dozen or so calls to the 202 and 617 area codes, and one for $57.28 to the 703 code. Joanie had called Washington, D.C., and Boston for the Sasquatch story, and I knew from my time covering the auto safety regulators that 703 was in Virginia near D.C. According to NLP Newspapers policy, because that single call was for more than $50, I was supposed to inquire about the purpose of the call and tell corporate. If I didn't, the people in finance would. They lived for it.

The faucet splashed on in the bathroom. I stared at the bill. If I didn't report the reason for the $57.28 phone call, would that jeopardize my chance at the executive editor's job? I couldn't believe I was worrying about this crap. The hell with it, I thought, and tossed the bill back on my desk.

Tillie appeared, holding a scrap of notepaper in one hand and a smoldering cigarette in the other. Now that I could clearly see her face, I could tell she'd been crying. "Is this a joke or something?" she said, waving the paper around.

"What?"

"This Sound Off question. The tunnels?"

Joanie emerged from the bathroom. "No joke," I told Tillie. "It's news. Use it. And keep the smoke out there, please."

She disappeared.

"What's her problem?" Joanie said.

"No idea." I picked up the dossier on Soupy's marina troubles and held it up for her. My phone rang. "Did you happen to borrow this?"

Her face said yes, but before she could say anything, Tillie ducked in again. "Gus. Scott Trenton?"

Joanie turned for the door, grinning. "Not saving you this time."

I picked up the phone and punched the blinking light. "Hello, Scott."

"You don't return calls."

"When I don't have anything to say, no."

I heard the wheels on Trenton's swivel chair squeak. "We have a meeting tomorrow," he said.

"Who's we?"

"Me and you and a bunch of lawyers. Superior. All-Media. The Hanovers. Noon."

"Scott, I have a paper to—"

"Listen to me, Gus. You will be in Detroit tomorrow for this meeting or you won't have me as your attorney anymore. You don't have to say a word, but I want you there to show good faith, one way or the other."

"The Hanovers are coming? Doug and Julia?"

"Yes."

"Jesus."

"Yeah."

"Why didn't you ask me first?"

Trenton let the silence answer.

"OK," I said. "What's the agenda?"

"This is our last shot at getting Superior off your back. We're going to tell them whether you're going to give up your source or not. It would be good if you could tell me your intentions now so I can position us for a decent outcome."

Now I let the silence speak.

"Gus?" Trenton said.

"I don't know yet. Sorry."

"Gus—"

"Most reporters would go to their grave before they burned a source."

"We've been through this. I appreciate your good intentions and your"—he paused—"integrity. But they're superfluous here, friend. This guy, or woman, or whoever your source is, burned *you*. Your obligation to protect their identity is frigging kaput."

"That's what you say."

"That's what I say."

"Where's the meeting?"

"You're not going to give me an answer now?"

"Unless you want one you don't want to hear."

"Let me be clear, Gus. If you don't give them an answer tomorrow, or you give them the wrong answer, count on Superior seeking criminal charges against you. Believe me, they can make that happen. The Hanovers won't be happy either. They want that settlement set in concrete before the appellate court rules."

I didn't care about Superior. The Hanovers were a different matter. "Where's the damn meeting?"

"Superior's law firm, Eagan, MacDonald & Browne. Comerica Building. Are you going to be there?"

"We'll see."

"You know," he said, "all you hockey players are nuts. You're a goalie, right? My partner had a goalie once for a client. Just a kid. He and the other goalie on his team were butting heads in the locker room. Like a couple of frigging rams, lining up in nothing but goalie masks and jock straps and running at each other with their heads down. Then, wham! The one breaks his nose pretty bad and his parents have us sue the frigging company that made the mask. Can you believe that?"

"Did you win?"

"Nah. Settled."

The morning had turned bad fast. I dialed our corporate office, got a machine, hit zero, got an operator, and asked for Jim Kerasopoulos.

"Yes," the lawyer's voice boomed out of the phone. He was on the speaker.

"Gus Carpenter, Jim."

"Gus." He picked up the handset. "How's the snowmobiling?"

What snowmobiling? I thought. He was the one who'd been snowmobiling. I remembered the egg pie I didn't get to eat and felt suddenly hungry.

"Um, fine. You called?"

"I did. I would really have appreciated a heads-up on the paper this morning."

"How's that?"

I pictured him stuffed into a black leather chair behind a pin-neat desk with a brass letter opener resting atop a stack of freshly opened letters, behind his head a framed etching of mallard ducks landing on a pond.

"I thought we had a good talk about communication between you and us folks here at the mother ship," he said. "Then I pick up the *Pilot* this morning and see murder splashed all over the front page."

"There's no—"

"All over the page."

"Jim, the word 'murder' does not appear."

"Gus, if you're going to write about murders in small towns and quote anonymous sources, you're going to let us know before you do."

"We shouldn't have run the story?"

"Gus?" A squeak made its way into his foghorn. "You're really disappointing me here, especially after Henry's been singing your praises. What I'm asking is pretty simple, sir. I want to know when any of our editors is running a story that could stir up the masses, or people who might want to sue us, especially if we have zero sources confirming it on the record."

"I'm confident in the story, Jim."

He paused for a moment, then said, "That's nice that you're confident, but frankly, Gus, in your case, that doesn't cut it. You have a past here, no? We're trying to accommodate you and your supporters here, and you're not meeting us halfway."

At last, the truth. Actually, all Kerasopoulos knew about my past was that I'd had an unfriendly parting with the *Times*. Depending on what I did in Detroit the next morning, he might know a lot more. I wanted to tell him my "past" had nothing to do with the Blackburn story, that this was just Newspapering 101 and we'd done our jobs. But I was worried that I'd gotten Henry into trouble too. So I swallowed hard.

"Jim," I said. "I understand. I wish I'd given you a call. It was hectic yesterday. Sorry."

"A call would've gone a long way, Gus. I'm not saying we would or wouldn't have run the story. Maybe we would've waited for the press conference. Excuse me."

He put me on hold. I decided it probably wasn't the best time to ask about the Sasquatch story. My other line started blinking. I couldn't risk cutting off Kerasopoulos, so I let Tillie get it. Kerasopoulos came back on, his voice calm with distraction. "OK, I've got to hop. I hope we understand each other."

Fleming picked up on the first ring. "Mr. Carpenter. Thank you for your message yesterday. It turns out that that matter has disposed of itself."

"Pardon?"

"We are still speaking off the record."

"Which matter?"

"Thank you. The matter we discussed in your office the other day with my client, Mr. Boynton."

Oh, no, I thought, thinking he'd given the dossier to Channel Eight. "I'm too late?" I said.

"Indeed, today was our deadline, but what I'm telling you now is, the issue is moot. We've done nothing with the documents we showed you, nor do we plan to."

"You don't want a story?"

"I'm running late for a conference call. Apologies."

seventeen

The Pine County Clerk's Office was exactly as I remembered it. Behind the frosted-glass windows set on the lacquered oak counter now stood twelve rows of filing cabinets instead of eight, a testament to the growth and prosperity the county had enjoyed when Jack Blackburn and Francis Dufresne, and later Teddy Boynton, were stumping for progress. All that was missing, for the moment, was County Clerk Verna Clark. Instead I was greeted by Deputy Clerk Vicky Clark, Verna's daughter.

As a teenager, Vicky Clark had played the piano well enough to win a scholarship to a prestigious out-of-state music academy. But she'd gotten pregnant with triplets, no less, and enjoyed a brief moment of triplet celebrity before sinking back into anonymity in Starvation Lake. She never went to the academy. Now she was a heavyset woman who dyed her blond hair black, streaked it purple and scarlet, and drew it back into a spiky leather catch. She wore a black T-shirt, black jeans, black lipstick, black stud earrings, and black mascara on her eyes, which were pinched nearly shut by her fat cheeks. A plaster cast painted black encased her right arm from the wrist to just above the elbow. Spackle, I thought. I couldn't help it. When we were kids, Soupy had dubbed her Spackle for all the makeup she plastered on her face.

"What happened to your arm?" I said.

She held it out, bracing it with her left arm. "Fell off a ladder at my boyfriend's house. Taking down Christmas lights."

"Your boyfriend puts up Christmas lights?"

"His kids like them. Mine could give a crap. But here I'm trying to help him out, and he's in the house watching hockey. I'm laying out there in the snow for like an hour before Sully comes out and says, 'What happened to you?' I broke my damn arm is what. He ain't my boyfriend anymore. I'm going to sue him. Know any good lawyers?"

"Nope."

"Well, I might get one if it doesn't cost me an arm and a leg—I mean my other arm and a leg. Dad said I could probably get some money out of Sully's homeowner's. Fine with me. Help me get the hell out of here."

I wasn't sure whether she meant the clerk's office or Starvation Lake, but I would've bet she'd never leave either. Despite what she said, she was probably back with Sully, or would be soon. I wouldn't have been surprised to hear he'd put her up to suing so they could split the insurance money.

"I hope your arm gets better," I said. I told her I needed to see the minutes for all the town council meetings from March through August of 1988. Just as her mother had fifteen years before, Vicky handed me a public-information request form.

"Boy, Vicky, do I really have to do this?" I said. "I'm in kind of a hurry."

"Sorry. It's policy. My moth—my boss would kill me."

She folded her hands on the counter while I filled it out. She looked bored. I'd almost finished when she leaned across and said, "Can I ask you something?"

I looked up from the form. "Sure."

"Why'd you come back?"

"Come back?"

"Here. Why'd you come back here? I heard you had it made downstate, then you got fired."

What the hell happened to you, Spackle? I thought. Didn't you have it made? Then I immediately felt bad for thinking it.

"Fired?" I said. "Not really. I just wasn't seeing eye to eye with my bosses, and I thought it'd be good to come back here and regroup before I get out in the real world again."

She knew I was lying. She gave me a little smile, seeming comforted to know that she had a kindred spirit, someone else who appreciated the dull pain of being stuck forever in Starvation Lake. "Give me that," she said, taking the form. She looked around the room. "Hang on."

Fifteen minutes passed as she went through drawer after drawer of filing cabinets in the back of the room. She came back to the counter empty-handed. "I'll be damned," she said. "They aren't hard to find, everything's filed by year, but there's a whole big folder missing from 1988. Maybe somebody from Town Hall came over and—uh-oh." She was looking past my shoulder. I turned around to see Verna Clark, lips pursed, hands on her hips. She didn't look pleased, but then I wouldn't have known what she looked like when she was pleased.

"What's going on here?" she said.

Vicky said, "Gus was asking for some—"

"If a customer wants some archival files," her mother said, "we have them prepare a public-information request, don't we?"

Vicky waved the sheet of paper. "He did."

Verna stepped forward and grabbed the form without the slightest glance at me. She skimmed it and, for the slimmest sliver of a second, I thought I saw Verna Clark smile. "Unfortunately," she said, "these particular files are unavailable at this moment." She gave me a look that felt like a slap. "I haven't forgotten you, Mr. Carpenter."

She was still as thin as a hockey stick, still wearing a gray dress and glasses that dangled at her neck. "Nice to see you again," I said.

She turned to Vicky. "As a matter of procedure, we don't go digging around in files until we've completed the proper processing of the form." She turned back to me. "That normally takes three to five days."

"Gus works for the newspaper, though, Mother, and he—"

"I thought we'd spoken about how you should address your superiors in the workplace. And I'm well aware of where Mr. Carpenter works. In fact he worked there once before, many years ago, and now that he has decided to come back, he'll find that our procedures have remained consistent."

"Yes, they have," I said.

"In any event, the files you're requesting were needed elsewhere this morning. I would've had them make copies, but our copier has been malfunctioning and we haven't been able to get it serviced yet, what with the budget cuts."

I thought it strange that someone from Town Hall would want to see ten-year-old minutes at the very moment that I wanted them. It had to be Dingus, working through channels.

"Can I ask who took them?" I said.

"You can ask, but I'm unable to furnish a reply," Verna Clark said. I looked at Vicky. She obviously didn't know. Her mother said, "If Town Hall follows procedures, we should have the documents back and ready for you to view in approximately seventy-two hours, no earlier."

Back at the *Pilot*, Tillie's little television showed frosty wisps of breath rippling around the perfectly round face of TV reporter Tawny Jane Reese. Her shiny mahogany hair framed a look of near constant surprise, accentuated by her slightly upturned nose. "Dumber than a bag of hockey pucks," Soupy liked to say about Tawny Jane. "But who cares?"

She was talking into a Channel Eight microphone in front of the sheriff's department. "Within minutes," she said, "Sheriff Dingus Aho is expected to talk about the discovery of a snowmobile at nearby Walled Lake. As exclusively reported by Channel Eight, police have determined the snowmobile belonged to legendary youth hockey coach Jack Blackburn, who drowned in an accident . . ."

Though she screwed up facts like Walleye Lake and took credit for "exclusive" stories she'd actually read in the *Pilot*, I had a soft spot for Tawny Jane Reese. Sometimes I just turned the sound down and watched her practice those TV moves: The punctuated nodding of the head. The furrowed brow of concern. The everything's-going-to-be-OK flash of smile. Tawny Jane had them down. Sometimes I tried to picture her having dinner with me. Would she chat with the same furrowing and nodding? I supposed she wouldn't. Other times I wondered if she was still young and perky enough to land a job in a big city. I supposed she wasn't.

Now she knitted her penciled-in eyebrows as the camera dollied in. "Local news reports have pointed to the discovery of a bullet hole in Blackburn's snowmobile as evidence that the coach has been murdered. However, sheriff's department sources are telling Channel Eight this may be premature. In fact . . ."

"Bullshit," I said. "We didn't say he was murdered. Read the story."

Tillie stubbed out one cigarette and lit another. "You and your little friend may have gotten a little ahead of yourselves this time, huh?" she said.

Where's that coming from? I thought. "No," I said. "Joanie nailed the story and Dingus knows it, but it drives him crazy so he gets Tawny Jane No-brain to piss on us."

"You have no idea what Dingus knows."

"Do tell. Is there something else we should be reporting?"

"Maybe. Maybe this isn't quite as horrid a place as you'd like to imagine."

"What is that supposed to mean?"

"Look around, young man. When Jack Blackburn died, this whole town went into mourning. While you were downstate chasing your little dreams, this place was falling apart. So now we're finally getting ourselves together, and you come back here with your little friend and dig up this cockamamie story about Jack getting murdered."

"The cops found the snowmobile, Tillie, I didn't."

She expelled a cloud of smoke. "Oh, please, save the 'don't-shoot-the-messenger' claptrap. The police find plenty of things we just plain ignore. The cops go out to Tazwell's damn near every weekend when Lloyd's whacking Ellie around, but do we write about that? And how about the Barbie heads?"

I was still working in Detroit when town council member J. Rupert "Woody" Woodhams had to have his stomach pumped one night and doctors found eleven shaved Barbie-doll heads he'd apparently bitten off. Neither the cops nor the hospital would confirm the story. The *Pilot* never wrote it. Everybody knew anyway.

"So," I said, "we should've ignored the snowmobile?"

"Hey, you're the big-city reporter here, I'm just a stenographer. But let's face facts. You hate this place. Stop taking it out on the rest of us who don't mind it so much."

She turned away. She was obviously upset, and it was obviously about more than just *Pilot* coverage. Maybe, I thought, it was just the whole spooky reemergence of Blackburn. She had dated him way back when. I'd seen her around the rink, her black leather jacket cinched tight beneath her bosom, watching from the uppermost row of the bleachers with an enormous Coke that all the Rats knew was laced with whiskey.

"Till," I said. "I don't mean—"

She pointed at the TV. "Listen."

Now Tawny Jane was standing inside the sheriff's department cafeteria. The lunch tables had been folded up and stacked against a pop machine in a corner behind her. Folding chairs were set up in three semicircular rows in front of a lectern surrounded by TV microphones. I counted eight reporters sitting in the chairs, a pretty strong turnout. I couldn't see Joanie.

"We're live at the Pine County Sheriff's Department," Tawny Jane said. "Let's join Sheriff Aho."

The screen framed Dingus in his brown-and-mustard uniform. An accordion folder bulged under his left arm. He'd waxed his handlebar mustache. Deputies Frank D'Alessio and Skip Catledge stood behind him with their hands behind their backs. Dingus set his folder down, removed a sheet of paper, and nodded at the reporters and TV cameras. "Good morning," he said. "I have a brief statement to read and then I'll be glad to take your questions."

He cleared his throat. "On Friday, February twenty-seventh, at approximately twelve fifty-eight a.m., the Pine County Sheriff's Department was notified that a number of unidentified objects had appeared on the shore of Walleye Lake. Sheriff's deputies were dispatched to the scene, arriving at approximately one-eleven a.m. Upon further inspection, it was determined that these objects were components of a snowmobile. This snowmobile had possibly been submerged in the lake for a lengthy period of time. The objects were classified as evidence and removed to—"

"Excuse me, Sheriff?"

I cringed. The camera stayed on Dingus, but the voice was unmistakably Joanie's. "Didn't you go out to Walleye yourself that night?" she said. "Can you tell us what prompted that unusual step?"

"Joanie, no," I said. Tillie was shaking her head.

Dingus's eyebrows and mustache rose as one in surprise. "Pardon me, young lady," he said. "I'll be taking questions after I've finished my statement." He glared at Joanie briefly before continuing.

"After further investigation and testing, it was determined that the snowmobile had once been registered to John David Blackburn, a former resident of Pine County who drowned in an accident on Starvation Lake early the morning of March 13, 1988. Our investigation—"

"Excuse me, Sheriff, but everybody already knows it was Blackburn's snowmobile." It was Joanie again. I couldn't believe it. "What we don't know is why you personally went out there, and why you would send the snowmobile for forensics."

"Forensics are—hold on—excuse me, Miss McCarthy, I will get to your questions at the proper time. But I—"

"Your deputies this morning have been telling TV"—here she turned and looked directly into the camera—"that my paper prematurely reported that Blackburn was murdered. We said nothing about murder, Sheriff. But since it's apparently on the table now"—Clever, I thought—"would you confirm that Blackburn was *not* murdered? Some people are saying this whole thing has been ginned up to help you get reelected. Could you respond, please?"

"Joanie!"

The camera zoomed in on Dingus's face, which was florid with disbelief and anger, as animated as I'd ever seen it on TV. The camera turned to the right, and there was Joanie. I wanted her to just shut up, but seeing her there with her legs primly crossed, her notebook propped on her right knee, I couldn't help but feel a little rush of admiration for her sheer disregard of Dingus's authority.

"Miss McCarthy," he said. "I'm going to ask you one last time to allow me to finish. Or you can leave."

Joanie, unfazed, scribbled in her notebook and continued as if she were conducting an interview. "Sheriff, haven't you questioned an acquaintance of Blackburn about the very possibility that he was murdered?"

"Holy shit," I said.

"Kick her little ass out, Dingus," Tillie said.

The camera swung wildly back to Dingus. He blinked once, hard, and said, "This briefing is over. Deputies, clear the premises."

I grabbed my jacket and ran out the back door. I thought I knew who Joanie's last question was about. I had to get to the rink, fast.

I was too late.

By the time I crept in, the Zamboni shed had been cleared of nearly everything that belonged to Leo. The police scanner. The little fridge. The old River Rats cap hanging from a nail. The addiction aphorisms. Only his cot remained.

"Leo," I sighed.

I glanced out at the rink through the little hexagonal window over the workbench. Young girls in short pastel skirts and white skates were cutting backward figure eights while their skating coach, a woman named Roberta, shouted instructions. My watch said 12:37. I figured Leo had resurfaced the ice for the noon session, then bolted. No one would notice he was gone until he was next scheduled to run the Zamboni at 1:00 or 1:30.

I had a few minutes to look around. I didn't want to be seen if Leo really had left town. I wondered, was I obliged to alert the police to his parting? No, I quickly concluded. If they thought Leo had murdered Blackburn, they could've arrested him. I knew this was a rationalization, but I still wasn't ready to believe that Leo had killed his best friend, regardless of what the cops thought.

I rifled the drawers and cubbyholes around Leo's work area. Greasy parts, tools, and containers of lubricant and paint littered the bench. Leo had taken the jar of disinfectant that held his stitching utensils. I touched the sutures still in my jaw. I'd planned to have Leo remove them before the game that night.

Next to Leo's cot stood a wooden filing cabinet. I tried a drawer and it gave. I pulled the drawers out one by one and peered inside, finding nothing. The last one, on the bottom, stuck when I tried to push it back in. I kept trying and it kept sticking. I pulled it back out, set it on the floor, and knelt to look inside the cabinet. The smell of mildew filled my nose. I couldn't see for the dark inside. I found a flashlight on the bench and shined it inside the cabinet on the side where the drawer seemed to be catching. Taped on the inner wall was a torn piece of paper. I reached in and peeled it away. Another piece of paper was taped beneath it and, beneath that, two more. I peeled them all away and replaced the drawer.

I laid the yellowed, palm-sized pieces of paper out on the bench. They looked like they'd been scissored out of looseleaf pages. Each was inscribed in red ballpoint ink with short lists of similarly arranged letters and numbers: F/1280/SL/R4.F/1280/SL/R5. F/1280/SL/ R6. They made absolutely no sense to me. I stuffed them inside my jacket and hustled out to my truck.

. . .

Leo's mobile home sat in a clearing encircled by pines off Route 816 three miles west of town. When two sheriff's cruisers blasted past me headed in that direction, I veered off the main road and looped behind Leo's place on DiRosa Drive. I parked on the shoulder and trudged up a snow-covered hill. At the crest I crouched behind an oak tree with a view down to Leo's. Dingus stood in front of the trailer directing D'Alessio, Catledge, and Darlene. They were carrying out boxes of things and stacking them in the back of a sheriff's van. I was too far away to hear much of what they were saying, but I did catch two words—"fucking disgusting"—uttered by D'Alessio as he moved past Dingus lugging a computer monitor. They had filled up most of the back of the van before they locked Leo's door and pulled away.

Driving back to town, I tried to imagine Leo on the lam. It was ludicrous. Leo hadn't left Starvation Lake for more than a weekend in thirty years. He hated driving cars because he had to sit. Leo drove a Zamboni; he liked to stand. He used to joke about cutting a hole in the roof of his car so he could stand while he drove. As I eased to a stop in front of the high school, I remembered how, when Leo was resurfacing the ice, we'd be perched at the rink's edge, Soupy and Teddy and me and the other Rats, dying to jump on, and Leo would be making slow circles like an old lady in a church parking lot. Just before he pulled off, he'd yell at us, "Not one skate out here until I say, or I'll do it all over again." And we'd wait while the fresh water hardened. Leo said that's what it took to put down a great sheet, and Leo put down a great sheet. It stayed hard and smooth and slick even after we'd chewed it up for an hour.

"Fucking disgusting," D'Alessio had said. And a computer? I had no idea that Leo, who wouldn't even get himself a new police radio, was interested in computers. If he really had fled, I hoped it was just irrational panic and not guilt that drove him. But even if he was just afraid, even if he really wasn't Blackburn's murderer, he evidently knew something no one else knew, or why would he have run? Again I thought of the Rats waiting to jump onto the ice, Leo on the Zamboni, Coach behind the bench. I remembered peering out at that little world through the eyeholes of my goalie mask. What had I failed to see?

eighteen

When I walked into the auditorium at Pine County High School, Teddy Boynton was on his feet, in a business suit, calmly addressing the five members of the zoning board. I slipped into a folding chair in the back and scanned the room. About seventy people were in attendance. Soupy Campbell was not one of them. Nor was Francis Dufresne.

Soupy needed to be there. After months of dithering, the board finally was disposed to grant the variance Teddy Boynton needed to build his marina. Most people thought it would provide an economic boost, and plenty were fed up with the erratic service at Soupy's marina. The board members liked Soupy, though—most had known his dad—and they wanted to be sure Soupy was taken care of before they effectively handed his future to Boynton.

" . . . found a way to invest a few more dollars to address the environmental concerns that the board has raised," Teddy was saying. His lawyer, Fleming, sat at his right elbow. The board listened from behind a long table draped with a green felt banner bearing the legend "Your Zoning Board of Appeals: Smart Growth Good Growth." Teddy brandished a large manila envelope. "The board has talked about an amount in the neighborhood of fifty thousand dollars. If the board can compromise a bit, we can pledge ten thousand dollars now and the rest over the next three years. We are committed to making the Pines the most environmentally friendly marina in Michigan." Boynton laid the envelope in front of the chairman, Floyd Kepsel. I was recalling what Francis Dufresne had told me about Teddy's precarious financial position.

"In addition, Mr. Chairman," Teddy continued, "we have come to an amicable agreement with Mr. Campbell and the Starvation Lake Marina. We recognize that the old marina, though sorely in need of renovation, is a treasured local resource, and our fervent wish is to work closely with Mr. Campbell, not against him, toward the betterment of our community. Mr. Campbell now agrees, and has indicated his desire to withdraw his concerns with our project."

A murmur rose in the room and heads craned around, all looking for Soupy. Teddy himself surveyed the room and our eyes met briefly, but he looked through me and turned back to the board.

"Well, Ted," Chairman Kepsel said, "not that I doubt your word, but I'd sure like to have Mr. Campbell here to vouch for himself."

Teddy reached into his suit jacket and produced a thin white envelope. "I agree that would be best, Mr. Chairman, but we have it here in writing." He handed the envelope to Kepsel.

I sat up in my chair. Kepsel slipped a single sheet of paper from the envelope, read it quickly, and passed it to the board member to his left, Vice Chairman Ralph Dexter. Dexter read it and handed it back.

"There's just one sentence here, Ted," Kepsel said. "For the record, I'll read it: 'I, Alden Campbell, hereby withdraw my opposition and urge the zoning board to extend to Boynton Realty Corporation the requested zoning variance necessary to enable development of the Pines at Starvation Lake.' Dated Sunday. Yesterday."

"It isn't even notarized," Dexter said.

Fleming stood. Boynton motioned for him to sit. "Mr. Chairman," Teddy said. "We've been in negotiations with Mr. Campbell for several weeks. We are deeply concerned about the future of the Starvation Lake Marina, and we've made several proposals to address that. Yesterday we finally—"

"Excuse me, sir," Dexter interrupted, "but I fail to see what's in this for Mr. Campbell."

"Vice Chairman Dexter," Teddy said, "we haven't quite worked out those details in writing yet, but we will very soon."

Dexter sat back and spread his arms wide. "Very soon? But you expect us to grant your variance *now*, and then when 'very soon' turns into a month or two or three and Mr. Campbell shows up later telling us he hasn't withdrawn a thing, his lawsuit will just be our problem, right?"

"No, sir, we fully intend—"

"Well, I think it will be our problem, Mr. Boynton, I think it will be."

A lengthy discussion followed. I kept looking for Soupy. Why wasn't he here? Had he changed his mind and accepted that settlement I'd seen when I sneaked into his office? If he had, why didn't Boynton just spell it out?

Kepsel finally rapped his gavel. "I would dearly love to get this business behind us, Ted," he said. "But I do wish Mr. Campbell was here. We'd all like to hear a little more about this settlement. I know you'd like to see a vote, but I'm afraid it might not come out how you'd like just yet. How soon do you think you can have an agreement all wrapped up?"

"Twenty-four hours, Mr. Chairman. But I don't see why—"

"That'd be fine, Ted," Kepsel said. "You wrap that up and we'll reconvene the board tomorrow for a vote."

"Mr. Chairman," Teddy said. He wrung his hands together behind his back. "The board asked for an additional commitment to the environment. We have provided that. You asked us to consider the future of the Starvation Lake Marina. We did. We're prepared to move forward and, frankly, we're at a loss to understand why we would be delayed by, of all things, the very sort of irresponsible behavior that has created the need for a new marina."

Dexter spoke again. "If we gave you the variance this minute, how long would it be before the first shovel went into the ground?"

Maybe it was because of what I'd heard from Francis, but I thought Teddy hesitated before he said, "We can't do a thing until we have the variance, Mr. Vice Chairman. But when we do, I can assure you we'll move forward expeditiously."

"Uh-huh," Dexter said. "And where's Francis today, Mr. Boynton?"

The muscle along Teddy's right jawbone twitched. Fleming jumped up and said, "Mr. Dufresne had another pressing matter to attend to but sent his best wishes that the board would act in our favor."

Dexter smiled. "But you don't have *that* in writing, do you, Mr. Fleming?"

"No, sir."

"How's the theater renovation going in Sandy Cove, Mr. Fleming?"

"On schedule and under budget, sir."

"All of us in Starvation are so delighted to hear that."

"Look," Teddy said, "we appreciate the board's patience." The tone of his voice suggested otherwise. "But, frankly, if we can't get the support of the very people who stand to benefit from this, then, unfortunately, and with all due respect, we've run out of time, and we'll say, Thank you, no hard feelings." He picked up his briefcase. "Let me state this as clearly as I can. If we don't have a green light by close of business Wednesday, we'll cancel the Pines at Starvation Lake and move on."

He and Fleming started for the door. Everyone turned to watch them go.

"Hold on, Ted," Kepsel said. They ignored him.

"We will not be bullied, Mr. Boynton," Dexter shouted as they went through the door.

Soupy's absence clearly had thrown Boynton. Maybe Soupy was still drunk. Or was drunk again. Or maybe this had something to do with his outburst at my apartment the night before. I hurried out into the corridor. "Teddy!" I shouted after them. They were almost to the double doors that led out to the parking lot when one of the doors swung open and in stepped Joanie, backpack slung over her shoulder.

"It's already over?" she said.

Teddy stopped, briefly unsure of himself, and turned toward me.

"Hey," I said. "You're just going to walk away? That's it?"

"After six months of this crap?" Boynton said. "Now maybe they'll focus."

"Focus on what?" Joanie said.

"Could you give us some details of your agreement with Soupy?" I said.

"Why don't you ask him?" Teddy said. "He's your butt buddy."

Fleming interjected, "As Mr. Boynton said, the deal has yet to be finalized, although we are confident it will be."

"What *is* the deal, Ted?"

"What deal?" Joanie said.

Boynton clapped a hand on Fleming's shoulder. "We're done here." They turned for the outer doors.

"You were expecting Soupy, weren't you, Ted?" I said. It made Boynton stop. He wheeled around to face me again.

"Know what?" he said. "Better tell your buddy not to show up tonight, either, because he won't have the zoning board to protect his ass out on the ice."

"Please," Fleming said, tugging at Teddy's elbow.

The door swung closed. Joanie looked bewildered. "What was that all about?"

"We need to talk," I said. "Follow me."

"Look," she said as I ushered her into a classroom and shut the door. "They were lying about our story. I couldn't just sit there and—"

"I don't care about the press conference," I said. One wall of the room was covered with pencil drawings of historical figures: Lincoln, Napoleon, Kennedy. A history class? Art? I stood near the teacher's desk.

"Sit," I told Joanie. She sat on a student's desk facing me. "Let's talk about that document you took off my desk."

"What document?"

"You know. The thick one about Soupy Campbell and his legal problems."

"Oh." She looked a little sheepish. "I thought it might be good background if I had to cover the zoning board."

"Did you show it to anybody? Or tell anyone about it?"

"No—well, nobody who didn't already know."

"Like who?"

She let her backpack drop to the floor. "Boynton."

"You talked to him?"

"Yeah. Saturday night. Remember when my beeper went off?"

"Why did you have to tell Boynton about a document he already knew about?"

"I didn't." She chewed her lower lip. "I wanted to talk about Blackburn, he wanted to talk about Campbell. I thought I'd get him going on one and he'd talk about the other."

"But he didn't tell you a thing, did he?"

"Not really."

"I'll bet you told him a few things, though, huh?"

She shrugged, looking even more uncomfortable. "I just said I was working on this feature on Blackburn. I told him—he asked me what I knew about Blackburn. He said he'd never really gotten to know the guy because he was from out of state, and he wished he had, because he was such a great coach, yadda yadda."

"And?"

"And—and that Canada thing came up."

"Canada thing?" I thought of Soupy crying on my landing.

"You know, how Blackburn missed that year?"

"You told Boynton?"

"No—I mean—I just told him what I knew."

"What?" I said. "What the hell did you know? You didn't say a word to me."

"No, I did not," she said. "Because I didn't have it *nailed*. You told me not to bring you stuff unless it was nailed."

"OK, I'm an asshole. Tell me now, please."

She sat on the teacher's desk. "It's not—I don't have it quite right yet—but something screwy went on up there. I told you I talked to this lady in Canada. St. Albert, actually, Alberta. Blackburn's last team before here."

"Yes."

"She works at the newspaper there, in the library. She was the one who sent me to that local guy who's like the hockey historian, and he told me Blackburn 'skedaddled,' remember? And then he hung up? That made me suspicious, of course, so I called that woman back, pretending I wanted some clips. She said she didn't want to talk, but I could tell she did, so I got her to let me call her at home. It took a little bit to get her going, but she had—has—this nephew, her sister's kid, who supposedly was a big star player for Blackburn. Everyone was saying he was going to play in the pros. Then one day, he just up and quit. No more hockey."

"Why?"

"I don't know. She got kind of upset and got off the phone."

"Was the kid not getting enough ice time?"

"No, no, he was a star. He was the top scorer like two or three years in a row. Blackburn supposedly worshiped him. Called him—what was it?—'Tiger.'"

That's what Blackburn had called Boynton. Soupy was Swanny and Teddy was Tiger. I was just Gus.

"At first the kid told his parents he was just sick of all the pressure. I guess these kids played like a hundred games a year. His dad was ticked off, but his mom didn't buy it. She thought maybe he was into drugs or something. So she goes snooping around in his room and finds this diary."

"Boys don't keep diaries."

"My brother did. I once made the mistake of reading it."

"OK. What was in the kid's diary?"

Joanie shook her head. "She just basically broke down at that point, just started to cry. She said she didn't want to go through it again. I said, 'Excuse me, go through what again?' and she just cried harder. So I tried to steer away from the diary and back to Blackburn and then she got pretty angry."

"At you?"

"No. Wait a sec." She bent down and rummaged in her backpack, producing a notebook. She flipped through the pages. "Here," she said. "She told me, 'Everyone said that man resigned. He didn't resign. My brother-in-law rode him out of here on a rail. But first, of course, he had to win that last blessed championship. We had to win, at all costs, we had to win.' "

" 'Rode him out on a rail?' "

"Yeah. I don't know. I just know his team won the championship and then he was out of there for some reason."

"Did you talk to the nephew?"

"I don't know his name."

"So we don't really know what happened."

"Maybe, but the same thing happened in Victoria."

"To Blackburn? That was *before* St. Albert, right?"

"Yeah, I don't know, I thought I'd just try another place. I made a bunch of calls. The funny thing was, it's been like thirty years, but just about everybody remembers the guy. Most of them didn't want to talk. But what I could piece together was that he had a pretty decent team but he did something to make the parents mad and as soon as the season was over, he just slipped away and took a year off. That's the gap in his résumé. Then he got hired in St. Albert."

I stared at the floor, a dull linoleum checkerboard of beige and green. Who was this man? Coaches lost jobs all the time, of course, especially in the cutthroat Canadian junior leagues. But not after they won championships.

"This must be weird for you," Joanie said.

"It's fine."

"Well, it's all off the record anyway, for now at least."

"How much of this did you tell Boynton?"

Now she cast her eyes down. "Not much. I was just trying stuff out on him to see what he knew. I don't think he knew anything about the Canada stuff, at least not specifically. But he knew something."

"How do you know?"

"I could just tell. When I said Blackburn might have gotten into trouble in Canada, he just seemed to understand. Then he kept asking if we were doing a story."

"Did you tell Soupy Campbell?"

"Nope. Couldn't find him."

The picture was beginning to come slowly clear, like my truck windshield on a frosty morning. Soupy and Teddy were fighting over the marina settlement. Soupy told him to go to hell at the bar Saturday night. But Teddy had just been talking to Darlene, and then he talked to Joanie, whose address and phone number he had on that bar napkin. He then collected something from Joanie that he used to put the screws to Soupy. I had no idea what, but it had something to do with Coach's past, and it was enough to drag Soupy up my stairs to cry at my feet on Sunday night. There was also a bullet hole in Blackburn's snowmobile, Leo Redpath fleeing town, and the cops hauling a computer out of Leo's house.

Actually, the windshield wasn't clear at all.

"I hate to say this," I said, "but Boynton pretty much picked your pocket."

Joanie sighed. "Yeah. It won't happen again. And on the press conference—"

"Forget it. How'd you know the cops had interviewed Leo?"

"Oh, God. D'Alessio."

"Has he asked you out yet?"

"He asked me to come watch him bowl. I was like, kill me now, but I was nice, I just told him I couldn't do it while I was covering this story. Then he told Tawny Jane Twitchy-Butt our story was 'premature.'"

"Twitchy-butt?" I said.

nineteen

D eputy Esper, please."
         I'd let Joanie get ahead of me and pulled up to a pay
         phone outside the IGA.

"Esper," came that voice.

"It's me."

An awkward silence followed. If she'd been home, she would've just hung up the phone, as she had every time I'd called her when I first came back to town. At work a hang-up might have attracted attention.

"What?"

"I just wanted to say thanks for giving me the heads-up the other night."

"I shouldn't have."

"Well, thanks anyway. I wondered—"

"Gus, this is not fair."

"Listen, this is work and we're off the record, OK? I've just got to ask, Darl, you have to trust me, when you were talking with Boynton at Enright's"—I felt a stab of jealousy—"he wasn't—"

"I'm going to hang up, Gus."

"It's not what you're thinking. He wasn't asking you about Coach, was he?"

"I can't talk."

"Darlene, please, you've got to help me."

After our sweet tryst in the county courthouse all those years ago, we'd begun dating. Around town we became, officially, an item, and there was talk that we would marry and settle on the lake. Not surprisingly, followers of the River Rats laced this talk with sarcasm about my gaffe in the state final. There were jokes about me falling down at the altar and dropping wedding rings. As for me, I can't honestly say that I fell in love with Darlene then because I think I'd always been in love with her, as far back as the day I rescued her bike from Jitters Creek. Whatever I felt, it wasn't enough to keep me in Starvation. We always knew I was going to leave, but even after I accepted the job at the *Times* and started preparing to move, we never talked about it. The pain we'd avoided for so long finally settled upon us. My last week in town, we didn't speak.

Only after she married did she deign to talk with me again, but even then only in short, strained snatches, like the conversation we were now having. Most of the time, it was as if we were talking on a bad connection. Emotional static obscured our voices and blocked our ears. Darlene wavered between anger about her lousy marriage and fear that somehow the sound of my voice might lure her back to me and whatever sorrow I might inflict on her a second time. I waited apologetically for her walls of resolve to crack so that I might hear the slightest echo of her old kindness. In a way, the worst of returning to Starvation Lake was facing Darlene, whose icy distance accused me of having been a fool for ever leaving.

She was right, of course, that it was unfair of me to call her like this. I felt I had no choice.

"I told him no," she said.

"No what?"

"No, I wasn't going to tell him anything about your coach."

"You didn't tell him anything?"

She hesitated. "No, not—"

"Come on, Darlene."

"I don't have to talk to you at all."

"I saw you taking the stuff out of Leo's house today."

The phone went silent. I waited for a dial tone. I heard Darlene sigh. "Boynton called me yesterday," she said. "I told him to go to hell again, but he said he had information."

By then Boynton had spoken with Joanie. He knew a little about Canada.

"What information?"

"It's pretty creepy. He was asking—hold on." I heard her close a door. She picked up the phone again. "He wanted to know about Blackburn's criminal history."

"Criminal history? Like felonies?"

"Blackburn didn't have a record, though."

"No record of what?"

"You can't print this, Gus."

"Darlene, I'm not going to print what Boynton was asking you."

"He—darn it, hang on." I heard knocking on her door. She covered the phone. I waited. She came back on. "I have to go."

"What did he ask about?"

Now I got the dial tone.

My story about Boynton's ultimatum to the zoning board went on the front page along with Joanie's story about Dingus's aborted press conference. Kerasopoulos read Joanie's story before it went to print. He made us redo a few lines so it didn't look like Dingus had walked out in a huff, even though he had. Joanie wasn't pleased, but at least she didn't blame me. Before I left, I made sure Tillie had put the underwater tunnel question in Sound Off. I also made arrangements for some editing help in Traverse City so I could make the trip to Detroit the next morning. I didn't say why I had to take the day off, just that I had some personal business.

The phone on my desk rang as I was climbing the stairs to my apartment. I let it. I wanted a nap before the game. Upstairs I packed my gear and lay back in the recliner. My eyes fell on the boxes supporting the table. The one marked "Rats" held one big part of my life, the others marked "Trucks" held another. Neither seemed to have worked out very well. I flicked off the lamp and closed my eyes. But I couldn't sleep.

By now, I thought, the police might have caught up with Leo. Or maybe they weren't even pursuing him. Maybe he'd left for some other reason, something that had nothing to do with Coach. Maybe he'd gone because he could no longer bear staying in Starvation Lake now that his old friend had returned, albeit in shadow.

I got out of the chair and called Mom, whose mile-a-minute message informed me that she was out. I couldn't tell where. I left a message that I'd try to stop by Tuesday evening. I didn't want her to know I was going downstate. She'd worry. I set my alarm for 5:30 a.m.

I had to tape Eggo's thumb. I unzipped my hockey bag, set the glove on the table, and rooted in my bag for the shiny black tape I always used. Barely any was left on the roll. I'd been meaning to buy more. I peeled off Saturday's tape and started winding the fresh stuff on. I ran out before I'd gotten around the thumb twice. Even though the tape didn't really hold anything, I liked to have it go around at least three times. Tonight, two would have to do.

When I walked into dressing room 3, the Chowder Heads were having the sort of discussion that passed for philosophical in a place that reeked of old sweat and mildew. Wilf was telling of a friend who'd skated on a minor-league team where it was customary for a rookie, as part of his ritual initiation, to come to a game and find his skates filled with a veteran's dump.

"Jesus, Wilf," Stevie Reneau said. He was smearing toothpaste on the inside of his plastic face shield so it wouldn't fog. Stevie had no stomach for these sorts of stories, which was one reason why Wilf took such glee in telling them. We never knew whether Wilf was making stuff up just to make Stevie sick, but this particular story was, unfortunately, plausible.

"So this rookie's cleaning out his skates, you know, while my buddy and all the other dudes are laughing their balls off," Wilf said. "Then the guy goes out and—what do you know?—scores a hat trick. No shit. First of his career, eh?" He grinned widely, knowing Stevie would reach the conclusion any superstitious hockey player would.

"Don't tell me," Stevie said.

"Oh, yeah," Wilf said.

Stevie's face contorted with pain. "The guy had to keep putting shit in his skates? Get the fuck out of here."

Wilf laughed while Stevie impulsively grabbed his own skates and stuffed them back in his hockey bag. "You've been in a bit of a scoring slump, Steve-O," Wilf said. "You never know what might help."

Although Zilchy thought it bad luck to speak a word just before games, this opportunity was apparently irresistible. "What do you think, Stevie? Would the guy have to have the same guy's shit in his skates before every game?"

"And what if the shitter got traded?" Danny Lefebvre chimed in.

Wilf's eyes lit up. "I guess the rookie's career would go right down the shitter!"

"Goddamn it, Wilf," Stevie groaned.

Soupy walked in, dragging his hockey bag and a cooler.

"Soup," Danny said.

"Spoons," Wilf said.

Soupy dropped his bag and slid the cooler to the middle of the room. He sat down, as always, to my left. He looked tired. It wasn't like him to be late for a championship game, even if it was just the Midnight Hour Men's League.

"Soup, you got to hear this," Wilf said. He started to retell his story, but Soupy stopped him in midsentence.

"Not now."

Wilf looked offended. "Fuck's your problem?" he said.

"The Zam's on."

"Leo finally show up?" Danny said.

Soupy kept his head down as he pulled gear from his bag. "Ronny's doing the ice," he said. Ronny was a high school kid who worked for Leo.

"So the ice'll suck," Wilf said. "Where the hell is Leo? It's a championship game, for fuck's sakes."

Soupy gave me a sharp sideways glance, as if I knew the answer. I flipped my mask down. "So, Soup," I said, changing the subject. "Mom's thinking of getting a boat, now that I'm back. Maybe a nice speedboat."

He grunted as he struggled to jam his left foot into his four-sizes-too-small skate. "Mrs. C's got the cash for a speedboat? I doubt that. You seen Leo?"

"No," I said. "What do they run these days?"

"A good speedboat? A lot. But, between the two of you, we could probably put you in an inflatable raft."

"So, like, what? Ten grand?"

He was forcing his second skate on. "Twice that," he said.

"Huh," I said. "So do you sell boats for, like, twenty-five thousand dollars?" That was the number on the receipt Dingus had given me.

"Sure," Soupy said. "Nicer, bigger ones. You used to work there."

"You don't sell ferryboats, do you?"

"Ferryboats? What the fuck are you talking about?" He directed himself to the entire room. "Was Gus already drinking? Goalies aren't supposed to drink pregame."

"Never mind," I said.

"Look, Trap, if Mrs. C really wants a boat, you know I'll work something out. Have her call me. But, Jesus, you're getting weird. Everything's getting weird around here. Where the hell is Leo anyway?"

Most of the room had emptied. I could hear sticks cracking pucks and pucks booming off sideboards. Soupy pulled on his Chowder Heads jersey, red and white, with a logo of a soup spoon made to look like a hockey stick.

"You were a little weird yourself last night, man," I said.

"You mean Saturday?"

"No, last night. On my stairway. You were shitfaced."

He popped his taped-up helmet on his head. "I don't know what you're talking about."

"And what about today? The zoning board missed you."

"Ain't lucky to talk business, Trap."

"Ain't lucky to talk luck."

He wrapped his arm around my shoulder as he always did just before we went out to play. But this time he squeezed hard and pulled me in close to him and peered in through the eyeholes in my mask.

"Where's Leo?" he said. "The Zam shed's cleaned out."

"I didn't notice."

"Bullshit. You notice every goddamn thing."

"We've got to get out there. I'm a brick wall, right?"

"Yeah," Soupy said, standing. "And I'm a rubber band, liable to snap any minute."

We came out fast. Zilchy scored on a rebound to make it 1–0 and then Stevie deflected a low shot by Soupy over Tatch, the Land Sharks' goalie, for a 2–0 lead late in the first period. I had to make only one tough save when D'Alessio got free and swung in untouched from my left. He shot low and hard to my stick side and I barely got my right toe on it. The rebound went right to Boynton, who tried to jam it just inside the goalpost, but I dove and smothered it for a whistle.

"Fuck you, Carpie," I heard him tell me yet again.

As we took the lead into the second period, Teddy started playing more and more like the Teddy he'd grown into. He kicked Stevie's legs out from behind. Elbowed Danny Lefebvre in the face. Clipped me with a butt end as he skated past. All when the refs weren't looking, of course. Mostly, though, he gunned for Soupy. He cross-checked him in the neck, whacked him in the back of the knees, yapped at him at face-offs. "You think this is a fucking game?" he shouted once. Soupy did not reply, which wasn't like him. He was no fighter, but he rarely shied from yapping at a yapper. Boynton kept it up. Soupy kept turning away.

Midway through the third period, Loob took a pass from Boynton and fired a slapper just to my right. Loob had a cannon, but I saw this shot cleanly and flicked out Eggo to block it. I thought I had it easily, but it deflected off Eggo's bottom edge, ricocheted downward, and bounced off the side of my right leg pad and into the net. While the Sharks celebrated, I stared at Eggo in disbelief, wondering if the lack of one wind of tape had cost me.

When I looked up, I saw blue and red police lights flashing through the glass at the other end of the rink. Everyone stopped to watch the sheriff's deputies, five or six of them, trot into the Zamboni shed. They got Leo, I thought. One of the refs skated down there, and D'Alessio jumped off the Land Shark bench and joined him. I could see the cops stringing up yellow crime-scene tape. D'Alessio turned and directed everyone, even the referees, over to the benches. He left the ice and clomped into the Zam shed in his skates. I went over and leaned against the boards by our bench where the rest of the Chowder Heads were quietly watching. Soupy gave me a look. "What?" I said, and he turned away. The police lights kept flashing. Finally D'Alessio emerged from the Zam shed, shaking his head. He called the refs over. They had a brief conversation. D'Alessio skated off the ice and into the dressing room. I watched Soupy watching him. One of the refs came over and said, "They're going to close the place, but we can finish."

A little more than six minutes remained. The police lights kept flashing. The skaters lined up for a face-off to my right. As the ref held the puck out over the face-off dot, Darlene, in uniform, stepped into view outside the glass in the corner. Stevie won the face-off back to Soupy, who slid the puck immediately to me. I froze it for another face-off, which is what Soupy wanted. "Hang on," he told the ref, and then skated over to Darlene. They had a brief exchange that I could not hear. Soupy punched the glass with his right fist and yelled, "No!" The ref's whistle shrilled. "Today, gentlemen," he said. Darlene hurried away, and when Soupy turned back to the game, his face was a pale mask of anger.

I felt certain then that something bad was going to happen.

From the next face-off, Stevie shoveled the puck ahead to Wilf, who banged it into the Land Sharks' end. Zilchy chased it down in a corner and slid a quick pass back to Soupy waiting just above the face-off dot to the left of the Land Shark net. From there he could've had a clear shot on goal or he could've passed it to Danny Lefebvre at the far goalpost. Instead he lifted his stick an inch and let the puck slide beneath it. He tried to make it look like a mistake. Inexplicably, he waited a beat while Boynton rushed past and scooped up the puck. Soupy turned in pursuit.

Boynton had a breakaway. Soupy was faster, though, and could have overtaken him easily. Instead he maintained his pace two strides behind, waiting for something. What are you doing? I thought. I slid out to cut down the angle, my eyes darting between Boynton and Soupy, still trailing. Boynton veered to the middle of the ice. I stopped and squatted, prepared to push backward, catching glove high, Eggo in position, eyes now on the puck. I was guessing that Boynton was preparing to shoot rather than deke when his legs buckled and the puck squirted away.

The heel of Soupy's stick caught Boynton just under the right eye. Soupy swung it like a baseball bat, following through as Boynton cried out once and crumpled. Soupy raised his stick again and brought it down like an ax on the side of Boynton's head. Boynton was wearing a helmet, but again I heard the crack of wood on bone.

"Soupy!" I screamed. I dropped my stick and gloves and rushed to grab him before he swung his stick again. I had a fistful of his jersey when someone tackled us from behind. In an instant, other Land Sharks and Chowder Heads were piling on, screaming and cursing. A whistle was blowing. I heard someone saying, "Oh my God, call an ambulance, call an ambulance." Somebody was punching me in the back, but I hung tight to Soupy, my mask pressed against the back of his neck. He was muttering to himself, "Leo, they fucking killed Leo. I'll kill you, motherfucker, I'll kill you."

The refs peeled us apart. Somebody pulled me away, and Loob and Wilf grabbed Soupy by his arms and he let them. "That's all, Soup, settle down," Loob said. Boynton lay motionless on his side. A scarlet smear streaked the ice where he'd slid after falling. One of his teammates crouched next to him and removed his helmet. The side of his face was covered in blood.

"Fuck him," Soupy said. "I hope he fucking dies."

A ref stepped in front of him. "Game's over," he said. "Sharks win by forfeit." Soupy didn't care. He looked at me. "Happy now?"

I had no idea what he meant. D'Alessio reappeared. He showed Soupy a pair of handcuffs. "Easy way or hard, Soup?"

Soupy held his hands out impassively. As D'Alessio cuffed him, Soupy looked down at the unconscious Boynton. "Guess it ain't a fucking game, is it?"

Two paramedics rushed through the front door of the rink, followed by two sheriff's deputies and Sheriff Aho. But why would Dingus come for a lousy assault and battery? It wasn't the first time a skater had gone a little crazy. Then a light like a car's headlamp went on just over his shoulder, and I saw a bearded guy in a hooded green parka shouldering a TV camera pointed at Dingus. Walking beside him and speaking into a microphone was Tawny Jane Reese. A TV crew for a stick fight? I looked at Boynton. He still wasn't moving.

Dingus walked out onto the ice and knelt next to Boynton, shaking his head. He looked up at Soupy. "You guys never grow up, do you?" he said.

Tawny Jane minced onto the ice, trying to keep her balance while she spoke into her microphone. Her cameraman aimed at Teddy as the paramedics secured him to a stretcher and hauled him out.

Dingus stood and walked over to Soupy and me. Tawny Jane and the cameraman followed. Dingus motioned to D'Alessio. "One minute, Deputy." They stepped aside and talked. Dingus turned to Tawny Jane and said, "Give us a minute." The camera light went out. Tawny Jane whispered something into the ear of the cameraman. She seemed excited.

D'Alessio moved back behind Soupy. He put one hand on the cuffs and one on Soupy's shoulder. Dingus pointed at Tawny Jane and the cameraman. He stepped in front of Soupy. The camera light went on again. Tawny Jane stepped closer and stuck her microphone out for what Dingus was about to say.

Soupy spoke first, though. "Leo, Dingus?"

Dingus held Soupy's gaze for a second, then he said, "Alden Campbell, you are under arrest for first-degree murder in the March 1988 death of John David Blackburn."

"Fucking-ay," Soupy said.

I had to lean on my stick to keep from falling over. I looked at Soupy. I wanted him to tell me this was all bullshit. His expression didn't change. It was as if he expected this.

"Get him out of here," Dingus said.

Tawny Jane narrated while the cameraman backpedaled in front of Dingus and D'Alessio walking Soupy off the ice.

I skated up behind them. "Dingus," I said. "What about Leo?"

"They fucking killed him," Soupy shouted.

Dingus stopped and turned to me. His face did not contradict what Soupy had said. "Later," he said.

I followed Tawny Jane to the edge of the rink. She was telling her microphone: " . . . bleak chapter in the history of this down-on-its-luck resort town, here in the place named for the man who, we're now being told, did not die in a snowmobile accident ten years ago but was, shockingly, murdered. Among the spicier ingredients in this torrid potboiler of a tale: A beloved coach, a disgruntled former player, and a twenty-two-caliber bullet. Channel Eight's exclusive coverage . . ."

The damp hair around my ears froze as I stepped out of my truck in the parking lot of the Pine County Sheriff's Department. I remembered the time Soupy and I had a playful hockey fight on the rink in his backyard. My hair had frozen to my helmet and, when Soupy tore the helmet off, some of my hair came with it. Soupy thought it was hilarious.

Now he was inside somewhere, in an interrogation room or a jail cell. And something terrible had happened to Leo.

The glassed-in sheriff's department lobby glowed with fluorescent light. Inside, Joanie spotted me approaching and hurried out.

"Are you OK?" she said.

"What's going on?"

"Dingus is supposed to be out in a few minutes."

"We better get in there."

"Wait." She put a hand against my chest. "Are you all right to cover this?"

Of course I wasn't. But what was I going to do? "I'm fine."

"Do you really think Campbell killed Blackburn?"

I hesitated just long enough that one of her eyebrows crept higher. I couldn't imagine what Soupy's motive would be, but I'd been surprised by so many things in the last few days that I wasn't sure what to think. I'd always thought of Soupy as gentle. He'd never been one for the rough stuff in hockey. Then came the sneak attack on Boynton.

"No," I said.

"Well," Joanie said, "I'm sorry about your friends. And I'm sorry about getting scooped. I've got to wait a whole damn day to catch up."

No doubt Tawny Jane's report was already on the air. At that hour, maybe twenty people were watching. "Forget it," I said.

"I come in tonight and she's like, 'Oh, this must be terrible for you, your stories today were so great,' and I'm like, you little slut."

"Just lock down your sources in the department now so we don't have Tawny Jane attached to Dingus when the rest of this plays out," I said. "Also, in case he has another press conference—"

"Yeah, yeah, I got it."

"Hey, guys," came a voice. We turned to see Skip Catledge leaning out the door. "Sheriff'll be out in a minute."

. . .

When Dingus emerged, his brown tie was still tied and clasped and he moved with purpose I had never seen in him before. He raised his hands as the four of us—Tawny Jane, the cameraman, Joanie, and me—stepped toward him.

"Before you start asking questions, this is not a press conference," he said. "Kill that, please." He pointed at the cameraman, who lowered his camera. "Rather than have you sit in my lobby all night, I'm going to tell you a couple of things and then you're all going home. Understood? No notes, Miss McCarthy. And no interruptions. This is totally off the record, just for your planning and information. There'll be plenty on the record tomorrow."

"As you know, we have in custody Alden Campbell. Most people around here know him as Soupy. He will be arraigned tomorrow at two p.m. before Judge Gallagher on a charge of murder, first degree, as well as assault and battery related to the incident during the hockey game this evening."

"Sheriff?" It was Joanie.

Dingus looked at her in disbelief. "Miss, I'm giving you a second chance here. It will also be your last."

"Sorry."

"This is my investigation, OK? *My* investigation." He waited for that to sink in. "We believe the murder did in fact occur on the same night as the snowmobile accident in which Mr. Blackburn previously was believed to have died. Again, I'm not going to go into a lot of detail. Suffice it to say that we believe the accident itself was fraudulent, and we're attempting now to determine the location of Mr. Blackburn's remains. As you know, there is no statute of limitations on murder."

The word "fraudulent" shivered through me like a fever chill. I thought of my mother and the floor that wasn't wet, and of Leo running. "In a related matter," Dingus said, "we attempted this evening to apprehend an individual who we believe had material knowledge of the events in question. That individual had fled the local area and was located by the Michigan state police on U.S. One Thirty-one about thirty-five miles south of the Mackinac Bridge. He resisted attempts to apprehend him peacefully. An unfortunate incident occurred, which we continue to investigate. We hope to have more for you on that tomorrow."

Of course it was Leo.

Dingus held up a finger. "That's all for now, but I will allow one question." He looked directly at Joanie and said, "Ms. Reese?"

Joanie frowned at the floor. Tawny Jane stepped forward. Her hair was tangled in a maroon scrunchy at the back of her head.

"Sheriff," she said, "do you have any idea of motive?"

Dingus pursed his lips. "We might."

"Can you say what?"

"I'm sorry. That's two questions."

"Sheriff—"

"Don't make the same mistake Miss McCarthy made, Ms. Reese," Dingus said. "OK, I'd like you all to clear out now—except you."

He meant me.

I waited in Dingus's office in the same angle-iron chair I'd sat in a few days before. In my mind I scoured the Zam shed for any clue that I'd been there that morning. Had the cops dusted for fingerprints? I remembered the pieces of paper with the strange lettering I'd taken from Leo's file cabinet. They were still in my coat pocket. What if this were some sort of interrogation? What if they searched me?

Dingus came in. He sat on the edge of his desk facing me and folded his thick arms across his chest. "We've got to talk," he said, "but first you need to know what happened to Leo Redpath. Off the record. You were supposed to be his friend. But you didn't do him any favors."

"What does that mean?"

"It's a tragedy, really. An unnecessary tragedy. We had questioned Redpath in this matter. Apparently he got scared for some reason, which is unfortunate because we didn't regard him as a suspect, at least not for long."

"Why did you—"

"Quiet," Dingus said. It was sometimes hard to take Dingus seriously because of that singsong Scandinavian accent of his. Not now, though. "Late last night, we got an anonymous tip that Redpath knew more about this incident than he'd let on in the original investigation. This person suggested maybe the original incident didn't happen the way everybody thought it did."

"Who was this tipster?" I said. I thought I knew: Teddy Boynton, after all of his snooping around between Darlene and Joanie.

"Doesn't matter," Dingus said. "As I said, Redpath was a suspect, but only briefly. After we heard from this caller, we definitely wanted to speak with Redpath again. But when we went to see him this morning, we found his room at the rink empty. We put out an APB. Two state police cruisers caught up with him. They had the squawk box going, trying to get him out of his car, and he reaches into his glove box."

My stomach dropped. "Jesus, Dingus. They shot him?"

Dingus leaned forward until his face was just a few inches from mine. "No, Gus," he said. "The wound was self-inflicted. Redpath had a pistol in his glove box. He discharged it into the side of his head above the right ear."

"Oh my God," I said. A prickle of heat ran across my shoulders and up my neck. An image flashed in my mind of the first time I'd seen Leo, standing at the wheel of Ethel, circling the ice, and then of one of the last times I'd seen him, leaned in close to my face as he sewed the stitches into my jaw. "What the hell is going on around here?"

"I wanted to ask you that, Gus, because you know what?" Now he reached up and grabbed my coat collar in his beefy hand and yanked me up off the chair. "I think you had something to do with this."

"What? Take your hands off me."

He tightened his grip. "I ought to strangle that little redhead. Somehow she spooked Redpath."

"Bullshit. He wouldn't even talk to her."

"He didn't have to talk to her. He just had to hear her questions. She asked him something that spooked him. We'd already talked to him. He didn't run. She goes to see him, he runs. I want to know what she asked him, Gus."

"I wish I knew, Sheriff."

Dingus swung me away from the chair and slammed me against the wall. "This man is dead," he growled. "I have to contact his family, whoever and wherever they are, and we're out a material witness in a murder case. All because your little reporter is sticking her nose in places it shouldn't ought to go. What did she ask him, Gus?"

"I don't know, Dingus, and I wouldn't have to tell you anyway. She was doing her job. Or are you just worried about getting reelected?"

I knew that was a mistake the second it left my lips. He hammered me against the wall again and pushed in close enough that I could smell his Tiparillo breath, see the tiny yellowed teeth hidden by his handlebar. I thought he might punch me. "This is not about a goddamn election," he said. "It's about a murder investigation. It's not your job to conduct murder investigations. It's not your job to embarrass me in front of the public when I'm trying to do *my* job."

"And you didn't embarrass us with those bullshit leaks about our stories being 'premature'? And then the TV chick gets a front-row seat for the arrest? Have hot lips D'Alessio take a cold shower, will you?"

He dropped me and stepped back and pointed a finger at me. "You know the meaning of 'is'?" he said. "Until I say something *is*— like a murder—then it *isn't*, understand? Or maybe you'd like to learn more about the case from Channel Eight. You guys are always talking about the public's right to know. Don't you think the public has a right to know what you know?"

"We know squat, Dingus. From what I can tell, Leo's obviously the one who killed Blackburn. He was there that night. He lied about it. He ran, and then he killed himself. But you have Soupy in jail."

"Where he belongs," Dingus said. He sat back down on his desk.

The framed photograph of his ex appeared over his left shoulder. I wondered if Barbara Lampley had still been talking with Dingus, or even married to him, when he was investigating the first time around. It was her dalliance with Blackburn, after all, that had effectively ended their marriage. I decided that I wanted to talk with her.

"Sit," Dingus said. I sat. "Gus," he said, "I have tried to help you out where I could because I think you can help me. What the redhead did was no help."

"Her name is Joanie."

"Uh-huh. Get her out of my way."

I wasn't about to accept responsibility for Leo's suicide. But I thought I was beginning to understand Dingus. His original inquiry into Blackburn's death obviously had missed the mark. Cops who messed up like that usually made excuses or tried to cover their tracks. Instead Dingus was doing everything he could to blow up his old case. It was as if he'd never believed the original conclusion, as if his hands had somehow been tied, and now that pieces of Blackburn were resurfacing in our little town, he was determined to set things right. I couldn't promise Dingus anything, and I didn't appreciate being roughed up, but I couldn't help but admire him a little.

"We'll try not to mess you up," I said, "and you try not to mess us up."

"Fair enough."

"Can I ask one thing?"

"One thing."

"Don't get upset. I watched you guys today hauling stuff out of Leo's house, including a bunch of computer stuff. What's the deal?"

Dingus considered it. "Redpath had issues," he said.

"What issues?"

He stood. "It's late. I'll see you tomorrow."

I drove directly to the pay phone outside the IGA. Joanie picked up on the first ring. "What happened?"

I told her what happened to Leo.

"Oh my God, that's terrible," she said. "I'm really sorry."

"Let me ask you. What did you tell him when you talked to him?"

She hesitated. "He wouldn't talk."

"You must have said something to *try* to get him to talk."

"I told him I was trying to find out more about what happened that night. He said he didn't want to dredge it up, he wasn't—how did he put it?—he wasn't 'a dweller in the distant past.'"

It sounded like one of those sayings he had pasted over his workbench. "And what'd you say?"

"I may have said something about Canada, the missing year and all that."

"Same as with Boynton."

"Yeah."

I didn't see necessarily why that would have spooked him. Leo wasn't with Blackburn in Canada, so far as I knew. "I know a little more," I said. "The cops searched Leo's house. They confiscated his computer."

"Why didn't you tell me?"

"I just did."

"Why'd they take his computer?"

"No idea. Dingus said Leo had issues."

"No, duh. Isn't it pretty obvious he's the killer?"

"Seems to make sense, but Dingus says no. Supposedly we'll learn more at the arraignment. You'll go?"

"Yeah."

"While you're at it, why don't you do a little more checking into Blackburn's background? I think he had a brother-in-law in Kalamazoo."

"Wife's brother or sister's husband?"

"No idea. I don't know if he was ever married."

"Gus?"

"Yeah?"

"I don't want to get scooped again."

. . .

In the darkness of my mother's bedroom, I gently jiggled her bed. She lurched awake. I laid a hand on her shoulder. "It's Gus," I whispered.

"Son. You scared me."

"Sorry." I sat down on the bed.

"What's wrong?"

"Leo."

Mom sat up in her flannel pajamas. "What?"

I didn't tell her about the computer, just the suicide. As she listened, her eyes grew slowly wider. She drew her hand up over her mouth. "No," she said. In her eyes in that instant I could see she knew things she'd never told me, and I wanted to ask her then, I wanted to demand she tell me whatever it was she had held back, but all I could do was let her fall into my arms and hold her as she cried. She hadn't sobbed so hard since Dad died. It surprised me only a little that I could not manage a single tear.

twenty

My alarm buzzed the next morning at five-thirty. I bolted up in my bed, startled and groggy. Then I remembered: I was supposed to go to Detroit for the meeting with Superior Motors and the Hanovers. "Oh, God," I said, lying back on my pillow. The night flooded back: Soupy was in jail. Boynton was in the hospital. Leo was dead. My mother had cried herself out and then I let her go back to sleep. I heard a snowplow rumble past my window. The clock said 5:46. If I was going to Detroit, I had to get on the road.

But why, really? The Superior Motors lawyers didn't care whether I showed up; they just wanted the name of my source, which I could supply easily enough over the phone, if I was so inclined. And I was beginning to think I was so inclined. What difference would it really make if I ratted out the sleazebag V? Joanie would be disappointed, but she'd be gone soon enough, chasing her career. Kerasopoulos wouldn't be concerned in the least that I had burned a confidential source at another paper. He'd care a lot more if cops showed up at the *Pilot* to arrest me for stealing Superior voice mails. The pointy-headed gods of journalism would undoubtedly denounce me if the news from Starvation Lake ever reached them, but I couldn't see how that would affect me in any tangible way. My career already had hit bottom. Giving up V's real name would help the Hanovers nail down the settlement they wanted, which might actually succeed in getting some of those killer trucks fixed.

I walked into the kitchen and dialed my attorney. Outside, a few snowflakes wafted through the streetlamp glow. "Snowing like a bitch up here," I told Scott Trenton's answering machine. "Tell the lawyers

I'm stuck but, listen, you wanted a show of good faith, so you can tell them"—I paused—"I'll have a decision on the name by tomorrow at noon. I know they wanted it today, but they've got a few days yet before the judge rules. Anyway, I've given your advice some thought and, you know, you're probably right."

The *Pilot* was empty when I walked down just after seven. I was hungry for a bite at Audrey's, but first I wanted to check on a couple of things.

Down in the basement I scanned paper after paper from 1988 and finally found what I was looking for. The story by Mildred Pratt, one of our blue-haired stringers, ran on the inside. It said the town council had decided against dredging the lake "due to budgetary constraints." That was pretty much it. Mildred didn't record the vote or supply any detail of the council's discussion, assuming there was one. Normally Henry would've covered the council meeting, but the story ran in April, around the time Henry was usually on a golf vacation in Florida. The story told me nothing I didn't already know. I had to get those meeting minutes.

I went back upstairs to see if we had a recent photo of Dingus. Morning light eked through the blinds and across the filing cabinets where Delbert Riddle kept the *Pilot* photos. I'd heard Tillie complain about Delbert's filing system, but I had yet to experience it myself because she was always the one who retrieved photos. At first glance, it looked simple. Taped on the front of each of the four drawers in each cabinet was an index card marked with letters in alphabetical order. I opened the drawer marked "A-Am." I found the file marked "Aho, Dingus" and laid it atop the cabinet.

Most of the folders were marked in the same simple way as Dingus's file. But others, scattered throughout, were identified with a series of letters and numbers, such as one stuffed just behind Dingus's file, marked Ai/0685/SL/W. I pulled it out and opened it. The first photo in a thick stack showed a beaming young woman in a wedding gown feeding a piece of cake to a man in a tuxedo. It was Dale and Sheila Ainsley. They owned the Dairy Queen. The stamp on the back said June 6, 1985. "I get it," I said aloud. Delbert's Ai/0685/SL/W signified Ainsley/June 1985/Starvation Lake/Wedding. So he was using the *Pilot* files to keep track of his freelance work. No surprise there. I slapped the file closed and stuck it back inside.

I spread Dingus's file open. There were only three photos. One showed a much younger Dingus, without the handlebar, accepting a plaque for being Deputy of the Year in a grip-and-grin with then-sheriff Jerry Spardell. An ink stamp on the back showed it had been taken January 31, 1987. The others were simple mug shots, both more than five years old. I left the file open and walked over to Tillie's desk to make out a photo assignment sheet. I figured Delbert could catch Dingus at the arraignment. As I jotted instructions down, I thought it also would be good to have some photos from the rink. I remembered the yellow tape strung around the Zamboni shed.

Then it hit me.

I hurried back to my desk and grabbed my coat off of my chair. In the pocket I found the three scraps of paper I'd removed from the inside of Leo's cabinet in the Zam shed. I rushed back up front and laid them next to Dingus's photo file. Scratched in red ballpoint were the numbers and letters that had flummoxed me the day before: F/1280/SL/R4. F/1280/SL/R5. F/1280/SL/R6.

Now I thought I understood.

I opened the drawer marked Ep–Fe. In the middle of the drawer where the F files began sat two accordion folders. I pulled out the first one. It was stuffed with thin white cardboard boxes marked on one end with Delbert's peculiar indexes. Opening a box marked F/0279/SL/R1, I slipped out a reel of what looked to be 8-millimeter film. So the F stood for film, I thought. I opened another box, marked F/0279/SL/R4. It, too, contained a reel of film. The 0279 apparently referred to February 1979, when I was in high school and playing for the River Rats; the SL, again, signified Starvation Lake. As Joanie had told me, Delbert developed film for Blackburn. These had to be films of our practices.

But why would Leo scribble down just those three indexes and then hide them? None of the numbers on the boxes in the first accordion folder matched the ones on the scraps of paper. I pulled the drawer all the way out, put the first folder back inside, and peered into the others. The second folder contained nine similar boxes from 1980 and 1981. Three were marked with the same numbers and letters written on the scraps. I removed the entire folder, carried it back to my desk, and stashed it in a drawer. I put Dingus's file back in the cabinet, then finished the photo assignment and dropped it in Tillie's in-box before heading across the street.

The first person I saw when I walked into Audrey's was me, a blurry image in my goalie gear on a small black-and-white TV someone had set up in the back. A dozen codgers clustered around, some still in overcoats and scarves, watching Dingus march Soupy out of the John D. Blackburn Memorial Ice Arena while Tawny Jane Reese narrated. Elvis spied me as I took a seat at the counter.

"Look who's here," he said. "An eyewitness to history, though you'd never know from reading his paper."

All the gray heads turned my way. What was I thinking coming in here? "Morning, folks," I said.

"Quite a night there, Gus," one of them said.

"Soupy Campbell wouldn't hurt a flea," another said. "Ain't no way he killed Jack Blackburn. Dingus is off his nut."

"Poor old Leo."

"Hoo-hah, I'll bet Leo's the one what killed Blackburn."

"Blackburn wasn't killed. He's in the lake. This is all a conspiracy cooked up by the sheriff to make sure he gets reelected."

"If Teddy dies, God forbid, we got a double murder in Starvation Lake."

"Ain't no double murder if one of them happened ten years ago, Elvis."

"Far as I'm concerned," Elvis said. "But like I said, you wouldn't know a thing from reading our local paper. Looks like another one got behind you, Gus."

It was all I could do to keep from screaming.

"The presses run at seven p.m., Elvis," I said.

The blue-and-white cap perched on his head read Pekoe Hardened Tools. "I hear other papers actually stop the presses and start them up again when they have big news, like maybe a double murder," he said. "But maybe you just don't want your drinking buddies looking bad, huh?"

"Elvis!" Audrey shouted it from behind the counter. "Keep harassing my customers and you can have McMuffins for breakfast." She pointed at the TV. The weather turtle was predicting a snowstorm. "And I don't want to see that thing in my place tomorrow, I don't care how big the so-called news is."

Somebody turned it off.

I turned to face Audrey. She was wearing a sky-blue apron and her hair was pulled back in a tidy bun. As she picked up two platters of eggs, bacon, and fried potatoes, she said to me, "You know what you want, honey?"

"Cinnamon bun, warm, and a coffee to go."

A *Pilot* rested on the stool two down from me. My eyes wandered past it to the autographed photo of Gordie Howe. He was winding up to shoot on a goaltender for the Montreal Canadiens. The goalie was still on his feet, probably backing into the cage. I wondered for the hundredth time if he'd made the save.

Audrey returned with my bun and coffee. "Audrey?" I said. "Can I ask you something?"

"Sure, honey."

I leaned closer so no one else would hear me. "You know Barbara Lampley? Dingus's ex-wife?"

"Mm-hm."

"She was still with Dingus when Coach died, right?"

Audrey scrunched up her face. "I can't recall, exactly. Why?"

"I thought maybe she'd remember something from back then. Maybe not."

Audrey glanced over at Elvis, then back at me. She didn't tell many tales, certainly not with Elvis within earshot. But her look told me enough.

"Does she work over at Sandy Cove?" I said.

Audrey nodded yes.

"At the IGA? Think it'd be worth my trip?"

"She's at Glen's now, dear. And yes, my guess is, it would be worth it. Be careful in the snow."

I stopped for a minute at the *Pilot* on the way to my truck. Tillie had called and said she'd be late. Joanie was going to the clerk's office to check on Blackburn's old property records, then to Soupy's arraignment. I reminded her to keep working the Canada angle and see what else she could find out about Leo's computer. When my phone started ringing, I figured it had to be Trenton and headed out.

In the parking lot I spotted Tatch trudging past and shouted at him. He heard me through his sweatshirt hood and veered in my direction, hands jammed in his jeans pockets. His name was Roy Edwards, but Soupy had long ago dubbed him Tatch, short for attachment, as in vacuum cleaner attachment that sucks pucks into the net. Although he worked for Soupy at the marina, he tended goal for Boynton's Land Sharks and had skated the length of the rink to join the melee the night before.

"Hear anything on Teddy?" I said.

"Ain't woke up yet's all I know." A tiny circular scar pocked his forehead, the lingering imprint of a goalie mask screw that had been pressed into his head by a Loob slapshot. "Total drag about Leo, man."

"Yeah."

"So what the hell are the cops thinking, taking Soup in? Seems to me, Leo kills himself, case closed, he whacked Jack."

I reached through my truck window and cranked the ignition.

"Maybe the cops figure Soup done it to Jack because he damn near killed Ted," Tatch continued. "But, hell, Soupy could barely kill a flea. Too drunk." Tatch mustered a chuckle. "Him and Teddy don't get along so well, but shit, you don't need to half kill someone. Man, did you see that? He wound up on him like Babe Ruth."

"Did you see Soupy yesterday?" I said. "Did he say anything?"

"Funny." Tatch scratched at the silver whiskers on his neck. "Before a game, Soup's usually giving me all sorts of shit about how he's going to light me up. But yesterday he didn't say nothing. Hell, he barely come out of his office. I asked him if he wanted to go over to Enright's for a burger and he said, naw, he had to go to the rink and then he had the zoning thing."

"He went to the rink during the day?"

"Said he had to check in on Leo."

"For what?"

"You know, some damn superstition."

Soupy had Leo sharpen his skates every Monday, whether they needed it or not.

"About when did he go over?"

"I guess about one or so. This some sort of interview?"

"No. I was over there myself about then and wondered why I didn't see him." So Soupy had discovered Leo gone, then apparently changed his mind about going to the zoning board. I got into my truck. "I'll see you around."

"Yeah, better get to work," Tatch said. "Looks like I'm the boss today."

Glen's Supermarket anchored a strip mall along the highway a mile from downtown Sandy Cove. I parked next to a beeping dump truck.

Barbara Lampley was working the register in the cash-out lane next to the bakery. I waited in line behind a woman unloading a cart full of groceries. Her little boy sat in the cart gnawing on a glazed dough-nut.

"Hi," he said.

"Hi there," I said.

"Hi."

"Sir?" Barbara Lampley said. "The express lane is open."

"That's OK," I said.

I waited while Barbara Lampley shared a laugh with the woman in front of me, who was telling how her husband had nearly sliced off his arm while using a chain saw to cut an old sofa in half so it would fit it in the back of his pickup. Barbara Lampley had a big, throaty laugh that I was sure they could hear at the other end of the store. She was tall and big-boned in her creamy yellow Glen's smock, with a fresh, childlike face barely betrayed by the spidery crinkles at the corners of her eyes and the silver wisps in her chestnut hair. I could see why Dingus, and maybe Blackburn, had fallen for her. I wasn't interested in her affair with Blackburn so much as how Dingus might have reacted. It wasn't the easiest thing to ask about, but I had noth-ing to lose.

When the mother and her boy left, I grabbed two Snickers bars and set them on the conveyor belt. Barbara Lampley watched the candy bars feed toward her. "That do it?" she said.

"Yes," I said. I looked around and saw no one was behind me. "You're Barbara Lampley, right?"

"Yes?"

She smiled while the rest of her tried to remember whether she should recognize me. I'd never gotten used to confronting people cold, especially people who'd never had their names in a newspaper and didn't care if they ever did.

"Gus Carpenter," I said, offering my hand, which she took. "I'm with the *Pilot*."

"The newspaper? Oh."

"Sorry, ma'am, I won't take much of your

story—"   working on a

"Wait. You're Bea and Rudy's boy."

It felt strange but good to hear my father's n

ma'am."   rain. "Yes,

"How is your mother? I haven't seen her in ages."

"She's good, thanks."

"We used to go to bingo together. That woman can talk,   ell
you. I used to think she was trying to distract me from my b
cards, but she's just your basic gabber. I mean in a good way. She's
nice."

"Yes, she is, ma'am."

She finished ringing me up and handed me the candy bars in a
small brown paper bag. "Give your mother my love, won't you?"

"I will."

I stood there holding the bag.

"Is there something else, um—?"

"Gus. Yes, ma'am, actually, I'm working on a follow-up story to
the arrest last night—"

"And you want to ask me about Jack Blackburn."

"Well, not exactly, ma'am, I—"

"Please call me Barbara, Gus. I'm not that old yet. You obviously
know I knew Jack, and Leo. Not very well, it turns out, but if that's
what you're looking for, I don't know that I can help you very much."
She gave a little laugh and put a hand to her breast. "I'm not a suspect,
am I?"

I almost laughed myself. "No. No, ma'am—that is, Barbara—
not that I know of. I was actually hoping to ask a couple of questions
about Sheriff Aho."

Her voice softened then. "What is it you want to know?"

I looked around the store. I didn't want to interview her there. "I
wondered, do you think we could—?"

said. She turned around and shouted down the
"Never nes, "Bert, I'm going out for a few." She set a This
row of cash on the conveyor belt and told me, "This way."
Lane Clos

Aike's, the submarine sandwich shop next door, Barbara
At Ma pointed me to a booth and asked what I wanted.
Lamp Coffee," I said. "I'll get it."

e ignored me and walked briskly behind the counter, where she
the teenage girl working there, "Hello, dear," before she poured a
ee and a Diet Coke. She carried the drinks back to the booth.

"You must be a regular," I said.

"Pretty much. I own the place."

"No kidding?" I pulled a notebook out of my back pocket and set
it on the table. I had to make it obvious now or risk unsettling her
after she started talking. Barbara gave it a glance and continued.

"Yeah. Dingus and I had some land that I got in the divorce.
Turned out there was a whole bunch of natural gas beneath it. I
sold the mineral rights and took the cash and put it all down on this
place."

"But you still work at Glen's?"

"Just a few hours, Tuesdays and Thursdays. I worked there a long
time before I got this place and I liked it. Anyway, I just can't be in
here all day." She leaned in like she was divulging a secret. "I never
thought I'd learn to hate the smell of Italian dressing." She laughed
her big laugh again.

"Hey, I love Italian dressing," I said. I reached for the notebook
with one hand and took a pen out with the other. "Do you mind?"

"You won't say anything bad about me?"

I really didn't know, but I said, "I doubt it."

"You're Bea's boy. I'm sure you'll be nice."

"Can you spell your name?"

"Are you going to put my name in the paper?"

"I might."

She thought about it for a few seconds, then spelled her name. I wrote it and the date at the top of the first page in my notebook. "So," I said, "just so I understand, you were living where when Blackburn died?"

"I was in Starvation, but that's not what you want to know. You want to know whether I was still married to Dingus then, and the answer is yes, barely."

"Barely?"

"Feel free to come to the point, Gus."

"Yes, ma'am. For some reason, I'd thought maybe you divorced earlier."

"Barbara, please. You thought we split before Jack died, because Jack and I, we had this, this relationship." She stopped and drew on the straw in her drink. She sat up straight. "Good Lord, I sound like I'm on Oprah. Jack and I had been fooling around. Everyone knew that. You probably knew it."

"I was living downstate then."

"Why am I talking to you about this?"

"I'm sorry. I was just trying to get a time frame."

She gave me a dismissive little wave. "You want to know what's really silly? This is going to sound like bull, but you'll just have to take my word."

"OK."

"Everyone thought we were fooling around, if you know what— well, of course you know what I mean—but we never actually did *fool around*. You see, Jack . . ." She fixed her gaze on the ceiling for a second. "Oh, good Lord," she said. "Why am I telling you this? Jack's idea of fooling around . . ."

I was leaning into the table for the end of her sentence, telling myself to keep my mouth shut and let her talk. Nor did I dare turn the page in my notebook lest I remind her that all of Starvation Lake was listening. Again, I felt like I was hearing about a stranger, a man I'd never known. Barbara seemed as frustrated as I was.

She shook her head. "No," she said. "I can't tell you that. That'll just have to do. We didn't really fool around, per se, OK?"

"Sure." I turned the notebook page.

"He had plenty of girlfriends. Jack could be a very charming man, but—well, let's just say he was a very complicated man."

"Can I ask how you got to know him?"

"You just did. Back then, I worked at the IGA in Starvation. He always seemed to come in when there was no one around, and Dingus was always working nights, and I was going out of my mind with boredom. We'd talk. One time—oh, God—I was the only one there and he opened two bottles of beer and we sat there drinking and talking." She looked past me out the window toward the parking lot. "It was one of those things, you know, my midlife crisis? Women can have them, too, you know." She looked to me like she was in her early to mid-fifties, which would've made her about forty when she and Blackburn had their dalliance, or whatever it was.

"And all this happened when?" I said.

Instead of answering she said simply, "Dingus," punctuating it with an exasperated sigh. "He just gave up. I thought he was a man's man, too, but he just gave up." She reached across the table and grasped my free hand. "Don't ever do that, young man. Everyone goes through a stupid period in their lives. Hopefully only one. You have to hang in there with them."

"So you were actually with Dingus when Blackburn died?"

"Yes, yes, I'm sorry, I'm rambling." She let go of my hand. "Dingus and I got married in 1978. He joined the department right before our wedding, and he just loved his job, just loved it. Jack and I had our little whatever you want to call it beginning in eighty-five or so, and it lasted about a year, no more. And, yes, before you ask, I actually left Dingus for a while, but just a couple of weeks, and then I didn't really stay with Jack, only for a few days, and I didn't really *stay* with him, if you know what I mean. It was weird, anyway, with those little houses and the boys around."

The billets. His players. His hockey.

I stopped writing. "Why are you telling me this?"

She looked at the table and decided not to answer. "I went back to Dingus eventually, for a little while. Things seemed to get better at first, and I thought we'd be OK, and then Jack died."

I must have looked confused then. Barbara said, "Gus, I know what you're thinking, but Jack's dying didn't help Dingus a bit. It might have been better if the sheriff had let Dingus do his job, but he didn't, so Dingus just never got over the whole thing, despite Jack's being dead and gone—*especially* because he was dead and gone."

"The sheriff?"

"Jerry Spardell. What a dope. He had to have his blessed cruiser. I'm sorry—do you want anything to eat?"

"No, I'm fine, thanks. What about Dingus? Are you saying the Blackburn case bothered him? Kept him up nights?"

"Oh, yes," Barbara said. She leaned in closer and whispered. "When he came home that morning Jack died, the first thing he said was, 'Leo is lying like a rug.'" She imitated the lilt of Dingus's voice, affectionately, not mocking. She sat up straight again. "God," she said. "I've never told anyone that."

I told her about Leo.

"Gracious," she said. "They were such a strange pair, he and Jack. I used to tell Dingus, like an old married couple. I mean, Leo, the only woman he was ever with was his silly ice machine. What did he call it? Agnes?"

"Ethel."

"Oh, of course, Ethel. How ridiculous can you get? I swear that man was jealous of me. Jack would make all these sneaky arrangements to meet me, and it was like he was more worried about Leo finding out than Dingus." She shook her head and laughed. "What an idiot I was."

"What was it Leo lied about?"

"I don't remember exactly. Dingus may not have told me. He may have just had a feeling." She stared into her paper cup as if the answer might be there. "Didn't Dingus go to your house that night?"

"My mother's house. Yes. That's where Leo went to call the police."

Barbara screwed up her face as if she were trying to remember. "I think that may have been it. Your mother told him something. Oh, God, Gus, please don't tell your mother I told you that."

"Don't worry. So what did Dingus do?"

"Not much. Spardell wouldn't let him."

"The sheriff didn't want to solve a murder?"

"Oh, no, there was no murder to solve. Not in Jerry Spardell's Starvation Lake. We hadn't had a murder here in a million years, and Spardell—who had a pretty tough election that year, as I recall—wasn't about to have one on his watch. He told Dingus he believed Leo. After all, they used to play poker Friday nights, and what better bona fides are there than that?"

"And that was it?"

"No, actually, it wasn't. Dingus wanted to drag the lake as soon as the ice was gone. But Spardell wouldn't let him. He had to have his cruiser."

"What cruiser?"

"Spardell liked to have a brand-new patrol boat every few years. He had one locked into the budget that year, and he went down to Detroit for the boat show and picked out the model and the town council was just about to approve the purchase when Dingus says he wants to drag the lake."

"Wait. Why was the town council buying a boat for the county sheriff?"

"Oh, they were always fighting about that back then. Now nobody's got any money for a new cruiser. Anyway, the sheriff's department did all the policing on the lake, so they insisted that the town pay for the boat."

"And any dredging would have cost Spardell his cruiser."

"Exactly. So that ended that. No body, no weapon, no motive. No murder charge."

And no wonder Dingus had shut down the press conference when Joanie suggested he was incompetent. And fell to his knees that night at Walleye Lake. All these years, he'd been forced to live with the memory of a man he'd despised, who wouldn't really be gone until someone solved his demise. The snowmobile washing up onshore had given him another chance to bury Jack Blackburn properly. But in a way, first he had to exhume him.

"Did Dingus consider quitting?" I said.

"No. What would he do? Dingus loved putting that silly uniform on every day. He also thought Spardell might be out of there soon enough, and he'd be sheriff. Of course old Jerry hung on just about forever."

"I guess I should talk to him. Where is he now?"

"St. Michael's." The cemetery. "Lung cancer."

"Oh. When did you and Dingus divorce?"

"In 1990. I couldn't live with Dingus *and* Jack."

"You know," I said, "he keeps a picture of you in his office."

She tried, without success, not to look surprised. "How is he?" she said.

"OK, I guess. He's certainly getting out more than usual."

She laughed. "Is he going to figure it out this time?"

"I'm sure he will before I do."

We sat there for a minute in silence. Then Barbara said, "I've heard people saying Dingus is just stirring the pot. Even though I haven't talked to him in God knows how long, I know that simply isn't true."

"I believe you," I said, and I did.

She walked me out to my truck. Barbara drew her arms around herself, shivering without a coat. "You seem like a nice man," she said.

"Thank you," I said. "I don't know if you knew, but I played for Blackburn."

"Hockey? Really? I never paid much attention. I'm sorry." She looked inside Glen's, then back at me. "Could I just say one more thing?"

"Sure."

"Dingus is a better man than Jack Blackburn ever was. You can quote me on that."

I wrote it down when I got in my truck.

Before going back to the *Pilot*, I went up to my apartment to call my attorney.

"Scott Trenton," he answered.

"It's Gus."

I heard his chair creak. Then he said: "She called you a coward."

"Excuse me?"

"Julia Hanover. She called you a coward. In front of everyone. 'How can he just hide like this?' she said. The Superior guys loved it."

I looked out the window at the falling snow. "If it weren't for me," I said, "she wouldn't even be in this position."

"Don't kid yourself, son. You don't have a friend on either side of the courtroom anymore."

"Reporters aren't supposed to have friends."

"Thanks for the totally useless information," Trenton said. "Look. Those people are counting on you to help them get their settlement done now, before the appellate court rules."

"Are you still going to be my lawyer?"

"With great reluctance. I'm sorry, Gus, but you ignore my calls, you blow off an absolutely crucial meeting, you don't answer questions. If it wasn't for that family, I'd be out of here, friend."

"Sorry."

"No, you're not. But you will be if you don't listen this time. I got your message, and I got you one more day. You have until noon tomorrow. Superior will seek a warrant for your arrest at one second after noon if they don't have a name. They're not screwing around, Gus."

"Why do they care, Scott?"

"About the name? I have no idea. Maybe they think the guy leaked other sensitive stuff. Maybe they're just messing with you. A bigger bunch of frigging pricks I have never met. They don't even get along with one another."

"How so?"

"The lawyers and the PR guys obviously aren't on the same page. The lawyers seem pretty cocky about their chances for winning the appeal. But the PR guys want a settlement so they can have a big press conference and let the Hanovers tell the world what a wonderful frigging company Superior is."

"Really?"

"Really. But get this—the big press conference could be as far it gets, because the PR guys are betting these class-action lawyers who have filed their own lawsuit out in Philly will come in and challenge the settlement because it isn't enough."

"Isn't enough in attorney fees, you mean."

"Precisely. It's all about checks and balances. But mostly it's about checks."

"Those flacks must think they're pretty clever."

"Oh, yeah. Clever guys. Is it true what I've heard that a lot of PR types are former reporters? How does that happen?"

"It happens when a reporter wants to be able to buy a house and isn't good-looking enough for TV."

Trenton chuckled. "Not bad," he said. "I'm due in court. Noon tomorrow, Gus. Any later and you'll be wearing a baggy orange suit."

Downstairs I found Tillie leaning against her counter, smoking, riveted by the TV. Over her shoulder I saw Tawny Jane Reese standing in front of the courthouse steps. " . . . arraignment of Alden 'Soupy' Campbell, charged with the murder ten years ago of revered hockey coach Jack Blackburn. Judge Horace Gallagher has rejected Channel Eight's request to place a camera in the courtroom, but we'll be bringing you updates throughout the day in this shocking . . ."

Behind her, a line of people waiting to enter snaked up one side of the stairs and clustered at the courthouse doors, where Sheriff's Deputy Skip Catledge stood guard. County workers in dingy red coveralls spread rock salt on the steps, barely keeping pace with the falling snow. A short man the shape of a beer keg, wearing a fedora and sunglasses, with two cameras slung around his neck, appeared on the top step, puffing on a fat cigar. It was Delbert.

"Did he kick and scream about having to shoot Dingus?" I said.

"You were in the photo file, weren't you?" she said, ignoring my question. "Didn't I tell you to stay out of there? You'll just mess it up."

"I was just checking on—"

"I'm the only one here who has taken the time to understand the very peculiar way that Delbert keeps those files organized. I would appreciate it if you would do your job and let me do mine."

"Sorry," I said. "So what do you think?"

"About what?"

"Do you think Soupy did it?" I really didn't care what she thought; she'd been behaving strangely, and I was more interested in seeing whether the question would upset her. She took a long drag on her cigarette and then stubbed it out. "I wish it all would just go away," she said.

twenty-one

Seven dead judges peered down on the packed courtroom of the Pine County Courthouse. The portraits hung on walls of polished walnut, circa 1950, rising two stories from shellacked wood floors to a ceiling of pressed tin. Beneath the paintings, townspeople filled every one of the fold-down wooden chairs in ten rows of wrought-iron frames. Elvis and the Audrey's crowd took up two rows on the prosecution side, just behind Dingus, D'Alessio, and Darlene. Joanie sat across the aisle one row behind the defense table, scrawling notes. I squeezed next to Neil and Sally Pearson standing along the wall on the prosecution side. I scanned the room for my mother. I figured she'd be there, if not for the action then at least for the socializing. A bunch of her bingo partners were sitting in the back, but Mom was not among them.

The room was dead quiet. Atop his tall wooden bench, Judge Horace Gallagher sat reading a piece of paper. On the brown leather of his chair back was the familiar dark spot left by the Brylcreem he wore on his just-so silver hair. Soupy sat before him with his head bowed slightly, his uncuffed hands flat on the table. I couldn't see his face for the blond locks drooping around it. He wore an orange jumpsuit inscribed Pine County Jail on the back in big black letters. His attorney, Terence Flapp, sat next to him, digging in a folder.

Soupy had pleaded not guilty to a charge of second-degree murder. That was a bit of a surprise, or so thought Sally Pearson, the town florist who in a rushed whisper filled me in on what had transpired so far. Everyone had expected a first-degree charge, but Sally said the prosecutor had cited "mitigating circumstances," as yet unspecified, that dictated the lesser charge. The assault charge against Teddy

Boynton had been dropped. He was now fully awake and feeling somewhat better, despite a slight skull fracture, a broken jawbone, and thirty-six stitches. I didn't mind hearing about the jaw.

The unpredictable was as integral to Judge Gallagher's courtroom as the delicate shapes of roses he had personally carved into the front of his bench. He was a distinctive man in Starvation Lake. He did not smoke, drink, swear, or cavort with women, but somehow he had been married six times. All of his ex-wives still lived in town, and all still claimed to be fond of Horace Gallagher, despite their apparent inability to live with him. His house on Main Street, one of the oldest in Starvation, was furnished almost entirely with items he had procured at a rent-to-own store in Traverse City, items that he frequently swapped out for even newer items two or three times a year.

In thirty-two years as a county judge, Horace Gallagher had won a reputation for driving lawyers crazy with his inscrutable questions and head-shaking rulings. He had a habit of interrogating prosecutors and defense counsel alike, even at pretrial proceedings. He was known for ordering hearings moved outside on balmy days— "Let's play hooky," he'd say—where he'd then indulge his hobby of bird-watching by noting in the middle of a lawyer's disquisition that a pileated woodpecker had landed in an oak behind Fortune Drug. (This practice finally came to a halt when the state judicial commission got wind of it.) Yet for all of his eccentricities, he was a judge's judge. He frequently took months to issue decisions that would be so precise and legally airtight that he had been overturned on appeal only three times, and in one of the cases he was later upheld by the state supreme court.

Now he was about to consider whether to grant bail to Soupy. "OK," he said, handing whatever he'd been reading to the court reporter sitting below his bench. He squinted at the prosecutor. "Bond, Miss Prosecutor?"

Eileen Martin stood at her table, tall and gawky and looking like she might tip over in her heels. Leave it to Soupy to be prosecuted by a woman he'd once dated, cheated on, and then christened "Rudder Lips" to her face one night at Enright's in front of five or six of her friends.

"Your Honor," she said. "The county believes the defendant, Mr. Campbell, poses an unusually high flight risk. He is an unstable man with a long record of unpredictable behavior, as suggested by his various drunken driving arrests, as well as incidents as recent as last night in which—"

Flapp stood. "Objection, Your Honor."

"Sustained," the judge said. Sitting back, he looked as neckless as a turtle in his billowing robes. "Confine yourself to the case at hand, Miss Martin."

"Thank you, Your Honor," she said. "Your Honor, the prosecution urges that bond be denied altogether and Mr. Campbell be returned to the county jail until trial."

As she was speaking, I noticed Peter Shipman, who had been Leo's attorney, slip into the jury box and sit down, alone.

Judge Gallagher turned to Flapp. "Counselor?"

Flapp stood, even taller and gawkier than Eileen. "Your Honor," he said, "I can understand the court's reluctance to grant bond where there's an allegation of second-degree murder. Of course we expect at trial to show that my client is innocent. But for now, I beg the court's mercy. Mr. Campbell is in a precarious time as regards his business, the Starvation Lake Marina. As you may know, Your Honor, the county zoning board is preparing to render a decision that could have a profound effect on this business and, frankly, on the entire town. My client would like dispensation merely to put his affairs in order. We would request forty-eight hours, Your Honor."

"You want your client freed for forty-eight hours, then he goes back to jail?" Gallagher said. It was an unusual request but, as Flapp well knew, Gallagher was an unusual judge.

"Yes."

"Your Honor," Eileen said. "This is preposterous. There is no legal—"

"One moment, Miss Martin," the judge said. He leaned forward and a sliver of neck appeared. "Mr. Flapp, if we're going to consider something so out of the ordinary, I think it fair to everyone involved to hear a little more about the charges. This is a hearing, after all. Would you have an objection to hearing the affidavit for the arrest warrant read, or at least parts of it?"

Flapp looked flummoxed. "Well, Your Honor—"

"What I'm thinking, Mr. Flapp, is that perhaps we'll hear something that might make me more inclined to be, as you say, merciful. Or I can simply rule now, and on the basis of there being a murder charge, I can assure you that your client would be headed directly back to the pokey."

"No objection, Your Honor."

Eileen stepped to a lectern in front of the judge and removed a thin sheaf of papers from a file folder. She cleared her throat. Everyone in the gallery leaned slightly forward. This was why they'd stood in line.

"Your Honor," Eileen said. She began to read aloud. "At approximately eleven thirty-five p.m. on the date in question, the decedent Blackburn was in the forest approximately five miles northwest of the town of Starvation Lake, Michgan. He and an acquaintance, Leo Redpath of Starvation Lake, had been riding snowmobiles. They had stopped in a clearing to build a bonfire. The decedent Blackburn and Redpath heard the sound of a snowmobile approaching. The snowmobile was being operated by the defendant Campbell. The defendant Campbell stopped the snowmobile in the proximity of the bonfire. He appeared to be intoxicated. The defendant Campbell and the decedent Blackburn exchanged words. The defendant Campbell became highly agitated and—"

"Pardon me, Miss Martin," Gallagher interrupted. "Tell me now, why is it that the county didn't see fit to bring a charge of first-degree murder? Was this not a premeditated act?"

Flapp stood.

Eileen said, "Yes, Your Honor, we believe it was."

Gallagher propped his glasses on his forehead and covered his face with his hands. I felt myself holding my breath. He removed his hands and his huge glasses fell into place. "Tell me, Miss Martin," he said, "the prosecution does have a motive in this case, does it not? You plan to demonstrate precisely why Mr. Campbell would want to kill a man who had been his coach and, presumably, a mentor, even a father figure of sorts, for many years?"

"Yes, Your Honor, we do."

"And these motivations," he said, "would these prompt, say, a neutral observer—not an officer of the court, mind you, just regular folk; the lady at Ace Hardware, say, or the propane delivery man—would these prompt that person to conclude that what Mr. Campbell allegedly did was justified, in some, let's say, moral sense, setting aside the law for the moment?"

"Setting aside the law, Your Honor?"

Gallagher waved her up to his bench. Flapp followed. As the judge listened to what Eileen Martin had to say, his face remained a blank. He glanced past them once at Soupy and nodded before sending them back.

"Miss Martin," he said. "Please continue reading."

"Yes, Your Honor," she said. "Picking up where I left off . . . The defendant Campbell became highly agitated and produced a twenty-two caliber pistol . . ."

In the jury box, the lawyer Shipman was motioning toward the bailiff, who was sitting to Gallagher's right. The bailiff stepped over to Shipman. Shipman whispered in his ear and handed him a piece of folded yellow paper. The bailiff walked it over to Soupy's table and handed it to Flapp.

" . . . The defendant Campbell brandished the firearm in a threatening manner. The decedent Blackburn and Redpath attempted, without success, to persuade the defendant Campbell to disarm himself . . ."

Flapp unfolded the paper and read it. He showed it to Soupy, who glanced at it and turned away, pressing his eyes shut.

"... The defendant Campbell then fired two shots. The first bullet missed the decedent Blackburn and lodged in his snowmobile ..."

Flapp stood. "Your Honor," he said, brandishing the note. Gallagher had followed the note-passing and was now glaring at Flapp.

"... The second bullet struck the decedent Blackburn—"

"Excuse me, Miss Martin," Gallagher said. Eileen Martin looked over at Flapp, annoyed.

"Mr. Flapp?" the judge said.

"Your Honor," Flapp said. "May I approach?"

"This had better be good, Mr. Flapp."

A murmur rose in the gallery as Flapp and Martin stepped to the bench. Gallagher tapped twice with the butt end of his gavel. "Quiet, please."

Flapp handed him the paper. Gallagher read it once, then again, and offered it to Eileen Martin, who read it and handed it back. I couldn't see the attorneys' faces, but Gallagher looked perplexed. The three of them had a brief, whispered discussion, then the judge looked over at Shipman and said loudly enough for everyone to hear, "Mr. Shipman, can you tell me why the deceased here would need a lawyer? Are you representing his estate?"

"Your Honor," Shipman said, "Mr. Redpath retained counsel approximately one day after the snowmobile washed up at Walleye. I was asked to deliver this note should any tragedy befall Mr. Redpath."

"He wanted you to deliver it to the defendant, Mr. Campbell?"

"To his counsel, Your Honor."

"I see," Gallagher said. "Approach, please."

Shipman eased out of the jury box and went to the bench. The judge leaned down and asked him something. Shipman nodded emphatically. His lips said, "Yes, Your Honor."

Gallagher sent them all back. Eileen motioned to Dingus, who stood and leaned close to her while she whispered something. He immediately looked over at Shipman. Dingus kept his eyes on the lawyer as he sat back down.

The judge took his glasses off and directed himself to the court reporter. "For the record, Miss Reporter, I have just been handed a note from the attorney, Peter Shipman, who is representing Leo—excuse me—the estate of the late Leo Redpath. I have disclosed the note's contents to counsel for the prosecution and the defense."

Flapp whispered something in Soupy's ear. Soupy put his head down on his clenched hands and shook his head an emphatic no. The gallery leaned closer still.

"So, Miss Martin," Gallagher said. "What do we do now?"

"With all due respect, Your Honor, this note is merely hearsay at this point. Until we've had an opportunity to verify—"

"Yes, yes, Miss Martin, don't worry, I'm not about to dismiss the charges, but let me ask you this: You have no body, is that correct?"

"That is correct, Your Honor, but the county is prepared to dredge Walleye Lake at the first opportunity."

Gallagher turned to Dingus. "Is that right, Sheriff?"

Dingus half stood. "Yes, Your Honor."

"Had we only pursued such a seemingly logical step ten years ago, yes, Sheriff? Maybe we'd all be out watching the winter storm today. Instead, we're here. So." He looked at Eileen Martin. "Do we have a weapon?"

"Yes, we do, Your Honor."

One of the other lawyers at the prosecution bench handed Eileen a clear plastic bag containing what everyone could see was a pistol. She held it up for the judge. "The county has marked this Exhibit 1-A," she said. "It is a Browning Challenger III .22-caliber pistol, manufactured in 1984. Although it was most recently in the possession of Mr. Redpath—our ballistics analysis indicates that he used it to inflict a fatal wound on himself—the gun was registered to the defendant, Alden Campbell, in January of 1988, and we have reason to believe it was used on the night Mr. Blackburn was killed."

Another murmur rose and again Gallagher rapped with his gavel's butt end. He looked skeptical. "Miss Martin, why would Mr. Redpath have had Mr. Campbell's gun ten years later?"

Eileen lowered the bag. "Your Honor, what we believe we will elicit at trial is that Redpath had it for safekeeping."

I looked at Soupy. His eyes were fixed on the table.

"Do you have other evidence, Miss Martin?"

"Your Honor, we have a witness who has additional testimony that, albeit indirectly, bears on the night in question. We would have had him here today but"—she turned and looked directly at Soupy—"he was detained."

"Detained?" Gallagher said. "Just who is this witness?"

"Theodore Boynton, Your Honor."

Of course. Boynton had known something himself and embellished it with whatever he'd picked up from Joanie and used it to blackmail Soupy. After Soupy stranded him at the zoning board, he'd gone to the police.

Gallagher turned to Flapp. "So what do we do, Mr. Flapp?"

Flapp stood. "Your Honor, based on the contents of the note delivered by Mr. Shipman, I would offer a motion to dismiss—"

"I wouldn't do that, Counselor. Despite the fact that the circumstantial evidence in this case could just as easily point the finger of guilt at Mr. Redpath, and that this note proffered by counselor Shipman could just as easily be a cover for Mr. Redpath's culpability, I am nevertheless inclined, for now, to give the benefit of the doubt to the prosecution out of respect for their professional integrity as well as that of Sheriff Aho, who in my experience does not bring defendants willy-nilly before this court."

"Yes, Your Honor," Flapp said. "In the alternate then, this note, as Your Honor suggests, does raise serious questions about my client's guilt in this matter. So again, addressing the question of bond, I would ask merely that Mr. Campbell be granted time to deal with the pressing matters pertaining to his livelihood."

I didn't think bailing Soupy out for even a few hours was a good idea. If he really cared about his business, his affairs would already be in order and he would have been at the zoning board meeting. The way he'd been acting of late, I thought he'd be safer—less of a threat to himself—behind bars.

Gallagher hitched himself forward. The faintest hint of a smile played on his lips. "Tell you what, Mr. Flapp, I'm certain that everyone in the courtroom would love to hear what it is we're talking about." He produced the note Shipman had given him and held it out to Flapp. "Would you do me the favor of reading this aloud?"

"Objection," Eileen Martin said.

"Overruled. Counselor?"

Flapp stepped forward and took the note from Gallagher. The judge motioned for him to turn and face the gallery. The judge then said, "Mr. Flapp will read into the record a one-page note, as yet unauthenticated, handwritten in pen on yellow legal paper, purportedly by the late Mr. Redpath. Is it dated, Mr. Flapp?"

"Yes, Your Honor. Sunday. Two days ago."

"Proceed."

Flapp cleared his throat and read:

To the good people of Starvation Lake,
Today, I trust my higher power to guide me to a realm of peace, light, and rapture. No longer will I allow shame and guilt to control my feelings, nor will I willfully prevent myself from grieving the losses in my life. I am fully human on this day, and every day going forward.

Jack Blackburn was my mentor and my friend. He taught me many things about life. Knowledge can be a gift, and it can be a burden. Everything Jack did was rooted in the desire to live life to its fullest possibilities. This on occasion led him to places of shame and hurtfulness. He was human. He meant harm to no one. His knowledge became a burden he could not bear. On that night in the woods,

Jack and I entered into a suicide pact. Jack honored his end of our agreement. I was weak at the time, and did not, until now.

You should look for Jack's body in Walleye Lake, if it hasn't been swept into the river by now. I pray I'll be forgiven for keeping this to myself for so long. I pray this will satisfy those who want the truth, and release any and all who might mistakenly be held responsible. I am now willing to surrender to the darkness with the knowledge that light awaits me.

Flapp handed the note back to the judge. The gallery sat silent, stunned. I had begun to transcribe Flapp's reading in my notebook but had to stop when he came to the suicide pact. I listened in a daze, without believing, without knowing what to believe. Nothing added up. I tried to picture Coach putting the pistol to his temple. I imagined Leo depositing the snowmobile in Walleye Lake. What "knowledge" could have prompted such an end? Why had Leo let Blackburn end his life if he didn't think he could end his own? And why now, ten years later, had Leo felt the need to "honor" his end of the pact? Why hadn't he simply confessed to what happened and let it be? What was he afraid of? Jail? The town's recriminations? How had he concluded that a journey to peace, light, and rapture led down the barrel of a gun? Even if what he said happened had truly happened, there had to be something more, something darker and more sinister that he had determined to take with him to his grave. I looked at Soupy. He had lowered his head to the table and was gently shaking it, no.

Gallagher broke the silence. "I will be giving this note to the county for handwriting analysis. We'll deal with that at trial, which I'm setting for March seventeenth, nine-thirty a.m. Mr. Flapp, I'll give your client twenty-four hours, bond one hundred thousand dollars. Naturally you'll need to post ten percent. When the twenty-four hours is up, he goes back to the county jail. Mr. Campbell, do you understand?"

Soupy's answer was barely audible. "Yes."

The judge looked at Eileen Martin. "Objections, Counselor?"

"Your Honor—"

Gallagher stopped her. "Keep in mind, Miss Prosecutor, that you have no body. You might have the weapon, or you might not. Many of the people in this courtroom, and in our town, are probably wondering why we're dredging this up at all. Because it's the law, of course, and the law is sacred. But the fact is, Miss Martin, I could shut this down right now, and the law would be served well enough."

"No objection, Your Honor."

Cigar ashes and snowflakes flecked Delbert's steel-wool beard when I found him outside the courthouse. An unruly gray mane spilled from his black fedora. He wore his camouflage jacket open and hid his eyes behind Ray-Ban shades.

"You know," he said, "we had a perfectly good picture of the sheriff on file. Did you even bother to look?"

A few feet away, gawkers crowded the courthouse steps to eavesdrop on Tawny Jane Reese interviewing Flapp. With one hand Delbert raised his camera to his shades and snapped off a clicking whir of pictures. Behind me I heard someone call out, "Hey, Gus," and I turned to see Elvis, grinning and pointing toward Flapp. "The puck's over here," he said.

I turned back to Delbert.

"Well," he was saying, "if you have a bottomless budget for film stock and developing chemicals, fine with me, I'll just keep shooting these people over and over again. Maybe you could make a flip book."

"I have to talk to you," I said.

"Talk."

"Over here." I motioned him toward the street. Standing close, I smelled the cigar smoke clinging to his beard. "You knew Blackburn, right?"

"Yes, sir," Delbert said. "Fine man. Fine businessman."

"You did some business with him?"

"Now just hang on, sir, I had permission from the publisher himself, Mr. Nelson P. Selby, to do my freelance work with whomever I chose. It didn't cost the *Pilot* more than—"

"I don't care about that, Delbert. What was it you did for Blackburn? Take pictures? Develop film?"

"Both, actually. I shot stills at hockey practices, a few things out at his place when he was building. I made him some prints. Mostly I sent stuff away for him."

"You took pictures when I was playing?"

"That's right, you played, didn't you. Yeah, I was out there a few times."

"And what stuff did you send away?"

"All film. Eight-millimeter. Sent it for developing."

"You didn't develop it yourself?"

"Nope. Wasn't my thing. I got it done by a guy downstate. Cheap and reliable. But"—he chuckled—"he was mixed up with some shady characters. Like the Mafia or something. I think he got whacked."

"Whacked?"

"Killed. Someone killed him."

"How do you know that?"

"I don't know. I made a delivery down there once. Wasn't pretty."

"Uh-huh. What was on the film?"

He tilted his head forward so that his pinprick eyes appeared between the brim of his hat and the rims of his shades. "Why do you care?"

"Look, Delbert, I don't care if you did it on the *Pilot*'s dime, OK? Like I said, I played for Blackburn. He meant a lot to me. I noticed some film in boxes in the photo files and wondered if it had anything to do with the team."

"Jack thought it'd be safer, better organized, filed at the paper."

Safer? I thought. From what? "Of course," I said. "Did you ever look at any of it, by chance? The film, I mean?"

Delbert snorted. "A bunch of runts playing hockey? I hate hockey. You can't see the damn puck. No, I just sent it to my guy."

"And you think your guy got whacked because of a film of kids playing hockey?"

"That's not what I said."

A sheriff's cruiser slid up to the curb where we were standing, Darlene at the wheel.

"Can I go back to doing my job?" Delbert said.

"Get the sheriff," I said.

Dingus was coming down the walk toward us. He didn't look happy. Tawny Jane followed along asking questions Dingus ignored.

"Sheriff?" I said as he neared me. I thought he was going to brush past, but he stopped. For a second I thought he might grab me again. He kept his voice low.

"What made you think you could go see my Barbara?" he said. Before I could answer he got in the car and slammed the door as Darlene pulled away.

My mother's Jeep wasn't in the driveway when I approached her house ten minutes later. Good, I thought. The fresh snow, now nine inches deep, groaned beneath my tires as I parked on the road shoulder. While the truck idled, I unlocked the back door and hurried into Mom's basement. Mildew hung on the dank air. I reached into the dark and pulled the string that lit the ceiling bulb.

The 8-millimeter Bell & Howell projector was sitting atop a stack of boxes in the storage room Dad had built next to the water heater. I wrapped the cord around my left hand and gathered up the projector, rushing to get out before my mother came home. Halfway up the stairs I realized I hadn't turned off the basement bulb. Hurrying back down in my wet boots I lost my footing and fell smack on the same spot I'd banged when I slipped on Boynton's fish. "Son of a bitch," I grunted. I stood, grimacing and rubbing my butt, snapped the light off, and struggled back up. At the top I looked out the kitchen window to see my mother pulling into the driveway.

"Gussy," she said as she stepped into the kitchen, stamping the snow off her boots. She stared at the projector bundled under my arm. "What's that for?"

"Oh," I said, "I found some of these old films of our hockey practices and I thought, you know, with all that's going on, it might be interesting to watch them."

In silence she hung her coat and scarf in a closet by the door. She knew I was lying. She shut the closet and went to the kitchen sink to wash her hands. "Can I fix you something to eat?" she said.

"No, thanks, I've got to get back. I didn't see you at the hearing."

"I didn't go."

"I thought I'd see you."

"Well, maybe I've had enough of the past for one week."

She was upset. She closed her eyes and leaned against the counter, letting her hands hang over the sink, dripping. I set the projector down, stepped behind her, and put my hands on her shoulders.

"Are you OK?"

She shook her head. "It just seems like the whole town is falling apart."

"Come on."

"Leo. All these questions about Jack. Everything was fine before that snowmobile. Now wherever I go, everybody's talking about what *really* happened to Jack, what *really* happened to Leo, and I know they're all thinking I have the answers, just because I happened to be here that night, trying to get some sleep. But I don't have any answers. I don't have any answers, Gus."

She pulled away and went to the fridge and removed a carton of orange juice. As she took a glass from the dish drainer and poured, I saw that her hands were trembling. I grasped her shoulders and gently turned her to face me.

"Mom."

"Dingus called," she said. She took a sip of the juice, then set it on the counter. "The police want to see me. And that TV woman called."

"You didn't talk to her, did you?"

"I'm afraid I wasn't polite."

"What can you tell Dingus that you didn't tell him ten years ago?"

Her eyes flitted over the projector on the floor. "I worry," she said.

"About what?"

She folded her arms. "Do you remember the time you called me a bitch?"

Of course. We'd been fighting for the hundredth time about whether I could spend the night in Coach's billets with the other River Rats. Unlike other kids my age, I didn't fight much with my mother, maybe because since Dad died we were all each other had. But this time I might as well have slapped her across the face. We didn't speak to each other for two days. When I finally apologized, all she said was, "You're too young to understand," and it made me so mad that I almost called her a bitch again.

"Yes," I said.

"I wasn't just being a bitch."

"I know. I'm sorry."

"No. You don't know."

"What? Why do you keep talking in riddles?"

She took my hands off of her shoulders. "Those little houses," she said.

"What? It's not like we had to go there to drink and smoke dope."

"Never mind," she said. "Why do you care if I talk to that TV woman?"

"I don't."

"Please." She turned back to the sink and started wiping the counter, which needed no wiping. "Don't you need to get to work?"

"Mom," I said. "Tell me."

"That night," she said. "Leo . . ." She dabbed at an eye with the towel. "Leo told me . . . he said he did a terrible thing."

"What terrible thing?"

"I wouldn't let him," she said. "He kept trying to tell me. I wouldn't let him. Then the police came, and we never talked about it again."

"Do you mean he killed Coach? Is that what you're saying?"

"I don't know what I'm saying." She put the towel down. "Go to work."

"Mom."

"Be careful with your father's projector."

She pushed past me and disappeared into her bedroom.

When I walked into the *Pilot* newsroom, Joanie was on the phone, frantically scribbling notes. I went up front and found Tillie hunched at her computer, smoking and typing. "You have a message," she said, gesturing toward a pink While You Were Out sheet on the counter. Someone had scribbled on it, "Mr. Carpenter, I'm a reporter with the *Detroit Times*. Any chance I could borrow your newsroom to file a story this afternoon? Many thanks, R. Kullenberg."

"Someone from Chicago called too," Tillie said. "Didn't leave a message."

"They're descending," I said. The out-of-town reporters would come and interview the regulars at Audrey's and Enright's and then write their overwrought stories about the little town with the big trial. And in a day or two they'd all be gone again, and I'd be stuck putting out the *Pilot*. I tossed the message in the garbage. "Did all the stringers' stuff come in?"

"Except for the wrestling meet, yes," Tillie said.

"Can you handle the wrestling story?"

"I cannot wait."

On her phone the number 38 glowed red in the message window. "Whoa," I said. "Did we get that many Sound Off calls?"

"It's not many more than we usually get," she said.

I let it go and punched the button to hear the first message: "This is Phyllis T. Fraser of 661 Oak Lane." The elderly woman sounded like she was underwater. "My opinion is that of course there are tunnels in the lake. In point of fact my uncle Sherman's boy Kevin, a graduate of the Michigan Technological University, says it has been studied by hydrogenists from his institution. And anyway, the tunnels are a tradition we've held dear for as long as I can remember, and I'm seventy-six, actually almost seventy-seven. We've always believed it. Who would think—"

"Hydrologists?" I said, while pushing the button for the next message. A man's voice came on. "Can I ask you something?" he croaked. He cleared his throat, coughed, coughed again. "May I ask why you waste valuable space on items like this? Who cares about tunnels when we have a Social Security system that is—" I shut the machine off. Tillie was smiling.

"Any good ones?" I said.

"I'm on deadline." She waved her hand in Joanie's general direction. "Worry about your star reporter. She's getting her precious career started, and what better way than to shovel dirt on a dead man's grave?"

"What's with you?" I said.

"Gus!" Joanie called out.

I went back to her desk. "What's her problem?" I said.

Joanie glared past me in Tillie's direction. "She spends most of her day eavesdropping," she said. "My sources are always asking why I'm whispering."

"What's up?"

She lowered her voice. "The lawyers are going to be too chicken to run this story. Maybe you will be, too."

"Thanks for the vote of confidence. What is it?"

"I got the kid in Canada."

"Which kid?"

"The kid who was a big star for Blackburn and just quit? The one with the diary? He's an adult now, of course. His aunt, the newspaper lady in St. Albert, told him about me. He just called me out of the blue."

She seemed at once excited and oddly put off, almost as if something had offended her.

"What'd he say?"

"I'm warning you. This is nasty stuff."

"What?"

She made me sit closer to her on her desk and whispered, "This kid's name was—is—Brendan Blake. He was a good player. A really good player. Pro scouts were watching him. I guess Blackburn knew some of the scouts, and he got them to come out. That's about when the weird stuff started. A couple years later, Brendan was out of hockey altogether."

"What weird stuff?"

"Bad stuff, Gus."

"OK. Just tell me."

She took a deep breath. "Blackburn started getting this kid alone," she said. "Mostly on road trips. Sometimes at home. He was abusing him."

"You mean—"

"Sexually, yes. It's all in the diary."

"Jesus. How?"

She told me in a flat, clinical whisper. As I listened, I felt my throat constrict. How could a teenaged boy write such things down?

"Why would a kid—why wouldn't his parents have called the cops?" I said.

"Come on, Gus. These are hockey parents in a hockey town. How do you think their kid would've been treated?"

That I could certainly imagine. Regardless of what happened to Blackburn, the kid would've been branded a pansy who should have fended off his coach's advances. The players, some of the other coaches, even some of the fans would have called him "fag" and "homo" and worse. He would've had to leave town himself. Which he apparently did anyway.

"So they just got Blackburn to leave?"

"Yeah."

"Like in the other place."

"I'm betting. I'm not sure yet. I have some calls in."

"Do you think he's telling the truth?"

"Why wouldn't he? What's he got to gain now? It was like he was glad to talk to me, like he'd been waiting for me to call. And he was dying to know what happened to Blackburn. Said he was sorry to hear it."

"He was sorry to hear the guy who supposedly abused him was dead?"

"Not supposedly."

"You look a little pale. You all right?"

She shook her head. "You know," she said, "we had a priest like this at my high school."

I imagined a middle-aged man, baggy-eyed and paunchy in a black cassock. "Was Brendan angry?" I said.

"I don't think so. At least not anymore. I mean, it's been thirty years."

"What's he doing now?"

"He's an electrician. Married. Two little girls."

I'd heard enough. "OK," I said. "Write it."

"Write a story, Gus? Are you sure?"

"He's on the record, right?"

"Yes."

"And his story checks out with the folks back in St. Albert?"

"Yes, I went back to them."

"And it goes to motive, right?" Soupy's motive, I had to admit.

"Well, only indirectly, unless we know that Blackburn sexually abused players here in Starvation Lake." Her tone was expectant. But I had no answer for her. This man she was describing was not the one who'd taught me to play goalie and sat at my Sunday dinner table.

"If it happened here," I said, "I didn't know about it. Just write it. Straight and simple."

"OK. I already filed the arraignment story. Boy, was that weird. Do you believe this suicide pact stuff?"

"I don't know what to believe," I said. I went to my desk and sat down. And I remembered.

twenty-two

M en," Coach Blackburn said. We were gathered around him at center ice, having just finished practice the day before the 1981 Michigan state hockey championship was to begin on our home rink in Starvation Lake. Coach held his stick high over his head, pointing at the four blue-and-gold banners hanging in the rafters. Behind the one that said, "Regional Finalist, 1977," we saw Leo crouched on a narrow catwalk.

"You've heard me say it a million times," Coach said. "Losing is good for winning. You know I believe that. Losing has made us strong. It has helped us see our weaknesses so we could eliminate them. It has made us keenly aware that at any moment the thing we desire most can be snatched away." He paused. "Now, men, we are done with losing. We have learned its lessons. Now it is time to win."

After four years of lobbying, Coach had persuaded Michigan's amateur hockey officials to hold the state tournament in Starvation Lake. Players, coaches, families, and fans from across the state jammed the town's only hotel and all the motels along Route 816. A line spilled out the door of Audrey's by seven each morning. Visitors clamored for the glossy tournament program, the souvenir pucks embossed with the River Rats logo, the kielbasa and bratwurst sizzling on grills in the rink parking lot. All week, people from Grand Rapids and Marquette and Trenton and Ann Arbor sought out Coach to tell him what a great tournament and a beautiful place this was.

But for all the good cheer and money flowing down Main Street, the tournament would not be a success unless the River Rats won it in front of our own fans, in our own rink, with all of Michigan's hockey establishment watching. Coach knew that. And he thought—everyone in Starvation Lake thought—that we had a good chance to win. We'd lost just six of the fifty-seven games we'd played that year. Three Rats—Soupy, Teddy Boynton, and Jeff Champagne, the kid who'd been cut and then reinstated at that uneasy meeting after our first season—had been named to state All-Star teams. And we'd come so close the year before, only to lose to the Pipefitters in the semifinals.

"Remember what we said all those years ago?" Coach said to us. "We said we came together to achieve the ultimate goal. And what was that?"

"To win one game, Coach," we answered in unison.

"Not all the games. *One* game. Now we're going to play that game." He lowered his stick. "We're going to play it tomorrow in the quarterfinals. We're going to play it again Friday in the semis. And on Saturday afternoon, we are going to win that one game, the state championship. Do I have that right, men?"

"Yes, sir," we yelled.

He gazed up into the rafters. "Leo," he called out. "Now."

We all looked up and watched as Leo scuttled from banner to banner, undoing their fastenings. One by one they fluttered down to the ice. Coach gathered them up and carried them away.

Naturally he had a plan for defeating each of our opponents. In the quarterfinals, we came out hitting against quick but small Fife Electric of Detroit and wore them down, scoring twice late to win 3–1. Soupy scored the winner. Against Copperstone Sporting Goods, we frustrated their two high-scoring centers by giving them the outside lanes while jamming up the front of our net. Soupy scored two goals in our 4–1 win. As we did in all of our games, we used the Rat Trap to clog the middle of the ice and make it hard for teams to break out of their own zone cleanly. Our opponents and their fans loathed the Rat Trap, just as our own parents and fans once had. Now, of course, our parents and fans loved the Rat Trap because it helped us win. As Coach was so fond of saying, "They don't care how, just how many."

We were to play the Pipefitters in the state final. They had dispatched their first two opponents with ease, 5–0 and 7–1. They were big and fast and intimidating in their goatees and sideburns and long hair hanging down over the numbers on their jerseys. Mostly they were good. To beat them we knew we would have to execute the Rat Trap to perfection and take advantage of whatever scoring opportunities we could muster. Even if we did all that, we would not win if we did not stop number 17, Billy Hooper.

College scouts had started watching Hooper when he was just thirteen. That year he scored 127 goals in eighty games for Paddock Pools. The Pipefitters lured him away by making his father an assistant coach. By the time he was sixteen, colleges were begging Hooper to enroll, and he was projected as a number-one draft pick in the Canadian junior leagues. But in an accident that summer, Hooper lost the sight in his left eye. As Pipefitter fans told it, Hooper pulled over on the Ford Freeway near Detroit to help a woman whose car had broken down. When he tried to jump-start her car, the battery exploded. His face was somehow spared severe burns, but the hot acid splashed his eye. Outside Pipefitter circles, another story circulated. It involved Southern Comfort, jumbo firecrackers, and a neighbor's mailbox. Doctors told Billy Hooper his hockey career was over. But when the Pipefitters held tryouts that fall, he showed up wearing a black eye patch. He struggled at first. His impaired depth perception made it hard for him to feel how hard to shoot and pass. His coaches worried that his severely limited peripheral vision made him a target for crippling checks. Hooper played on. He removed his eye patch for games; his teammates took to calling him "Deadeye." In a few months he was turning defensemen and goalies inside out again and, by season's end, Billy Hooper was again one of the most talked-about players in Michigan. Still, nobody was talking anymore about college and the NHL. The scouts didn't believe a one-eyed skater could make it at those levels. They stopped coming.

In the Pipefitters' first two state tournament wins, Hooper was unstoppable, scoring five goals and assisting on four others. I saw him score on a wrist shot, a low slapshot, a deke, a high backhander. At one point, seemingly trapped behind the net, he caromed a goal in off a goaltender's calf. On breakaways, I noticed, he especially liked to try to stare the goalie down and then head-fake him into flopping, whereupon Hooper would come to a near stop and calmly flip the puck over the fallen tender.

Coach noticed, too. After our semifinal win, he squeezed between Soupy and me on the bench in dressing room 3. "Tomorrow night, Gus, number seventeen," he said. "Remember—you're a stand-up goalie. I've seen you watching him. He's got a lot of dipsy-doodles, eh? Every one's designed to make you fall on your face so he can go high on you. Don't take the bait, Gus. You're not a flopper. Hold your ground."

"I will."

"Good." He put his arm on my shoulder. "You coming tonight?"

Coach had invited us all to stay in his billets. He said it was important for the entire team to be together before its biggest game ever. Everyone was going—except me. My mother insisted that I stay with her, at home.

"I don't think so, Coach," I said. "My mother—you know."

"Yes, I know. You ought to be there tonight. I'll speak with your mom again."

That was the night I called my mother a bitch.

Soupy was quiet the next morning at our pregame skate-around. I sat down next to him in the dressing room as he struggled with his left skate.

"Have fun last night?" I said.

"Same old thing," he said. He kicked his skate heel against the floor to force his foot all the way in.

"I hope you guys got some sleep."

"I'll get a nap before the game."

"You OK?"

"Just nervous."

We weren't going to be playing for hours, but already my stomach was squirming like a bass on a fishing spear. Soupy never seemed to get nervous, though. He was always fooling around, throwing tape wads, telling jokes. He didn't really look nervous now, either; he just wasn't himself. Something wasn't right.

Coach walked in. "Good morning," he said. "Are we ready to win?"

"Yes, sir," we all said, except for Soupy, who was preoccupied with his skates.

"Swanny?" Coach said.

Soupy didn't look up. He plopped his helmet on his head, grabbed his stick, stood up, and brushed past Coach on his way out of the room. Coach silently watched him go. Teddy Boynton came in with his bag slung over a shoulder. Coach slapped him on the back. "Ready, Tiger?"

"Oh, yeah," Teddy said.

I leaned over to Wilf, who was taping his stick blade. "What's with Soup?"

"Hell if I know. Maybe he's pissed about Teddy shadowing the one-eyed guy."

"We're shadowing Hooper?"

A "shadow" would stay with Billy Hooper wherever he went on the ice, in the hope of keeping him from getting the puck in the open. It was a difficult but potentially glorious job. A shadow had to be fast and disciplined and utterly selfless. For a player as quick and shifty as Hooper, I couldn't imagine anyone but Soupy being the shadow.

"Don't know for sure," Wilf said. "But Coach had Teddy and Soup up at his house for a couple of hours last night, and when they got back, I thought I heard Teddy say something about it, but I was half asleep."

"Man," I said, "we never had a shadow before. Coach must think this Hooper is still hot shit."

"Fuck Hooper," Wilf said.

. . .

Eight hours later, we were back in dressing room 3, dressed and waiting to go out on the ice for the state championship game.

I sat next to Soupy, staring at the shiny black tape I'd wound onto
my waffle glove, Eggo. I was so afraid to play that I couldn't wait to
get out on the ice. That's how goaltenders think. My belly would keep
jumping around even after I got in the net and started roughing up
the ice with my skates and whacking the goalposts with my stick. The
butterflies would disappear only after the first shot on goal drove
into me and I swatted it down or kicked it away or grabbed it in my
catcher. If it hurt, even better.

The only sound in the dressing room was of stick blades being
tapped nervously on the rubber-mat floor. Through the closed door
we could hear the crowd's rumble, and when the door swung open
to let Coach in, we saw the throng in blue and gold squeezed in the
space between the room and the rink, clapping and yelling. Leo slid
in behind Coach. Coach threw the bolt on the door and stood before
us in a jacket and tie, a gold River Rats stickpin in his lapel. His eyes
scanned the room, falling briefly on each one of us. He clapped his
hands together in front of him and held them there.

"Men," he said. "Three things."

He held up an index finger. "First, as always, the Rat Trap."

He held up two fingers. "Second, the Fitter goalie's got a good
glove and two left feet. Make him use those feet. Shoot low and crash
the net for rebounds."

He held up three fingers. "Last, we're going to shadow number
seventeen. Teddy the Tiger's our man."

I looked at Soupy, who was sitting, as always, to my left. His eyes
were on the floor. "Seventeen's got some speed and a few moves," Coach
said, "but he doesn't much like the rough stuff, does he, Tiger?"

"No, sir," Teddy said.

"Truth is, he's a little fag, isn't he, Tiger?"

"He's a one-eyed fag with a lot of fancy-ass fag moves," Teddy said.

He looked across the room at Soupy, the hint of a smirk on his lips. The others egged Teddy on, saying "Yeah, Teddy boy!" and "Do it!" and "Kill the little fag!" Soupy kept his eyes down. I elbowed him. We couldn't win without Soupy.

"Soup," I whispered. "You don't want to be tied up covering Hooper. The guy's got one fucking eye. Hell, the Fitters'll probably have a shadow on *you*."

He ignored me.

"What do you say, men?" Coach said. That was our signal. It was when Soupy usually clapped me on the shoulder and said, "Tonight, you're a sponge . . ." Now he didn't move. Everyone was up, crowding around Coach. I stood. "Soup?" I said. Still he did not move.

Coach stuck out his right hand and we all reached in to touch it, glove on glove on glove. Coach got up on his toes and looked over our heads at Soupy. "Swanny?" he said. Soupy slowly stood without raising his eyes and placed a glove on my outstretched forearm. Coach watched. Then he looked at the rest of us and said, "One game."

"One game!" we yelled. Everyone but Soupy.

When one hockey team faces another that is clearly faster and more skilled, the job of the goalie on the lesser squad is to keep his team close until they catch a break that might shift the momentum in their favor. Keep your team within a goal, even two goals, and they play with the proper balance of patience and urgency needed to come back. Get behind by three and despair begins to take over. You start playing stupid. Then it's over. In hockey there is no better match for superior speed and skill than a hot goalie.

I was never hotter than during the first two periods of that state title game.

The Pipefitters won the opening face-off and flung the puck hard into the corner to my left. While two Fitters gave chase, Soupy tried to rifle the puck around the boards behind the net. But one of the Fitters slapped it out of the air and the next thing I knew it had bounced out in front of me and onto the stick of Hooper, not fifteen feet away, all alone. His rising shot caught me on the left side of my neck, hitting me so hard that it popped my mask clear off my head. The puck deflected downward and pinged off the goalpost as I tumbled backward, grasping at the crossbar for balance, determined not to go down. The refs were whistling play dead, but Hooper skated up and deliberately banged into me. I saw his left eye up close, phlegmy and gray as the innards of a clam. He wanted me to see it. "Fuck off," I said, pushing him away. He laughed and kicked my mask aside. Then Soupy and Teddy and Wilf and two other Fitters converged, shoving and swearing as the refs pulled us apart. When we'd separated and I leaned over to pick up my mask, Soupy turned to Boynton and punched him once, hard, in the chest, nearly toppling him right there in front of all the Pipefitters and the Rats and the fans standing three deep along the glass. "Where the fuck were you?" Soupy said, and I heard Hooper laughing again as Teddy turned and skated to his position. "Guys, what the hell?" I shouted. My neck was burning and my butterflies were gone.

For the next fourteen minutes, it seemed like the Pipefitters never left our zone. It was as if they had ten skaters to our five, as if there were an invisible wall at our blue line that kept the puck from going to the other end of the ice. I scuttled furiously back and forth between the goalposts, trying to stay square and upright between the puck and my net as the Fitters relentlessly circled, quick as bumblebees, the puck flashing from one Fitter's stick to another, corner to slot to point to dot, behind me, in front of me, and back again and again and again. The shots came from everywhere, two and three at a time. I kicked them into the corners. I snatched them from the air. I deflected them off my shoulders, chest, Eggo, mask. Whenever I could, I gathered the puck into my chest or my glove to freeze it for a face-off so we could get fresh legs on the ice. The Rats were gasping for air.

Teddy got better at staying with Hooper, but it didn't matter much because that just left their four players against our four, and almost all of theirs, skater for skater, were better. Part of our problem was Soupy. He was as good as any of the Fitters, even Hooper, but he wasn't playing his game. He wasn't controlling the puck and leading the charge out of our zone. He was hanging back. Coach Blackburn knew. I saw him glower when Soupy went to the bench. I saw Soupy ignore him.

With two minutes to go in the period, the Fitters' enormous defenseman, the aptly named Wallman, stepped between Teddy and Hooper and suddenly Hooper was free. Someone got Hooper the puck and he faked out the last man, Zilchy, as if his skates were tied together. Now it was just Hooper and me. I slid forward to cut down the angle, hearing the crescendo roar of the crowd even as I heard Coach in my head: "Hold your ground." Hooper dropped his left shoulder to fake a shot. I felt my right knee buckle. I slid to my left as Hooper dug his blades into the ice and cut in the same direction. In a flash the puck was on his backhand. It was just how I'd seen him deke the other goalies. Like them, I wanted to go down, my legs wanted to, my body wanted to. Hooper flicked the puck at my right shoulder. My knees were giving way, my butt was dropping, and momentum was taking me to my left, away from the puck, when I flung out my right hand, the one inside Eggo. As I fell to the ice, the puck just barely caught the edge of the waffle and skipped higher. I craned my neck to look back as I sprawled and saw the puck—or maybe I just heard it—clang off the crossbar and fly up and over the glass behind the net. Whistles shrieked. I jumped to my feet. I'd gotten away with a flop, a sloppy one at that. The crowd began to chant: "Gus! Gus! Gus!" Hooper spun on his skates and stopped, looking straight at me. Our eyes met. He grinned and winked his good eye. I looked away.

Finally, we caught that break. Wallman crushed Jeff Champagne against the boards on my left as Champy tried to scoop the puck out of our zone. But Wallman's stick blade snagged in a seam of the boards and snapped off. He dropped the broken stick and tried to kick the puck as Champy fell to a knee, poked it past him, jumped up, and wheeled around him on a breakaway. The poor Fitter goalie must have been cold; he hadn't seen a shot in ten minutes. He flopped, of course. Champy waited till he was down, then fired a shot over his right shoulder. As the goal light flashed red, I raced out of my net to the blue line with my stick raised in celebration. I couldn't believe it. The Fitters had put twenty-two shots on net to our two. But we led, 1–0.

The lead held well into the third and final period. The Rat Trap really took over then, taking the edge off the Fitters' offensive game. Their passes went awry, the open man wasn't so easy to find as he was in the first period. Within our zone, Coach drew us into a defense designed to jam the front of our net and force the Fitters to take low-percentage shots from the perimeter.

The clock wound down—ten minutes to go, seven, five. The Fitters were gasping now, and growing frustrated. They seemed astonished that they could be losing to our team. With three minutes and sixteen seconds to go, their astonishment turned to exasperation—one of them took a cross-checking penalty. Their coach nearly vaulted the boards to assail the referee. Now the Fitters were playing stupid. We'd have a one-man advantage for two minutes. In the stands, our fans began to celebrate. The state title was within reach. All we had to do was keep the puck out of our net.

I don't know why Teddy Boynton chose that moment to leave Hooper alone and chase a loose puck in the Fitter zone. Hooper was as tired as the rest of his teammates. He hadn't had a clean shot on me since that breakaway I had barely stopped. Maybe Teddy thought, with the one-man advantage, he could take a chance on scoring the goal that would put the game and the championship away. But when he abandoned Hooper in pursuit of the open puck, he left five strides between himself and his man. I heard Coach scream, "Tiger—no!" As Teddy reached the puck, Wallman snuck up on his blind side and flattened him. The Rats fans howled for a penalty. Wallman whacked the puck off the glass and it slid to Hooper in full stride. "Tiger, get up!" Coach yelled. But Hooper was gone.

Teddy's gamble left the rest of the Rats flat-footed. Soupy gave futile chase from the opposite side of the rink as Hooper swooped in from my right. I pushed out. He wound up. I never saw the puck. I heard three distinct sounds, barely a second apart. First was the thunderous *thwack* of wood on rubber. Then the sickening ring of the puck inside the juncture of the goalpost and the crossbar. Then the roar of the Fitter fans. As Hooper whipped past me, his stick raised high over his head, he looked over and again winked his good eye. "Can't see it, can't stop it," he said.

I felt a hand grab me by the back of my jersey. It was Soupy, red-faced and furious. "Fucking Blackburn," he sputtered, his spittle flecking the skin behind my mask. "I knew this would fucking happen."

"Forget it, Soup," I said. "We're going to win."

"You don't understand," Soupy said. Past him I could see Blackburn and Leo calling out from the bench, Zilchy and Wilf skating over. "Blackburn fucked us, Trap."

"Calm down, Soupy."

"Like fuck," Soupy said. He turned to skate away and then, as Zilchy and Wilf caught up to him, he wheeled around and yelled, "Watch. I'll show these motherfuckers a fancy-ass fag move, all right."

I knew immediately what he meant.

When it happened, we were five minutes into sudden-death overtime. We had just dumped the puck into the Fitter zone. Number 25 slapped it high on the glass around the back of the net and up the opposite boards. Champy stopped it with his chest and shoveled it back across the ice into the corner left of the Fitter net, where Soupy, having snuck in from his defensive post, now appeared. Two Fitters converged, but Soupy sidestepped one, then the other, cut left, and scooted behind the net. The two Fitter defensemen momentarily froze in front of their net. The goalie grabbed his crossbar and looked frantically over one shoulder, then the other, trying to anticipate which way Soupy would go. But I was the only one in the rink who knew what was about to happen, the only one in the theater who'd seen the movie before, who knew how it was going to end, who knew that Soupy, no matter how Coach had upset him, was going to be the hero.

He scooped the puck up in his stick blade, lacrosse-like, in a motion so fast that only someone who'd seen it before could fathom what was happening. To me, it was all in slow motion. It was Soupy all alone in the rink that afternoon months before, flinging pucks into the goal mesh from behind the net. It was Soupy practicing the same utterly absurd, utterly sublime move, unbeknownst to Blackburn or anyone else except me, in the moonless cold on the frozen patch behind his garage. The Rats and Fitters crisscrossed in my line of sight. I squatted low and eased forward so I could see through to Soupy. He raised his stick, the puck a black blotch on the white tape on his blade, and snapped it around the wide-open upper corner of the Fitter net. I raised my arms over my head and took a big stride, then another, waiting for the goal light, the last whistle, the explosion of the crowd. We were going to win the state title.

But none of it came.

Instead of the fans' roar, I heard the clank—I would learn only later—of a puck bouncing off the crossbar. When I looked for the goal light, I saw instead the Fitter goalie pointing his stick in the air high above the rink. Everyone on the ice turned in my direction, looking for the puck.

Billy Hooper found it first.

He appeared, alone, legs in full churn, tearing down the boards to my left, Zilchy and Stevie in hopeless pursuit. Coach was yelling, "Back, Gus! Back! Back! Back!" I looked down to see that my celebration had taken me almost to my blue line, a good forty feet from the net. The puck fell from the sky and plopped to the ice about fifteen feet to my left and in front of me, directly in Hooper's path. For one foolish instant I hesitated, thinking I could beat him to it. Another mistake. I started backpedaling as Hooper snatched up the puck. Coach yelled. The Fitter fans shrieked. There were still twenty feet between me and the empty net when Hooper pulled nearly even on my left. I was never going to outrace him. I had no choice.

I threw the lower part of my body across the ice, stacking my leg pads to form a sliding blockade. I hoped to flummox Hooper enough that he might hurry a shot that would hit some part of me or skitter wide. The crowd's roar swelled in my ears. Hooper leaned hard to his left while keeping the puck just out of reach of my outstretched stick. His blades dug in and I felt the spray of snow like needles across my neck and face. He lost his edge. He fell. I ground my slide to a halt and twisted around and propped myself on Eggo. Other skates were scraping toward us. The puck had come to a stop ten feet from the open net, just out of Hooper's reach. If I had jumped up at that very instant and dove and threw my stick at the puck, I might have been able to smack it out of his way. But I didn't. Instead, in that sliver of a split second, I looked at Hooper. Our eyes met again. This time, his eye startled me more. Maybe it was because I realized then in the back of my mind that he had lost most of his dreams forever, and there I was trying to take the last one away. Or maybe I just choked. Whatever the reason, I froze. Not for long. Half a second maybe. But it felt for that half a second as if my arms and legs were stuck to the ice. In the years to follow, that half a second would become a full second, five seconds, a minute, a lifetime in the town's collective memory. Elvis Bontrager got used to telling people, "I could've rotated my tires in the time he laid there staring at that damned puck." To the people of Starvation Lake, in the wake of Soupy's heroic effort, and despite my own heroics earlier in the game, I'd had a chance to keep the River Rats, and our state championship dream, alive. And I'd blown it.

The puck sat between us. Hooper lunged and caught the puck with the heel of his stick. I dove, finally, but the puck crossed the goal line inches ahead of my stick. Whooping Pipefitters piled on Hooper as I dragged myself away.

We sat in the dressing room, dazed and silent but for a few muffled sobs. Coach and Leo left us alone. After what seemed like an hour Coach came in and packed up the tackle box he used to carry tape and first-aid supplies. He looked around the room. "We're done here, boys," he said. "Get dressed and get out." He turned to leave.

"Get the fuck out yourself."

It was Soupy, sitting on my left. Blackburn stopped and turned around. "Excuse me?" he said. Behind him the door opened and Leo stepped inside.

"You heard me. You cost us the fucking title." Soupy threw his runner-up plaque to the floor at Blackburn's feet. "You put the wrong guy on Hooper and you know it."

"Fuck off, Campbell," Teddy Boynton said.

Blackburn set the tackle box down and walked over to Soupy. He leaned down until his face was barely two inches from Soupy's. "I cost us the game?" he said. He smiled in a way I'd never seen before. It made the hairs stand up on the back of my neck. He took Soupy's chin in his hand. Soupy tried to pull away, but Blackburn held tight. "You pull that selfish little fag move of yours and I cost us the game?" he said. "You are a joke, son, you know that? A joke. Maybe when you realize that, you'll be able to make better use of your God-given talents instead of wasting them on hot dog fag moves."

"Fuck you," Soupy said, still trying to jerk his face away.

"Coach," I blurted. "Leave him."

Coach let Soupy's chin go and turned slowly to me.

"What did you say?"

"Shut up, Trap," Soupy said.

"He's upset," I said. "Leave him. He didn't lose the game. I lost the game."

"Trap, shut up."

"You," Blackburn said. He reached across Soupy and jabbed a forefinger hard into my chest. "Jack!" Leo admonished, but Blackburn ignored him. "What the hell were you thinking, Gus, when you were just lying there staring at number seventeen? Huh? Why didn't you kiss him?" He jabbed me again and I flinched.

"I couldn't get up. I tried—"

"You tried?" He pointed his stabbing finger at the door. "Well, you know what? All those people out there who thought we were going to have a state championship in this town? They don't give a damn if you tried or what you tried or how hard you tried. Because you failed. That's what they know, and that's what they'll always know. How many times do I have to tell you, Gus? Nobody gives a good goddamn *how*. They only care *how many*. And you know what? I'm with them. Because right now we could have a state championship trophy in this room, but we got a little piece-of-shit plaque and it doesn't mean a goddamn thing *how* anymore. Do you hear me?"

Soupy leaned between us and directed a low, hoarse whisper at Blackburn, as if he wanted no one else to hear. "He knows," he said.

Coach's head snapped back to Soupy. "What?"

Their eyes met. Blackburn backed away, raising his palms in a gesture of angry surrender. "Fine," he said. "Fine." He picked up his tackle box and walked out with Leo.

Soupy drove me home in silence. When he pulled into my driveway, I turned to him. "What was going on back there?" I said.

"When?"

"When you told Coach, 'He knows.' What was that all about?"

Soupy kept his eyes on the road. "Nothing," he said. "Just that you already knew all that crap he was saying. I just wanted him to shut up."

I wasn't sure whether to believe him, but I just said, "Thanks." We never spoke about it again.

twenty-three

I was editing Joanie's story on Brendan Blake when she tapped me on the shoulder. She whispered, "Is there a way to listen to the messages without using the phone up front?"

"Why?"

"You've got to hear one of the Sound Offs."

I found an instruction book for the message machine in a pile next to the copier. Joanie sat next to me as I dialed. She had a folded map in her hand.

"OK, I'm in," I said. "What am I listening to?"

"Can you skip through the messages? You want number thirty-four." I kept hitting buttons and hearing beeps until the automated voice said, "Message number thirty-four, received today at three twenty-seven p.m."

The recording began. At first, all I heard were indistinguishable voices in the background, then what sounded like a car passing. The call must have come from a pay phone. "Yo," came the voice, a male rasp carrying the hint of a southern accent. "Tunnels? Y'all must be joking." He cackled. "Ain't no tunnels, ain't no Blackburn. Time to maybe make a deal." He hung up.

"Know that voice?" Joanie said.

"I don't think so."

I pushed replay and listened again while Joanie spread the Pine County map on my desk. Two X's were marked in green Magic Marker a quarter inch from the western edge of Starvation Lake. One X was just above and to the left of the other. She pointed to the lower one. "That's where Blackburn and Redpath and Campbell were the night Blackburn died."

"OK." Though I had snowmobiled plenty in the woods between Starvation and Walleye, I had no idea where Coach and Leo might've built their midnight fire.

Her finger moved to the other *X*. "This is where Clayton Perlmutter lives."

The Sasquatch hunter. "No way," I said.

We made a plan to visit Perlmutter after deadline. No need to call ahead, I told Joanie, he obviously was expecting us. She went to Audrey's for sandwiches while I wrapped up her stories on the arraignment and Brendan Blake. We quoted Blake saying Blackburn had sexually abused him, but left out the details. I scheduled the story for the front page, just below the fold. Prominent play, but not too.

I dialed Kerasopoulos on my main phone line. His secretary would be gone. I put that call on hold, pushed the button for my second line, and dialed his number again. While the first line blinked, I waited on the second. One ring. Two rings. Three. A pause. Voice mail. "Evening, Jim," I recorded. "Gus Carpenter. Sorry to miss you, but wanted you to know we have a somewhat controversial story for tomorrow's paper, slugged BLAKE. Just sent it. You might want to take a look. Thanks."

If Kerasopoulos checked his voice mail, he'd have his heads-up, and he might well kill the story. If he didn't, the story would run. He couldn't say I hadn't warned him. As I hung up the phone, I felt someone standing behind me. It was Tillie, holding another pink message slip.

"Jesus, you scared me," I said.

"I'll bet," she said. I didn't like how she was smiling. "This woman called again."

"What woman?"

"From the *Chicago Tribune*. I told you before."

"What does Chicago care about Starvation Lake?"

"How would I know? Can I please go?"

"Wrestling story in?"

"Sent it."

I stared at the slip. The number was long distance, so the woman wasn't in town. Might she be calling about my problems with Superior Motors? The *Trib* probably had subscribers in northern Indiana. Maybe the Hanovers had called the paper to say I was the coward who'd used their tragedy to get some big stories and then walked away when they needed me.

I put the slip on the stack of papers next to my computer. Joanie burst in through the back door, panting. "Let's go," she said.

"So, guess what the cops found in Redpath's computer," Joanie said.

I was steering my pickup onto Main Street toward Route 816. She was handing me a pasty. Warm grease bled through the wax paper as I propped the meat pie on my knee. "What?" I said.

"OK," she said. "So I go over to Audrey's and I see the TV slut's in there with her camera guy. I order my usual Swiss cheese on pumpernickel. Audrey's all weird, she leans across the counter and says she's totally out of Swiss. So I say cool, make it with American, but Audrey says you can get Swiss over at Enright's. I say American'll be fine, and then she says, well, she might be out of that, too, and I'm like, what's up?"

"So who was at Enright's?" I said, biting into the pie. It needed ketchup.

"A source."

"Deputy Esper, maybe?"

"You want to know what was in the computer?"

"Please."

"Porn."

"What?"

"Porn. All sorts of it."

It pained me to hear that, but for some reason it didn't surprise me. "What kind of porn?" I asked.

"What do you think?"

"Boys?"

Joanie nodded. "More bad stuff, Gus."

We drove for a while in silence. Then I said, "Do you think Blackburn really killed himself?"

"Well," Joanie said, "before I was thinking, no way, this suicide pact thing is, like Gallagher said, a cover. I mean, if Blackburn really killed himself, why wouldn't Redpath have just told the cops back then? Why would he have gone to all the trouble of getting rid of the body and making up a snowmobile accident? Plus, Redpath had the gun, not Campbell. But now, I'm not so sure. You've got these two guys, buddies, and they're apparently into some pretty deviant stuff. Odds are pretty good that if Blackburn was fooling around with boys, Redpath might've been too, right? So maybe—I don't know, I shouldn't say."

"What?"

"Maybe—look, sorry, I know this guy was your friend, but maybe these guys—maybe they both had, like, some sort of, you know, *thing* for Campbell. Maybe they were rivals. Maybe this was some sort of weird triangle."

I was gripping the steering wheel so hard I thought I might break it. "Aren't you jumping to some conclusions here?" I said.

"Maybe." She shifted around in the seat to face me. "What do you think?"

I fixed my eyes on the headlamp beams cutting through the dark. What did I think? That wasn't really what Joanie was asking. She was asking, what did I know? What did I know of what went on between my best friend and my coach and his assistant? The answer, unbelievably, was that I knew nothing. The day's events were beginning to sink in. All those years, Soupy had known. And he'd never given me the slightest hint. We'd sat there in the second-floor window at Enright's, watching Blackburn's funeral procession, Soupy with his hand on my neck, a comfort. And he knew. And maybe my mother knew, too.

"Gus," Joanie said. "Are you all right?"

"No. I'm pissed and embarrassed. All this shit was happening right under my nose."

"Come on. It's not your fault. I mean, you weren't—"

"No, Joanie, I was not part of it, whatever it was."

I eased around a snowplow that was pitching sheets of snow onto the six-foot walls along the shoulder.

"Take a left up here," Joanie said.

At the corner where I turned, a neon vacancy sign burned red in front of Jungle of the North, a tourist trap motel. A menagerie of concrete statues crouched in dim light thrown by flood lamps tacked on birches: An orange hippopotamus. A white tiger striped in purple. A pink-and-black giraffe, missing the lower section of one leg, steel reinforcement rods showing where the hock once was. A giant, leering alligator, his back and snout covered with snow.

"Whatever happened to the priest at your high school?" I said.

"Oh, he's still there," Joanie said.

I turned onto a two-track past hand-painted wooden signs warning of dogs and guns. I hadn't gone far before I stopped and parked. "I don't want to get stuck coming out of here," I said.

As we trudged up the road to Perlmutter's, the night was so quiet you could hear the snow falling. "Oh, yeah," Joanie said. "Campbell's out. Guess who posted bail?"

"Boynton?"

"How'd you know?"

"The zoning board meets again tomorrow. Teddy wouldn't let something as minor as a hockey stick to the head interfere with business."

"You know," Joanie said, "Boynton might know a lot more about all this, too."

"The thought has crossed my mind."

A few steps farther, a light flashed in our faces. We stopped and raised our gloved hands to shield our eyes. Over the menacing growl of a dog came a man's rasp: "You can stop right there or I can let go of this here leash."

The shadows in Perlmutter's living room danced along the knotty-pine walls with the flickering in his fireplace. He was squeezed into a rocking chair, shotgun across his lap. His chest strained at the snaps of the down vest he wore over a red flannel undershirt. The German shepherd he called Shep crouched at his feet, glowering. Perlmutter reached behind his chair and fished a can of Bud Light from a cooler.

"Frosty, anybody?"

"No, thanks," Joanie said. She sat in a chair Perlmutter had taken from the kitchen, its dull yellow vinyl seat back torn and peeling. I'd sunk into an armchair that sagged so badly that my butt rested below my knees.

"I'll take one," I said. I hoped the smell might cut the stench of cat stinging my eyes. He tossed the beer at me, hard and a little high. I snatched it out of the air as if I were wearing my catching glove.

"Whoa," Perlmutter said. "Still got a little of that, huh? I saw you play a bunch of times, kiddo, including that last time. You played one hell of a game until the end there. What happened?"

"I screwed up."

Perlmutter rocked back chuckling. "Well, I'll be. That's good. I didn't figure anybody screwed up anymore. Every time I turn on TV, there's somebody saying it wasn't their fault, it must've been some-body else. Good for you."

I saw little evidence of Perlmutter's Bigfoot passion in his liv-ing room. An enormous rifle hung over the fireplace. On the mantel below sat a police radio next to a copy of the infamous fuzzy black-and-white photograph showing what purported to be a Sasquatch walking through a forest. An inscription etched across the top of the frame read, "The Truth Will Set You Free."

Perlmutter rocked forward into the light, and the shadows fell away from the acne scars beneath his scraggle of a beard. He crushed his empty beer can with one hand and tossed it at the fireplace. Shep immediately rose, picked the can up in her jaw, and carried it into the kitchen.

"You folks in a trading mood?" Perlmutter said, dipping back into the cooler. "I got something to trade, but I ain't talking unless it's even-steven."

"We don't do trades," Joanie said.

"Well, little Miss Mike Wallace, I'm talking to the boss here," Perlmutter said. Shep came back and lay down by the fire. "And I'd appreciate it if you wouldn't be writing in your little book anymore."

Joanie gave me a sidelong glance as she shut her notebook. Perlmutter looked at me. "Didn't you used to write for one of them Detroit papers?"

"Yep."

"What was your byline?"

"A. J. Carpenter."

"What's Gus come from?"

"Augustus."

"Augustus. Sounds like a Roman emperor. And the *J*?"

"James."

"So you weren't named for your daddy?"

The question startled me. "Actually I was," I said. "My dad was Augustus Rudolph, after my grandpa, but they called him Rudy. My grandma's dad was a Rudolph. My mom's was a James."

"And your momma's daddy, that would've been Jimmy Damico?"

Again he surprised me. "That's right," I said. "You knew him?"

"My daddy and him used to hunt rabbits up around Sunset Trail where it zigzags there past Twin Lakes. Jimmy and his brother Bill. One of them had a kid who bought it over in Nam. I tagged along once or twice before I moved out here by myself. Ain't sure they cared so much about the hunting, but they sure liked sitting around on the tailgate of Jimmy's old Chevy wagon till dark, telling stories and drinking."

"You knew my dad?"

He looked down at Shep. "A little. Bumped into him once or twice at the titty bar in Alden."

"What titty bar?"

"Tit-for-Tat," Perlmutter said. He'd noticed the surprise and disbelief in my voice. "Wasn't there long. The cops got the owner for running coke and that was that."

"It couldn't have been my dad." Mom had said he worked at a restaurant on those weekends. She had never mentioned naked dancers. But she wouldn't have, would she?

Perlmutter took a long, slow sip of his beer. "Maybe I got it wrong," he said.

"So, Clayton," Joanie interrupted. "Why don't you tell Augustus here how you got into the Sasquatch business?"

"Hah," Perlmutter said. "This the interview part? Well, you know, as I told little Miss Wallace here, everybody's got to do something. I used to work for the county extension service, and I'd see all these professor types coming up from downstate in their duck shoes and camo hats, getting all these grants and such to go chasing after mosquitoes and lily ponds and algae. I figured that money'd be better put to use looking for something ain't nobody found yet."

"Like Bigfoot," I said.

"Yes, sir. You see that there on the mantel?" He pointed to the picture. "That's a joke. A friend gave me that to remind me of my mission, because that picture, y'all seen it before, if that ain't a guy in a gorilla suit, I'll eat my gun."

"Think so?"

"Aw, heck, the Sasquatch ain't been definitively discovered. He's no doubt out there, and me and Shep have set ourselves to the task of finding him, and we won't give it up no matter what y'all put in your paper, will we, Shep?" He reached to pet the dog, but the dog turned its head away. "I got a whole museum in my garage and my tool shed and I showed it all to the little missy, but she don't want to believe what she can see with her own eyes."

With a glance I warned Joanie to keep quiet.

"You know, Augustus," Perlmutter continued, "we all got stories to tell. Some are true and some ain't and some are only half true, and those last ones are most liable to get us in trouble. Ain't that right?"

"Yes," I said, because it was. "But you've got to admit, Clayton, it's pretty impressive how you've kept this museum going all these years."

He grinned. "Well, it don't hurt to have friends in high places. And that's all I'll be saying about that."

"How did you know Blackburn?"

Perlmutter picked a birch log off a stack next to his chair and flung it onto the fire. The papery bark spat flames. "Not well. Saw him when I went to games, of course, and I'd say hello. I don't think he was much for socializing. Now, I ought to talk, but Blackburn and his pal there, the guy who went and killed himself, I figured they were a little like me, they liked to go out and rough it up in the woods and have a few beers. I could see them out there at their bonfire once in a while, ain't far from here. I tried to join them once or twice, but I could tell pretty quick they didn't want me around."

"They didn't like you?" Joanie said.

"Who wouldn't like a guy who rides up with a cooler full of cold ones?" He swigged his beer. "They had their own little club. Then one night I guess it kind of broke up." He chuckled.

"What do you know about that?" I said.

He straightened in his chair, a movement I'd seen in many a source who knew something I wanted to know. I disliked them for it even as I tried to flatter them into telling me. "Well," he said, "I might have seen a bit of it."

"Come on," Joanie said.

"Maybe this is where we talk about what you're bringing to the table," he said. "I believe you have an article you're fixing to write about my livelihood."

I pointed at the door. "Can we have two minutes?"

Out on the porch, the cold air sucked the cat smell from my nose.

"Does he have a cat too?" I said.

Joanie looked annoyed. With me. "About a dozen of them," she said. "He says they have a special sense for Sasquatch. You'd probably buy that, huh?"

"Voice down, please."

"What the hell are we doing here, Gus?"

"We're getting the Blackburn story."

"And we're going to trade in my other story, which is dead solid, for something that could be total crap?"

"Quiet. Yes, we are. For now."

"It was never going to run anyway, was it?"

I chose not to answer.

"Gus, this is a scumbag who insists he has a pile of Bigfoot crap. Now because he happened to know your dad, we're going to trust him?"

I grabbed her elbow and steered her away from Perlmutter's window to the edge of the porch. An automatic security lamp flashed on over our heads. The beam illuminated the ground through the trees all the way down to a corner of Walleye Lake.

"Yes, he's a liar," I said, speaking as quietly as I could. "But he's capable of telling the truth. If he lies about Blackburn, our deal with him is immediately off, and I'll fight like hell to run your Bigfoot story, I promise."

"He's *capable* of telling the truth? You know, it's one thing to steal voice mails from a bunch of liars. It's another thing entirely to make deals with one."

"Cheap shot," I said. It didn't matter at the moment that she happened to be right. "Look, I'm going back in. You can wait in the truck if you want."

"Whatever."

"OK," I told Perlmutter. I was sitting on the arm of the sagging chair. Joanie stood next to her peeling one. "I can tell you—and I shouldn't be—that we've written our story on your so-called museum, and the lawyers don't like it."

"What good's that do me?" Perlmutter said.

"Look, Clayton," I said, "if Joanie and I go back and do some screaming, we'll turn the lawyers around." Joanie nodded on cue. "Or we could just stay on the Blackburn story, if we have something fresh to write. Anyway, Joanie's going to be leaving the *Pilot* soon, and that'll pretty much assure your story will die."

"Where's she going?"

Joanie blinked twice but kept her gaze on Perlmutter. "Who knows?" I said. "Someplace bigger. She's the one breaking all these Blackburn stories. If it wasn't for her, we might not even have had an arraignment today."

"Huh," Perlmutter grunted. "Don't break your arm patting yourself on the back."

"Anyway," I continued, "it was nice chatting about my family, but if you aren't going to help us, we're going to go do some screaming."

It wasn't the most ethical way to go about things, but I'd done worse. Anyway, if the people of Starvation Lake and the fools in the state capital who had showered money on Perlmutter wanted to think he was running a museum, maybe they deserved to get ripped off.

Perlmutter gazed at Shep for a long minute. He undid the top two snaps of his vest and produced a black-and-white photograph that he handed to me. Joanie got up and looked at it over my shoulder. Through a thicket of trees, the blurry shape of a man appeared on the shore of a lake. He was bent over another, indistinguishable shape, hidden in shadow. The perspective was similar to the one from Perlmutter's porch. The trees were lush with leaves. A dull streak of moonlight glimmered on the water's edge. "You took this?" I said.

"Yessir."

"But this wasn't *that* night?"

"No, sir. That was spring, couple of months later."

"But what did you see *that night?*" Joanie said. "You said you saw something."

Perlmutter ignored her, pointing at the photo. "You recognize the guy?"

"No," I said, squinting.

"Here's a hint. He was one of the four I saw at their little bonfire that night."

"Four?" Joanie and I said in unison. "No," Joanie said. "It was just Blackburn, Redpath, and Campbell."

"That's all I'm saying about that," Perlmutter said. "Look at the picture."

I knew it couldn't be Blackburn. It was too bulky to be Soupy. "Leo?" I said.

"Give the man a cigar," Perlmutter said. "Yessir, old Leo snuck down to the lake to dispose of a little something."

"Blackburn's snowmobile," Joanie said.

"Another winner," Perlmutter said, holding his beer up in salute. "Old Shep was just a puppy that spring, and Redpath wasn't making that much of a racket, but Shep about tore her chain off the house, didn't you, girl?"

"So," I said, "you're saying Leo killed Blackburn—or Blackburn killed himself—and then Leo waited a few months to dump the snowmobile and, presumably, Blackburn."

"No," Joanie said to me. "Remember what he said on the answering machine."

"Hey, maybe I'm all wet," Perlmutter said. "Try this." He held out his hand. Lying in the palm was a .22-caliber bullet. "Found it out by their fire," he said.

"When? That night?" I said.

"The morning after."

"The morning after the fire, after Blackburn died?"

"In the winter, yeah."

He handed me the bullet. I examined it and gave it to Joanie.

"When I heard about the snowmobile dunking on the squawk box"—Perlmutter jerked a thumb at the police radio—"I got myself out to their campsite for a look-see. The cops were still messing around at Starvation. It was a sunny morning, and I caught a glint of the bullet, stuck in a tree."

"In a tree?" Joanie said.

"Fourteen of my steps from the fire pit."

"Must've been buried pretty good," I said.

"Yep. Took a little work to dig it out."

"Why didn't you tell anyone?" Joanie said.

"Maybe I did. As I think you know, missy, I am nothing if not opportunistic."

"Amen," she said. "I'll bet you're the one who called the cops last week when the snowmobile finally washed up."

"You never know."

She held up the bullet. "We have to take this."

"Not a chance."

"This could be anybody's," Joanie said. "The cops have to look at it before we could write about it."

"Ain't going to happen," Perlmutter said. He leaned forward, his hand open. "I'll take that picture too, if you please."

"Joanie, give him the bullet," I said. The cops eventually would come for it anyway. "But let me keep the picture, Clayton, just for a little. I want to look at it some more in some better light." If Delbert blew it up, we might be able to tell if it was a fake. Or it might actually give us a little leverage with Dingus. And maybe it could help Soupy, too, though it was pretty flimsy as court evidence went. "It will not appear in our paper unless you yourself give me permission, I swear on my father's grave."

"Your daddy's grave, huh?" he said, chuckling. "Let me think about it."

"Joanie," I said.

She handed him the bullet. "So," she said, "we've got a Bigfoot-like photograph and a bullet that could've come from Kmart."

"Hah," Perlmutter scoffed.

"Clayton," Joanie said. "The cops say there were only two bullets—one in the snowmobile, one in Blackburn's head."

"But they ain't got no bullet from Blackburn's head, now do they, missy?"

The police radio sputtered to life. I heard Darlene's static-riddled voice, calling for assistance at a fire.

"This bullet doesn't mean diddly, Clayton," Joanie said. "Who was the fourth guy?"

"I don't remember saying it was a guy. Anyway, I think I'm done talking for now, missy. Obviously you ain't smart enough to figure it out. I think I'll just hold on to what I got until I know I'm not going to get crucified in the paper."

Joanie turned to me. "We're wasting our time."

Perlmutter looked at Shep and shook his head. He looked as disgusted as he did amused. "The little missy's just plain young, girl, but what do you figure is *his* excuse?"

He was trying to tell me something, but I was straining to hear the police radio. "Listen up," I said. Darlene, louder now, was calling all available deputies to the old Blackburn property. Fire trucks and ambulances were on their way. A man had ignited some buildings and appeared to be trapped in one, but he was to be considered armed and dangerous nevertheless. I hoped it wasn't who I thought it was. "Let's go," I said, jumping up. I must have spooked Shep, who leaped up snarling from where she lay and lunged at me, jaws agape, just as a fat black cat sprang from my right, flying straight at my head. My arm instinctively shot out and whacked the cat out of the air. It screeched as I drove my right boot into Shep's ribs and yelled, "Get the hell away!" Shep yelped and skittered toward Perlmutter, who grabbed her collar while shouting, "No, down, girl, down!" I raced out the door behind Joanie and kept running off the porch and into the darkness, grabbing her by the arm as we struggled through the knee-deep snow, saying, "Go, go, go, before he realizes I have the picture."

twenty-four

W hat a load of crap," Joanie said. "We traded a perfectly good story for that?" My truck bounced along the snow-covered gravel road two miles from Blackburn's old place. "Third bullet, my butt. Probably just another drunken miss."

"We got the photo."

"I bet it's rigged. And this fourth guy—or girl, or, heck, maybe it was Bigfoot—why didn't he just tell us? I'll tell you why. Because he didn't see a thing. He was working us."

She looked at me for a reply, but I was going over what Perlmutter had told us while dreading what we might find at the old Blackburn place. Yes, his "third" bullet could have been a fake. But the photograph intrigued me; the figure in the photo seemed to have that hunch Leo had in his shoulders. As for a fourth person, I didn't want to think about it too hard without knowing who it was. Boynton? Dingus? Elvis Bontrager?

"Did you ever find out anything about Blackburn's family?" I said.

"Nada. If he had a brother-in-law in Kalamazoo, he isn't there now."

I swung the truck onto Route 571. A dim orange glow pulsated in the sky ahead. "How about the property?" I said. "Who owns it now?"

After Blackburn's death, the county had boarded up his house and the billets and declared the property off-limits. Now and then some kids would break into one of the billets and have a party. It had all since been purchased, or so the rumor went, by an out-of-state real-estate investment firm.

"Some company in Virginia," Joanie said. She flipped through her notebook. "It's in my backpack. Something like Richards Incorporated or Richards Company."

"You got this at the clerk's office?"

"Yeah."

"How'd you get past Verna? Vicky?"

"Yeah—holy crap!"

We crested a hill and in the clearing below orange flames and billowing black smoke leaped into the sky through the falling snow. Swirling police lights painted the bare trees in scarlet and blue while the fire hoses etched silver arcs of water catapulting over Blackburn's house and the three billets.

Everything was burning.

I stopped the truck on the horseshoe drive that looped in front of the cabin, where our parents had parked their cars when we were kids playing at Make-Believe Gardens. A cluster of deputies swung around and pointed flashlights our way. "Stay back," one said, but it was only Skip Catledge, so I moved ahead of Joanie into the reek of charred wood and gasoline.

Catledge turned and shouted to another deputy, "Tell Sheriff the press is here." He turned back to me and said, "Not another step, buck."

"What the hell's going on?" I said.

"Judge never should've let him out."

So it was Soupy, as I had feared. This was how he put his affairs in order. "Where is he?"

"One of the little houses in the back. Said he isn't coming out, but the firefighters are going in before the smoke kills him."

I tried to move past Catledge, who put a gloved hand firmly in my chest. "Back off, Gus. If this isn't evidence of guilt, I don't know what is."

"Come on, Skip, I've known the guy for thirty fucking years."

"I've known him just as long, and he's an idiot," Catledge said. He turned around and surveyed the scene, then grabbed me by my jacket shoulder. "All right. Come on."

We trotted up to within fifty yards of the billets. The heat and smoke stung my face and the inside of my nose. "Far enough," Catledge said. "Stay here." He jogged off toward the fire.

Cops and firefighters encircled the burning billets. I imagined Soupy crouched inside, the fire and smoke closing in on him, his idiotic bravado vanished. I thought of his estranged daughter in Flint and how even though she hadn't seen him in years she would be crushed to hear how her daddy had died. I wanted to run into the burning buildings and punch him to death. And I wanted him to come out, sputtering for breath.

Just then a firefighter, followed by a second one, burst from the front door of the nearest billet. They stumbled awkwardly off the porch into the snow, hefting a body wrapped in a blanket. Two paramedics rushed past us with a stretcher.

"They got him," Joanie said.

I walked in a daze of fury and relief toward the paramedics. They laid the body on the stretcher and unwrapped the blanket. It was Soupy, all right. His eyes were shut. He was limp and motionless. A flap of thick hair fell over one side of his face. The hair on the other side was singed off. Charcoal smears blackened his nostrils and upper lip. Dingus emerged from the smoke to our right. He was waving and yelling something I couldn't make out. He saw Joanie and me approaching and held up a hand as if to stop us. Catledge jumped in front of us. "You're gonna get me in trouble," he said.

"Is he alive?" I said.

"No idea. Get back."

The paramedics closed around Soupy, blocking our view. All I could see was Soupy's arm dangling lifelessly off the stretcher. In all of our years of playing hockey, I'd never seen him on a stretcher, not even close. He was lucky that way. Other things didn't hurt Soupy. Mostly it was Soupy who hurt Soupy.

One of the paramedics leaned away and I saw Soupy's arm jerk up and down, once, then again. Then Soupy's head rose a few inches off the stretcher. He coughed a moist wad up on his chest. He leaned over the edge of the stretcher and spit more in the snow, struggling for breath. I felt myself exhale before the anger rushed back in.

"Soupy," I yelled. "What the hell are you doing?"

Dingus pushed in front of me. "Deputy, get them out of here."

"Trap," I heard Soupy say. "Trap. Man, I'm so, I'm so sorry, man."

"Deputy!"

Catledge put his hands on my shoulders. "Let's go, buddy," he said. He pushed me back a step and I stiffened.

"Soupy, why?" I said.

Catledge pressed against me. "Don't make me, Gus."

"I got to talk to you, man," Soupy said.

Catledge shoved me back another step. "Now, Gus," he said. "You want the cell next to his?"

I let Catledge push me back and away. The paramedics strapped Soupy down and lifted him into the ambulance.

"Sorry, man," Soupy cried. "I'm sorry about, about—fuck, man, my fingers burn!"

As the ambulance pulled away, a bright white light shined on us from across the horseshoe. Tawny Jane and her cameraman were walking up. Dingus turned to Joanie and me, the fire raging behind him, his face flushed crimson, his mustache drooping with a crust of ice. "Go home," he said.

We rode to town in silence. I let Joanie out at her car in front of the *Pilot*.

"Long day," she said.

"Yeah. Good job. The Blake story's going to look great."

"Thanks."

I parked in back. I pulled Dad's Bell & Howell out of the back-seat and lugged it into the *Pilot*, where I retrieved the boxes of film I'd found in Delbert's files.

Upstairs, I poured myself a jar of water and drew the shades. From the wall facing the kitchen counter, I removed two pictures—one of my parents sunning on a pontoon boat, my mother pregnant in a pink one-piece swimsuit; the other of my old dogs, Fats and Blinky, asleep on a rug. I set the projector on the kitchen counter, facing the wall. It took me a while to make it work. I got a little thrill of accomplishment seeing the bulb flash a white square on the wall. But I discovered I did not have a take-up reel. Probably dropped it when I slipped on Mom's basement steps. I toweled out my sink and plugged the drain, figuring I'd run the film into the sink and untangle it later if need be.

I inserted the reel marked F/1280/SL/R4. I assumed it was from December of 1980, when I had just turned seventeen. The projector whirred and rattled. A grainy black-and-white image blinked on the wall. I saw our indoor rink viewed from the bleachers, where Leo must have been sitting. On the ice, the River Rats—my River Rats—were practicing. Most of the skaters huddled near the penalty boxes on the opposite side of the ice. Five others stood spread out between the blue lines at center ice. I saw myself standing just outside the blue line on the right of the screen, looking too skinny, even in my goalie gear, to be playing hockey. The shaggy head of Blackburn's mutt, Pocket, poked up from the bench behind the boards.

In the middle of the ice, Blackburn, in skates, hockey gloves, and a blue-and-gold Rats sweatsuit, pointed and waved and shouted direc-tions. The film was soundless, but I could tell he was drilling us in the Rat Trap. He held a puck over his head and skated across the blue line on the left, where he set the puck down on a face-off dot. Then he went to each of the five players and showed him exactly where he was supposed to be. It was hard to make out individual players. I rec-ognized Teddy, who didn't look skinny at all, and Soupy, with his hair splayed across his shoulders. When Blackburn wasn't looking, Soupy would turn and mug for the camera. Blackburn finally caught him, of course, and ordered us all to the end of the rink for sprints.

I didn't recall this particular scene, but it happened often enough. As we lined up to skate, I saw Boynton barking at Soupy, who shrugged and said something back, probably something like, "Twelve-pack on this one, boy-O?" Sometimes I wondered if Soupy deliberately got us into trouble so he could win his Friday night ration of beer from Teddy. I watched us sprint. Once. Twice. Three times. Four. Blackburn presided at the blue line, stick at his side, whistle in his mouth. So many times he'd watched from there while we stood shoulder to shoulder between sprints, leaning on our sticks, gulping at the Freon air.

As Blackburn raised an arm to call for another sprint, the screen went blank white again. I looked at the projector. The spinning reel was still nearly full of film. Could that be all? Maybe Leo didn't want to waste film on sprints. I waited. For a few seconds, the screen went black and the room dark. Then the wall began to flicker with jagged fragments of light. The white square reappeared, followed by a fuzzy new image.

It focused. The camera was now peering into a room. The frame contained a shadow frame within, as though the camera had been aimed through a window. At the center of the picture stood a pool table, covered with a blanket. On the wall behind it hung a bar sign advertising Jim Beam Kentucky Bourbon. "What the hell?" I said aloud. I knew this place. Coach usually didn't have enough out-of-towners to fill the third billet, so he made part of it into a playroom. This was it.

The body of a woman moved languidly into the picture, her head cut off by the upper limit of the frame. Her hair, the color of day-old snow, cascaded down to the tops of her bare shoulder blades. The rest of her was covered in a bedsheet she held in a bunch at her breasts. She stood with her back to the camera, obscuring most of the picture. The way she'd strutted slowly into the picture, then held herself there, as if on display, suggested to me that she wanted to be there, that she belonged. Behind her someone else entered the frame. I spied enough of a forearm to think it was male. His head, too, was cut off by the frame. She let her arms fall to her sides. The sheet fell away. On her bottom's right cheek I glimpsed a tattoo, too small to see clearly, though I thought it might be a four-leaf clover. She gestured toward the pool table. The man seemed frozen in place. The woman moved toward the table, leaving the frame. Now I saw that the man was not a man but a boy. His face still wasn't visible, but I knew his chest and shoulders and the way his boxers drooped on his thin hips.

It was Soupy.

The woman reentered the frame. She was crawling naked across the pool table toward Soupy, her head down, her hair hiding the corner of her face included in the frame. Soupy turned toward her, tentative, and hooked his thumbs inside the waistband of his boxers. Her head snapped up then, the hair flipping back, but the camera slid downward and she was headless again. She slithered across the table, took Soupy by his shoulders, and pulled him toward her.

He obeyed with the shy reluctance of a child. He lay motionlessly on his back while the woman slipped his boxers off and mounted him. I wanted to turn away but instead I reached into the drawer next to my head and grabbed a pen and notebook and began taking notes. The woman pressed the heels of her palms flat against his belly and writhed, her hair tossing back and forth on her shoulders. There still was no sound, but the way she moved suggested she was enjoying herself. Soupy's arms lay still at his sides as he gazed blankly at the ceiling.

A man entered the frame from the right, fully clothed. His face was clearly visible. It was Jack Blackburn. Soupy closed his eyes. The woman continued to grind against him while Blackburn propped his thighs against the side of the table behind the woman, over Soupy's bare feet. I knew what was going to happen then. It had happened to Brendan Blake. Blackburn unzipped his pants and took his erect penis in both hands. Now I closed my eyes, though only briefly. With the celluloid piling up in the sink, I felt it was my duty to compile a record. I forced myself to watch as Blackburn masturbated. He ejaculated on Soupy's pale feet. The toes curled. Soupy twisted his face away from the camera.

I thought of him in our dressing room, jamming his too-small skates onto his feet, and I jumped up and lurched around and leaned into the sink, trying to keep from vomiting. My breathing echoed on the stainless-steel walls. Beneath my face the unspooled film was heaped like dead snakes in a sewer. I pushed away and stumbled into the bathroom, where I flicked on the light and splashed cold water on my face and the back of my neck. Staring into the mirror, I drew deep breaths and watched the water trickling down my cheeks and off the stitches still in my jaw. I wiped my face and brought the towel with me into the kitchen.

For the next two hours I filled most of the notebook with everything I saw on the three reels. I had to stop now and then to collect myself. On every reel, scenes of River Rat practices were spliced with scenes of Soupy in the playroom. The woman was in some of the scenes, some not. Blackburn performed in every one. The level of light and the camera angle varied slightly from one reel to the next, suggesting that there had been numerous sessions. In one scene a whiskey bottle and a glass appeared on a shelf in the background. In another, Blackburn's little dog, Pocket, jumped onto the table and licked Soupy's face; Soupy, showing the only emotion I saw in any of the films, angrily swatted the dog away. I scribbled it all down.

I concluded Blackburn had placed the camera behind a mirror on the wall—a one-way mirror, obviously. Was Leo behind the camera? Or had Blackburn set it up and let it run while he participated? The wall was common to a bunkroom. For his last two years on the Rats, Teddy had stayed in that bunkroom alone while other out-of-town players shared the other billets. Imagining Teddy there aroused my nausea again, and then a searing wave of sympathy I'd never before felt for him.

Each time a reel finished, I lifted the snarl of celluloid from the sink and packed it gently in a brown paper bag that I then stashed in a Cheerios box in the back of my pantry. After stowing the last film, I unplugged the projector, wrapped the cord around it, and stuffed it under my bed. Then I lay down without taking my clothes off. I couldn't sleep, though. Every time I closed my eyes, I saw Soupy and that tattooed woman writhing on the pool table. I tried to focus on the ceiling, but that didn't work. It was too quiet and too dark. I reached under my bed and pulled out the projector. I set it up again on the kitchen counter and turned it on. The empty white square appeared on the wall. I sat down on the floor and leaned back against the cabinets beneath the sink. The projector *click-click-clicked*. I stared at the blank light until my eyes wouldn't stay open anymore.

twenty-five

I woke with my face pressed against the scratchy wool braid of a throw rug. The phone was ringing. I shut off the projector and grabbed the phone. "Yeah?"

It was Joanie. She was angry. "Brendan Blake is not in the paper."

"It's on the front below the fold."

"No. On the front below the fold there's a high school wrestling story. The Blake story isn't in the paper anywhere. I even looked through the classifieds."

"A wrestling story?"

"By Matilda P. Spaulding."

"Goddammit," I said. "Goddamn Tillie."

Tillie must have eavesdropped on me leaving the message for Kerasopoulos. That's why she'd been smiling that smile I didn't like. Then she'd obviously called him, and he killed the Brendan Blake story. With nothing else handy at the last minute, the printers substituted wrestling. No doubt I had a message from Kerasopoulos waiting downstairs.

"Come on," Joanie said, incredulous. "Tillie wanted a front-page byline?"

"Of course not," I said. A bit of the previous night's queasiness returned. "Tillie didn't give a damn about the wrestling story. She's just kissing up to the bosses."

"You're her boss."

"Yeah, right."

The line went silent. Then Joanie said, "You know what? Fuck Tillie. Fuck Kerafuckface. Fuck the fucking *Pilot*."

"Joanie!"

"Yeah, yeah, I know, everything'll be fine, you'll get all my stories in the paper. I don't even care anymore. I'm so fucking out of here."

She slammed the phone down before I could say anything else.

I opened a cabinet and took out my only liquor, a dusty plastic bottle of vodka. I poured a little in a coffee cup and took it into the bathroom. I dipped some tweezers in the vodka and plucked the stitches from my chin. I didn't know the trick of removing them without pulling part of the suture back through the wound, so I applied a dab of vodka after each one came out.

I took a shower and dressed. In my bedroom closet I found the knapsack I'd used to carry the Superior transcripts out of the Detroit bus station. I filled it with underwear, white socks, three T-shirts, and two flannel button-downs. I zipped a toothbrush and toothpaste into a separate pocket.

I lifted the plywood sheet off the boxes marked Trucks and Rats. One by one I hauled them down the outside stairs. The wind whistled around me as I loaded them into my truck's flatbed, where my hockey bag still sat, covered with snow.

I did it all without really thinking. It felt like I was getting ready to leave, but I had no idea where I was going, or even if I was going. I just felt like I might have to leave, and quickly. I had to supply the name of my Superior source by noon or face arrest. I still wasn't sure what I was going to do, and I wasn't stupid enough to think I could run, didn't even think I wanted to. But something was telling me to be ready. A lot of things I'd never expected had happened in the past few days.

A few minutes before eight, the phone rang again. I picked it up expecting Joanie. "Are you in the office?" I said.

"Excuse me? Mr. Carpenter?"

"Oh, sorry. This is Gus."

"It's Terence Flapp, attorney for Alden Campbell."

Flapp told me Soupy had spent a few hours in the hospital but now was back in lockup. Soupy wanted to see me. Flapp wasn't sure why. He had advised Soupy against seeing anyone. But Soupy was Soupy.

"Judge Gallagher will have my head for this if he finds out," Flapp said. "Although I should tell you I do not intend for this to become an interview for your paper."

I actually had no great desire to see Soupy. But I did have some questions. "Dingus doesn't mind?"

"You tell me. When I told him I wanted to bring someone in, his first response was, 'Over my dead body.' But when I told him who, suddenly it was fine."

"Huh."

"Yes, well, meet me at the jail at ten-thirty."

I had another stop to make first.

Gloria Lowinski, R.N., answered the door of her pink frame house in a white housecoat decorated with faded pink flowers. Pins and curlers knitted her hair, dyed the color of rust, tightly to her scalp. I hadn't even introduced myself when she opened the door wide and beckoned me in. "Oh, oh, oh, you're the man from the newspaper, aren't you?" she said. Her eyes were exceptionally bright for a widow in her eighties. "I've seen you at the diner. Come in, come in. Would you like coffee? I'm a tea drinker myself, but most people drink coffee. Are you like most people?"

"No, ma'am," I said, meaning I didn't want coffee. "Sorry to bother you so early."

"No bother. I adore having visitors anytime. Sit."

I sat in a wing-backed chair covered with more pink flowers. Issues of *People* magazine covered the end table next to me.

"I have to say, young man, you have quite a popular newspaper," Gloria Lowinski said. "I've been on the phone all day every day since I was in that article. It's been absolutely astonishing."

"I'm glad. What you said about the president was very interesting."

"Oh, oh, yes, the way of the tantric, I think that most definitely would help him with his, shall we say, waywardness, and it certainly would be appreciated by his wife, I can you tell from glorious experience." She closed her eyes and pressed a hand dramatically to her breast. "As in *Gloria's* experience."

"Yes, ma'am. I was wondering if you could help me with a story I'm working on now. It's about tattoos."

I had an idea about the tattoo I'd seen in the films. I'd come to hear Gloria Lowinski tell me if I was right. I wouldn't have minded being wrong.

"Tattoos? Young man, your timing is perfect. My granddaughter just got a tattoo on—well, I shouldn't tell you, but, oh, what the hang—it's just above her privates on the left side. Here." She pointed to a spot on her bathrobe. I focused on my notebook. "Would you like to speak with her? It's Priscilla Lawlor, 1209 Fletcher Street."

"Thanks, Mrs. Lowinski, but actually, I'd—"

"Oh, I know, I'm prattling on, you want to ask me something." She sat down on a sofa facing me. "I should tell you, Mr., Mr. . . ."

"Carpenter. Call me Gus."

"Of course, Bea and Rudy's boy. How is your mother? She used to come to our office but she stopped. She never said why."

"She's fine, thanks. You were saying . . ."

"And you, weren't you going to marry the Bontrager girl, the buxom one, Deborah or Deirdre something?"

"Darlene."

"Yes, Darlene. That wasn't so long ago."

"About fifteen years."

"Oh, well, that's not so long. My husband died twenty-three years ago and it still seems like yesterday."

Everything in my past was beginning to feel like yesterday. "I'm sorry, ma'am. You were saying you should tell me . . . ?"

"Yes, yes. What I meant was, I'm no expert in tattoos. I don't have one myself, but of course, as an obstetrical-gynecological nurse, I have seen a few."

"I figured," I said, and we both smiled. She was indeed a blabber-mouth, as Mom had said.

"Now," she said, "are you interested in what sorts of tattoos I've seen? Or the most, shall we say, interesting places women have them? Oh, oh, I remember a woman—Doris, yes, Doris Kellogg—an exceptionally large woman who had a tattoo of a large beautiful butterfly right where her—"

"Actually, Mrs. Lowinski, I have a specific tattoo in mind. We, uh, we have a photograph of a tattoo we're trying to identify. It's quite pretty and we'd like to contact the owner."

"Please call me Gloria. Are you going to put me in the paper again?"

"We might."

"Good," she said. "Because, if I may say so, it sounds a bit, shall we say, farfetched, that there would be some local collection of tattoos"—she raised an eyebrow—"but if you're looking to quote an expert, or, maybe not an *expert* but certainly an *observer*, then perhaps I can help you. If it's a woman and she's local, chances are I've seen her and her tattoo."

"Of course. I'm sure you can help."

"Can I see the photograph?"

"Unfortunately, no. I don't have it with me."

"Well, whose collection is it? Why wouldn't they know whose tattoo it is?"

"That's a little complicated, Gloria." I was dancing as fast as I could. "I'm really not at liberty to say."

"Are you sure the tattoo is from someone around here?"

"Pretty sure."

I described the tattoo I'd seen on Blackburn's films. Though I'd thought at first that it was a four-leaf clover, I'd caught a few other glances of it during the films, including one fleeting close-up, and decided it actually looked more like a star with something inside it. Gloria listened. I tore a page out of my notebook and drew a crude version of it for her. She took one look and gave me a sly smile.

"You're not really doing a story, are you?" she said.

"Pardon me?"

She leaned closer. "You are a devil. Are we—are you playing a practical joke? Is it a certain someone's birthday?"

"Uh, no, I'm not sure what you're—"

"Come on, Gus. There's only one person in this town with a tattoo even remotely like that, and you darned well know who she is."

I wasn't going to say it.

"Why don't you guess?"

"I'd rather not, Gloria. Guessing gets newspaper people in trouble."

"Really?" she said, laughing. "You are a devil. You're here enchanting me with a chance to get in your paper again, but really you have some other secret agenda. OK, I'm game. It wouldn't be the first time a man has bamboozled me."

"So," I said, totally unsure of myself now, "can you tell me?"

She shook her head and laughed again. "Hand me one of those." She meant the *People* magazines stacked on the end table. "Any of them."

I gave her one. She flipped through it, came to a stop, and showed me a photograph. "Here's a clue," she said. In the photo a young actress I didn't recognize was stooping to admire her freshly implanted star on the Hollywood Walk of Fame.

I looked up at smiling Gloria Lowinski.

"That's what your tattoo looks like, doesn't it?" she said. "Makes sense, doesn't it? How else could our beloved beauty queen have gotten one of those?"

"Right," I said.

Gloria stood. "You're not going to put me in your paper, but this was fun anyway. And what a coincidence! She was just here the other day, sitting on that very chair."

I didn't really need further confirmation. But inside my truck, I flipped back to the notes I'd taken in my semistupor the night before.

I wanted to see if I had written down the brand of the whiskey in the bottle standing on the shelf in the background. I had. My barely legible note read, "gntlmn jac." Or, as Soupy put it that night on my stairway, "Gentleman-fucking-Jack," the brand of Starvation Lake's very own beauty queen, Tillie Spaulding.

twenty-six

Some things were beginning to make painful sense. Now I understood why Tillie had been behaving strangely, why she'd been so protective of the photo files, why Soupy had always resisted meeting me at the *Pilot*. Blackburn had stashed his film at the paper so Tillie—a movie star at last, in thrall to her director—could keep watch.

I was glad to see she wasn't in yet when I got back to the *Pilot*. I was a little angry and a lot uncomfortable and I might have fired her on the spot, which would have been foolish. Better that she didn't know what I knew, at least for now, although she had to be suspicious if she had noticed the missing films.

Joanie sat reading *Newsweek* with her feet up on her desk. Her clutter didn't usually allow space for feet, but today she appeared to have cleared her desk onto the floor. I walked up and stood silently regarding the mess.

"In case you're wondering, those are my notes from the story we're supposedly covering," she said, without looking up from her magazine.

"Nice. Why not just toss it all in the garbage?"

"I'll get around to it." She snapped a page back. "By the way, there's a press release in the pile about some New York bank buying a bunch of little banks up here. Sounds like something tame enough for us."

On my desk lay that morning's paper. Across Tillie's wrestling story Joanie had scribbled in red ink, "Pulitzer?" Higher up the page, that old picture of Blackburn in his slicked-back hair stared up at me. The caption read, "JACK BLACKBURN, Jan. 19, 1934–March 13, 1988." Something about it bothered me.

My message light was on. I dialed voice mail. Kerasopoulos had called at 7:14, saying, "Please call the minute you get in." I wandered back over to Joanie. I didn't blame her for feeling the way she did. But I needed her to get over it.

"Hey," I said. "I got a jailhouse interview with Campbell."

"Great. You can add to the pile."

She kept reading. I stooped down to look at what was on the floor. Seven or eight notebooks, half a dozen file folders, a smattering of other papers. One was a photocopy of a tax document that had to have come from the county clerk's office. I picked it up.

"This from the old Blackburn land?" I said.

"If it's that Richards Company, yep."

"Boy. The assessed value's almost five hundred grand." My eyes went to the line identifying the owner. "It's actually Richard Limited, singular, not Richards," I said. There was an address in Springfield, Virginia.

"Who cares?"

I stood, letting the paper drop. "So what are you doing today?"

"Hmmmm. First I thought I'd finish reading this story about how everyone's going to get rich selling poodle sweaters on the Internet. Then I was thinking maybe Audrey's for a leisurely brunch or maybe just straight to Enright's for a double Bloody Mary. Maybe Dingus'll join me and I can at least tell *him* what I know."

"That reminds me," I said. I grabbed Joanie's phone and dialed the county clerk's office, hoping Vicky would answer. I was in luck.

"It's Gus Carpenter," I said. "How are you?"

"Sick of snow," Vicky said.

"Me, too. Listen—remember that file from eighty-eight I wanted the other day? Did you ever find out who took it?" Dingus, I'd figured.

"Oh, God, I've got to get that back before my mother kills me," she said. "Dave from Town Hall has it and he's not returning my calls."

"Dave?"

"Dave, you know, the bartender?" She meant Loob. He worked part-time for the tax assessor. But why in the world would Loob need those minutes? "If you see him, will you tell him to bring me my folder?"

"Sure." I hung up the phone.

"Tell me," Joanie said. "Why do you keep doing this?"

"Doing what?"

"Doing *this*. Being a reporter. Chasing this story. Why bother? Nobody here wants to know the truth anyway. They don't care what we have to say unless it's to tell them where's the Rotary lunch or what's showing at the movies or who caught the biggest fish. I mean, sorry, but this is it for you, isn't it? You had your shot at the big time and you blew it. Now you're in piddling little Starvation Lake, the denial capital of the world. Why do you keep going?"

It was a good question. My old coach was a pedophile. My receptionist was his beard. My closest friend and maybe others I knew were their victims. My mother knew things I didn't. I had been blind to it all. For years I had been walking around in the middle of the truth and I could not see it. True, I was just a boy but, even now, I could see only the blurred contours of the truth. From within its darker core a thousand questions taunted. Joanie was right. Even if I answered every question, no brighter future awaited, not in what I'd chosen to do with my life thus far. There was just the knowing. Somehow, I had to hope, the knowing would make things better. I was no longer on a mission for clips or prizes or raises or the envy of my peers. There was just the knowing. And it wasn't even the knowing of the who-what-where-when-why of Blackburn's life and death. I wanted to know why I wanted to know.

"I don't know," I said. "It pays the bills. But thanks for asking." I meant it. "I've got to call Kerawhatshisfatass."

I dialed at my desk. His secretary answered and put me on hold. As I waited, I doodled "Richard Ltd." on my blotter. He picked up.

"Gus Carpenter, Jim," I said.

"Excuse me," he said, "I'm going to close the door." He set the phone down, picked it up again. "Last night was not good, Gus."

"This morning's not so hot, either. We had a hell of a front-page scoop someone obviously killed."

Out of the corner of my eye I noticed Joanie put her magazine down.

"You bet we killed it," Kerasopoulos said. "I thought we had a talk—two talks—about certain stories. I thought we had an understanding."

"We did. I was going to let you know when we had something out of the ordinary. Last night we did, and I let you know."

"On voice mail? Not good enough. Not even close. I don't want to hear from your secretary about the most inflammatory story in the paper."

"I'm going to fire her."

Joanie rolled her chair over next to my desk. I pointed toward the front counter. She shook her head no, meaning Tillie wasn't in yet.

"Let's just calm down now," Kerasopoulos said.

"Let's not. My job is to put news in the paper. We had legitimate news that had a direct bearing on something very big going on around here. We checked it out and we decided to run it. That's what reporters and editors do. Anybody can kill stories."

I knew I was treading on thin ice, but I no longer cared. "Careful, Gus," Kerasopoulos said. "It is simply not sufficient to quote one person who is thousands of miles away, whom we've never even seen, whose credibility we have not tested—"

"Others corroborated it."

"Really? How about the police up there or, whatever, the Mounties? Did this guy ever think to tell them about his, his encounters, if in fact they happened? What use is there in dredging all this up now?"

"If Blackburn was a child molester, it could suggest a motive. The person charged with his murder played for Blackburn."

"You played for him, too, didn't you, Gus?"

"Yes, I did."

"Exactly. So let me ask you, and you obviously don't have to answer, but did your coach ever do anything to *you* to suggest he was, you know, a little off? Did he ever come on to you?"

"No, he did not."

"Well, excuse me, Gus, but you were there. If you didn't see anything, why are you so all-fired sure it happened? What hard evidence links this guy in Canada—and, again, we don't know what ax he might have to grind—to what tragedy may have befallen Blackburn? Anything?"

I'd had enough of this jerk. Maybe I was blowing the chance to be executive editor of the *Pilot*. I'd made worse career moves. "An ax to grind?" I said. "You've got to be kidding. Let me tell you, Jim—" As I spoke the words, I pressed the cradle down to end the call. Hanging up on yourself was an old newsroom trick. You used it to get rid of late-night weirdos claiming to have seen Elvis at Burger King.

"You hung up on him?" Joanie said, incredulous.

"Fuck it. Better get out of here before he calls back." I grabbed a fresh notebook and a couple of pens. "I'm going to the jail."

D'Alessio led Flapp and me into the windowless room where Soupy waited at a small steel table. "I'll be out here if you need me," the deputy said.

The first thing I noticed was Soupy's head. It had been shaved down to tiny bristles. "What happened to your hair?" I said.

"Cops took it," he said. "Thought I'd use it to hang myself or something."

Flapp pulled a chair next to Soupy and sat. I sat facing them. The room smelled vaguely of paint. I recalled an item in the *Pilot* about the county setting aside money to repaint the jail. Then I remembered Tillie had written it. Pinpricks of heat tingled at the back of my neck.

"How are you?" I said.

"Flapp and Trap," Soupy said. He grinned. "Head hurts, but other than that I'm fine." He wore an orange jumpsuit, white sneakers, shackles on his wrists and ankles. Bandages covered both of his hands. He looked OK for someone who the night before had barely escaped from a burning building.

"You remember last night?" I said. "You were pretty wasted."

"You know, I didn't really mean to burn all those shacks. Just the one."

"Excuse me," Flapp interjected. "Can we discuss a few ground rules?"

"Relax, Flapjack," Soupy said. "This ain't business. It's personal. I got a few things to say."

"Splendid," Flapp said, the muscles in his jaw pulsing as he ground his molars, "but do you want everyone in the county listening in on your personal conversation?"

"Gus and I'll work it out."

"Once it goes in the paper, it's fair game—"

"Look," I said, "we can do this off the record and if there's something I really want to use, I'll run it by you first, Terence."

Flapp looked at Soupy. "Fine."

"Great," Soupy said. "See you in a bit, Flapjack."

"You want me to leave?" Flapp said. He looked horrified. "Absolutely not. I cannot advise that."

"OK, you didn't," Soupy said. "I want to talk with my man alone."

Flapp picked up his satchel and left, shaking his head.

Soupy leaned back and looked up at the ceiling, where lightbulbs glowed in little cages. "Things are pretty fucked up, Trapezoid."

"Yep."

"How's Boynton?"

"Not dead."

"The prick had it coming."

"Yeah," I said. Soupy watched while I pulled out my pen and notebook. "What about Coach, Soup? Did Coach have it coming?"

"You sound like Dingus. Man, he doesn't quit."

I doubted now that Dingus really believed Soupy killed Black-burn. It was looking as though he'd arrested Soupy to shake him down.

But I was going to ask anyway.

"Did you kill Coach, Soupy?"

He laughed. "Jesus, Trap, I asked *you* here, man."

"Did you or not?" I didn't usually start by asking the biggest question, but I'd wasted enough time already with Soupy and his shenanigans.

"Trap," he said. "Don't do it. Don't even try."

"Try what?"

"To save me."

I knew what he meant. "I'm not trying to save you," I said. "You can save your own sorry ass."

"Right," he said. "Look, either I don't need to be saved or I'm beyond saving. So just forget it. I asked you to come because I want to tell you something."

"Why don't you just tell me the goddamn truth?"

Soupy laid his manacled, bandaged hands on top of the table. "No," he said. "All right? I did not kill Blackburn. But I'll you what. I wish I had. I should have."

"So it was Leo?"

"No, no. Leo was protecting me. Leo—"

Soupy suddenly bowed his head. He was gathering himself. I decided to change the subject. "Boynton blackmailed you, didn't he?" I said.

Soupy shook his head, embarrassed. "The bastard," he said. "I should've let him. Maybe I'd be sleeping in my own bed now."

"That's what the other night was about, right? When you came over to my place shitfaced?"

"Trap, this ain't what I asked you here for. But since you asked. Remember me and Boynton bitching at each other the other night at Enright's? Sunday morning, he shows up at my place. Remember now, everything is about his goddamn marina. He says, look, we got to work this out, blah blah—"

"I know. He was going to give you a piece of the action, and you were going to tell the zoning board to go ahead with the new marina."

"How'd you know?"

"Doesn't matter. So Boynton comes over Sunday morning . . ."

"He brings buns from Audrey's, for Christ's sake. He wants coffee, but all I got is Blue Ribbon, so we drink a couple with the buns and he says I got to reconsider and I tell him to basically go to hell. I know I'm not so hot at running the marina, but it's all I got. And Boynton says, well, maybe you ought to consider some new information."

I added it up quickly in my head. By then Joanie had talked to Boynton, and Boynton had talked to Darlene, or tried. An echo chamber in the service of blackmail. I told Soupy, "He said the *Pilot* was going to run something bad about Coach."

"Yeah. About . . ." He stopped. "I ain't going to talk about that."

I didn't need him to talk about it just yet.

"So eventually you told him you'd do the deal, right? You were supposed to go to the zoning board and tell them the marina was fine and dandy."

"Something like that."

"Did you tell Boynton anything else?"

"About what?"

"About anything, Soupy. About Blackburn or Leo or whatever the hell happened in those billets you tried to burn down."

"I don't remember."

"Fuck you. Did you hear the prosecutor say she's got testimony from somebody who spoke with you recently? Who the hell do you think it is?"

"Sorry."

"Why didn't you show up at the zoning board?"

"I was planning to, I was. But I go to get my skates sharpened, like I always do, and Leo's gone. The Zam shed's cleaned out. I figure he hit the road because Boynton went to the cops with . . . with what he knew. So I go to Boynton and blow a gasket. He swears he didn't talk but says I better have my ass at the zoning board or he will. But now I'm like, fuck him, it's over, so I blow off the zoning board. And then . . ." All the blood went out of his face. "Fucking Leo, man."

"Soup," I said. "Leo was my friend, too. I hate what happened to him. But do you think it's even remotely possible that he killed Blackburn? Is that why he killed himself? You said he was protecting you. From what? What did Teddy know? Why did you let him bail you out?"

"So I could burn down that goddamn building."

"Soupy." I reached across the table and grabbed his shoulder. Then I spoke as slowly and evenly as I could. "I know, OK?" I said. "I know what happened in the billets. I know about Coach and Tillie and what you meant the other night about the whiskey."

"What whiskey?"

"Gentleman Jack."

"Oh, fuck," Soupy said, yanking his shoulder back.

"It's all right, Soup. You were just a kid."

He looked away for a while. Then he wiped a sleeve across his face and propped his elbows on the table. "All right," he said. "Put the pen down a minute."

"Why?"

"Just put it down."

I obeyed. Soupy told me what he saw that night with Blackburn and Leo in the woods between Starvation and Walleye lakes.

twenty-seven

On that March night in 1988, the pistol felt cold against Soupy's palm. He gripped it loosely, nervously, in his coat pocket as he emerged from the trees at the clearing's edge. "Hello," he said.

Jack Blackburn and Leo Redpath barely heard him over the crackle of the fire in the rusted oil barrel. The glow of the flames played across their faces where they sat on their snowmobiles.

"Look who's here," Blackburn said. "Old Swanny."

"The returning soldier," Leo said, waving a flat, clear glass bottle. "Welcome home, Mr. Campbell. Come toast the Ides of March. We're celebrating early this year."

The knee-deep snow felt like mud as Soupy stepped toward the men. He was sweating. He'd been building up courage at Enright's.

"What's up, Jack?" he said.

"What's up, Jack?" I said. "You've got a gun in your pocket and you're saying, 'What's up, Jack?'"

"I know," Soupy told me. "I didn't know what the hell I was doing. I almost bolted right there."

"Almost?"

He shook his head. "Fuck him, Trap. I hope he's frying in hell."

"Jack?" Blackburn said. He smiled and raised his own brown bottle to his lips. His hair was matted from wearing the wool cap and helmet that rested in his lap. "How'd the season go, Swanny? Still in Harrisburg?"

"Hershey," Soupy said. His last season in the minors. The booze churned in his belly. His hand was now shaking so badly that he let the gun go and clutched the inside of his pocket. "Got hurt."

Blackburn grunted. "I'll bet. You were never too big on the conditioning. You just wanted to play." He took another drink. "Just wanted to show off for the girls." He and Leo laughed.

Soupy felt a surge of anger and took hold of the gun again, his index finger resting on the trigger. "Champy says hello, Jack," he said.

"Pardon?"

Something rustled in the bushes behind Soupy. He looked around, keeping his hand in his pocket, and saw nothing.

"Just a deer that wants a beer," Blackburn said. "He won't hurt you, Swanny."

"You don't remember Champy, Jack?"

"What's got you so hot under the collar?" Blackburn said. "Who?"

"Champy, Jack. Played for the Rats. You cut him, remember? But he turned out to be a player. Good wheels. Awesome hands. Better hands than me."

Blackburn propped his bottle on his knee. "I had a lot of players, down here and up in the homeland. I don't remember all of them. But nobody had better hands than you."

"He had the stuff to make it big, Jack," Soupy said. "But he's all done now. Like me. He was pretty much done when he got to Hershey this year. You know, Jack, if we had a three-day break between games, Champy could blow through a pile of coke bigger than your head."

"I'm sorry to hear that. What's your point?"

"When Champy showed up in Hershey, I hadn't seen him in years. We talked a lot, Jack. Talked a lot about you."

Blackburn shifted the bottle to his other knee.

"Worried?" Soupy said. "You can probably figure what we talked about, huh, Jack? You probably thought nobody would ever talk about it. You were wrong."

Leo stood. Blackburn looked at him and then back at Soupy. He said, "Spent the evening at Enright's, eh, Swanny?"

"Don't fucking call me that anymore."

"Soupy," Leo said. "What's the matter?"

"Quiet, Leo," Soupy said. "Don't fuck around with me, Jack. You stayed in pretty close touch with Champy, didn't you? Real close. His parents must have loved you helping him get the full ride to State. I wonder what they would've thought about you going to visit him now and then. Do you think they would've been happy about you fucking their son? Huh, Jack?"

"Jack?" Leo said.

Blackburn twisted the cap onto his bottle. "Let's go, Leo. The boy's had too much to drink."

"No," Soupy said, taking a step forward. He pulled out the gun and pointed it at Blackburn.

"What the hell?" Blackburn said.

Leo took a step toward Soupy. "My God, son."

Soupy waved him back with the pistol. "Sit down, Leo. Ain't about you. This is all about Jack. And Champy. And me."

"What do you want?" Blackburn said.

"Hah," Soupy said. "Whatever it is, Jack, it's way too fucking late for you to give it to me. Or give it back."

"You know what? I think you're drunk, eh? I think you're a little pissed off about your shitty little career and you'd like someone to blame. You might want to go look in a mirror, eh? As for your friend, Champy or whatever, I don't know what you're talking about."

Tears had begun to burn in Soupy's eyes. He lowered the gun barrel until it was aimed at Blackburn's crotch. "What was his name, Jack?"

"Put the gun down, Swanny."

"I'm going to blow your dick off, Jack."

Blackburn lowered his voice. "You little shit. I never did anything you didn't want me to."

"Jack?" Leo said.

"What was his name?" Soupy said.

"Jeff," Blackburn said. "Jeff Champagne, all right?"

"Fuck you, Jack."

The shot went off as Blackburn somersaulted backward into the snow. The bullet missed him and pierced the snowmobile. Soupy aimed to fire again but Leo had jumped in his way, crying, "Oh, my God." Blackburn scrambled out from behind the snowmobile and flung his bottle at Soupy's head. Soupy ducked at the same time that something whacked him hard behind his left ear and he fell. In an instant Blackburn was on top of him with the pistol. He grabbed Soupy's coat collar with one hand and pointed the gun at his head with the other. "You little shit," he said. He forced the gun barrel into Soupy's mouth. The metal banged against his teeth. "Suck on this," Blackburn said. Soupy closed his eyes. He heard another voice, maybe Leo's, he wasn't sure, shout, "Get off that boy!" and then another—not Leo's, not Blackburn's, not one he recognized in his drunken grogginess—say, "You took it too far, Jack. Too damn far." Then Blackburn cried out and his weight fell suddenly away and Soupy half opened his eyes to see Leo standing with the pistol in hand and Blackburn sitting in the snow, rubbing the back of his head.

"Get up, Soupy," Leo said.

Soupy struggled to his feet. Blood was dripping from his left ear. Leo pointed the gun at Blackburn. It shook in his hand.

"You lied, Jack," Leo said. "You didn't stop."

Blackburn groaned. "Jesus, Leo. You hit me."

"You said you'd stopped."

"It's not my fault his life is all fucked up."

"Enough," Leo said. He swung the pistol awkwardly across Blackburn's eye, as if he didn't want to hurt him. Blackburn grunted and keeled over, his blood coursing red into the snow. Leo turned to Soupy. "Get out of here."

"What are you going to do?" Soupy said.

"Just go."

"I ran like hell," Soupy told me. "Had to puke before I got to my truck."

"Did you hear anything?"

He paused. Then he said, "A shot."

"One shot? You didn't turn around?"

"No way. Didn't even stop."

"Just one shot?"

"Yeah."

That made for only two shots, as the police had concluded: one in the snowmobile, one in Blackburn's head. It didn't account for the bullet Perlmutter supposedly found embedded in the tree. Were there two bullets or three? Three people or four, as Perlmutter claimed?

"How come nobody else heard shots?" I said.

"What difference would it make? Drunk assholes are always shooting their guns off around here."

"And the only ones out there were Blackburn and Leo?"

"All I saw. I might've heard someone else, but I don't know for sure."

"You didn't hear somebody else running away?"

He shook his head.

Even though I'd never heard the story before, never came close to imagining it, hearing it made enough sense now that it gave me an eerie sense of déjà vu, as if I'd been standing there myself, watching from the clearing's edge.

The door opened. D'Alessio ducked in. "Carpenter," he said.

"Our time's not up."

"One minute."

In the hallway, he looked around to make sure no one was listening. "We got a call from the state police," he said, his voice edged with irritation. "They want our assistance in case they have to make an arrest."

"Yeah?"

"They wanted your place of residence, Gus."

Superior. That's what a company that sold a lot of discounted cars to the state police could do. My watch said I still had more than an hour before I had to give up my source's name. "OK," I said.

"I don't know what the hell you got going with the state boys, or why the sheriff would care, but he told me to tell you. Now you know."

I sat back down with Soupy. "So what about this suicide pact Blackburn and Leo supposedly had?" I said.

Soupy shook his head. "That's bullshit. Why would Leo make a deal like that? He wasn't doing any of the shit in the billets."

"Are you sure he wasn't working the camera?" It came out before I could stop it.

"What camera?" Soupy said.

"Shit," I said. I told him what I'd seen. "I found them totally by accident."

"Did you watch them by accident too?" Soupy said.

"Soup, nobody else has seen them, so far as I know. Obviously Blackburn, but he's dead."

"Fuck it, man, don't worry about it." Soupy shoved his chair back. "Everybody's probably seen those things."

"Everybody who?"

"Every twisted fucking pervert who goes for that shit."

"How?"

"Blackburn. The motherfucker was selling them, making money off them."

So Soupy knew all along.

"No," I said.

"How do you think he afforded all those houses, Trap? He was a goddamn air-conditioning guy. He was selling those films. To whoever buys that kind of shit."

"How do you know?"

"Leo. Jack cut him in when he first got started. You know Leo; he went along. He was a great guy, but that porn shit got to him, man, he got to love it, like a drug. He finally went to a shrink. Took him a while, but he got better. He tried to get Jack better too, but Jack just pretended. He was a hopelessly sick fuck. He was still fooling around with Champy after Leo thought everything was cool. Then when Leo found out that night at the fire, they blew up like they did. Leo never told me what happened after I bolted that scene. But these last couple of years, he was trying to help me find those films."

"How?"

"The new way, man. The Web."

"The Internet? You can do films on the Internet?"

"Nah, but they can pick stills out of them. And of course all the slimeballs who crave this shit can communicate real fast and easy without leaving much of a trail. Anyway, Leo thought we might be able to track down my films, or maybe the guys who had them, and maybe buy them up. It was pretty stupid. Like we were going to buy up every little piece of me out there. Never did find me. But there was plenty of porn. Little boys. Little girls. Cats. Dogs. Ducks. Pigs. Fucking pigs, man. The whole world is a goddamn porn freak show now." He stopped and thought for a moment. "Leo got hooked on that shit all over again. He said it wasn't a problem. But it was a big problem. I wish I'd thrown his damn computer in the lake with Blackburn."

So all that happy blather pasted over Leo's workbench had nothing to do with alcohol, but pornography. Maybe he *had* been behind the camera in the billets. Maybe he had expected that everything he had on his computer would have come out in the courtroom. Maybe he had killed himself out of pure suffocating shame.

"Leo never told you what happened?"

"Never."

"Come on."

"Nope. Neither one of us ever said a word. Even when we were hunting around on his computer, we acted like that night never happened."

"So you always knew the snowmobile accident was bullshit."

"Yep. And that pisses you off, doesn't it, Trap? Sorry, man. You got your job, I got mine. Leo saved my goddamn life. I couldn't take a chance on getting him in trouble. Turns out I did anyway."

It infuriated me that I had no choice but to understand. "What about that other voice you heard that night? Was it Leo?"

"I don't know. Maybe. I was half blind."

"So there might've been somebody else out there? Is that what you're saying?"

"I don't know. Why do you keep asking that?"

"Somebody . . . I heard there might've been somebody else."

"From who? Boynton?"

"No."

"Well then, hell, Trap, maybe it was Boynton out there. Maybe he just showed up late with the marshmallows."

"You know," I said, "maybe it was. He certainly seems to have known a lot about all this stuff. Enough to blackmail you and get Leo in trouble with the cops. I wonder if he tipped them off to the computer. Would he have known about that?"

"Ah, fuck, man," Soupy said. "Listen."

The night before the state title game, Blackburn had Soupy and Teddy leave the rest of the team in the billets and come to his house. Over cocoa in the kitchen they argued about how we would cover Billy Hooper. Soupy insisted that only he was fast enough to stay with Hooper. Coach said he thought Teddy could handle it. Teddy sat there smiling, letting Coach do his talking. Coach said he'd sleep on it. He told Soupy to go back to the billets and get to bed, Teddy would be along soon.

Soupy fell asleep listening for Teddy to come in.

The next morning, Teddy sat next to Soupy on the bus to the rink. Soupy looked out the window. Teddy leaned over and whispered: "Guess what I watched last night?"

. . .

"So he knew everything?"

"Pretty much. And he loved it. He told me if I ever fucked with him, he'd tell the whole world."

The films flickered in my head. "Blackburn had to have been pulling the same stuff on Boynton, Soup," I said.

He chuckled bitterly. "Maybe I was just jealous."

"Why didn't you tell somebody?"

"Why do you think, dipshit? You think I was proud of it?"

"It wasn't your fault, Soupy. Why didn't you tell someone?"

"I told my fucking father, OK? And, as you can imagine, he was so understanding. First he wanted to hear all about Tillie's tits, then he told me to stop making things up. I never brought it up again."

"What about your mom?"

He shook his head.

"Have you told anyone else any of this?"

"Nope."

"Not even Flapp?"

"Not much."

"Well, what the hell are you thinking, Soup? Are you thinking you're going to go to prison for Leo? Leo's dead and you aren't bringing him back."

"You know," he said, "none of this is why I asked you here. I wanted to tell you something else. So shut the fuck up a minute."

He tried to stand, but the manacles on his ankles made it difficult. "You know?" he said. "The guy was my coach. I did what he said. You did what he said, too, Trap. You worshipped the guy and you could've been on that table if it wasn't me. I worshipped him, too. He made me feel like I was fucking famous around here, you know what I mean? I was the man. You go look in Enright's sometime and you count who's got the most pictures on the wall."

"That's what you had to tell me?"

"No." He loosed a long, sorrowful sigh. "Ah, Jesus, Trap."

"What?"

"You remember the lacrosse shot?"

"In the title game?"

"Yeah. I missed it, man."

"I know. You hit the crossbar."

"No, man. I could've made that shot a thousand out of a thousand. I made a hundred in a row once behind my garage. But I was pissed at the world. I aimed for that crossbar."

I heard the puck ringing off the pipe again as my legs involuntarily lifted me out of the chair. I saw the puck flopping on the ice in front of me. I saw Hooper's dead eye, felt myself freeze, saw the puck trickle into the goal, heard the sickening roar of the crowd.

"You missed it on purpose?"

"Sorry, man."

"You never told me."

"I'm telling you now."

"Thanks," I said. I stuffed my notebook in my pocket. "I'm damn sorry for everything that happened to you, Soup. Good luck."

Outside I stared at my steering wheel. I screamed as loud and as long as I could. Just once. Nobody but me could hear it over my idling truck and the hum of the wind.

I parked next to a green Dumpster behind the IGA. I got out and threw the lid open, then reached into my flatbed and unzipped my hockey bag. I removed each piece of stiff, frozen gear—leg pads, chest protector, arm pads, mask, baggy pants, skates—and heaved each of them, one by one, into the stinking void. Last out was Eggo. A scrap of shiny black tape remained stuck to the thumb where Darlene's mom had stitched it. I put my right hand in the glove and stuck it out in front of me, flexed my fingers inside, turned it back and forth as I would during pregame warm-ups. I opened the truck door and tossed the glove onto the floor. Then I grabbed my empty bag and hurled it into the Dumpster before I slammed the lid shut and pulled away.

twenty-eight

Tillie was standing at my desk when I walked into the *Pilot*. She wore a dress of faded turquoise that drooped to her knees, a white silk scarf, and rubber boots still slick with melting snow. She was slightly stooped, her shoulders gathered into her chest. I forced myself to look at her. She was no more or less Blackburn's tool than Soupy or Teddy. She'd kept watch over those films. She'd called Kerasopoulos to stop Joanie's story. Maybe she had loved Blackburn, too.

"Good morning," I said.

"Your big-city friends keep calling," she said. She handed me two pink While You Were Out slips. "This from Chicago, and this Trenton man again. And Jim Kerasopoulos. He said he got cut off before."

"I see your wrestling story made the front page."

"I really haven't looked at the paper yet."

"Looks like someone in Traverse killed Joanie's story."

"Well, maybe somebody with some sense read it and decided it didn't belong in a family newspaper."

I went to my desk. After my earlier conversation with Kerasopoulos, I figured I wasn't long for the *Pilot*. Maybe I had another day or so to get some truth into the paper. Starvation Lake had to hear it. How Blackburn really died. What happened in the billets. How the new marina, if Boynton really planned to build one, would be anchored in an ugly past. Some would say there was no use in revealing these secrets. I wondered if a few of those people already knew, or at least suspected. I blamed them for not knowing and for not putting a stop to it long ago. I suppose I blamed myself, too. Kerasopoulos had one thing right: I had been there. Why hadn't I seen it for myself? In a matter of a few days, all these people I'd thought I'd known—Coach, Leo, Tillie, even Soupy—had been transformed. Now I saw strangers walking around in my memory. Maybe they'd been there a long time and I'd refused to see. No more, I told myself.

I had a problem, though. The state cops were ready to pounce if I didn't reveal my source's name. I'd never get Blackburn's story into the *Pilot* from jail. But I still didn't know if I could bring myself to give up the source. I was in this mess because I'd broken the rules of my trade. Now I had to break yet another to get out of it? In my head, I kept going over what Soupy had told me. It was all beginning to follow its own perverse and disgusting logic. But did I have it exactly right yet? Was Soupy telling me the whole truth? He'd held out on me for years and might be holding out still. Or maybe he just didn't know everything.

I had twenty-three minutes to decide what to do. I looked at the *Tribune* message slip and considered again whether that woman was calling about my Detroit problems. Maybe she could help. I dialed her number. While her phone rang, I gazed idly at what I'd scratched on my blotter earlier: "Richard Ltd."

"*Tribune.* Sheryl Scully."

"Hello. It's Gus Carpenter at the *Pine County Pilot.*"

Richard, I thought. Or, as any hockey player might see it, REE-shard, the French pronunciation.

"Thanks for returning my call," Sheryl Scully said. "I called to ask about one of your reporters: M. Joan McCarthy?"

"Joanie," I said. But I was still thinking REE-shard. Like the great Montreal Canadiens Maurice "The Rocket" Richard and Henri "The Pocket Rocket" Richard.

"Are you her direct supervisor?"

"I'm her only supervisor," I said, but I was barely listening. I was thinking that Blackburn had named his mutt Pocket for Henri Richard, his favorite NHL player.

"I see," Sheryl Scully said. "We've got a position in one of our suburban bureaus we're considering her for. What can you tell me about her?"

An image of the dog popped into my head. I saw him sitting on our bench watching us practice, his head swiveling back and forth with the motion of the puck.

"Mr. Carpenter?"

"Oh, I'm sorry. Are you going to hire her?"

"She's a candidate. Her clips look promising."

Joanie really was out of there. I should have felt the envy then. But in my head the image of Pocket now was jumping and yelping. REE-shard, I thought. Like Blackburn's mutt, like his favorite player, like Ree-shard Ltd., the company in Virginia that owned Blackburn's property.

"Oh my fucking God," I gasped.

"I'm sorry," Sheryl Scully said. "We're really not here to steal your reporters, Mr. Carpenter. Is that—is that an endorsement?"

"Ms., um, I'm sorry?"

"Scully."

"Ms. Scully, I'll have to call you back. I'm on deadline."

I went to Joanie's desk and riffled through the documents I'd seen earlier on the floor. I found the one listing Richard Ltd., with an address and phone number in Springfield, Virginia. I went back to my desk and dialed the number.

It was disconnected.

I grabbed the front page of the *Pilot* and looked again at the dates that had bothered me beneath the photo of Blackburn. "January nineteenth," I said to myself. His birthdate. I rummaged through the junk on my desk and located the phone bill with all those long-distance calls. I ran my finger down the list. The call I was looking for went to a place called Fairfax, Virginia, with a 703 area code. The charge was $57.28, for 176 minutes. The date was January 19.

I wanted to call the Virginia number immediately. But the clock said 11:51. I dialed Trenton. I could not get arrested now.

"Got to push it, don't you?" he said.

Tillie appeared. "Hang on," I told Trenton. "What?"

"Joanie said to tell you she's over at Audrey's," Tillie said.

"OK," I said. I watched until she left the room. "Scott?" It was eight minutes to noon. "You want a name? Here's your name."

"Hold on," he said. "I know what I've advised you, but are you sure?"

"What choice do I have?"

"You say it could cost you your career."

"Going to jail isn't going to help it much either." Seven minutes to noon. "Got a pen?"

"Yeah."

"OK," I said. "The name"—I hesitated for just a second—"is Durnan. D-dog, U-underwear, R-Robert, N-Nancy, A-apple, N-Nancy."

"First name?"

"William. Regular spelling."

"Middle initial?"

"No idea."

"How about a title?"

"The deal was for a name."

"All right. I've got about three minutes to call Superior. Sit tight. You did the right thing, Gus. This guy's a sleaze."

"Do me a favor," I said. "Tell the Hanovers I wish them well. Tell them everything in my stories was true, and I'll come and testify to it if they want me to."

"Will do."

"And tell them I'm sorry."

"For what?"

"For their loss, Scott."

I didn't want Tillie to hear, so I went up to my apartment to call the Virginia number. It rang once then burst into the middle of a recorded announcement.

" . . . located just off Route 50 in Fairfax. For directions, press one. For the pro shop—"

I pressed zero. It rang another four times before I heard the cracked, indifferent voice of an adolescent boy.

"Fairfax," he squawked.

"Hello," I said. "What's Fairfax?"

"Excuse me?"

"I'm sorry, what's this place I'm calling?"

"Fairfax Ice House."

"You mean a rink?"

"Uh, yeah. Can I help you?"

"Like a hockey rink?"

He paused, probably thinking how stupid is this guy. "Yeah, a hockey rink."

"When are you open?"

"We're open now."

"No, I mean, what time do you open?"

"Seven on weekdays, six Saturdays and Sundays."

"So you're open tomorrow at seven?"

"Yeah."

I hung up and dialed my mother. Her answering machine picked up. Of course I could barely make out her message, but I heard enough to remind me it was her bowling day. After the beep, I said, "Mom, I've got to make a little trip. You might hear some things, but don't worry, OK? I love you."

Back down in the newsroom, I grabbed my coat and swept past Tillie and out as if she weren't there. After closing the front door behind me, I patted the pocket that held Perlmutter's photograph. I was filled with a strange mixture of excitement and dread. Leo had told my mother that he did a terrible thing on that night in 1988. It was terrible, all right. Worse than if he'd just put that bullet in Blackburn's head. But that bullet was never shot.

Crossing Main Street, I saw two blue-and-gold state police

cruisers parked front to back near the marina. The officers had their driver's-side windows down and were talking. Instinctively, I ducked my head.

Inside Audrey's, Joanie was at the counter digging into a grilled Swiss on pumpernickel. Behind her hung the old photo of Audrey's girlfriend's uncle, the great Gordie Howe. I sat down next to her and whispered, "I'm going out of town."

She stopped chewing. "Now? Where?"

"Keep it down, please," I said. Elvis Bontrager was sitting at his usual table nearby. "Just for a couple of days. I've got an emergency to attend to."

"For the story?"

I couldn't tell her yet, certainly not in Audrey's. "Sort of," I said. "I'll have to fill you in later. Hey, Audrey."

Audrey poked her head out of the back. "Hello, Gussy."

"Could you wrap me two tuna fish on whole wheat to go?"

"Toasted?"

"No, thanks."

Joanie grabbed my arm. "You better not be going to Detroit. You're not going to give up your source."

"No. But you've got to take over for now. I've made arrangements for Traverse City to handle our copy, but I need you to get a Blackburn story in shape. It probably won't run tomorrow, but Saturday for sure."

"Gus—"

"Your best story, Joanie. Everything you know. Put it all in. File it directly to Traverse. Then I want you to call Kerasopoulos directly and tell him what you've filed. Make sure you get him on the phone."

"I'm not talking to that stiff."

"Just do it. Which reminds me." I leaned closer. "See if you can find a guy named Jeff Champagne. He used to live here. Played for Blackburn with me."

"Champagne? Like bubbly? Where is he?"

"Like bubbly. And I have no idea."

"Why do I care?"

"Think Brendan Blake."

"No."

"Yes. And the Perlmutter story—get that ready too."

"Didn't we promise him—"

"Not a damn thing. Get it ready."

"What about the lawyers?"

"Fuck the lawyers. Even if it doesn't run, you can show it to the *Chicago Tribune*. A woman from there called me today. I'll call her as soon as I get back, and I'll say good things."

Joanie blushed. "Um, thanks."

"One more thing," I said. "I think I know what Perlmutter was trying to tell us."

"Let me guess: Bigfoot killed Blackburn?"

"There were only two bullets."

"I know that, Gus."

"No, you don't know. There were only two bullets—the one he found in the tree, and the one in the snowmobile."

"What about Blackburn's head?"

I stood. "Write your stories. You'll hear from me."

"I'd better."

The coming storm had turned the afternoon to dusk. The state police cruisers now were parked at either end of Main. As I crossed, exhaust plumed from the back of one car. Don't hurry yet, I told myself.

The bells on the door jangled as I stepped into the *Pilot*. Tillie was out. I turned around and reached up and tore the bells off in one staple-popping rip. I stuffed them in my pocket. At my desk I stopped for a fresh notebook and two pens. Tillie had left me another message from Trenton. URGENT, it said. I tossed it in a wastebasket on my way out the back.

Outside, snow had begun to fall again. I tied the bells to the radio antenna on my truck, hopped in, turned the key, and swung out onto

South Street toward the lake. I checked the rearview mirrors for state cops. None yet. I smiled when the truck hit a pothole and the bells jangled. I thought of the photo of Gordie Howe in Audrey's. He was winding up to shoot on a goaltender for the Montreal Canadiens. The goalie was one of the best ever. During the 1940s, he won two Stanley Cups and made the NHL All-Star team six times. He once went 309 minutes, including four entire games, without giving up a goal. His name was William "Bill" Durnan.

At the lake I turned left on Beach Drive. Walls of snow closed me in on both sides. I flicked my brights on. I'd hoped to get half an hour's head start before it dawned on Superior that I hadn't ratted my source out after all. But as the road crested just before Mom's yellow house, headlights blinked in my rearview mirror. They were fuzzy pinpoints, probably a mile back but gaining. Passing Mom's, I felt an urge to pull over and surrender. Instead I tapped the horn twice.

The headlights in my rearview had closed to half a mile when I spied another pair behind them. Without slowing, I veered left onto Jitters Trail. The back of the truck fishtailed on the snow, so I gave it a little gas and it swung back straight. The road dipped and swerved to the right and I had to slow down so I wouldn't miss the narrow opening in the trees. The two-track road burrowed through a canopy of snow-laden pines. As I slowed to turn, I saw the twin sets of headlights weaving erratically toward me. First one, then the other turned on the red-and-blue flashers. As the sirens began to wail I felt a surge of adrenaline like I'd felt a thousand times when a shooter bore down on me, alone in my goal.

My truck crashed down to Jitters Creek, the axles hammering the ground, my head banging off the cab ceiling as I bounced along. The sirens grew louder. Just short of the creek bank, I hit the brakes, put the truck in park, and left it running. Jitters Creek flowed too fast to freeze thick. At this spot, not far from where Darlene's bike had floated away, the water was deep enough to sink a pickup truck.

I reached into my glove box for the roll of hockey tape I kept there. The engine revved as I taped the gas pedal as far down as it would go. I didn't really know what I was doing; I'd seen it on TV. The grinding engine drowned out the sirens for a few seconds, but then I could hear them again, nearer still. The cops were probably having trouble getting their cars down the snowy two-track. I was hoping they'd have even more trouble getting back up.

I should have felt desperate. I should have felt afraid. Instead I felt calm and in control. It was like my best nights in goal, when everything was chaos around me, shooters flying back and forth, the puck zipping at me from every direction, and I could slow it all down to where the skaters looked like they were running under-water and the puck grew as big as a Frisbee and no matter where I looked through the tangle of legs and arms and torsos in front of me, I could always find it and stop it. I grabbed the sandwiches off the dash, stepped out of the truck, and snatched the duffel bag I'd packed out of the flatbed. I hadn't pictured myself leaving Starva-tion Lake this way. I was about to throw the truck into drive when I glimpsed Eggo on the passenger seat. The glove barely fit into the duffel bag.

The bells jangled one last time as my truck plunged into Jitters Creek. I heard the cops screaming from up the hill, "Stop right there, you're under arrest." The truck listed on its left side and began to sink, burbling. The bells came unfurled and drifted away. A cop cried out, "Oh, Jesus, he's in the river," but by then I was scrambling down the bank with my bag under an arm, ducking beneath pine boughs for cover. I followed the bank until it swerved right. I veered left and angled my body into the hill, sidestepping upward as fast as I could in the snow. I crested a ridge atop a meadow of untrammeled snowdrifts. I had to get to the other side of the meadow and then it would be a short dash to my destination. The cops probably didn't know these woods as well as I did, but I couldn't take chances, so instead of cross-ing the meadow I skirted it to stay in the trees. On the other side I stood behind an oak and surveyed where I'd come from. There were no cops in sight, but I could see the glow of their flashers blinking against the sky.

On the roof of Dad's garage the tree house was invisible beneath snow. As I approached the side door, I automatically reached for my keys, but they weren't there. They were in my truck ignition at the bottom of Jitters Creek. I grabbed the doorknob, knowing I'd locked it when I'd come to start the car on Sunday. It refused to turn. "Dumb shit," I said aloud, and for the first time that afternoon I felt a twinge of fear. I hurried around the garage and looked back again at where I'd come from. Still nothing but trees and falling snow. "OK," I said to myself. I snapped a branch off a dead tree and poked it through the lower left corner of the window. Delicately I brushed the glass shards away then reached in and unlocked the door.

I raised the big garage door and climbed into the Bonneville. It started easily. In the rearview mirror I saw my escape route buried in a foot of snow. How would the Bonnie plow through that? I didn't have time to shovel the entire driveway, but I hoped I could clear enough snow to give the Bonnie a chance. I grabbed a snow shovel hanging on a pegboard and cleared two parallel tracks extending about thirty feet from the garage. That would have to be enough.

I tossed the duffel bag in the backseat and got back behind the steering wheel. I had to gather enough momentum before I hit the downslope so the big fat Bonnie might make it over the fifty yards to the plowed road below. And I had to do it in reverse. At least that meant the rear-drive wheels would be going down first. I slipped the car into gear and eased the back wheels out of the garage. I twisted my body around to see out the back and slammed my foot down on the accelerator.

The Bonnie leaped out, gathering speed. Dad had told me many times that it was loaded with power, but I hadn't really understood until now. I clung to the steering wheel to keep the car on the tracks

I'd dug before it plowed into the deeper snow. The two-track dipped down and the Bonnie plunged down with it, churning snow left and right, the roof scraping against pine branches. "Come on, baby, you can do it," I yelled. I let up a little on the accelerator, then punched it, then let up again, trying to keep the car moving without setting the wheels to spinning in the snow. Out the rear window I could see Horvath Road. The county plows had cut an opening there where the snow was shaved down to just a few inches deep. If I could just get there, I'd be out.

"Come on!" I screamed. With twenty feet to go, I felt the left rear tire sink and grab and then spin in the snow. The Bonnie lurched out of my control and swerved left until the car was perpendicular to the two-track. I hit the brakes, rammed the gearshift into drive, and jammed the accelerator as I swung the steering wheel to the right. The Bonnie pitched forward a few feet and stopped, the left rear tire whirring.

I was stuck.

Leaving the car running, I stepped out and looked up and down Horvath Road, barely ten feet away. Nothing. But the cops wouldn't be long.

The Bonnie's front wheels had made the snow shallower, but the left rear tire spun in the deeper stuff when I tapped the accelerator. The right rear wheel had fetched up on a bump that gave it some purchase. I'd been stuck like this before and escaped by rocking the car between drive and reverse. A push helped. But there was no one to push. I squatted next to the left tire. If I had something solid to stick beneath it, it might give me enough traction to get unstuck. On hands and knees I dug out as much snow as I could from under the stuck tire.

I retrieved Eggo from my duffel bag. For old times' sake I slipped my hand inside and waggled the glove as I had so many times. Then I jammed it under the tire until it was wedged tightly between rubber and packed snow. "Sorry, old pal," I said. "One more save, OK?"

As the Bonnie popped out onto Horvath Road, I saw my glove fly up behind the car in shreds. I thought about going back for it, but only for a second. The snow was falling harder. The road was slick. I pushed the speed to thirty-five and hung on. Whenever the Bonnie started to fishtail, I dropped my speed a little and tapped my brakes and prayed I'd stay out of a ditch.

The quickest way out of Michigan was I-75, but the state cops would be lying for me there. I decided I'd take Old U.S. 27 as far south as I could and then wing it. The way the snow was blowing, I'd be lucky to make Ohio by 7:00 p.m. First I had to get to Old 27. I couldn't chance Route 816, because the cops would be waiting there, too, so I figured I'd zigzag along some back roads they probably wouldn't know. The falling snow enveloped me in a white cocoon. I pushed the Seger tape in and turned the volume up:

Go ahead and call me yellow
Two plus two is on my mind . . .

The snow let up south of Clare. I drove all night, stopping only for gas and coffee. A little after five the next morning, I pulled the Bonnie into the snowless parking lot behind the Fairfax Ice House. The trees in Virginia were still mostly bare, but the grass was beginning to turn green. I stretched out across the enormous front seat of Dad's dream car and fell instantly to sleep.

twenty-nine

The sun woke me a little after seven. The floor of the Bonnie was a mess of foam cups and cellophane wrappers. I sat up and rubbed my eyes and peered at myself in the rearview mirror. I couldn't look much worse than anyone wandering into a rink at this hour.

The lobby of the Fairfax Ice House was like most I'd seen. Black rubber mats covered the floor. Long benches waited for youngsters to sit and tie on their skates. The smell of popcorn lingered. To my right was a skate-rental window and hockey shop, closed at the moment, to my left a cluster of vending machines, video games, and pay phones. Facing me were two sets of double doors leading to the rink. Between the doors stood two banks of lockers, and over the lockers on the cinder-block wall hung five black-and-white photographs of people identified by name tags. Don Peacock managed the rink and Margie Peacock taught figure skating along with Kitty Petreault and Jeff Bender. Power skating was taught, appropriately enough, by Al Power. All of them wore white turtlenecks beneath purple nylon jackets.

No photograph accompanied the sixth name tag on the wall. "Richard Blackstone. Hockey Skills Coach," it read. I wrote it down in my notebook. On the wall next to the skate-rental window hung a bulletin board listing the week's activities: public skating sessions, figure skating classes, hockey leagues. On this Thursday, I saw Richard Blackstone was scheduled to teach a hockey class for kids aged five to seven at eleven forty-five, and another for eight- to twelve-year-olds at three forty-five. I wrote those down, too.

. . .

On a traffic-choked road called Route 50, I found a banged-up old
diner squatting beneath a sign that said simply, EAT. There was no egg
pie on the menu, and when I asked for fried potatoes, the waitress, a
tubby woman wearing a dirty yellow smock stitched with "Shirley,"
said, "Don't you want grits, sugar?" I ate them with a cheese omelet
and drank coffee reading the *Washington Post* until 9:00 a.m.. By then I
figured the Fairfax County Clerk's Office would be open.

The roads wound and twisted and doubled back in a bewildering
asphalt pretzel. Wherever I turned, it all looked the same, clusters of
townhouses squeezed between strip malls and fast-food joints and
car dealerships. A perfect place to disappear.

At the clerk's office, I paid for copies of every document containing the name Richard Blackstone. I went through them line by
line sitting in the parking lot. Now I knew where Blackstone lived
and what he drove. One piece of paper linked him to Richard Ltd.,
the company that owned Jack Blackburn's property near Starvation
Lake. The clerk gave me directions to a nearby electronics store.
There I bought a point-and-shoot camera, a video camera with a
tripod and zoom lens, and a tape recorder that fit into my breast
pocket. I stuffed it all in my duffel bag and headed back toward the
ice rink, noticing a FedEx store along the way. At a Mobil station
I filled the Bonnie's gas tank. Inside, I bought a cap adorned with
the logo for the Washington Capitals, the local pro hockey team. A
bony codger in an oil-stained sweatshirt changed my five-dollar bill
for quarters.

I backed away from the gas pump and slid in next to a pay
phone.

"*Pilot.* McCarthy."

"It's me," I said.

"Holy crap." Joanie lowered her voice. "Where are you? When I
got back from Audrey's yesterday, there were four cops waiting. You
didn't give up your source, did you?"

"Nope. What did you tell the cops?"

"I told them to call Kerawhatshisname. What a jerk. He just called me and said he'd spike any story with the name 'Blackburn' in it."

"Just keep writing."

"First I've got to do something on this bank thing. The jerk gave me a bunch of crap for not running anything on it in today's paper. And Tillie took off."

"What bank thing?"

"I told you, the New York bank buying the banks up here? I guess one of whatshisname's golf buddies is a banker."

"Keep it short. What about Tillie?"

"She's gone. Came back for about five minutes after you took off and cleared out. Didn't say a word to me."

The missing film files had finally spooked her. Or maybe my sudden departure. It worried me. Had she figured out where I was going?

"What else is going on?" I said.

"AP put out a short on the cops looking for you. Redpath's funeral is tomorrow. The zoning board got postponed yesterday because of the snowstorm. And the chick from the clerk's office dropped off a big envelope."

The 1988 town council minutes. "Vicky?" I said.

"Yeah. She said she was sorry but she had to go get them from that bartender guy."

"Loob. Can you open them up?"

"Already did. I don't see much. But I'll bet you wanted to know about the dredging vote."

She was good and getting better. "Yeah."

I heard her rustle some papers. "They voted on it at this April thirteenth meeting. Seemed like a no-brainer to me, like, duh, how else are you going to find a body? But the sheriff, this Spardell dude, was worried about how it might mess up his budget."

"Yeah. He wanted a boat."

"I'll get to that. Anyway, first they voted three to two to dredge the lake. But the sheriff made a fuss and then the mayor—excuse me, the mayor pro tem, because the mayor wasn't there—called the council into a closed session. They came out of that and voted three to two again, this time *not* to dredge."

"Who called the session?"

"Mayor Pro Tem A. Campbell."

"Soupy's dad? Shit, that's right, he was on the council. And who switched their vote?"

"You'll love this," Joanie said. "X. Perlmutter."

"Huh? Clayton's brother?"

"Oh, no, it's Clayton. His first name is actually Xavier."

I'd never known Clayton was on the council. But then I had been in Detroit. "What about the boat?"

"The last thing they did was authorize twenty-five thousand dollars for that, with Campbell abstaining since they were buying it from him."

"What an upstanding guy. What kind of boat?"

"Doesn't say. Just one 'appropriate to the tasks of policing the lake and its shoreline.' Why's the town buying a boat for the county sheriff anyway?"

A recorded voice was telling me I had to insert more quarters. "Listen," I said. "Go to my desk, second drawer on the right. Near the top you'll find a photocopy of a receipt from the marina. Get it. Hurry."

I waited. She came back on. "Got it. A receipt from the Starvation Lake Marina for twenty-five thousand dollars. Got to be for the boat, huh?"

"What's the date on it?"

"Let's see. April twelfth."

"But the meeting was the thirteenth, right? How could the town give Angus Campbell the money before the council voted?"

"Good question. What does it have to do with anything?"

"I don't know," I said. I really didn't.

The recorded voice said the call was about to end.

"Hey, that reminds me," she said. "On Perlmutter, I was going over some of the state grant stuff again and—"

"I've got to go," I said. "I'm going to be sending you something overnight. Look for it. And do me a favor and call my mom and tell her I'm OK."

"Gus, listen, one of the names on—"

The dial tone cut her off.

The Zamboni made its final circuit before the 11:45 a.m. hockey skills session. At the top of the bleachers, I placed the video camera on its tripod, slung the still camera around my neck, got out my pen and notebook. A dozen little skaters burst onto the ice in baggy socks and too-big pants, their faces obscured by cages. They swerved right and skated counterclockwise. I made sure the video camera was recording.

Behind the skaters, the door to their dressing room swung open and their teacher emerged. I tugged my Caps cap lower. Richard Blackstone wore his silver hair in a comb-over swept left to right and then back. My heart skipped a beat. Jack Blackburn never wore his hair that way. Blackstone seemed smaller and paunchier than Blackburn, and his face was obscured in a full silver beard. No, I thought. Is that really him? I zoomed the camera in on his eyes. They were downcast, watching his feet. Of course. Blackburn had just one superstition. Had he left it in Starvation Lake? Just before he reached the threshold, Richard Blackstone took a little hop and a skip to stagger his stride before he stepped out, so that his left blade would hit the ice before his right. A shudder went through me. I closed my eyes.

When I opened them again, he was circling behind the goalie net to my left and heading up the boards toward me. I took a deep breath and looked into the video camera. I caught a closer glimpse of his face, but he quickly passed. I watched him with my naked eye as he circled again. His black sweatsuit did nothing to hide the bulge at his waist.

His stride was still smooth, but his legs had to work harder to move him along. As he turned toward me, I leaned into the video camera and focused on his face. His teeth seemed whiter and more prominent, probably false. They set off the dull yellow that tinged his sagging cheeks and the creases at his deep-set eyes. I pictured him in his house at night, drinking by the arid glow of his television. It made me feel good to think of him as alone and pathetic, a dried-up old man unloved and anonymous. He circled again and as he veered my way a third time he turned toward me and looked straight into the camera. It startled me. Maybe I merely imagined it, but I thought I saw a faint, knowing smile play across his lips before he was gone again. Had he recognized me? Had Tillie gotten to him? I hadn't expected how hard it would be to see those eyes again as I'd seen them so many times across the Sunday dinner table.

Below me, three mothers in parkas stood along the boards, chatting, paying little attention to what was happening on the ice. As the coach gathered the boys around him, I felt the urge to walk down to those mothers and tell them everything I knew. I imagined myself talking and pointing, and the mothers' eyes darting between me and the ice, and the disbelief on their faces, followed by horror, either at the truth of the matter or at me for telling it. Twice I yanked my cap lower and coat collar higher and ventured down to the edge of the ice where I could get clearer shots of his face. I snapped shots with the still camera and, when his back was turned, took notes.

He ran some of the same drills the River Rats had run. He took the boys by the shoulders and steered them to specific spots on the ice and showed them where to look for the puck and which way to hold their stick blades. He arranged short stacks of pucks around the ice and made the kids weave between and around them without ever touching them with their sticks. If he told them they had to be hungry for those biscuits, though, I couldn't hear. Near the end of the session, he gathered the boys around him at center ice. Through the camera I watched their helmeted heads nod in unison as he turned this way and that, telling them they'd done well, patting each of them lightly on the head. I heard them laugh. I heard them shout, "Yeah!" I remembered standing there watching him reach out to the other Rats, waiting for his hand to touch me.

I felt a tap on my shoulder. One of the three mothers was standing next to me, wearing a nervous smile.

"Excuse me," she said. "May I ask who you are?"

"Oh," I said, startled again. "Just a second." I repositioned the video camera so it was pointed at the dressing room door.

"There," I said. "I'm, uh, I'm with a newspaper."

"I see," she said. I saw her friends watching. "You're doing an article?"

"Yes, ma'am."

"Are you with the *Post*?"

"I wish. I'm just with a little paper."

"Really? Which?"

Of course I had no idea what papers were in the area. "The *Pilot*," I said.

"The *Pirate*?"

"*Pilot*, ma'am."

"The *Pilot*," she repeated. "I haven't seen that one. But there are so many little papers around here, some days we get four or five on the drive. How could I get a copy of your article?"

"Well, why don't I send you one? Here." I handed her my pen and notebook. "Write down your address."

"I didn't know newspapers took video."

"They don't, usually, but it's a good visual aid. I don't take very good notes." The kids were heading off the ice.

"Mm-hm," the woman said. She handed the notebook and pen back and stuck out a mittened hand. "Well, I'm Miriam Belzer. If you'd like an interview"—she motioned toward her friends—"we'd be glad to help. What was your name?"

"A.J.," I said.

"A.J. what?"

I peeked into the camera. The coach was looking up toward us. "Oops," I said. "This thing is screwing up. Excuse me, ma'am."

"Oh, I'm sorry," she said. "We'll watch for your story."

She walked down. I hurried a fresh videotape into the camera. The first one wasn't nearly used up, but I was going to need two. I refocused the camera as the coach followed the boys off the ice toward the dressing room. At the door, he stopped and turned and looked at me again. I felt an involuntary shiver of fear while I zoomed in on his face, the hard, certain face that nobody in Starvation Lake could fail to recognize, no matter how much they might want to. He held the camera's gaze for a full two seconds before turning away. Again I wondered if he had recognized me. But this time I relished the thought that he might have stood there wondering, for even a split second, whether his past was about to crash down on him.

thirty

I pulled into another gas station pay phone and inserted the rest of my quarters. A man answered at Channel Eight in Traverse City. I told him Gus Carpenter was calling for Tawny Jane Reese. Five seconds later, a woman picked up.

"T.J. here," she said.

"I'm holding for Ms. Reese."

"That's me."

"T.J.," I repeated, liking it.

"You know, you're pretty famous around here." Her voice was just as soothing on the phone as it was on TV. "Where are you now?"

"Am I on the air, T.J.?"

"You are not."

"Good. I don't have much time, so listen carefully: I'm going to FedEx you something. You'll have it in the morning. But you have to promise you won't air it until eight a.m. Saturday."

As she thought about it, I imagined her furrowing her brow the way she did when she was telling her viewers about a bombing in Kosovo or a flood in Des Moines. The image appealed to me, at once so mundane and so glamorous.

"I don't usually make deals," she said.

"Really? So you just happened to be covering a men's hockey game in the middle of the night when the cops showed up to arrest an alleged murderer?"

"Ah, well, we all make exceptions, Gus, as you ought to know."

Touché, I thought. "Trust me, you'll want to make an exception for this. It has to do with Jack Blackburn."

"OK. What about you?"

"There's something else you need to do. After you get this FedEx and you're getting your story ready, you've got to call a guy for comment. His name is Kerasopoulos. He's the lawyer at the company that owns the *Pilot*."

"I know that blowhard. Why do I have to call him?"

I was liking her more every second. "For one thing," I said, "to find out what happened to Gus Carpenter." That was partly true. Really I wanted her to let Kerasopoulos know that Channel Eight was working on a story so he would have to run Joanie's story, unless he wanted to be scooped on the most explosive news ever to hit Starvation Lake. "The rest will be obvious once you see what I'm sending."

"You're just a voice on the phone."

"No, I'm a FedEx package on your doorstep tomorrow morning."

"OK, OK, it's a deal. But let me ask could we just run a teaser the night—?"

"No. No teasers. Eight a.m. Saturday."

"All right, but listen, we have a one-minute news break at seven-thirty that morning. Let me just mention it then. What difference will half an hour make? The *Pilot's* out by then. That's what you're worried about, right?"

Tawny Jane Reese was all right. And, yes, I just wanted to make sure Elvis read the story in the *Pilot* before he saw it on TV. "OK," I said.

I bought a Coke and a package of cheese crackers and ate as I drove to the FedEx store. I parked, pulled out my notebook, and transcribed my scribbling into readable print. Then I went inside and made a copy of the same notes on other pages. I slipped the copied notes, the videotapes, and the undeveloped stills into separate FedEx boxes and shipped one to Joanie at her apartment, the other to T.J. at Channel Eight.

I had originally planned to return to the rink and record Richard Blackstone's three forty-five session with the eight- to twelve-year-olds, but decided it might spook him. Instead I backed the

Bonnie into a spot at the rear of the rink parking lot with a clear view of his silver Toyota Camry. The sun was sliding down the sky when he emerged from the rink a little after five. He was carrying the puck bag, two hockey sticks, and his tackle box first-aid kit. A man and a boy walked along with him. The man carried a hockey bag. The boy, his dark hair matted with sweat, had a pair of goalie pads slung over a shoulder and a stick in his hand. He squinted up at the coach and the man as they talked. The coach lowered himself to a knee and put a hand on the boy's shoulder and spoke to him. The man regarded his son and the coach with a proud smile. The boy nodded.

I let anger rise up to suffocate my sadness.

I followed the Toyota at a distance of a few hundred yards. We ended up in a neighborhood of red-brick bungalows with greening end-of-winter yards, towering oaks, and one-car garages. The streets twisted and turned. At a four-way stop, a UPS truck got between me and the Toyota. Three houses down, the truck came to a lurching halt at an awkward angle and the driver hopped out with a package under an arm. With cars parked along both sides of the street, I couldn't pass. "Son of a bitch," I said, slapping the steering wheel as the Toyota disappeared around a curve.

I dug through my notes for the address I'd written down at the clerk's office and, after doubling back once, located Blackstone's house. I drove about half a block past it and pulled to the curb. As I waited for darkness to fall, I considered whether he'd seen me. Maybe as I sat there he was calling the police and I'd be hauled away before I could make anyone believe me. It didn't really matter. This neighborhood where I'd never been before and probably never would be again was exactly where I was supposed to be. When the streetlights blinked on, I stuffed my cap in a coat pocket and pushed the record button on the miniature tape recorder.

"Home of Jack Blackburn," I dictated, "214 East Luray, sub-urbs of Washington, D.C., Thursday, March fifth, five forty-nine p.m." I slipped the recorder into my breast pocket and stepped outside.

Four shaggy pines obscured the front of his house, making it impossible to see inside. A lamp over the concrete porch was unlit. I climbed the porch steps and rapped on the door, standing away from the peephole. The last time I'd seen Jack Blackburn up close was on the sidewalk outside Kepsel's Ace Hardware the summer before he left us. We'd said hello and nothing more.

I pressed my ear to the door but heard no stirring inside. I knocked again. Still no answer. I walked around to the backyard. The side drive was empty. Maybe he hadn't driven home. Maybe he'd noticed me following and decided to lose me in the maze of his neighborhood. I tried to peek into the garage but couldn't see a thing through the tinted windows.

Cyclone fence hemmed in the backyard. I unlatched a gate and stepped across a semicircle of turquoise patio stones to the back door. Laying an ear against the door, I heard only the flat ticking of a kitchen clock. I looked around at the shadows surrounding me, thinking maybe I had been foolish to come at night. I looked at the knob on the storm door. Did I really want to add breaking and entering to my list of crimes? I tried the door and it gave. The door inside gave, too. I eased it open two inches and called out softly, "Anyone here? Mr. Blackstone?" I stepped into the dark vestibule. A corn broom leaned on the wall beneath a flyswatter hanging on a hook. To my right was a sliding door, to my left two steps up into the kitchen.

I turned toward the kitchen, catching a whiff of Lysol. In my breast pocket, the record light on the tape recorder glowed red. I leaned my head down and whispered into it, "Inside now." The immaculate kitchen was dressed in snow-white Formica countertops, a white tile floor, white appliances, blond cupboards. On the counter sat a dish drainer holding a clean plate, a coffee cup, a fork, a steak knife. Next to it stood two bottles of Jim Beam, one nearly empty, one unopened. Impulsively, I opened a cupboard door. There was no River Rats sticker on the inside.

I stepped through the kitchen into a small living room. The front window curtains were drawn. The beige walls were bare. An unlit floor lamp stood behind a recliner, which faced a television that stood in a corner. A TV remote rested on a copy of *Business Week* magazine atop a small folding table next to the recliner. Along the wall to my right stood a table hockey game, the kind with a plastic bubble top I'd seen in bars. Beyond it in the corner stood a garbage can filled nearly to the top with empty Coke and Mountain Dew cans.

"Mr. Blackstone?"

Across the living room a doorway beckoned to a darkened corridor. I felt an involuntary urge to leave. I could go back to the Bonnie and stake out his house until he returned. But what if he didn't? What if he'd recognized me and was now fleeing? I might never find him again. I couldn't go back to Dingus and the rest of the town and tell them Jack Blackburn was still alive without being able to say I had confronted him in the flesh. They might not believe me. They might not want to believe me.

I crossed the living room and stepped into the hallway, stopping to let my eyes adjust to the dark. I could still hear the kitchen clock ticking. There was a closed door to my left, one to my right, and a third facing me at the end of the short corridor. Two bedrooms and a bathroom, I figured. As I reached for the doorknob to my left, memory sucked me back to the schoolhouse Soupy and I had broken into as kids. For an instant I could smell the mold and must again. I pushed the door open.

The bedroom, the size of a child's, had been converted into an office. A computer monitor and keyboard sat on a desk facing me. A stack of *Wall Street Journals* leaned against it. Next to the computer was a box containing what looked like blank VCR tapes, a telephone wired to the computer, and two black marking pens. To the right of the desk stood a small television equipped with a VCR. The TV was angled so that the person sitting at the desk could watch as he worked.

Against the far wall stood a bookcase holding five shelves of videotapes. A few of the tapes bore labels indicating they were instructional hockey videos: *Defense for Beginners. Shoot to Score. Dryden on Goaltending.* Some were unlabeled. Many had thin white stuck-on labels bearing tiny black markings. I leaned in close enough to read one and a shiver raced down my spine: LP/0293/FX.

Blackburn had borrowed Delbert's filing system. The numbers in the middle, as with Delbert's, signified a date. Virtually all of the tapes were marked FX, which I assumed stood for Fairfax. I wondered if the first two letters could have been someone's initials? A boy's? An empty tape box rested next to Blackburn's computer. I picked it up. "JJ/1297/ FX," the label read. I wondered why Blackburn hadn't brought his old River Rat films with him when he fled to Virginia. Maybe there was no time. Tillie could have sent them, of course, but it dawned on me that those were her last claim on Blackburn, the thing that kept him, however distant, in her life.

I was filled at once with dread at what I had found and exhilaration at what I could now tell the world. There was so much here, and there had to be more in Blackburn's computer and his video camera. If he had escaped, so be it; he'd left too much behind. I flipped open my notebook. As I put my pen to the paper, I felt something on my shoulder.

A hand.

"What?" I cried out. The hand firmed its grip, but I twisted away and stumbled backward against the wall, face-to-face with Jack Blackburn.

He wore black nylon sweatpants, slippers, and a faded gray Fairfax Hockey T-shirt puffed out at the waist to hide his paunch. He seemed to be smiling, though it was hard to know for sure because his upper teeth, obviously capped, stretched his mouth in an unnatural way, like a clown's. In one hand he held a glass of what I assumed was whiskey. The other he extended to me. I reached for it without thinking.

"Hello, Gus," he said.

"Going through my things?" The clown's mouth chuckled. "Should I call the police?"

"Do what you need to do."

"I hear some police may be looking for you, Gus." He looked at the videotape box still in my hand. "Kind of late in life to be boning up on your hockey skills, isn't it?"

I set the box down. "Those aren't hockey tapes, Jack."

"Jack?" he said. "The name's Richard. Or Rich, if you prefer." He laughed at this as if it were hilarious. "It's nice to see your dad's big boat again." He'd recognized the Bonnie. "It's looking pretty good for, what, thirty years old? Though it does stick out like a sore thumb around here. This is the nation's capital. Nobody drives American." Again he cackled. "So, what are you here for? An article? Is that what gives you the right to just break into somebody's house?"

"I know what you did."

That didn't seem to register. "Is it one of those where-are-they-now stories?" he said. "Wait—aren't you back at the little-league paper in Starvation again?" He took a sip of his drink and shook his head. "You remember how I used to say, 'Losing's good for winning'? Well, no offense, Gus, but I'm thinking maybe you're the exception. Losing didn't work so well for you, did it? You just kept on losing. The town goat. The hotshot reporter who let the big story go between his legs. Now here you are sneaking around an old man's house, looking for who knows what."

"I found what I'm looking for, Jack."

"Rich, please. And, by all means, let's talk if I can help with whatever you're writing. I'd love to hear your questions." He held his glass out and shook the cubes around. "Cocktail?"

"No, thanks."

"I'm going to have another myself."

I waited in the living room while Blackburn went into the kitchen. He was either perfectly at ease or putting on a fine act. I heard ice clinking and the top of a bottle being spun off. He emerged with a fresh drink, a second glass, one of the bottles of Jim Beam, and a kitchen chair. He put the chair down and motioned for me to sit. I remained standing. He set his drink, the other glass, and the whiskey on the table next to the recliner. Then he just stood there, looking me over.

"I owe you an apology," he said. "See how your body has a certain flow to it, how the shoulders flow so nicely into your arms, the arms so nicely along your sides and hips, your hips into your legs? All that nice muscle tone, all that wonderful sinew, even all these years later."

I wasn't going to let him make me squirm. "I've got you," I said. "I know everything you did."

Blackburn sat down in the recliner. "When I first saw you," he said, "way back when, I thought right off you'd be a flopper, because, you know, you were never too tall, and the stand-up goalies tend to be taller. Of course today they're all floppers, that's how it is. But the more I looked at you, the more I was convinced you were built to stand up. A runt, but a wiry runt. I figured you had the strength, you know, the sort of—what do you call it?—internal stature that makes a goalie unbeatable." He paused to lick the rim of his glass. "But you didn't, did you, Gus? You were weak. You're still weak. Aren't you?"

I sat down now and leaned forward, elbows on knees.

"I know what you did with Soupy," I said.

"Do you still have that glove? What the hell did you call it? You guys and your idiotic superstitions."

"And you and your films, huh?" I took out my pen and notebook.

He pointed his glass at me. "No notes. Or I can call the cops. You can shut off that tape recorder, too."

He wasn't going to call the police anymore than I was, but it didn't matter. I snapped off the recorder and put my pen and notebook away while he drained his glass in one practiced swallow, then poured again. My coach. The long-dead hero of Starvation Lake. He actually lived alone in a dark house in a place that knew little of the game he supposedly loved. His cheeks had turned the color of a fading bruise. He had a Toyota and a bottle and a TV remote and a bookshelf filled with tapes of naked boys.

"I may be a failure, Jack, but I am what I am," I said. "You call yourself a coach, but you aren't really a coach. You only pretend. You're a pedophile. You fuck little boys. You fuck their heads. Then you fuck their bodies."

He actually laughed again.

"I know about the billets," I said. "I know about Soupy and Tillie and Jeff Champagne. Pretty clever, put Champy back on the team so you could fuck him? I suppose he was weak, too, huh? I know about Brendan Blake, too. Remember him?" Now his defiant smile ebbed and an eyebrow twitched, once, then again, an insect shifting its weight. "I know all about your disgusting films, and how you sold them, and how you used the money to buy all your land and the billets and—Jesus, Jack—all that ice time you paid for. What a great guy, picking up the tab for the parents. I'm weak? Maybe so. But I'm not a disgusting, twisted old man who pretends to be something so he can have sex with boys."

He reached for the whiskey.

"And I am not someone," I said, "who would drive his best friend to suicide."

He finished pouring. Then he sat back in his chair, took a drink, and smacked his lips.

"You know fuck-all," he said.

"I know everything. I have your old films, with you in them. And there are others who are ready to speak up."

"Let me get this straight. I *forced* your worthless, drunk, pathetic friend Swanny to have sex with an older woman who, I think we can agree, was quite a looker then. Yes? Having sex with foxy older women is something a sixteen-year-old boy would never do? Is that it?"

"It's Soupy, not Swanny, and I think you—"

"As for my old friend Leo, when I came to town, he was working in the back of a dry cleaners or something. A nobody. I took him by the hand and next thing you know, he's basically running the rink and working the door for one of the best damn hockey teams in Michigan. He's a celebrity in Starvation Lake. A goddamn Zamboni driver." As he spoke, I repeated his words in my head so they would stick like ink on paper. "And then, there he is, my last night in Starvation, waving a pistol around my head, telling me, 'I'm drawing the line, Jack, I'm drawing the line right here.' *He's* drawing the line. What a joke. Come on, Gus. Leo didn't really pull the trigger on himself. He couldn't have. He didn't have the balls."

"He's dead, Jack."

"God rest his soul. He laid a damn good sheet, eh? Best Zamboni jockey I ever saw. But he got squirrelly on me. All that recovery crap. One minute he's the porn king of Pine County, next minute he's got all this horseshit religion and he's waving a goddamn pistol at me. What was I supposed to do? He could have blown me away and he and Swanny would've told the cops it was all in self-defense. So here I am, Gus. Here I am."

"I thought Leo didn't have the guts to pull the trigger."

"He didn't."

"Then why did you run?"

He hesitated. Then he shrugged. "I had no choice."

"Was someone else there? Someone who *could* have pulled the trigger? It wasn't Soupy. He ran before you did."

"No."

"You're lying."

"No. No one else." He stared into his glass. A bitter smile slowly creased his face. "Look around. I rent. Eleven hundred bucks a month. Can you believe it? Eleven hundred bucks in Starvation, you'd have a mansion on the lake." Again he gulped the rest of his drink, again he refilled, pouring carefully, as if he could not afford to spill one drop. "Let me ask you, Gus, do you ever *think* about these things you think you know? I know you believe I'm the bad guy here, I'm the guy who's done all these terrible things. But do you really think I could have done all this stuff I supposedly did all by myself?"

"You were the star of the films. I saw you."

"Do you know why you're such a pathetic failure? Take today. First you exposed yourself to me at the rink, then you talked to that very helpful young mother, then you let me lead you here and get the jump on you. You didn't see the big picture. All you could see was you and your little notebook and your little newspaper and your little ideas about what's right and wrong. And now you're missing the big picture again. All you see is your old coach, who let you down—poor Gus—because he blamed you for losing the only game that ever mattered in the whole damn history of your hometown. Which you did, son. You lost that game. Grow up and take the responsibility."

I couldn't help myself. "I kept us in that game. If not for me, we'd have been down five to zero before the second period."

He dismissed me with a wave of his glass. "Yeah, the Fitters had a lot of shots, but they were hitting you right in the breadbasket"—he thumped his chest—"you weren't making saves. Take a lesson from old Billy Hooper, Gus. Remember? 'Can't see it, can't stop it'? One eye and he saw things clearer than you. Sorry, but everything bad that ever happened in Starvation Lake ain't about me. There's a whole world of shit out there, and I'm just a little fly buzzing around it. I mean, did you ever *think* about why the sheriff wouldn't just drag the lake after I supposedly drowned in it? Seems logical, doesn't it? But what did they do? Nothing. Why? You'd think a few folks might know."

"Like?"

"Like, hell, maybe old Angus Campbell? Now there was one crafty sonofabitch. It wasn't two days after I'd supposedly drowned that Angus had all the angles figured out and got himself to the right pers—the right people. And just like that, he had a couple of big checks, one from the town for Jerry's boat, one from"—he hesitated—"'hell, it doesn't matter. Jerry got his blessed boat, Angus got his cash, nobody ever said a thing."

I shuddered. "Jerry's boat?"

"Spardell. The sheriff. He wanted his boat, boy."

Jerry's boat. How could I be so stupid? The scribble at the bottom of the receipt Dingus had showed me wasn't "Ferryboat." It was "*Jerryboat.*" Whoever had scratched it there—maybe Soupy's dad?—had made the *J* look like an *F.* I'd just read it wrong. And, as Joanie had told me, that receipt was for a check written April 12, 1988—the day *before* the town council appropriated $25,000 for a new boat—so it couldn't have come from the town. Angus had that check in hand when the next day, as mayor pro tem, he called for the executive session at which Clayton Perlmutter changed his vote and the council decided not to dredge. Soon Angus had a second check for $25,000. One, written by the town of Starvation Lake, paid for Jerry's boat. The other kept Angus's mouth shut. Who wrote that one? And what did Perlmutter get for changing his vote?

"How would Angus have known anything?" I said.

"Ask his worthless son."

"So it was hush money."

"Call it whatever you like. They don't care how, Gus, just how many. Remember?"

"Who paid the hush money?"

Again he peered into his drink, considering. "Let me ask you something," he said. "Do you know what it's like to be dead in the eyes of all of your friends? To be dead in the eyes of everyone you know and love? I know, you don't think I'm capable of feelings like that, but can you at least imagine it?"

I thought I could, actually, but I said, "I don't care."

"I left Starvation Lake. Isn't that enough? I had a good life. I was a good coach. I made all of you into better hockey players. I put that place on the damn map. Here, where a little shitbox like this rents for a thousand bucks a month, you got a lot of rich guys from Boston and New York who think their kids are going to be the next Wayne Gretzky. It's a joke. There ain't no Swannies here. No River Rats. No state titles. And me, I'm a nobody, skating around with a bunch of tripods. I'm teaching girls to play, for God's sake."

"And how about the little boys, Jack?"

"You ungrateful little shit," he said, thrusting his glass at me so hard that some whiskey slopped over the top. "I made you a goalie. You never would've started for the Rats—hell, you never would've made the team just to sit your ass on the bench—if it wasn't for me. I was like a father to you. I had to be a goddamned saint, too?"

"I had a father. You were not my father."

"Oh, listen, son, my daddy got hit by a train when I was six. He was stumbling around drunk in the dark and it came up out of nowhere and knocked him to Nova Scotia. So be it. All good things come to an end." He took a long swallow of whiskey. "I'm glad you brought your daddy up, though, since you think you know so much, I'm sure you know all about the Friday night poker games then, eh?"

"I know—"

"You know zip. For your information, those games were going on a hell of a long time before I got to town. And there wasn't a lot of poker either. The main attraction was your dear old dad—the late, great Rudy Carpenter and his late, great movie projector. Sometimes I'd even make popcorn. It wasn't poker night; it was poke-her night. Get it? Poke her?" He jabbed a forefinger at the air. "That was quite a crew—old Lenny Ziolkowski, Angus, Jerry. And your old man. That projector of his made a hell of a racket, but the pictures were"—he looked up at the ceiling, as if seeking inspiration—"exquisite."

He stopped and watched me, savoring my discomfort, then picked up the whiskey bottle, filled half of the other glass, and pushed it along the table toward me.

"Sorry, son," he said. "This film business was doing just fine before I arrived in Starvation. They had a healthy little network of flicks moving around the state, some coming up from the South, a few as far out as Iowa. A nice little market. But it was mostly run-of-the-mill stuff, you know, guys and chicks, chicks and dogs, same old same old. It was getting difficult to—what would the *Wall Street Journal* say?—differentiate the product. I saw an opportunity and was able to, as they say, leverage it for a more profitable market niche. Because, whether you like it or not, there's huge demand for that stuff out there. Huge."

"It's child pornography. It's perverted and illegal."

"Illegal if you get caught. And the rest, well, it really ain't for me or you to judge. You know, in hockey, you play the puck where it goes, not where you think it ought to go. Business is no different. Where there's demand, there's going to be supply, so you might as well supply, because people are going to get it anyway, one way or the other, just like they get their guns and cigarettes and heroin and"—he jiggled his glass—"this. Sure, my heating-and-cooling business was for shit because everybody and his brother up there was selling furnaces. Too much supply. So I found something with lots of demand and not much supply, at least not then. But remember, Gus, it takes a team to succeed. One guy can screw everything up—you ought to know that, eh?—but it takes a bunch of people working together to succeed. I had a good idea, but I had no money. And it doesn't matter how good your idea is, you don't have money, you're going nowhere. Which brings us back to your daddy."

"My dad had no interest in your disgusting business."

"You know, it's really too bad old Rudy isn't still around, because now we've got the Internet. Supply is so much more efficient. And demand is unlimited. Unlimited, Gus. And it's never going to stop."

"You're lying."

"I don't know where he came up with the money either. But your dad was obviously a pretty determined guy." He leaned forward in his chair. He grinned. "You don't actually take after him, do you, Gus?"

My father had wanted a Cadillac, if only just for Sunday drives to Lake Michigan. For years he saved to buy one. But when he finally had enough money, he chose instead to buy a used Bonneville so he could put the rest of the money into an investment. What investment? A retirement fund? My college education? Anything, I hoped, but Blackburn's "opportunity." Not my father. Even if he had misled my mother about where he worked those Saturday nights, it was only because of the looming death sentence of his cancer and the duty he felt to make sure Mom and I were cared for.

"You're a goddamn liar."

"You don't have to believe me," Blackburn said. He sat back again and lifted his glass to his lips. "Ask your mother."

"Fucking liar!" I leaped from my chair, knocking the table over and sending my untouched drink flying. I slapped his glass out of his hands and it shattered against the table hockey game. "This is not about my mother and father," I yelled, "this is about you and all the kids you fucked over. You're going to jail or I can take you out right here."

I was hovering over him now, breathing hard, heart pumping, fists clenched. I wanted to rip Blackburn's face off from the ears.

He didn't move. "Take me out?" he said. "Starvation ain't enough of a jail for you? What are you really going to do, Gus? You want to hit me? Go ahead. See what difference it makes in your life or mine."

"It's over. It's over now."

"That's right!" he shouted, and before I could react, he bolted up straight in his chair and grabbed my shirt collar and yanked me down close to him. I struggled to free myself as hairy knuckles scraped my neck and liquor breath slithered up my nose. "That's right, boy," he snarled. "It's over. Right . . . now!" In one motion he raised himself out of the chair and with a grunt from his belly flung me back against the wall. I righted myself and braced for him to charge, but he just stood there looking at me and gasping for breath. He leaned over and picked the bottle, unscrewed the cap, and took a long slug. Finished, he wiped his mouth with the back of one hand and let the bottle fall to his side.

"You know," he said, "it could've been you. It could've been you and not the others. You didn't see me over at Swanny's when he was a squirt teaching him how to play the game, did you? But that's the way you wanted it, or your mother wanted it, and now, here we are. You got away, I got away." He took another swig from the bottle. "Now go home. Nobody knows you were here. Go home to your mommy. Let your father rot in peace."

"My dad would spit in your face."

"Yeah? Well, we're done here. I'm calling the cops."

He took the bottle into his office. I heard the beeps of numbers being punched into a phone.

I crossed Blackburn's front lawn at a slow trot and hurried down the sidewalk to the Bonnie, relieved to have the cover of dark. I kept my headlights off until I was out of the neighborhood, where I pulled into a strip mall lot, parked, and wrote down everything I could remember.

The cop flashers blinked in my rearview mirror about an hour northwest of Pittsburgh. A tow truck dispatched the Bonnie while two Lawrence County sheriff's deputies ferried me to the Ohio border, where they stopped and took me out of their car and ushered me to the backseat of a Mahoning County sheriff's cruiser. None of the cops said much. Every hour or so, we'd stop and I'd be moved to a different car as one county sheriff handed me over to another and another until we pulled over at the southern border of Michigan. Through the windshield I saw two Monroe County sheriff's cruisers, one from Pine County, and a burly officer wearing an earflap cap and puffing on a thin brown cigar.

"You know a lot of sheriffs," I said.

We'd driven about half an hour into Michigan, Dingus at the wheel, me in the back. It was nearly three o'clock Friday morning.

"It was either that or let the state boys grab you," he said. "I have a little piece of paper here from Judge Gallagher that says you're mine until six o'clock tonight. Then I'll be having to hand you over to the state police, depending."

"Depending on what?"

"Depending on what you tell me."

Of course I was bursting to tell someone what I knew, and the longer I waited, the more time Blackburn had to get away. But I had no idea what Dingus was going to do with me. I wouldn't be able to help Joanie much with that FedEx delivery if I was in jail. And where would Blackburn go anyway? Once the world knew he was alive, he wouldn't be hard to track down.

I was thinking, too, about my father and what he had or hadn't done. I told myself that Blackburn was lying, that Blackburn was just trying to manipulate me yet again. But what if he wasn't? What shame might be brought down upon my father's grave and, inevitably, my mother?

"It's not my job to help you do your job," I said.

"Oh, really?" Dingus caught my eyes in the rearview mirror. "Did you think you fooled me on your way out of Starvation? Did you think I don't know those back roads?"

I didn't say anything.

"For the record, we had you at every turn until you hit Old Twenty-seven. Not too hard to keep track of a car the size of a battleship."

"Wait. You're saying you just let me go?"

He lit another Tiparillo. "Sheriff Aho declined to comment."

"You're a funny guy, Dingus."

The car filled with the smell of the cherry-sweet smoke. We drove in silence for a while.

"So," he finally said. His eyes were in the rearview again. "Are you going to tell me what you learned on your little trip?"

thirty-one

T he clang of a jail cell door woke me.

"You're up," Darlene said.

I looked around, blinking against the light from the caged bulbs. A little before dawn, Dingus had stuck me in a part of the jail I'd never seen before, away from Soupy and the other prisoners. In my cell there was a sink, a toilet, and, instead of a cot, a concrete slab where I had fallen asleep.

"I guess so," I said.

"You have visitors." She motioned down the corridor. Catledge appeared with my mother and Joanie.

"Oh," I said. "Mom." Her eyes were red around the rims. Joanie had an arm around my mother's shoulders. Two days before, they hadn't even met. Joanie was one great reporter.

"Skip, can you get a couple of chairs?" Darlene said. "Hold on, Mother Bea." Catledge went for the chairs and Darlene stepped into the cell and handed me an envelope. "Here," she said.

The envelope had already been sliced open. I took it and pulled out a note written on a piece of notepaper in pen.

Gus,
Very sorry to hear of your troubles. If you are in need of an attorney, don't hesitate to have the police contact me.

Sincerely, Francis J. Dufresne

P.S. Our friend Leo will be remembered at a service this afternoon. I will pass along your regards.

I set the envelope on the edge of the sink as Catledge returned with the chairs. Mom and Joanie sat facing me.

"What time is it?" I said.

"Where were you, Gussy?" Mom said. "Why did you go away like that without telling me? Why didn't you tell me the police were after you? Why are you keeping things from me? What's wrong, son?"

"Nothing's wrong," I said. "I'm fine."

"You are not fine. Dingus says they're going to take you to jail in Detroit tonight. He says he's trying to help you but you're not cooperating."

"Does he?" I said.

Dingus had persisted in his interrogation all the way back to Starvation. Whenever I dozed off, he roused me with more questions. I told him a little, though obviously not as much as he wanted to know. Hearing that Blackburn was alive didn't seem to surprise Dingus much; he kept asking who else was involved, who was the brains behind Blackburn. It was as if he'd listened in on Blackburn telling me he couldn't have been the only one peddling porn. I thought of my father and shut my mouth. Dingus deposited me in that jail cell.

"Gus," Mom said. "It's time to grow up now."

"I'm sorry you think that," I said. "But I'm not the only one who's been keeping secrets, am I?"

Tears welled in my mother's eyes. "It's all right, Bea," Joanie said. She looked at me. "Your mother has some things to tell you."

"Yes."

"Tell him about Leo."

Mom pulled a packet of tissues from her coat pocket and used one to dab at her eyes. "I think I told you," she said, "that on the night of Jack's accident, Leo tried to tell me he'd done a terrible thing."

"That's right."

"I'm not proud of this, son. As I said, I wouldn't let Leo tell me what the thing was. He was hysterical, one minute cursing Jack, the next near tears. I couldn't make heads or tails of what he was trying to say. But I knew, I mean, I didn't *think* I wanted to hear it. Then the police came. Leo must've gotten scared. But I'm not so dumb. I could see he wasn't wet."

"What are you saying?"

"I'm saying"—she stopped to collect herself—"I'm saying I knew what Leo was trying to say. I didn't understand until later, a lot later, when I didn't think it mattered anymore."

"What was it, Mother?"

"He meant he'd let Jack go."

"And why," Joanie said, "would Leo have thought this was so terrible, Bea?"

"I can't be sure. But I thought something—something that wasn't right—was going on at those little houses Jack had for the out-of-town boys. I was with him once at his own house after we'd gone to a show. I could just—" She paused. "He was a strange man. A very strange man."

My brain had begun to throb against the inside of my skull.

"You have to believe me, son," she said. "I didn't know for sure what was going on there. And, yes, maybe I didn't want to know. But at least I kept you away. I'm so glad I did that. Joanie told me about the young man in Canada."

"Did you tell all of this to Dingus?" I said.

"I told him I wouldn't talk until I spoke with you."

"Anything else?"

From a sweater pocket Mom produced a folded sheet of paper. She set it on her lap. "Your father," she said. "I know you've been looking for answers. By now"—she glanced at Joanie—"maybe you know some things."

I looked at Joanie.

"The delivery isn't in yet," she said. "Snowstorms."

Shit, I thought. I turned back to my mother. "I know Dad made some sort of investment in something that had something to do with Blackburn."

"No," Mom said. "Not with Jack."

"Mother, he made an investment. I knew it even back then."

"Whatever he did, he did for us. For you."

"Can we please stop this bullshit? Dad's gone. If you have something to tell me, just tell me. What was this second job he had on Saturday nights? What was the damn investment?"

"Settle down," Joanie said.

Mom continued as if she hadn't heard me. "On Friday nights, he went to those poker parties, and—"

"At Blackburn's?"

"Some. Remember, Jack was only here a year or two before your father passed. They were playing poker long before that."

"All right."

"Those nights, after a while your father started sneaking that old movie projector out of the house. The same one you were sneaking out the other day. He thought I didn't know. I wanted to think it was just some harmless boys' fun. But Rudy wasn't the sneaking kind."

"So what?"

"It wasn't like your father."

"What about *Saturday* nights, Mother? The job?"

"He just wanted some extra money. We were starting to save for your college. And there was that Cadillac he had to have. It wasn't a big deal."

"You didn't mind him working at a titty bar?"

"Watch your mouth," she said. I glanced at Darlene standing outside the cell and she looked away. "I didn't know that, at least not right away. He was in his funny period after Cousin Eddie died. Anyway, the money was very good. And he didn't work there long."

"Long enough to get mixed up with the wrong people?"

She ignored me and unfolded the piece of paper. "Your father wanted that Cadillac. After the doctors told him about his illness, I wanted him to have it. But he insisted on buying that other car and putting a thousand dollars into this business opportunity. I tried to talk him out of it, but you know your father."

"What opportunity?"

"You're not going to like this, son."

"What?"

"Rudy never told me. He never told me anything about our money. That's the way things were then. He just said it would pay off. He wouldn't do anything that would harm anyone. Your father was a good man."

"You said he didn't give it to Blackburn, though."

"No. He gave it to Francis."

I felt suddenly dumb. "Francis? Dufresne? What's he got to do with Blackburn?"

"Didn't they work on a lot of real-estate things?"

"Yeah, years after Dad died. Was Dad investing in real estate?"

"I told you I don't know. All I know is, after your father died, when I was having trouble making tax payments on the house, Francis came to the rescue." She handed me the paper. "This is from last year."

"You never said anything about problems paying taxes."

"You weren't around, Gus. You were in Detroit."

The paper was a photocopy of a receipt from the Pine County Treasurer's Office and a canceled check drawn on First Detroit Bank. The receipt confirmed a payment of $542.61 in taxes on property owned by Beatrice Carpenter on December 5, 1997. The check in the same amount was signed by Francis J. Dufresne. So my father had given Francis that thousand dollars for who knows what, and years later, Francis returned the favor by helping my mother with her taxes? Was that how the investment paid off?

"By the way," Joanie said. "I was trying to tell you something when we got cut off the other day. I noticed something in my Bigfoot notes I missed before. Dufresne chaired some little state committee that gave Perlmutter a bunch of the money he used for his Sasquatch stuff."

I was staring at Dufresne's signature. There was something strangely familiar about it. I grabbed the envelope off the sink and looked again at Francis's handwritten note.

"Joanie," I said. "Did you write that bank story?"

"What does that have to do with anything?" Mom said.

"Why?" Joanie said.

"Did you?"

"Yeah. Six inches."

"Which bank bought which?"

"Why?"

"Which, please?"

"Chill out. City-something from New York bought First Detroit. So what?"

"And First Detroit owned what or used to own what? Didn't Kerasopoulos have a buddy who's a big shot at one of the banks that got bought?"

"Yeah. It's just called First Detroit now, but it used to be called—"

"First Fisherman's Bank of Charlevoix."

"Yeah. So?"

I had to clutch at the slab to keep from doubling over. The paper fluttered to the floor. "Gus," Mom said. "You're pale."

The cell door creaked open. "Time's up," Darlene said.

My mother swung around. "Darlene Bontrager," she said, using her maiden name.

"Two minutes," Darlene said.

Mom got up and sat down next to me and put an arm around me.

"Gussy," she said. "What is it?"

"Why didn't you tell me these things? I asked you about Leo. Why didn't you tell me about Dad and his job and his movie projector and his investment?"

"Do you really want to know?"

"Yes. I do."

"All right." She gave me a look I hadn't seen since the day she told me Dad was gone. "It's simple, actually. You really didn't need to know, but even if you did—even when you were asking me—you weren't ready to know. You were too young."

"Too young at thirty-four?"

"Thirty-four, twenty-five, fourteen. What difference does it make? You boys, you and Soupy and the all the rest, you got out of high school and you had your chance to grow up but you chose to stay boys forever, playing your little games as if they really matter."

I fixed my eyes on the floor. "I know they don't matter, Mother."

"No, you don't. You're still acting like a boy. Running here and there instead of settling down and facing the facts of your life. You left this place, a place you loved, because of a stupid little mistake you made in a stupid little game. Instead of the people you loved"—she didn't have to look back at Darlene—"you put your trust in silly prizes and sillier superstitions, in, in, I'm sorry, whatever that foolish glove is you wear, as if those things could somehow make you more than what you are." She put the tissues back in her pocket. "I love you, son. But I was afraid that telling you what I knew would only drive you farther away. You were already far enough away for me."

I let her words sit there for a minute.

"Thanks a lot," I said.

"I'm sorry."

"Why did you come here?"

"I came here for you."

"Give me a fucking break."

"Gus," Joanie said.

"It was *my* fault that you kept secrets? Bullshit. I'll bet you still know more than Joanie's been able to wheedle out of you. And you've known it for years and years but old Spardell told you not to talk so you didn't talk, not even to your own son. Was that the right thing to do? Just keep your mouth shut and keep cashing the checks? Why don't you go see Francis? He paid your damn taxes."

Joanie stood and reached for my mother. "That's enough," she said.

My nerves felt as if they might poke through my skin. What could I tell them that would make them all happy? What did I really know that they didn't know already? Nothing had changed since Dingus marched me into that cell. Except, perhaps, this thing about Dufresne. I couldn't get that signature—Francis J. Dufresne—out of my mind.

"You're wasting your time," I said. "Sorry."

"Stop being sorry," Mom said. "Everyone is sick of it."

Darlene held the door for Mom. Joanie stayed.

"Remember that priest at my high school?" she said.

"What priest? What about him?"

"Here." She pulled a piece of paper from her jacket pocket and set it on her chair. "Not that any of this matters anymore," she said.

"What the hell are you talking about?" I said, but Darlene took Joanie by the sleeve and ushered her and Mom away.

I lay back on the slab and closed my eyes, but I couldn't sleep. Soon Joanie and Tawny Jane would be opening those FedEx deliveries. I wondered if Tawny Jane would come to the jail looking to interview me. Maybe I'd be gone to Detroit by then.

I sat up and grabbed the paper Joanie had left. It was a photocopy of a story that had run in the *Daily Press* of Escanaba, Michigan, three months earlier:

SEX OFFENDER
TO BE CHARGED
HERE TODAY

A local man is expected to be arraigned today in Delta County Circuit Court in connection with alleged sexual abuse involving a minor.

Jeffrey Donald Champagne, 33 years old, was arrested by Escanaba police yesterday at his rented cabin outside Escanaba, police said.

Police provided few details about the alleged sexual abuse except that it involved a 12-year-boy whom Champagne had become acquainted with while teaching physical education at Gauntlett Elementary School in Escanaba. Police didn't release the boy's name.

Champagne has been a part-time teacher and assistant baseball coach at the school since the fall of 1996. Police said he was previously charged with sexual assault involving a boy in Calumet, but those charges were dropped after the boy's parents declined to allow him to testify.

Champagne originally hailed from Starvation Lake, a small town in the northern Lower Peninsula.

"It's a sad story," said Delta County sheriff's deputy William Hooper. "From what we can tell, the suspect apparently had been drifting around for some years before he landed here. We've been diligent about determining when sex offenders move to this area, but unfortunately the suspect in question had not been previously convicted."

Champagne is being held in Delta County Jail.

"No way," I said.

"What?" Darlene said. She was still standing outside.

"Nothing."

I understood that the suspect was the very same Jeff Champagne who had played for the River Rats. I did not want to believe that the cop was Billy Hooper. There had to be a lot of William Hoopers in Michigan.

Darlene opened the cell door and stepped inside. "Come on, Gus," she said. "You don't really want to go back to Detroit."

"Call off the state boys."

"It's not up to us, it's up to you."

"I've done what I can. You'll see. What time is it anyway?"

She looked at her watch. "Time to go."

"Go where?"

"Leo's funeral."

"Right. Tell everyone I said hello. And to watch for the *Pilot* tomorrow."

"You can tell them yourself. Let's go."

She was serious.

"Come on, we're going to be late."

"Dingus said I could go?"

She came over and seized me by the elbow. "The hell with Dingus," she said.

She steered the sheriff's cruiser along Route 816 away from town and turned north on Ladensack Road. I sat in the backseat and gazed out the window. Darlene had squirreled me out of the jail and grabbed a sheriff's parka for me out of another car. As we passed Jungle of the North, I remembered turning there to go to Perlmutter's place and asked where we were going. Darlene didn't so much as look at me. Another mile ahead, she pulled onto the shoulder, stopped, and shut off the ignition. Seven or eight other cars and trucks were parked there, including my mother's Jeep.

Darlene got out and came around and opened my door.

"You're going to get me in trouble," I said.

"Not if you do the right thing."

She yanked me out and told me to wait on the shoulder. "Darlene," I said, "what's going on?" But she ignored me again and got back into the driver's seat and snatched up her radio transmitter. I couldn't hear what she was saying but there was something urgent in the way she shook and nodded her head. She hung up and got out and came around to me with a key in her hand.

"I'm going to take the cuffs off for now," she said. "Don't blow it."

"Why are you doing this?"

"Maybe I'm giving you one last chance."

We crossed the road and followed a path of freshly trod footsteps that wound through the woods. We emerged in a clearing where a dozen people stood in a circle around a patch of frozen brown earth from which the snow had been dug away. At the center of the patch lay a crude red-and-white container that I would later learn had been fashioned from a scrap of steel cut from the bumper of Ethel, Leo's Zamboni. It was filled with Leo's cremated remains.

In their search of Leo's home, the police had found another, type-written note in which he had requested that his ashes be scattered on the spot where he and Blackburn had built their midnight bonfires. Leo wasn't an ironic man, and I couldn't imagine now that his nostalgia for those nights had been anything but bittersweet. But Blackburn had been his best friend, after all. So there we were: Wilf; Zilchy; Tatch; Elvis Bontrager and Floyd Kepsel and their wives; Francis Dufresne; Judge Gallagher; and my mother, leaning against Joanie. Darlene steered me to the side of the circle facing Elvis and Dufresne. Every one of them looked me over.

"Sorry," Darlene said. "Please continue."

"No trouble, darling," Elvis said. He scowled at me while producing a Bible from under his arm. "We were just getting started."

If Leo had claimed a denomination, it would have resided in the church of the recovering addicted. He had insisted that no clergy officiate at his funeral and that the service be limited to the reading of a single Biblical passage.

"Blessed are the poor in spirit, for theirs is the kingdom of Heaven . . ."

The reading finished, Elvis made a few remarks. He called Leo a "pillar of the community" for the many services he had rendered and said his death marked the "passing of an era," Starvation's "last days of glory." Floyd Kepsel talked of how Leo's gentle nature had complemented Jack Blackburn's competitive intensity and praised Blackburn for recognizing that Leo could "bring something more to our boys than just the desire to win." Neither Elvis nor Kepsel alluded to the circumstances of Leo's death, how he had put a pistol to his temple and pulled the trigger. It was as if Leo had died in his sleep.

Francis Dufresne stepped forward. He clasped his hands atop his gut as he spoke in his hand-me-down brogue.

"This is another terrible day in our great town," he said. "A good friend—a good man—has fallen. Now I say 'fallen' because of course we all know the unfortunate details of Leo's death, how it shocked us all, how it grieved us to the very core. In a town like this, everyone knows the Zamboni driver, am I right?" A few heads slowly nodded. "But apparently, folks, none of us knew Leo Redpath well enough. And for that we have no one to blame but ourselves. I know I blame myself."

A sob tried to push up from deep in my belly, but I forced it down and stared hard at Leo's makeshift urn. I wasn't thinking about Leo, though. I was thinking about Jeff Champagne, sitting in a jail. I was thinking about that twelve-year-old boy in Escanaba. I was wondering if he played hockey, as Champy did when he was a skinny winger in Starvation Lake trying to land the last spot on the River Rats roster. I was imagining whether that boy looked up to his phys-ed teacher the way Champy once had looked up to Jack Blackburn.

But of course he did.

"It was ten years ago, almost to this very day," Dufresne was saying, "that we lost our dear friend Jack Blackburn—another good, good man—in a different but equally tragic situation. With due respect to all of you and to the deceased, I would argue, dear friends, that we would not be here today if we had taken better care of our friend Leo in the wake of Jack's passing." He paused to look around at the gathering. "In the past week, we have heard much theory and speculation about what happened to Jack and Leo all those many years ago— spurious theory and speculation, if you ask me. Now, I've gone back and forth on this, as Augustus here can tell you, and while I appreciate that he has a job to do, and that you, Darlene, and your boss have a job to do, I simply cannot for the life of me see what good any of this prodding and poking of the past has done. Indeed, I'd say it has brought us nothing but grief. I'd venture that we would not be standing here today, with Leo reduced to ashes and Augustus like that and the Campbell boy in jail and Theodore in the hospital if we'd all just left well enough alone."

"Amen," Elvis said.

What did Elvis know? Nothing. What did anyone in Starvation Lake really know? I couldn't blame the people of my hometown anymore than I could blame myself. Most of them were guilty of nothing more than ignorance. They wanted to go on with their lives and hope for the best. Did my father know where his thousand dollars would wind up? Maybe. Maybe not. But I couldn't save him anymore.

Dufresne unclasped his hands and raised them in front of him. "So now, my friends, I'm imploring you, and everyone in the good town of Starvation Lake, to honor the memory of Jack Blackburn and Leo Redpath by letting them rest in peace. They lived their lives, they were good men—not perfect men, mind you, but good men—and now they are dead and gone." He looked, in turn, at Judge Gallagher, at Darlene, and at me. "Wherever they are, I am sure they would ask the same simple favor. Let us bury them once and for all today."

I took a step forward.

Wherever they are, he'd said. I knew where Leo was. At this moment, I had no idea what had become of Blackburn. There was a truth I had been selfishly trying to deny: Blackburn was still out there, he would not be deterred because he was powerless to deter himself, there were many who would help him carry out his missions, and the terrors he wreaked would be repeated again and again and create more and more ruined boys like Champy and Teddy and Soupy.

"No," I said.

"Excuse me?" Elvis said. "Deputy, can you control your prisoner?"

"Sometimes," Darlene said.

"No, by all means, let the boy speak," Dufresne said. "Augustus knew these men well. Please. Son?"

He held his hand out to me, throwing a shadow across Leo's urn. I did not take it. He knew where Blackburn was. He had known for ten years.

I looked directly at Dufresne. "What happened to Leo was not our fault," I said. "It was not the town's fault. You know that."

"Well, son, I suppose we can agree to disagree."

"No. It's not a matter of opinion. You know."

"What is it that I know?"

"You know Jack Blackburn was not a good man."

"What the hell is this?" Elvis interrupted.

"Quiet, Uncle El," Darlene said.

"Gus Carpenter has had it in for Jack ever since—"

"Shut your fat mouth, Elvis Bontrager," Mom said. "Do you hear me?"

"Augustus," Dufresne said. "I thought we were friends. I tried to help you as best I could, didn't I?"

"Sure. Like you told me to look at the minutes of the meeting where the town council decided not to dredge for Coach's body. Then you had your bartender—Loob, for Christ's sake—go take the minutes so I couldn't see them. I guess you think I'm pretty stupid, huh?"

"Not at all, Augustus."

"How about that old calendar in your office?"

"A calendar? My God, what of it?"

"You got it from your bank, First Fisherman's of Charlevoix.

Then they got bought by First Detroit. And you stayed with them, right?"

"What in the world? We're at a memorial service. This is no place for business."

Judge Gallagher spoke up. "Why don't you answer the question, Francis?"

Dufresne turned to him, unable to hide his surprise. "Ah," he said. "Well, all right. Sure, I stayed with the bank, why wouldn't I?"

"You wrote a check on that account in April of 1988, just a few weeks after Coach's"—I hesitated—"incident. April twelfth, to be exact. For twenty-five thousand dollars. To Angus Campbell."

"I've written a lot of checks to a lot of people."

"Not for twenty-five thousand dollars in hush money."

Dufresne folded his arms. "Excuse me?"

In the distance a siren wailed.

"I'll show you," I said. "Joanie, somewhere in that backpack I'll bet you have a copy of that marina receipt we talked about."

"Sure," she said. It took her a minute, but she dug it out and handed it to me.

I held the receipt up for Dufresne. "See?" I said. "It says, paid in full, check 5261, written on First Detroit Bank. It's your handwriting, Francis, not Angus's. I guess you didn't trust him."

He chuckled again. "If that's my signature, I'll eat the receipt."

"The signature's smudged," I said. "But look here." I moved closer to Dufresne and pointed. "I'll bet you didn't think a word like 'Jerry-boat' could give you away."

It had come to me in the jail when my mother showed me the copy of the check signed by Francis J. Dufresne. The J on Dufresne's signature looked like an F. It had a little tail on it like a fishhook.

"I'm sorry," Dufresne said. "I don't follow."

"Yes, you do." The siren was upon us now, just beyond the trees ringing the clearing. "How about your buddy Clayton Perlmutter?

You helped get him a bunch of state money to stay quiet, too, didn't you, Francis? You paid a lot of people to keep quiet."

"Clayton Perlmutter? I haven't spent more than five minutes with that old hermit in my life." He looked at Darlene. "I think this foolishness has gone—"

"You were there, I mean *here*"—I pointed at the ground—"you were *here* that night at the bonfire." Some of the onlookers gasped. "There was Blackburn and Leo and Soupy and you. You were *here* the night Jack Blackburn supposedly died."

"Supposedly?" Elvis said.

"You waited in the woods until Soupy ran away. Then you made Jack Blackburn leave Starvation Lake forever. You told him he'd gone too far, Francis. He's not in any lake. He didn't commit suicide. You kept him alive. And he kept you in the porn business."

"Oh, my God," my mother said.

"This is insanity," Dufresne said.

"Sure as hell is," Elvis said. "But it's over now. Looks like you're going back to jail, Gus."

Everyone turned to see Dingus emerge from the snow-laden trees, trailed by Catledge and D'Alessio. The circle parted and the sheriff stepped into the middle. He gave Darlene a look, then addressed me.

"What are you doing here?"

"Thank God, Dingus," Dufresne interrupted. "Augustus must have gone stir crazy in jail and now he's dishonoring a good man— two good men—with a lot of crazy talk."

"I see," Dingus said. He plucked a pair of handcuffs from his belt. "Like what?"

"Francis," I said, "who owns the controlling interest in Richard Limited? Why has that company been paying the taxes on the old Blackburn estate?"

"Dingus," Dufresne said. Now I heard fear in his voice. It felt good.

"Where's Blackburn, Francis?"

"Get him out of here, Sheriff, so we can finish paying our respects."

"Where is Jack Blackburn?"

Dufresne took a step toward me. His eyes went cold.

"I don't know where he is. And neither do you. You don't know a damned thing, do you, Augustus?" He turned to Dingus. "Sheriff?"

Dingus moved between us and slapped on the cuffs.

thirty-two

With Dufresne in custody, Judge Gallagher issued more pieces of paper that prevented the state cops from collecting me. After a couple of loopy hearings in his courtroom, they, and Superior Motors, gave up.

Joanie and I wrote front-page stories about Blackburn and Dufresne every day for the next three weeks. Soon the networks had camera trucks crowding Main Street. Reporters from across the country were lining up for interviews with Dingus and egg pies at Audrey's. But the *Pilot* owned the story.

Darlene hadn't really snuck me out of the jail; Dingus was in on it all along. She'd listened carefully to my talk with Mom and, on a hunch, pleaded with Dingus to search Dufresne's home. Judge Gallagher came through with a quick warrant. Then Darlene left her walkie-talkie on as we stood at Leo's gravesite. Dingus heard everything. In the trunk of his cruiser were boxes of confiscated photographs and videotapes, labeled with the same cryptic markings I'd seen on Blackburn's bookshelves.

For years the legend had gone that Dufresne took five thousand dollars he inherited in the late 1960s and, by investing wisely time and again in real estate, turned it into millions. The truth was that he'd taken a thousand dollars from my father and a few other unwitting investors and, with the help of Jack Blackburn, turned that stake into a child pornography business. With Dingus's help, Joanie and I uncovered a far-flung network of pedophiles buying and selling films and photographs, largely via the Internet. Dufresne was at the center of a loose but sophisticated web of suppliers, distributors, and consumers. The FBI hauled him away on charges of mail fraud, income tax evasion, and possession of child pornography.

Agents found Blackburn, Dufresne's most reliable supplier, at a highway rest stop near Jacksonville, Florida, sitting on a picnic table eating a bag of fried pork rinds. He'd colored his hair and his beard a garish shade of red. He told the agents he was a recreational-vehicle salesman named James Graham, even producing genuine-looking identification. A cardboard box hidden in the spare-tire well of his Camry contained half a dozen videotapes and three manila envelopes stuffed with photographs.

The town council declared the day of Blackburn's arraignment an official day of atonement. More than five hundred people piled onto school buses to make the two-and-a-half-hour trip to the federal courthouse in Grand Rapids. An hour before the arraignment, they assembled along both sides of the sidewalk leading to the courthouse door. They stood in icy silence as federal marshals ushered Blackburn past, his head down, his eyes on the ground.

After Soupy was released from jail, he holed up in his marina office, shooing reporters away, too ashamed to talk. I left him alone. But that summer I returned to Grand Rapids and took notes as he gave testimony that would help send our old coach to prison. On the third morning of the trial, I spotted Dingus and Barbara Lampley at a coffee shop nearby, holding hands.

Joanie ignored the job offers pouring in while she worked on the Blackburn story. One night after deadline I sat her down with some Blue Ribbons and nacho chips, and we decided she should go to the *Chicago Tribune* to cover the police beat.

"All right," she said. "But not until we're done here."

"OK, boss," I said.

A few days after she left for good, I was named executive editor of the *Pilot*.

. . .

One afternoon, I walked up to my father's old tree house. Under my arm was his Bell & Howell movie projector. In my pocket was the key to the closet I had never been inside.

The reels of film, fourteen in all, lay in cardboard boxes on the closet floor. I hung a bedsheet in the garage and aimed the Bell & Howell. I ran every reel through it, or tried. A couple of them, rotting, disintegrated in my hands. Others shredded as they fluttered through the projector. Most were movies of Soupy and me and my other buddies playing at Make-Believe Gardens. I'd forgotten how Dad used to run up and down the rink trying to get all of us into the frame; one time he slipped and fell on his face, and we all laughed. Other films showed some grainy images of women and men having sex. But no boys.

I dumped all of it, including the projector, into an oil barrel behind the garage. I doused it with kerosene, lit it, and stepped back in the wet snow to watch it burn.

"Hey, Gus."

I looked up to see Darlene standing at the corner of the garage, wearing jeans and a denim jacket over a hooded sweatshirt. She walked up and stood facing me on the other side of the fire, a brown paper sack under her arm.

"What are you doing?" she said.

"Not much. A little spring cleaning."

We didn't say anything for a few minutes. I could feel her looking at me. The celluloid sizzled and spat.

"Brought you something," she said. She walked around the fire and held the bag out, smiling. She hadn't smiled like that at me in a long time. "I'm sorry," she said. "Even Mom couldn't fix her this time."

I looked inside the bag and saw the tattered remains of Eggo. Darlene must have retrieved it from Horvath Road. I reached inside and touched the scrap of black electrical tape clinging to the thumb. I looked up at Darlene.

"What?" she said.

"I don't know, Darl. Sometimes, I swear, I wish we'd just brought him back and drowned him in the lake."

"No, you don't."

"What the hell." I took the bag from her and tossed it on the fire. "I won't be needing that anymore."

"Gus. You can't quit hockey."

"I know. But I'm done playing goalie. Time to fire pucks at other people's heads for a change."

We stood there a little longer. The fire quieted until I could hear the melting snow dripping off the garage roof.

"Want to get out of here?" I said.

"Yeah. Want a ride?"

ACKNOWLEDGMENTS

Thanks to my agents, Erin Malone and Shana Kelly of the William Morris Agency; my editor, Trish Grader of Touchstone; her assistant, Meghan Stevenson; my copy editor, Amy Ryan; and my Web designers, Sunya Hintz and Justin Muggleton. They all made this book better. For her courageous book *Crossing the Line*, thanks to Laura Robinson. For their advice and encouragement, thanks to John Anderson, Shelly Banjo, Joe Barrett, Valerie Bauerlein, Michael Brown, Helene Cooper, Kimi Crova, Carrie Dolan, Sam Enriquez, the Gruleys (Danielle, Kaitlin, Joel, Pamela, David, and Terry), Matt Hulsizer, Greg Jaffe, Allan Lengel, Dan Morse, Bruce Orwall, Jonathan Pecarsky, Frank Provenzano, Mike Schroeder, Sean Sherman, Andrew Stoutenburgh, John Wilke, Jeff Zilka, and especially Jonathan Eig. Last but far from least, thanks to the Shamrocks, the Flames, the YANKS, and all the boys of Thursday hockey.

For the complete Reading Group Guide,
please visit www.simonsays.com.

A CONVERSATION WITH BRYAN GRULEY

**How has your background in journalism helped prepare you to
write mystery fiction? Is Gus inspired by anyone you know?**
My years working for newspapers small and large helped me invent
the *Pine County Pilot* and informed much of Gus's behavior and choices
relating to his journalistic present, past, and future. As for writing a
mystery novel, per se, I didn't set out to write a genre mystery; I just
wanted to tell a story. Storytelling has been a big part of my journalistic career, both as a reporter who loves to write nonfiction narratives
and an editor who encourages others to write them. Turns out the
story I chose to make up in *Starvation Lake* is a mystery. OK. I think
most novels are essentially mysteries, wherein authors pose questions
and answer them as they see fit.

The question about Gus reminds me of the time I told my *Wall
Street Journal* colleague Greg Jaffe, a great narrative writer, that I was
writing a novel. "Don't tell me it's about a hockey-playing journalist,"
he said. Very funny. Actually, though, Gus is an amalgam of many
people I have known, journalists and not, and just as all of them have
influenced who I am in one way or another, they have influenced
the way Gus apprehends and interacts with his world. So, I suppose
there's a bit of me in Gus, although I am not a goaltender, at six feet
two I'm a head taller than Gus, and almost none of what happens in
the book ever happened to me.

What is your personal connection to the setting of the novel? Are you a Michigander? Could you see this story taking place anywhere aside from Starvation Lake?

I grew up in Redford, a blue-collar suburb abutting Detroit on the west side. In 1971, my parents bought a cottage on Big Twin Lake, about forty miles northeast of Traverse City in the northern Lower Peninsula. It's probably my favorite place on earth. I'm writing the answers to these questions at that cottage, sitting on an oak swing that faces the lake between a pair of ancient birch trees. For dinner, I'm planning on a patty melt at the Hide-A-Way Bar on the *real* Starvation Lake a few miles from here.

Although *Starvation Lake* is purely fiction, the scenes, the food, the dialogue, the weather, the very streets of the town are inspired by things I have seen, heard, tasted, and smelled in the nearly forty years I have been visiting (and my summer spent as a reporting intern at the *Bellaire News*, not far from here). For instance, Bea Carpenter lives in a yellow house because there are a couple of yellow houses on Big Twin that I love looking at from the water. But this story could happen anyplace, small or big, where the need to win blinds people to the nefarious compromises that winning often requires. While I tried to create a little world that would be at once alluring and dangerous, the events and characters that populate it aren't necessarily peculiar to northern Michigan; I've never met anyone up here even remotely like Jack Blackburn.

Are there any mystery or thriller novelists you particularly admire? Are there any artists in other mediums who influence your work?

I read widely and eclectically, so many writers have worked their charms on me, from Franklin W. Dixon to Flannery O'Connor to Howard Norman to Pete Dexter. The older I get, the more I appreciate great stories told well, and the less patience I have for writers who, as Elmore Leonard says, engage in "hooptedoodle" (showing off). That isn't to say I'm not guilty, but I'm trying to beat the rap. A beach vacation introduced me to Thomas Harris, and I loved *Red Dragon* and *The Silence of the Lambs*. One thriller writer whose work gave me impetus is Michael Connelly. Reading his book *The Poet* some years back, while aware that Connelly is an ex-journalist, made me think I could take a whack at novels and have fun doing it.

Has anybody my age not been influenced by the Star Wars trilogy? OK, my wife, but I can watch the first three flicks again and again and love them every time. But really just about every damn thing influences me—movies, cartoons, commercials, songs on the radio, brief items I see in newspapers. I carry around a little notebook to jot things down I might want to use. And I keep my ears open in the rink dressing room and on the bench when I'm playing hockey.

Are the underground tunnels referenced in the book based on an existing urban legend? Why did you decide to include information about the tunnels but never prove or disprove their existence within the story?
A *rural* legend, but yes, the tunnels were inspired by tales my brother Dave told me about sunken boats disappearing on Torch Lake, a gorgeous expanse of water in the northern Lower Peninsula. I chose not to prove or disprove their existence because it wasn't necessary, and I'm not really sure yet whether they exist or not. There's a chance they'll turn up again in a future book.

Would you please discuss the Leo Redpath character? How does he act as a foil for Blackburn? How do you hope readers will judge him?
I love Leo Redpath. That doesn't mean I admire him, although he has some admirable traits. I love Leo just as I love many people in my life who have made mistakes, and just as many people in my life have forgiven my flaws and foibles. Although Leo shares—or shared—certain characteristics with Blackburn, he was trying to move in a different direction. I don't expect readers to admire Leo or even like him, but I hope they'll empathize.

Each character in the book is flawed in some way. Was it important to you that all of the characters were realistic, without one clear hero and one clear villain?

In retrospect, yes. I can't honestly say I had this sort of ambiguity in the forefront of my mind when I started to write *Starvation Lake*, but that's how it turned out. That could be because I love watching characters struggle against their imperfections, from Holden Caulfield to Christian Bale's Batman. It probably owes as well to my day job, where many of the most interesting stories are richly ambiguous. Besides, all goaltenders are flawed. Who in their right mind would play such a position?

What can readers expect next from you?

I'm back in northern Michigan trying to figure that out: What will become of Gus and Darlene? How might a rich ex–auto executive named Haskell help or hurt Starvation Lake? Why would Dingus and his deputies be called to a tree filled with old shoes outside of town? Has the ghost of a vengeful killer returned to haunt Starvation? How will Gus fare as a winger instead of a goaltender?